Advance praise for
Three Days to Dead

"Dark, dangerous and delectable. A fantastic debut, impossible to put down!"

—GENA SHOWALTER, *New York Times*
bestselling author of *Seduce the Darkness*

"Action-packed, edgy, and thrilling, *Three Days to Dead* is a fabulous debut! Kelly Meding's world and characters will grab you from the first page. You won't want to miss this one."

—JEANIENE FROST, *New York Times*
bestselling author of the Night Huntress series.

"*Three Days to Dead* is one of the best books I've read. *Ever*. Evy Stone is a heroine's heroine, and I rooted for her from the moment I met her. Kelly Meding has written a phenomenal story, one that's fast-paced, gritty, and utterly addictive. Brava! More! *More!*

—JACKIE KESSLER, co-author, *Black and White*

THREE DAYS TO DEAD

KELLY MEDING

DELL

Three Days to Dead is a work of fiction. Names, characters, places,
and incidents are the product of the author's imagination or are used
fictitiously. Any resemblance to actual events, locales, or persons,
living or dead, is entirely coincidental.

A Dell Mass Market Original

Copyright © 2009 by Kelly Meding

Published in the United States by Dell, an imprint of
The Random House Publishing Group, a division of
Random House, Inc., New York.

DELL is a registered trademark of Random House, Inc.,
and the colophon is a trademark of Random House, Inc.

ISBN 978-0-553-59286-3

Cover illustration: Cliff Nielson

Printed in the United States of America

www.bantamdell.com

2 4 6 8 9 7 5 3 1

For Tim—living proof that people can and do change

Acknowledgments

Part of me wants to take a page from actress Kim Basinger and thank everyone I've ever met in my entire life. However, too many people had active and important roles in getting this book into your hands, so I'll thank them the old-fashioned way.

Major kudos to my awesome agent, Jonathan Lyons, for having faith in a new author and your passion for this book; it has made all the difference. Mega thanks to super-editor Anne Groell, for your wisdom and support. And a round of applause for Pam Feinstein, copy editor extraordinaire.

To my crit readers, Sarah and Nancy—you ladies are the best. Thanks to Stacey G. for your awesome website design and for being an all-around good egg. A special shout-out to the folks at the AW Watercooler for being an incomparable source of information, resources, and support (especially Peter and the other peeps on the SF/F board). A hug to Kris Young, the first pro to tell me I could do this. You made a believer out of me.

Thank you to my best friend Melissa, the only person in the world who's read all of my fiction (and somehow maintains the impression that I'm a sane person). Mel, you always had faith in me, even when I didn't. For my sister, Dawn—you are one of the strongest people I know. As children we shared a love of reading and, as an adult, I am so proud to contribute to that literary landscape we adored so much.

And most of all, thank you to my parents. You never once told me to be an "Insert Financially Sound Career Choice Here," and you always supported my dreams. You let me be me, and I could not have asked for more.

Chapter One

71:59

I don't recall the first time I died, but I do remember the second time I was born. Vividly. Waking up on a cold morgue table surrounded by surgical instruments and autopsy paraphernalia, to the tune of the medical examiner's high-pitched shrieks of fright, is an unforgettable experience.

I vaulted off the table, my mind prepared to execute a move that my chilled body hadn't quite caught up to, and promptly lost my balance. My knees didn't bend; my ankles stayed stiff. I landed on my bare hip, earning another shock of cold and something quite new: pain. Sharp and biting, it lanced up my hip and down my thigh, orienting me to two facts: I was on the floor and I was completely naked.

Something metal clanged to the floor, rubber squeaked on faded tile, and the screams receded. Far away, a door slammed. The soft hum of machinery mingled with the hiss of my ragged breathing. Fluorescent light glared down from gray overhead fixtures. I smelled something sharp, bitter, and completely foreign.

My bruised hip protested as I sat up. The room tilted. A sheet dangled from the edge of the table I'd fallen from. I wrapped the thin, papery material around my shoulders. It did little to cut the chill.

Coroner's table. Naked. Scalpel on the floor. What the holy friggin' hell?

I searched my addled memory, hoping for an explanation as to why I was bare-ass naked on a morgue floor.

Nothing. Zilch. Awareness wrapped in cotton batting. No cinematic instant recall for me.

My chest seized and I began to cough—a wet rasp from deep inside my lungs. I spat out a wad of phlegm and continued coughing until I thought my chest would turn inside out. When the spasms ceased, I grabbed the side of the table and pulled. My feet responded. Knees bent. I managed to stand up, using the surgical table as a crutch, and found myself staring down at its shiny surface.

And a stranger's face.

A curtain of long, wavy brown hair framed a curved chin and high cheekbones. Not mine. A smattering of freckles dotted the bridge of her nose. Definitely not mine. I touched my cheek, and the stranger touched hers. All wrong. I was pale, with blond hair, blue eyes, and no freckles. And younger. The dark-haired woman with track marks inside her left elbow and an open, but healing, gash down the inside of her forearm was not Evangeline Stone. She was someone else.

Another sharp tremor raced down my spine, creating gooseflesh across my back and shoulders. Wyatt. I was on my way to see Wyatt Truman. We'd agreed to meet at our usual spot by the train yards. I arrived. Waited. And then what?

Something bad, apparently.

I gazed around the small autopsy room with its plain gray walls and yellow tiled floors. Two identical beds lay on either side of a floor drain. An instrument tray lay upended on the floor. A wall of doors, roughly three-foot-by-four each, had to be where they kept the bodies. How long had I been in there?

Why had I been in there?

Wyatt would know. He had to know. He knew everything. He was my Handler; that was his job.

Did he know where I was? Or who I was, for that matter?

Opposite the refrigeration unit was a desk and beyond that a door marked PRIVATE. I stumbled toward it, clutching the sheet around my shoulders, still having some trouble with my extremities.

I limped into a small bathroom containing a sink, two stalls, and a bank of four gray lockers. I tried each one. The last opened with a sharp squeal, and the eye-watering stink of old tennis shoes wafted out. My stomach churned. Inside I found a pair of navy sweatpants in XXL and an oversized white T-shirt. Nothing else useful.

I dropped the sheet and tugged the shirt on, not surprised that it swam all over my thin frame. I was a few inches taller than I'd been. Bigger breasts, rounder hips—less the blond waif, and more the curvy woman. Definitely an upgrade. I rolled up the extra material and knotted it around my torso. The sweatpants went on next, and even with a drawstring, they were ridiculously huge.

It didn't matter. The clothes just needed to get me out of there. I blotted my hair in the sheet, removing some of the excess moisture now that it was starting to thaw. The pants slipped, and I hiked them back up. A red hole peeked through the top of my belly button, hinting at a vanished piercing.

Voices bounced through the other room. I tiptoed to the door and pulled it open just far enough to peek outside. The technician was back, waving her hands wildly. Short, red hair bobbed around her shoulders each time she turned her head. Her companion was an older man, white-haired and wrinkled, dressed in surgical scrubs. He picked up the chart hanging from the end of the bed I'd previously occupied and skimmed the contents.

"Dead bodies don't just come back to life, Pat," the man said.

"I know that, Dr. Thomas, but she was dead. I was here when she was brought in early this morning. I pulled out the drawer when her roommate came to identify her."

Roommate? My roommates were gone. I didn't even have a couch to crash on anymore, now that the Owlkins were dead and their apartment building razed.

"She was still dead when Joe put her on the table for me," Pat continued, "but then I got a phone call. When I got back and pulled the sheet, she was pinking up. I swear, I thought I was seeing things, but then she sat up."

"I see," Dr. Thomas said, in a tone that clearly indicated he didn't believe her. "The physical examination showed that she died of acute blood loss. How do you think a dead body without blood sat up and walked out of the room?"

Pat gaped at him, her mouth opening and closing, but producing no response.

"The last thing we need," Dr. Thomas said, "is a lawsuit from that girl's family, because we misplaced the body. So I suggest you stop acting hysterical and find her, or you'll be looking for another job."

Dr. Thomas spun on his heel and stalked through a pair of swinging doors, leaving Pat behind. She stared at the settling doors, hands limp by her sides.

"I'm not crazy, you son of a bitch," she said in a small voice. Not much of a fighter, that one. Then her entire body went rigid. Slowly, she turned in a small circle, eyeing the room. Her head snapped toward the far corner, as though she'd heard a noise. I held my breath and waited.

"Hello?" she said. "Chalice? Chalice Frost? Are you there?"

Chalice Frost? I could only imagine the sort of teasing she'd endured as a child. Probably why she (I?) had turned to drugs. Not that I possessed any memory of such a thing; I only had the track marks on my arm as proof. The gash, too, and the longer I stared at it, the more convinced I became that the exposed flesh had knitted, drawing the skin closer together. Healing.

"Get it together, Pat. It's your blood sugar, that's all. It's off, so you're seeing things."

It was just too painful. I stepped into the autopsy room, still clutching the front of my borrowed sweatpants in an ongoing attempt to protect my modesty. The door shut with a solid thump. Pat jumped and spun around. Her mouth fell open, eyes widening to impossible proportions.

"If it helps," I said, the voice strange to my ears, "you aren't really crazy."

She adopted an unhealthy pallor, then fainted dead away. Her head bounced off the tiled floor with a sickening crack. I winced. She lay still, her chest slowly rising and falling.

"So much for not scaring anyone," I muttered. Chalice's voice was deeper than mine. It felt powerful, like I could scream to wake the dead. No pun intended.

I crouched next to Pat and checked her head, but found no gushing wound. Just a small lump. It's not every day that someone sees a reanimated corpse. Likewise, it's not every day a person becomes a reanimated corpse. My day was decidedly much worse, so I did the first sensible thing that came to mind. I stole her tennis shoes.

No way was I walking hell knew how far in my bare feet. The white canvas shoes fit snugly, unlike my clothes, and helped provide a bit of warmth for my ice-cube toes. I padded over to the medical examiner's desk. A cardboard box labeled "Effects" sat on the blotter, surrounded by untidy files, scraps of paper, and other office sundries.

Inside the box, I discovered a stack of manila envelopes, each one different in thickness and weight. I sifted until I found a slim one with "Chalice Frost" printed on the front. I tore it open and upended the contents onto the desk.

Out fell a pair of sealed plastic bags. Inside one was a gold hoop—the missing belly ring—and in the second a pair of silver cross earrings. No wallet or license. No scraps of information to tell me who this Chalice chick was, besides poorly named.

I needed an address, or even a phone number. I'd broken into morgues in the past, usually to check mutilated bodies for signs of Dreg attack, so this wasn't an entirely unfamiliar environment. I plucked her chart from the foot of the exam table. Chalice Frost, aged twenty-seven. She lived in an apartment in Parkside East, one of the last "nice" neighborhoods in the city.

The chart also listed a phone number. Pat said my—her—roommate identified Chalice's body. Was she at home? Would she pick me up if I called? Or would she freak out and faint like reliable old Pat?

The one thing I really wanted was a cell phone. Pat had a phone on her desk, but as I reached for the receiver, I couldn't think of a single number to call. Not even Wyatt's number. I should have known his number. I had dialed it a thousand times. But no, the little space in my brain reserved for that string of digits was empty.

This was bad.

I tore a piece of paper from one of the M.E.'s files and scribbled down the address and phone number. With no pockets in my extra-baggy clothes, I stuck the paper in my borrowed shoes.

A daily newspaper caught my eye. Ignoring the headlines about inflated gasoline prices, I checked the date. May twentieth.

"Twentieth," I said, trying it out. "May. Twentieth." Nope.

It had to be a mistake. My brain was fuzzy and my memories hazy, but I knew that I set out to find Wyatt on May thirteenth. It was the day that the Owlkin Clan was attacked; the entire nest was destroyed because of me. Everything had changed two days before that, the night my partners and I were attacked by a pack of vampire half-breeds. My partners had died; I hadn't.

The other Hunters had come after me, screaming for my head, and I'd run. I'd eventually gone to the Owlkins—a peaceful race of shape-shifting birds of prey. Then I'd been found and the Owlkins slaughtered. It hadn't made sense then, and it didn't make sense now. I'd given up and decided to turn myself in. To stop running. To stop getting others killed.

Had I gotten myself killed in the process? Chalice died last night, but when did I, Evangeline Stone, die? What had happened to the last seven days? And why the hell was I back?

Instinct told me that someone had screwed up. You didn't mess with a reincarnation spell without putting all of your ducks in a row, and while my new body was strong and young, it felt untrained. Unready for the physical, painful nature of my former job as a Dreg Bounty Hunter, and whatever task still lay ahead of me. Chalice Frost could not have been their first choice—whoever "they" were. Someone should have been there to greet me when I woke. Instead, I was rooting through a dead woman's personal effects, scaring the shit out of hapless coroners, and hoping I could get away without being caught.

Time to trek across town to Chalice's apartment for more cash and a change of clothes. Maybe I'd even remember Wyatt's phone number on the way. I just hoped that her roommate wasn't home. One freak-out per day was my limit.

From the desk drawer, I rustled a key ring that held at least a dozen different keys, all attached to a glittery metal P. One of them had a black, plastic sleeve around the top, engraved with a familiar logo. Car key. Bingo.

"Who the hell are you?"

The male voice echoed through the cramped room. I pivoted on one foot, dropping my shoulders and balling both fists. At least, that's what I did in my head. In reality, my gradually loosening limbs tangled, and I stumbled two steps forward, hands up like a drunk ninja.

Dr. Thomas stood just inside the room, a file in one hand and an expression of confusion painting his age-lined face.

No one had sneaked up on me in years. Not even a goblin, and they were built for stealth. I should have heard the squeak of the door hinge and ducked before he ever saw me. But I was listening with someone else's ears—untrained ears, without years of survival to make them sharp. Indecision froze me—not a place I liked to be.

Dr. Thomas shifted his confusion from me to Pat's sprawled body, his caterpillar eyebrows arching high on his small forehead. "Pat?" His attention reverted to me, widening both eyes. "What did you do to her?"

His voice quavered. He didn't launch himself at me or attempt to help Pat, further hinting at the total wimp beneath the angry bluster. I considered whamming him with the truth, but didn't really want a stroke on my conscience.

"I didn't lay a hand on her," I said, which was very much true. The next part, not so much. "I got lost."

He stared, not quite believing. His attention wandered, probably taking in my odd state of dress. He paused on my right hand. I looked down and groaned. The plastic I.D. bracelet still clung to my wrist, probably attached when the body was brought down to the morgue.

"Damn," I said, tugging at the reinforced band. It didn't give.

"That isn't possible," he said.

I smiled. "What's not possible? A frozen dead girl coming back to life? Doc, if you only knew half of the things that happen in this city after dark, you'd run screaming for the sunny south and never look back."

He continued to stare, all of the color slowly draining from his face. Better ask my questions before he did something crazy like scream for help or pass out.

"I don't suppose you know where Shelby Street is from here, do you? I'm a tad disoriented."

He jacked the thumb of his right hand over his shoulder—a vague direction at best—and grunted something. I took fast advantage of his incredulity, and headed for the door. On second thought, I about-faced and snagged Pat's keys off the desk.

"Wait," Dr. Thomas said.

"Can't; sorry."

"You were dead."

His plaintive tone gave me pause. For someone so intimidating only five minutes ago, he looked like a lost child. It made me want to put him out of his misery.

"Do yourself a favor," I said, crossing the distance

between us in three long strides. "Tell yourself some-one broke in and stole the body. It'll make it easier to sleep at night."

He blinked. I swung and caught him low in the jaw. The impact jarred my fist and shoulder—Chalice was definitely not a fighter—but Thomas went down like a stone. Two people unconscious in a matter of minutes was not a great start to the day.

No time to ponder the consequences, though. I had a former Handler to find, no idea where to start looking in a city of half a million people, and if any-one else in Chalice Frost's life knew she was dead, I was in for a very eventful day.

Chapter Two

I dumped Pat's car two blocks away from my destination and humped it through one of the nicest neighborhoods in the city to get to Chalice's building. Uncracked sidewalks, trees with little fences around them, neatly trimmed hedges, and graffiti-less walls surrounded me on all sides. So different from the rest of the city.

Few Dregs crossed the Black River, so I rarely ventured into Parkside East. I certainly couldn't have afforded the clean, spacious apartments that lined the streets on this side of the river—a slash of concrete and putrid water that divided light from dark, human from Dreg.

During the trip across the river, the gash on my left arm finished its annoying, itchy healing process. A pencil-thin scar remained, the only fading evidence of what Chalice had done to herself. Even the dappling of track marks had disappeared. I checked my belly button. The hole for the gold hoop was gone. Completely healed. So were my earlobes. Weird.

I double-checked the scribbled address against the apartment building, then went inside. The small lobby was tidy and smelled of furniture polish and glass cleaner. Even the elevator smelled fresh and new. I punched the button for the fifth floor and waited for the doors to close, completely lacking a plan for once I got up there. Knock and hope the roommate answered was my best option. Breaking and entering was possible, thanks to my day job. It was just made more difficult by my severe lack of tools to—

A hand jammed its way between the sliding doors and forced it back open. I tensed, instincts preparing me for a fight. A little girl, no more than ten years old, dashed inside, clutching a cloth grocery sack. She flashed me a pink-lipped smile.

"Thanks, Chalice," she said in a sunny, singsong voice.

Neighbor. Cute kid. "No problem," I said.

She eyed me over the lip of the sack and a protrusion of potato chips. "Your clothes look funny today."

"I'm in disguise." I held one finger to my lips, hoping the child played along. The last thing I needed was a pint-sized shadow, especially if I ended up jimmying the door lock. "Don't tell anyone you saw me, okay?"

"Like a game?" Her round eyes widened, delighted at having a secret with an adult.

"Absolutely like a game."

She giggled and nodded, her blond hair swishing around her cherubic cheeks. She shifted the bag into one arm and pretended to turn an invisible key in front of her mouth.

"That's my girl," I said.

As each floor lit up and passed us by, my anxiety mounted. She hadn't gotten off yet. Please, let her live on one of the floors above.

The elevator dinged on the fifth floor. I stepped out, and she followed. The corridor branched left and right, but had no signs indicating which numbers lay in which direction. I glanced at the plates on the two nearest doors: 508 on the left and 509 on the right. Chalice lived in 505, so I took a chance and turned left.

The little girl followed, still grinning like a lunatic, and stopped in front of 506. No wonder she seemed so friendly. We were neighbors.

They were neighbors.

Whatever.

She watched intently while I stared dumbly at an apartment I'd never seen, in a body that wasn't mine. I tossed her a sunny smile, turned the knob, and made a show of surprise. "Well, darn it," I said. "That's not supposed to be locked."

"Where are your keys?" she asked.

"I must have lost them. That was pretty silly of me, huh?" I turned, pretending to leave.

"You gave my mom a key."

Thank God. I turned back around. "Really? Gosh, I'd forgotten that."

"Yeah, when you and Alex were both gone a week last summer, we came over to water the plants. I'll get it!"

She was inside her apartment before I could respond, and back in seconds, sans groceries. She proudly displayed the round, copper key. "There, see?" she said.

"You're a lifesaver." I plucked the key from her small fingers.

"Grape or cherry?"

I blinked. "What?"

She grinned as if this was our own private joke. "What flavor Lifesaver, silly?"

"Definitely cherry."

She bounced, giggled, and let the euphoria dance her back into her own apartment. The door finally closed and stayed that way.

I pushed the key into the dead bolt, turned it, and the solid wood door opened. I stepped inside and closed the door.

The immediate odor of stale beer surprised me. I stood on the edge of a spacious, well-decorated living room. A matching striped sofa and chair coordinated with the dark wood tables. Lamp shades matched the shade of the throw rug. Framed prints of ocean scenes decorated the walls. It wasn't expensive, but definitely tasteful.

An open kitchen with eating counter was situated on the right side of the apartment. Directly ahead, sliding glass doors gave way to a patio of some sort, hidden behind gauzy mauve curtains. Three doors lined the left wall. Chalice's room lay behind one of them.

In the kitchen, a garbage can was overflowing with glass beer bottles. Two empty cases sat on the floor next to it. No other party evidence pointed to a recent, serious bender. A troubling thought.

A framed photograph lay facedown on the counter. I lifted it. My new face smiled back at me, happy and whole, arms around the shoulders of a very handsome man. He had vivid blue eyes, brown hair, and a cocky smile. Boyfriend? Brother? Hairstylist?

I wished for some of Chalice's memories; it would

make this part a lot easier. Of course, I didn't really want a dead woman's consciousness vying for control of this body. I had enough things to deal with without adding multiple personality disorder to the mix.

Door number one concealed an ivory and blue room with plain oak furniture, a desk covered with books, and very little in the way of personal items. Very male, and very likely not Chalice's. The middle door was the bathroom, squeaky clean and organized. Toothbrushes in the holder, no water marks on the mirror or dry toothpaste blobs in the sink. Chalice and her roommate must have been like-minded neat freaks to keep an apartment so tidy.

The third door opened easily, and I stepped into an unfamiliar world—a world of white carpet and pink-flowered wallpaper. Pink and red pillows rested on a white bedspread, and red curtains bracketed the room's single window. An enormous painting of a vase of flowers covered most of the wall above a white-washed desk. Every stick of furniture in the room was painted white. Stuffed animals lined a shelf high on the wall—bears and cats and puppies and pigs.

"Oh, ew," I said.

I marched over to the white-shuttered closet doors. If her clothes were mostly pink, too, I was going to throw up. I yanked them open and was presented with an array of colors and styles. Very little pink in the bunch. Disaster averted. I rifled through until I found a stretchy red tank top and a pair of black jeans. Comfort clothes, something I could easily move in.

A quick search through her dresser turned up the appropriate undergarments, and I changed. Money was next. I inspected the half-dozen purses I'd spotted in the closet. Where the hell was her wallet? I'd settle on untraceable cash hidden in a sock, but that drawer had, likewise, yielded nothing.

I poked through her jewelry box. Standard mall stuff, nothing of secondary market value. Wrapped in pink tissue—what else?—I found a tasteful silver cross necklace. Engraved on the back were three words: "Love Always, Alex." Sweet. I put it on. Crosses were an old joke in my line of work, a holdover from a time when people actually believed they warded off evil creatures. Silly superstitions.

Silver, on the other hand, is a potent weapon against the shape-shifters of the world. Weres are as allergic to silver as Bloods are to unpolished wood. I'd seen vampires stabbed with pine splinters as small as my pinkie who fell into their version of anaphylactic shock and died within minutes.

I used a pair of fingernail scissors to snip off the morgue bracelet. I tucked the creepy thing into the back of her jewelry box, glad to have it out of sight. Her desk yielded the jackpot—a slim, leather wallet and three keys on a C-shaped fob. One of the keys matched the one I'd gotten from the neighbor girl. They went right into my pocket. The wallet had a driver's license, a bus pass, a debit card, and twenty dollars in cash. Not much, but it was a start.

One last toss of the desk uncovered a lot of organization and nothing very personal. Not even a journal or an address book. Just a few photos of Chalice with other people, including a few more with the man from the picture frame. Had to be a boyfriend.

Her laptop was off. I left it alone, but made a mental note to snoop later. It was inching closer to five o'clock, and I needed to get in and out before the roommate came home.

I crouched down and reached under the bed. Nothing, not even dust bunnies. I turned around and flopped down on the floor, blowing hard through my mouth. My fingers curled in the thick carpet. I wanted to rip it up and fling it out the window, to stop feeling so helpless. I hit the side of the mattress with my elbow. The headboard cracked against the wall.

Is this what a suicidal person did? Clean her room spotless before slashing her wrist? She couldn't have done it here—no way the carpet would be so spotless. Bathtub, maybe. No streaks or overflowing water, not for such a tidy girl. And what about those track marks? I hadn't found a single syringe or bag of powder among her things.

"Why did you do it, Chalice?" I said, fingering the thin chain around my throat.

As much as the pink-loving contradiction of a young woman deserved understanding, I couldn't waste time on it today. Her body wasn't ideal, but it was alive and healthy (unusually so), and I had it on loan for a little while. Item number two on my list of things to find out ASAP: how long did I have?

I stood up and went into the kitchen. A basket of mail sat on the counter. I shuffled through it. Bills and official mail, all addressed to Chalice Frost. Near the bottom of the stack were three letters, sent to this apartment, under the name of Alexander Forrester. Same as the one engraved on the necklace charm. I remembered what the neighbor girl had said, about my roommate's name, and glanced at the framed photo on the counter. He kind of looked like an Alex.

No time, Evy, no time. Get the cash and get out.

Under the kitchen sink seemed like the next best place to check for stashed money. It smelled strongly of fresh cleaning solution. I pushed a bucket and sponge out of the way, both still moist. More bottles and a few empty coffee cans at the very back of the cabinet. Dish detergent and a box of steel wool. Nothing terribly useful.

The front door rattled. I froze, head halfway under the sink, heart pounding. A male voice was talking as the door opened.

"I appreciate it, Teresa, and I'm sorry I missed the lab," he said. "I—hold on, I have another call." Something beeped. "Hello?"

The door closed. I backed out as slowly as possible, careful to not knock anything over and give myself away.

"Yes, this is Alex Forrester," he said. "Yes, I was the one who— What?" Keys clanked to the floor. "What are you saying? She's alive?"

His shock-laden voice seemed to come from the center of the living room. I crawled to the edge of the counter and peered around, but I couldn't see him.

"How is that possible? We both—" He inhaled sharply. "Yes, if I see her, I'll call. I just . . . don't know what to say. Thanks."

A snap, probably his phone closing. Utter silence filled the apartment, interrupted every few seconds by a deep exhalation of breath. I silently urged him to leave, to run from the apartment in screaming shock, so I could escape undetected. But footsteps shuffled across the carpet, stopped.

"The hell?" he said.

The bedroom door. I had left it open. Shit. Might as well get this over with.

I stood up and moved out from behind the kitchen counter. A broad-shouldered man faced away from me, wearing tight jeans and a black polo, hands fisted by his sides, staring at Chalice's bedroom door.

"Alex?" I said.

He yelped and turned too quickly, tangling over his own ankles. He tripped, hit the wall with a rattling thump, and stopped. And stared. He was wild-eyed and red-faced, but definitely the fellow from the photos.

"Chal?" he asked. Beneath the spots of red on his cheeks, the rest of his face was taking on a frightening pallor.

"Breathe," I said. "Do not freak out on me. I've seen quite enough of that today, thanks."

He took direction well and began sucking in large amounts of air. He straightened and pushed away from the wall, but did not approach. So far, so good. His eyes roved all over my body, taking in the details. Assuring a confused mind that it wasn't seeing things.

"It's really you?" he asked.

"It's me." I hated lying to him; he seemed like a genuinely nice man.

"How?"

"No idea. I honestly don't remember much about the last couple of days. It's all a blank."

He blinked hard. "You don't remember yesterday?"

I shook my head. He stepped toward me. I backed up, and he stopped his advance, hurt bracketing both eyes.

"I have to go," I said.

His hand jerked. "Go where?"

"I can't tell you."

His hurt and confusion became palpable. He seemed fragile. Scared. Great, he just had to be the sensitive type.

"Do you trust me, Alex?" I asked, taking a step toward him.

"With my life, Chal."

"Then please trust me now." Another few steps. He let me close the distance between us. "I need to go and figure out a few things, and I'll try to explain all of this later. Okay?"

"You'll come back?"

I stopped at arm's reach. I could smell his cologne and see the razor nick on his throat. He had a few inches on me, and muscular arms that seemed ready to sweep me up into a protective hug and never let go—something I didn't get often enough in my line of work.

"All my stuff's here, isn't it?" I said. "Where else would I go?"

"You're leaving now."

I sensed a challenge in his words, only I had no prior experience with which to judge them. "Yes, I am, but I'm coming back." Maybe. "This is going to sound strange, but who else thinks I'm dead?"

His lips puckered. "The cops and EMTs who came when I called."

My stomach roiled. So he had found her with her wrist open and called for help. He'd probably spent the entire night cleaning the bathroom, trying to erase the blood from memory and sight.

"The coroner's office, obviously," he continued.

"Jenny called this morning when you didn't show for work, but I didn't pick up. I hadn't . . ." He inhaled, held it, and blew hard through his nose. "I hadn't called anyone else yet. Good thing, huh?"

"Yeah. Good thing."

"Are you sure you don't remember—?"

"I don't." I held up a hand. Twenty questions dangled on my lips, but Chalice was not my priority. "I really don't. Later, okay?"

"Okay." His hand rose up, away from his hip. I tensed. He stopped, fingers hovering inches from my face. I forced myself to relax, to give him this little thing. The tip of one finger traced a line from my cheek to my chin, feather light. Sweet. "I can't believe it's really you," he said.

Instinctively, I reached up and grasped his roaming hand. Squeezed. He clutched it like a lifeline, his eyes sparkling with moisture.

"I've never been so glad to be wrong about something in my life," he said. "When I saw you like that, the tub full of blood, I almost died. You're my best friend, Chalice. I don't know what I'd do without you."

My heart broke for him. For a brief, blinding moment, I considered spitting out the truth. But it would do me no good. He would return to mourning for his friend sooner or later. Today, he had the luxury of make-believe. Sometimes denial was better than reality.

"Me, too," I said, forcing out the lie. "Just . . . don't tell anyone you saw me?"

"Okay."

I released his hand. He watched, silent but intent, as I laced up a pair of running shoes. I kept my eyes forward, away from him, pretending that I belonged there as much as he did. He bought the illusion, every scrap of it.

Still wishing I had a cell phone and more cash, I headed for the front door. Alex watched me go from his spot by the bedroom door. I stopped with my hand on the knob and looked back at him. He smiled. I smiled back, then ducked out into the hallway.

Chapter Three

70:33

Once I crossed the Black River and retreated to the east side of the city, I lost the keen sense of displacement that had haunted me since waking up in the morgue. In its place, I discovered something new and barely detectable. The air around me seemed alive, energized, like an impending lightning strike. It might have been a side effect of the resurrection, but I doubted that. It hadn't started until I crossed the river again—until I found myself downtown, in the neighborhood known as Mercy's Lot. It was where I belonged, among the hopeless and the damned. Angry human souls without privilege, living side by side with creatures they couldn't comprehend and chose not to see.

The real cause of the city's sharp contrasts between prosperity and decay isn't unemployment or a police department impotent to stop rising street gang violence. It's the Dregs: creatures of nightmare and legend, eking out their existence with the rest of us. Some are friendly to humans—gargoyles, the Fey, and most of the were-Clans are tentative allies. Other races, like gremlins and trolls, just don't care; they leave us alone and we leave them alone.

But vampires, goblins, and some weres longed to see us wiped out, and that's where people like me came into play. Dreg Bounty Hunters. Enlisted young and trained hard, we are the only defense between the violent Dregs and innocent humans. Our credo is simple: they break the law, they die.

The fun part was deciding *how* they died.

I took the Wharton Street footbridge across a spiderweb of intersecting railroad tracks. The heavy odor of metal and burning coal tingled my nostrils, familiar and welcoming. Far away, a train whistled. I paused and looked at the tracks, the warehouses on both sides of the stretch of sandy ground, and the rows of abandoned boxcars.

My first kill as a trainee had been down there. Six months of Boot Camp hadn't prepared me for working as part of a team. It taught me to defend myself, to think on my quickly moving feet, and to kill. Teamwork is learned in the field or you die fast.

Two days after being assigned to Wyatt and given a room in a shabby apartment above a hole-in-the-wall jewelry store, our Triad went hunting. Physically, we were an odd group. Ash Bedford was senior Hunter, but she barely hit the five-one mark; black hair and almond eyes hid a wealth of savagery always tempered by a sunny smile, present even when killing. Jesse Morales, conversely, towered at six-one—with dark hair, dark eyes, and smoldering cynicism that hid his marshmallow center.

I hadn't known those things at the time. My impressions were less than sparkling, as were theirs of me—the skinny, blond-haired, blue-eyed bitch from the south side, with a huge chip on her shoulder and enough ice around her heart to sink a luxury liner.

Our first assignment: two rogue vampire half-breeds had crashed the local prom. We had to kill them before they could turn their dates into midnight snacks.

I hadn't expected much from my new partners that night, so I ignored Ash's plan and barreled into the open, blades flashing. I never expected one of the two unsuspecting victims to hit me in the head with her rhinestone clutch. Teenage girls are, apparently, protective of their boyfriends, vampire or not.

Jesse had yanked me out of the way before Halfie Number One could sink his half-formed fangs into my elbow and leave me to a fate worse than dying.

Halfies are easy targets for a rookie, because they're often young, always dumb, and, once in a while, completely insane from the infection. Creating half-breeds, though, is a major no-no, and the vampire Families, like the Hunters, make it their business to thin them out. Even more than humans, they disdain the mixing of species. Tainting bloodlines, so to speak, and it's one thing on which I actually agree with them.

For almost four years, Jesse, Ash, and I had been the most feared Hunter Triad in the city, our kills more than double that of the next team. The Dreg populations knew our faces and our reputations, and for the first time, I had a family. The first family to truly accept me.

My mother had ignored me in favor of a string of live-in boyfriends and, later, a heroin addiction, leaving me to fend for myself at the ripe old age of ten and a half. Seven months after my stepfather left us, she became Jane Doe Number Twelve, dead a week before the body was found. I became a ward of the state, and their rules and I did not get along. Bitterness was my only friend for seven years, until the Triads found me.

Ash showed me how to apply mascara. Jesse taught me how to whistle. For all their trouble, I watched Ash get stabbed in the throat, and then I shot Jesse in the back. Nothing puts your allies on you faster than being accused of turning traitor and murdering your teammates.

Even if that's not what happened.

The only advantage to walking around the city in Chalice's body was anonymity. If both Triads and Dregs knew Evangeline Stone was dead, they'd never see me coming.

Unless Chalice was a klutz, and I couldn't get her body to do what needed to be done.

At the far end of the bridge, a sharp tremor tore up my spine. I grabbed on to the handrail, certain I'd been attacked, but no one was within a dozen yards of me. Traffic continued past, paying me no mind. I looked for shadows, strange shapes, prying eyes, anything out of the ordinary. Nothing.

"You're being paranoid, Evy," I muttered, and kept walking.

Four blocks from the train yards, the ground began to slope. On the east side of the river, the city had dozens of hills and dips. Some streets followed the natural curve of the ground, and others crossed above the city on elevated bridges, in a maze of over- and underpasses.

Cars and trucks drove past. Once or twice I earned a honk. I discounted hitching on the grounds that, in the middle of a fight, I didn't need to discover that Chalice had a glass jaw.

My progress took me into a residential area on the north side of Mercy's Lot, full of weekly apartment rentals and cheap motels that advertised hourly rates. Many of them rose ten or more stories into the sky. Already elevated on hills, they appeared to tower over the rest of the city. Then a gap appeared in the distance, a block to the west of my current position. As I continued up the sloping street, the gap became more pronounced, like a missing tooth in an otherwise perfect mouth.

Yellow tape cordoned off the block. Sawhorses stood a weak sentry line across the sidewalk that ran parallel to the wreckage. It looked like no one was willing to pay to have the site bulldozed, so a mass of burnt wood and brick and metal lay where the Sunset Terrace apartment complex had once stood.

I stopped across the street, hands shaking, overcome by a wave of grief. Many were-Clans lived together, finding comfort and safety in their own kind. The Owlkins—a race of gentle shape-shifters who took on the form of owls, falcons, eagles, and other birds of prey—had once lived in Sunset Terrace. The community had thrived, because they chose neutrality over hostility. Levelheaded and fair, they often served as negotiators between disputing weres.

Now, because of me, they were gone. I didn't know if any had survived the Triads' assault.

I could still hear their screams. Feel the scorch of the fire on my face. The smell of burning wood and flesh. Danika's voice telling me to run. Three hundred dead. It was the price they paid for harboring a fugitive Hunter. Fugitive for a crime she didn't even commit.

I hadn't understood it then, and I still didn't. We'd been lured to Halfie territory and attacked. So why come after me less than ten minutes after I reported the assault? Why was I dodging the bullets of other Hunters, instead of working with them to learn who set us up in the first place?

If I knew any of that before I died, it was lost to a well in the Swiss cheese mess of my memories. All I recalled was going to the Owlkins for protection, being tracked there by the Triads, and running yellow while three hundred gentle souls were burned alive for their kindness. A hostile and over-the-top reaction I just did not understand. And I couldn't imagine how the Triads had justified it to themselves.

"Now what?" I asked the wreckage. The faraway beep of a car horn was the only response given.

Behind me, a door slammed. I jumped, pivoting on one foot with a surprising amount of grace. A woman in a short skirt, wearing makeup piled on with a shovel, clacked down the sidewalk in high heels, away from the building behind me. She paid no attention to me, but even from a distance, I sensed something off about her. It was the way she walked, holding herself a little too upright, too stiff-legged—the way a goblin female walked when she was trying to pass as human.

Only goblin females could pass and, even then, it was a rare feat. Goblins had naturally curved spines, which accounted for their hunched-over appearance. Some females were able to overcome the curve and maintain a straight posture. Contacts covered red eyes, dye took care of the blue-black hair, and files flattened sharp teeth. Males were incapable of passing. They had more severe hunches, oily skin, pointed ears, and rarely grew taller than five feet—even when standing straight up.

On a normal day, I would have slipped into the shadows and tailed Madame Goblin until I discovered why she was wandering around the city in broad daylight, dressed like a hooker. But today was hardly normal, and I had no proof she wasn't just bad at walking in heels.

She disappeared around the block. On the same corner stood an old-fashioned telephone booth. Dialing Wyatt's number should have been as natural as breathing, but even if I could remember it, what would he say? When had I last spoken to him? What did we say? He had been a driving force in my life for the last four years. At once fiercely supportive and shatteringly critical, and somehow he always made it work. We worked as a Triad because of him.

Only now his team was dead, and nothing was how it used to be. Now I had no one to turn to, except for Chalice's roommate, and he was likely to have me committed if I tried to tell him the truth.

At some point, I'd started walking toward the phone. I stopped halfway there. Turning myself in to the Department was giving up. It meant that the Owlkins died—no, not died, they were slaughtered—for nothing.

No. They died for something: me. A debt worth more than I could possibly repay.

The wind shifted, pushing the acrid stench of burnt wood and tepid water in my direction. I sneezed and bit my tongue. My eyes watered.

Overwhelming loneliness—something I hadn't felt in a very long time—crashed over me like a wave. I was crushed beneath it, helpless and alone. The world grayed out, at once fuzzy and keenly electric. I held on to consciousness until the dizzy spell passed. Fainting in the street was not on today's To Do list. Getting answers was.

I grabbed the pay phone's handset, unaware that I'd entered the booth until I touched the grimy plastic. I lifted it, then dropped it back into the cradle. Was getting those answers worth probable execution? The Department would file me away as Neutralized. Normally they allowed Triads to operate under our own rules, answerable only to our Handlers, who answered to the brass—three key people in the Metro Police. Until someone really, truly screwed up.

The phone rang. I yelped and jumped back, slamming my elbow into the corner of the door. Needles lanced up my right arm, numbing the nerves. Fucking funny bone.

Two rings, sharp and clear.

I spun in a complete circle, halfway in the booth, surveying the surrounding buildings. No one came running to answer the call. The street was quiet, empty.

Three rings. Insistent.

My fingers closed around the mouthpiece.

Four.

I picked it up, silencing the offending noise. Gingerly, I held it to my ear. The line was open, but I heard nothing. Not even heavy breathing. Seconds ticked off, each one stretching out in a lengthy silence.

Frustrated, I swallowed my doubt, and said, "Hello?" Silence. I took a chance, not daring to hope. "Wyatt?"

Click.

Shit.

I dropped the phone and backpedaled out of the booth. My foot stamped down on something hard. The warmth of an arm wrapped around my waist, while a hand clamped over my mouth. Panic hit like ice water. One of my hands came up, clutching at what my eyes couldn't see. Years of training told me that screaming was futile, but Chalice's body refused to cooperate.

I shrieked against my human (I hoped) gag, and tried to bite the palm and failed. I ground the heel of my sneaker down, longing for my heavy combat boots. My captor grunted, but didn't loosen his ghostly hold.

Broad daylight. He was attacking me in broad daylight.

I hooked my left ankle around his, shifted my weight backward, and pulled. We fell over. I drove my elbow into his ribs just as he hit the sidewalk. The pained grunt it elicited was music to my ears. I landed a second jab. His hold loosened.

"Will you stop? I won't hurt you."

I froze, surprise replacing my fight instinct, and marveled at the most beautiful sound I'd ever heard. Rolling sideways, I dropped into a crouch and found myself face-to-face with—

Dead air. And the sidewalk. Lots of empty sidewalk.

"Wyatt?" I asked. Had I hallucinated the whole thing as preparation for my loony bin audition?

Warmth brushed my hand. I jerked.

"Evy?" asked Wyatt's disembodied voice. He could have been right in front of me, as the direction of his voice implied.

Wherever he was, he shouted a sudden warning. "Behind you!"

The air behind me shifted, and I flattened myself to the sidewalk. Something sailed over my head, "oofed!" as it hit a person who wasn't even there, and skidded on its scaly ass until it slammed against a trash can.

The goblin was young and stupid to be attacking me alone. He scrambled to his feet, standing barely four-foot-five hunched over, which made him tall for a goblin. Ruby eyes glared at me from beneath bushy black eyebrows. He snarled, lips pulling back over jagged teeth.

Bile scorched the back of my throat. The unexpected reaction came without explanation or emotion—just immediate and profound revulsion at the sight of the angry goblin male, a simple leather loincloth the only thing between him and immodesty.

Goblins never attacked in the open, or during the day.

Air swirled behind me. I spun around, anticipating an attack from behind. The assumption proved correct, but the additional pair of goblins who appeared to assist their friend were already sprawled on the sidewalk. Like they'd run headfirst into an invisible brick wall.

I pivoted again, but turned too late. Two inches of a dagger blade sank into my left shoulder, just above the cleft of my armpit. Pain shrieked through my chest. I spun the other way and clipped the goblin square in his pointy nose with my elbow. His head snapped backward. Fuchsia blood spurted from his nostrils. I continued my pivot and landed a roundhouse kick to the side of his head. He tumbled ass over teakettle into the street.

Chalice's untrained legs almost tangled together, but I kept myself upright. Inner thigh muscles screeched, protesting the acrobatic move. I grabbed the narrow hilt of the goblin's blade and yanked. It slid out neatly and with only a minor amount of additional pain. I charged the downed goblin, intent on slitting him from sternum to scrotum.

Wyatt cried out—a pained sound I knew too well. Attacker forgotten, I fixed my attention on the other two goblins, who appeared to be hanging in midair, attached to some invisible object. An object that was bleeding from a dagger, which dangled from nothing about four feet off the ground. The smaller goblin's head was snapped back by an invisible blow, followed by a second that dislodged him. He hit the pavement and took off running.

The remaining goblin snapped his cone-shaped teeth at the air. The blade of the embedded dagger became suddenly visible, coated in red blood. It turned and buried itself to the hilt in the throat of the trapped goblin, splattering fuchsia blood across what looked

like a pair of human legs. The dead goblin was tossed
to the sidewalk.

Blood-soaked shoes took a step toward me. I
stepped backward. Red, human blood continued to
ooze into thin air, outlining a man's torso.

It couldn't be. He was Gifted, sure, but his power
was summoning inanimate objects. Since when could
Wyatt turn invisible?

The retreating goblin had almost reached the end
of the block. I stepped into the quiet street, took aim,
and with every bit of concentration I could muster,
loosed the knife. It sailed straight, but arched down
at the last instant. Instead of hitting the goblin square
in the back, it buried itself in the creature's leg. He
stumbled forward, into the road, and was flattened
by a speeding pickup truck. Brakes squealed, and the
truck fishtailed out of sight.

From a distance, the mess looked like the remains
of someone's dog, all black and pink and grotesquely
inhuman. The truck's engine continued to rumble just
out of sight. I waited for the driver to back up or walk
over, to see whose pet he'd just mangled. Instead, the
engine roared and was gone.

Typical.

"Where's the third?" Wyatt asked.

Shit. The one who stabbed me had gotten away.

"We need to get off the street," he said. "Now."

I wasn't about to argue. I followed the free-floating
bloody torso toward the nearest apartment building,
trying to reconcile my eyes with my senses. I smelled
the blood, both human and goblin, and something
else, so familiar—a spicy aftershave, like musk and
cinnamon, unique to Wyatt. The continued invisibility

frightened me, even though I'd never admit it. I wasn't the only one who had changed.

He led me through a narrow, musty lobby, past a row of mailboxes, toward a door marked with a laundry machine symbol. I followed him into a dank stairwell. Down we went, into a gray and damp world of concrete floors and cement-block walls. A chill wormed down my spine. At the bottom of the stairs, the room opened up. Four washing machines lined one wall, with four dryers opposite. A long, wooden table divided the room. There were no windows and no chairs.

"It is really you?" his disembodied voice asked.

I nodded at the blood. "It's me, and if it's really you, I could sure as shit use some answers. Maybe a face to talk to."

"Right; sorry."

He spoke words I didn't recognize. The air around him shimmered and rippled, like heat off the surface of a desert road. A body materialized, faded, and then appeared with perfect clarity. One hand pressed against his wounded side; the other clutched a glowing yellow jewel. He desperately needed to shave the dark stubble that shadowed his chin and cheeks—as black as his short hair and intense, thick-lashed eyes. Blood of two species had soaked the legs of his jeans, staining them purple.

Hurt and surprised and staring at me with open curiosity, Wyatt Truman smiled. It was such a familiar gesture of affection that my reaction to it was entirely unexpected. Something started in my stomach and surged upward, then came back down to settle deep in my abdomen—an instant and instinctive reaction to the mere sight of him, unlike anything I'd ever experienced.

Wyatt had been my boss, my friend, and my confidant. Besides Jesse and Ash, he was the closest thing to family I'd ever known. I crossed the short space that separated us and flung my arms around his shoulders, ignoring the blood as I hugged him. Hard. One arm snaked around my waist. His breath tickled my ear.

"You have no fucking idea how glad I am to see you," I said. "I thought I was going crazy."

"I'm sorry, Evy," he whispered. "I am so sorry."

"For what?"

He stiffened. I pulled away to arm's length. He pressed his lips into a thin line, black eyes searching mine for . . . something. Bright spots of color darkened his cheeks, and the intensity of his stare sent little niggles of doubt worming through my stomach.

"Evy, what do you remember?" he asked.

I didn't like the sound of that. I backed up, putting another few feet of space between us. "I remember the Triads attacking the Owlkins, slaughtering them because they were hiding me. I called you, because I didn't know what else to do." But the memories still ended with me sneaking through a city street toward our meeting place.

"That was a week ago," he said.

"No kidding. Do you mind filling in the blanks?"

Despair crumpled his face. I bit the inside of my cheek, clenching my fists to resist the overwhelming instinct to hug him again. Something had happened to me, something very bad.

"Wyatt, what happened? How did I die?"

His eyes flickered toward my shoulder. "You're hurt."

"I'm fine." Strangely enough, the knife wound didn't hurt anymore. It sort of itched. "How did I die?"

He limped over to one of the dryers and opened the door. Wrinkled laundry spilled onto the floor. He put the yellow jewel on top of the dryer and began sifting through the clothing. I eyed the precious gem, wondering if that was the source of his invisibility cloak, and how much he'd paid for it.

"Wyatt?"

"Nice necklace."

I fingered the cross around my neck. "Don't change the subject."

He checked the waistband of a pair of jeans and, determining them appropriate, tossed them onto the room's center table. "I should have been there when you woke," he said, returning to his search. "But you didn't come back where we thought you would. Even dead, you're pretty damned contrary, you know that?"

I smiled at the familiar jab. I always preferred questioning his orders over following them, and it drove him bat shit. Drove my partners bat shit, too, when they were alive. Even if I was wrong, the fun was in the argument.

"Next time leave a better trail of bread crumbs, and I'll try resurrecting to the appropriate body," I said.

He threw a cotton shirt on top of the jeans and stood up. Pain bracketed his eyes and pinched his mouth. My stomach tightened. I was such a bitch. Here he was, bleeding to death in front of me, and I kept nagging him for answers.

"Take off your shirt," I said, closing the distance between us.

Wyatt arched an eyebrow.

I rolled my eyes. "Let me see the wound, jackass."

I reached for his shirt, but he caught my hand. A tremor danced up my arm, awakened by his touch. I looked up, startled. Something dangerous flashed in his eyes, there and gone in a blink. Warning bells clanged in my head.

"I did it," he said.

"Did what?"

His shoulders drooped. Agony radiated off him. He dropped my hand, and I mourned the loss of his touch. Only for a moment, though, because he spoke three words that shattered everything.

"I killed you."

Chapter Four

69:47

"That's not funny," I said, fingers clenching into fists. A shiver wiggled down my spine.

Wyatt frowned. "It wasn't a joke, Evy. You died because of me."

A tiny bit of fear evaporated, replaced by annoyance. I could have belted him in the jaw. "Then why didn't you just say that? 'You died because of me' and 'I killed you' do not imply the same thing."

"It means the same to me."

"You aren't the one who died!"

He flinched as though slapped. Uncertainty flickered across his face, but the agony never wavered. Nor did the utter certainty that my death was somehow his fault—a fact that remained to be seen, since my Swiss cheese memory was missing a couple of important details.

He put his back to me and tried to take off his blood-soaked shirt. It rose halfway up, revealing a crisscross of pencil-thin bruises. They decorated his lower back like graffiti, dark blue and painful-looking.

His arms caught in the tacky sleeves, trapping them above his head in a tangle that would have been comical if he hadn't suddenly cried out.

The knife wound gaped open just below his rib cage and still oozed blood. Deep, but not jagged or life-threatening, as I'd first assumed. I turned him around and helped him pull his head and arms through the shirt, finally freeing him of the ruined cotton. More bruises, identical to the others, marked his chest and well-defined abs. He'd gone through some form of hell. And if I found out he'd gone through it solely for me, I'd give him a matching black eye.

"You might need stitches," I said, tossing the old shirt to the floor in a soggy heap.

"It's fine."

"Really?" I planted my hands on my hips and fixed him with my hardest stare, hoping the stance was as effective on Chalice as it had been in my old body. "Since when do you downplay a wound of any kind, Wyatt?"

His mouth opened and closed several times in succession, until he finally gave up on a response. I rifled through the recently laundered clothing until I located a plain white cotton T-shirt. I ripped it into one long strip, and then folded the rest over into a makeshift bandage. When I returned my attention to Wyatt, he'd already stripped out of his bloody jeans and slipped into a new pair.

"Arm up," I said.

He followed direction, folding his arm up and around his neck, giving me a clear field. I pressed the makeshift bandage against the wound. He hissed; I flinched.

"So are we going to talk about this?" I asked. "Hand."

He pressed his palm against the bandage. "You know, I imagined this conversation a dozen times, how I'd try to explain everything to you. Now it's just . . . hard."

"Use small words." I looped the strip around his waist and positioned it over the bandage. Twisted the ends. Pulled it into a knot.

He grunted. "Where should I start?"

"How about what day I died?" I suggested, doubling the knot. I didn't need the bandage shifting.

"May seventeenth."

Three days ago. Four days after the last I remembered. My mouth felt suddenly dry. "Okay, good. Let's go further back, then, shall we? Why in the blue fuck did the Triads go in and murder the Owlkins? Because if we talked about it, I need a refresher."

Wyatt reached for the fresh shirt, but didn't put it on. He fingered the blue material, turning something over in his mind. I recognized his thoughtful face. One advantage to having a new body was that he didn't know my tics and foibles anymore, the way I still knew his.

"I honestly don't know why, Evy, but it was excessive," he said. "The official story was that the Department brass wanted you neutralized at any cost. They think you killed your own Triad teammates. They blame you for Ash and Jesse."

Well, they were half right.

"Apparently the Fey Council got wind that a Triad member had, as they put it, turned traitor," he said.

"When they found out about the trouble at the bridge, and that you were involved, they stepped in."

Damn me and my infamous reputation.

He continued. "When one of the Council leaders calls up the brass and demands that their secret stash of Bounty Hunters Neutralize a threat, they listen. When the brass found out where you were staying, they planned an assault and ordered the Triads to carry it out."

"Yeah, I remember that part."

The sounds of my friends screaming as they died would never fade from my mind. Danika, barely sixteen by human years, had forced me to run. I never should have left the Owlkins alone to fight the Triads, who shouldn't have attacked in the first place.

Putting aside the simple question of how they tracked me to Sunset Terrace (even I can make mistakes when caught in the clutches of grief), the attack made no sense. The Fey Council is to the Department what soft money donors are to politicians—silent partners who occasionally benefit from offering their support, but nonetheless hold sway. They also hold magic over our heads like a toy on a string. Giving us occasional swipes, but never sharing their intimate knowledge. Not even to our human Gifted, who struggle to understand and live with their unusual powers.

Considering the steady increase in Dreg-on-human violence over the last six months, a holy smack-down may have seemed inspired to the brass. The perfect excuse to nearly wipe out a species and send a very clear "Don't fuck with us" message to the other were-Clans.

"Did anyone survive?"

"I don't know, Evy. I'm sorry."

"I called you. We were supposed to meet. Did we?"

"Yeah, we met." He slipped one arm into the shirt and through the sleeve. Slow, calculated movements designed to mask the flood of emotions running across his face. "You wanted to turn yourself in, and I tried to talk you out of it. I'd heard rumblings of a major deal going down between the goblin Queens and some of the Bloods, and thought if we could get something solid, the brass would be lenient."

Goblins and vampires? Sure, they were united in their hatred of humans and Fey, but they rarely worked together. Both species were fiercely independent and proud. Teaming up was like admitting to weakness— something neither liked to do.

His other arm went into the shirt, and he didn't bother hiding a pained grimace. "You said you would make contact, see what you could find out. The next day, you were captured by goblins. They tortured you for two days before we found you. You died before you could tell us anything."

Tortured and killed by goblins. That explained my instant revulsion on the street. I forced away any speculation as to just what that torture had entailed. I knew goblins and their ways. Any details would probably make me curl into a fetal position and cry for a few hours. Perhaps memory loss was better for my sanity.

Still, it didn't explain why I hadn't been allowed to rest in peace. "So why bring me back? Resurrection spells aren't cheap, Wyatt. Did I learn something about the goblins and the Bloods? Something important enough to pay the price?"

"I think you did, but you wouldn't tell. At least,

not around the people who were there when we found you. Even though you were dying, you didn't talk. I could see in your eyes that you wanted to, but something frightened you into silence."

"Something or someone," I said, uncertain which I preferred. "So that's why you brought me back? To pick my brain about those final moments, only I can't remember them?"

"That was the plan. Obviously we didn't account for this specific contingency."

"That's a pretty big fuckup, Wyatt."

He had the temerity to smile. "You don't look like you, but you sure as hell sound like yourself."

I flipped him a one-fingered salute.

"And I get to be selfish about something," he said, fishing his wallet out of his old jeans. "I can apologize to you."

A novel experience: bringing someone back from the dead to apologize for getting them killed in the first place. "Well, you're forgiven."

"You may want to wait on that until you get your memory back."

I didn't know if that was simply self-deprecation (not something he did well or often) or said in earnest (much more likely), so I kept quiet.

"Let me see your shoulder," he said.

"It's fine."

"Now who's downplaying?"

I turned around. He lifted my hair up and away, so much more than used to be there. I had kept my straight blond hair cut short, just above the shoulder. The weight of Chalice's wavy locks continued to startle me. Gentle fingers stroked my shoulder around the itchy spot. My stomach again fluttered at his touch. That was weird.

"Incredible," he whispered. "It's already starting to heal."

"Really?" I reached back and touched the wound. Sure enough, a thick scab had formed, and it was barely sore to the touch. I checked the laceration scar on my arm—gone. Track marks, as well. "Cool. So is this a side effect of the spell, or does Chalice have superhuman healing powers we didn't know about?"

"Who?"

I spun, striking a pose for him. "Chalice Frost, the chick we brought back to life. And since we've circled back to that, how did I end up in her and not in someone . . . I don't know, graceful?"

"I'm not sure. We had a former Hunter ready for you, a girl about your age who had died two days ago. She was trained. I don't know why you jumped to this body, and neither does the Elder who performed the spell."

I studied his face, searching for truth and finding a blank stare. He was trying so hard to keep emotion out of this, but it continued to leak through in his words and his actions. Maybe he didn't know what went wrong, but it was high on my list of things to find out. Soon.

"In the long run, I guess it doesn't matter why," I said. "Granted, having a body that does what my brain tells it would be nice, but we all have our crosses to bear. So if the Department put up for the spell to bring me back, is it safe to assume they won't kill me on sight?"

Wyatt flexed his jaw, then chose that moment to

pick up his soiled clothing and dump them into the room's only waste can. Slow, deliberate movements. He was buying time again.

"Magic has a high price, Wyatt, and nothing is more costly than this." I poked myself in the chest, smearing a spot of blood that had transferred from him to me. Ick. "Who paid, Wyatt?"

"The brass doesn't know," he said, back still turned. "Neither do any of the other Triads. I don't trust them, not right now. It's one of the reasons I was staying cloaked."

I got into his face, pleased that I now stood eye-level to him, rather than six inches shorter. It made intimidation easier. Height and size made up for the brute strength Chalice's body lacked. He didn't back down, but he did keep his eyes fixed on the floor.

"Who paid?" I growled, both eager and terrified to hear his reply.

His nostrils flared as he exhaled hard through his nose.

I moved in, leaving only the tiniest cushion of air between us. I could smell him—blood and sweat and aftershave, the barest hint of coffee on his breath. The minuscule space was alive with electricity. The short hairs on the back of my neck tingled. Was he doing that, or was it my imagination? I hooked one finger beneath his chin and pressed until his eyes met mine.

Inky black pools teemed with frustration and worry, and with something else I didn't dare label. Something so close to desire that it scared me.

"Who?" I asked.

He swallowed. "Me."

I stepped back, eager for distance after hearing the

response I both wanted and feared. Wanted because it meant he was convinced of the importance of what I knew—convinced enough to put up an enormous price. Feared because of the price he had likely offered in return. I thought of those bruises, and my stomach roiled.

For humans, the use of magic exacts a physical toll—always painful, sometimes even crippling. Gifted have little choice in the matter, but magical spells can be purchased for the correct price; often the price includes a promise of silence, because black market magic is frowned upon by the Council. Faeries selling spells will up the ante to include proof of sincerity on the part of the buyer. Sadistic creatures, no matter what books say, faeries are rumored to require a physical beating as that proof.

Fey magic isn't cheap. What the hell had he gotten himself into?

"I must be repressing one hell of a secret," I said, hoping to de-emphasize the enormity of what it meant to me.

He tilted his head up slightly, then back down in a curt nod. "You were with them for almost three days, Evy. When we found you, you were dying. You were mostly lucid, but someone in that room scared you into taking your secret to the grave."

"And you thought that I'd wake up and give you all the answers you needed, right?"

"Something like that." He furrowed dark eyebrows. "I never expected memory loss."

I hopped up onto the wooden laundry table and leaned back on the palms of my hands, legs swinging freely. "Guess you should have used your price for a séance and saved the trouble of resurrection, since it's obviously doing neither of us any good."

His hand jerked. I'd struck a nerve. Good. My own nerves were well frayed. I wanted to share the wealth.

"We just need to jog your memory," he said, slipping first his wallet and then the yellow jewel into his jeans pocket. "I'm not calling this a loss yet, Evy. Not until the clock's run out."

Breath caught in my throat. Right; the clock. I forced an exhale, but my heart continued to beat too fast. "Wyatt, how long do I have? I know that spells like this have a shelf life, and if you were expecting an instant replay, you wouldn't have bargained for a lot of time. A week? Five days?"

His shoulders slumped. "Three days."

Hell. Seventy-two hours. I shivered. Was that enough time? It didn't feel like enough, not if we were running cold.

His hands gently squeezed my knees, offering silent support. I looked up, right into his eyes. One of his hands reached up and brushed a lock of hair away from my cheek, carefully tucking it behind my ear.

I caught myself staring at his slightly parted lips, wondering . . . what? No, not wondering. *Wanting.* Wanting something I had never wanted before.

No. "Do you have a plan?" I asked.

He nodded, the intensity of his stare never wavering. "I want you to talk to Smedge. He would always talk to you, give up what he knew when you asked. He won't talk to me. I've tried."

Smedge, one of my most loyal informants. One of my strengths as a Triad Hunter was my ability to get Dregs to trust me, even if they had no reason for it. Maybe it was my smile, or my all-American blond-haired, blue-eyed looks. It didn't matter, as long as they talked. But I hadn't spoken to Smedge in weeks.

"I don't think Smedge ever liked you," I said.

"Bridge trolls don't tend to like human males, period."

"Too true, but he *really* didn't like you." I nudged his leg with my foot. "Can't imagine why, though. You're such a charmer in person."

He quirked an eyebrow. "I insulted his bridge once."

"You didn't!"

Wyatt shrugged. I punched him in the shoulder.

"What?" he asked, drawing back.

"You never insult a troll's chosen bridge, you idiot. Hell, even a trainee knows that." Of all the stupid things to say to another species . . .

"I apologized later on," he said.

"Smedge's bridge is across town from here. How are we going to get there?"

"I have a car parked the next block over." He hesitated. "Something else is out there hunting and it's not human, so we need to be careful."

"Something?" I recalled how I'd felt crossing the Wharton Street Bridge. The oddest sense of being followed, contrary to physical evidence.

"I haven't seen it, but I've heard rumors. Some call it an interspecies breeding, but they don't know of what. Just that it has a keen sense of smell and can track anything."

"No one's ever heard of a successful interspecies breeding."

"Like I said, it's a rumor. I haven't seen it."

"Sounds charming."

"Did I mention the double rows of razor teeth?"

"Are you trying to get me all hot and bothered?"

He rolled his eyes. "I know you like to kill things, Evy, but this one's different."

"If it's real."

"It's real."

"Okay, it's real. I take it you have weapons?"

A sly smile confirmed it even before he replied. "You'd better believe it."

Chapter Five

Calling the stockpile of weapons in the trunk of Wyatt's car a "cache" only insulted the variety and care that had gone into the selection. "Arsenal" painted a better picture of the plethora of weapons stored in cases beneath the trunk's false bottom. There were revolvers and rifles, each with multiple-round clips. Regular and fragmenting bullets for thinner-skinned targets like goblins and gremlins—although in five years I'd never had to hunt a gremlin, much less shoot one. Anticoagulant-coated bullets for the Bloods. Silver nitrate tips for weres. Acid tips for gargoyles.

Grenades and flash bombs were lined up in fleeced cases next to smokers. My personal favorites were the blades—sharp enough to slice paper on their edges. A variety of smaller knives, smooth edge and serrated, came in a variety of sizes. There were also two sharpened broadswords—I was trained for them, but hated their weight—and a pair of machetes on velvet pads, next to a row of throwing stars and brass knuckles. I spotted a couple of dog whistles tucked into the corner, gleaming silver—with their heightened hearing, it was an easy and underrated method of knocking Halfies and Bloods for a loop.

I took a sheathed serrated knife the size of my palm and strapped it to my right ankle. A closed butterfly knife went into the back pocket of my jeans. Wyatt strapped on a shoulder holster for one of the revolvers and grabbed a fragging clip and an anticoag clip—standard gear for Handlers, since they acted more like a guide for the Triads than an active participant in our activities. I had never seen Wyatt fire a gun in my life, but things had changed. He looked completely able to pull the trigger and mean it.

When we were safely in his car and cruising toward downtown's Lincoln Street Bridge, I asked, "So what did you do? Raid the Department vault before you went rogue?"

"Of course not," he said. Pity. "I raided them afterward."

He smiled as if joking, but something in his voice hinted at sincerity.

"How about that cloaking jewel? You get that there, too?"

"No, I traded it for a favor."

"Yeah? What was her name?"

"His name is Brutus." The annoyance in his tone came out of nowhere.

I turned sideways in my seat, less interested in the scenery than in the subtle changes peeking through the man I thought I knew. Only three days and he seemed a different person. "What was the favor?"

He grunted. "I summoned something, and he gave

me a one-shot cloak. I needed to stay off the radar for a while."

"Until you had me back?"

"Something like that."

"So the jewel?"

"Useless."

Of course, because having an invisibility cloak at our fingertips was too damned easy. "So you going to tell me about those bruises?" I asked.

His hands white-knuckled the steering wheel. "Does anyone else know that Candace—"

"Chalice."

"That Chalice is alive?"

I tilted my head to one side. "You mean besides the two morticians who nearly died of heart attacks when I came to life on their table?" Another half smile from him.

"Yeah, besides them."

"Chalice's roommate."

"How did she find out?"

"He. Since I woke up butt-naked and abandoned in a morgue, I needed money and clothes. I found Chalice's address on a chart, so I went home to change. He interrupted me."

"He saw you naked?"

"No, pervert." I rolled my eyes. "And Alex does get points for neither passing out nor screaming like a little girl, since he both called the ambulance and later identified the body. He saw her—saw me—dead."

"How did she die?" Wyatt made a left-handed turn at a four-way intersection.

"Does it matter?"

"Guess not. Yet."

We had left the high-rising apartment complexes behind for the darker, grittier streets of Mercy's Lot. Ancient brick buildings, many of them old industrial shops that had closed at the turn of the century, lined the streets. Sidewalks held broken benches and overflowing waste cans, gutters filled with trash and standing rainwater. In a few hours, when the sun went down, neon lights would blaze and welcome people inside to rid them of their hard-earned money.

A hustler's paradise; a hooker's best corner. The city would be teeming with life and light and sin, and things that went bump in the night—creatures I would normally be prepared to hunt. Only tonight, under the cover of darkness, I would be the hunted.

"Do you think it was murder?" Wyatt asked.

What was his obsession? "I really haven't pondered it, Wyatt, but next time I see Alex I'll be sure to ask him how he felt when he found his roommate with her wrist slashed. I'm sure that conversation will go over real well."

Wyatt grunted, eyes on the road. "I'm sorry, Evy. All I was getting at is that if it was foul play, then whoever did it could get really annoyed when they find out that Chalice is alive and well and running around the city. We've got enough people gunning for us that we know about, you know?"

"Good point." Lucky us, then, that Chalice's worst enemy seemed to be herself.

Silence filled the car for the remainder of our trip. We drove past a raggedy newsstand, stuck between a Chinese take-out restaurant and a bar advertising "Adult Dancers Live." I briefly considered turning on the radio, but changed my mind. Wyatt's firm grip on the steering wheel betrayed his anxiety, reinforced by the slight twitch of a muscle in his lower jaw.

He drove southeast, toward the lower end of downtown where the Black River intersected a tributary of the Anjean River, before continuing south. Downtown was surrounded by water on three sides, with mountains creating a northern border. Uptown was, ironically, southwest of the Black River, and as we approached Lincoln Street, the tall, shiny buildings rose up high on the opposite riverbank. New and safe and well fortified—nothing like Mercy's Lot.

The bridge had two lanes for traffic, and a separate train bridge that ran parallel. Wyatt turned at the last exit before the bridge that would have taken us into the industrial parks and factories that were housed on the southeast bank of the Anjean River. The side street curved down one hundred and eighty degrees, turning us in the opposite direction. Another left and the underside of the Lincoln Street Bridge came into view.

The one-way street passed beneath the bridge, leaving little space between the cement underside and the gray water of the Anjean. Wyatt pulled onto the narrow shoulder, still half on the road, but with enough room for another car to pass. I climbed out to the cacophony of bridge traffic rumbling overhead and the smooth rushing of the river. The odors of oil and rotting fish tingled my nose, as familiar as it was disgusting.

"And you wonder why I insulted his bridge," Wyatt said.

"I never said I wondered." I walked around the front of the car to join him. "I just knew better than to say anything to his face."

He cocked his head to the side, regarding me with some amount of amusement. "That's my girl."

I smiled, warmed by his praise. Even as a rookie, I'd wanted only to make him proud. He was only ten years older than me, but was one of the rare Gifted. He could tap into the organic source of the Fey's power and manipulate it in a limited way. One in about thirty thousand humans have that ability, many of them under surveillance by the Triads—or like Wyatt, under contract for services. The Fey can sense them, but the only surefire way for humans to identify a Gifted is the birthmark—the size of a halfpenny, usually located midway down on the left buttock.

Magical hotspots exist all over the city, undetectable by normal humans. Only the Dregs, the Fey, and the human Gifted can sense them. I'd heard once that the Gifted were all born over one of those hot spots—breaks in the world where magic bled through. Even as a rare Gifted, inorganic summoning was a talent Wyatt seemed hesitant to use, even in his role as a Triad Handler.

It was, in some ways, a curse to the Gifted. While they possessed extraordinary talents, the human body was not designed to filter that sort of magical energy. Manipulation was often painful and took a physical toll. It also (according to rumor) made them sterile. And that was something likely to remain a rumor for the time being. I knew no other Gifted, and it wasn't a subject I was willing to broach with Wyatt. Ever.

The bridge thrummed thirty feet above our heads. A chain-link fence bordered the opposite side of the road, supposedly to prevent graffiti-happy teenagers from plastering their artwork all over the underside of the bridge. The metal support beams and concrete slope remained devoid of spray paint, but dozens of footprints marred the dust on the other side. Artists came, but something chased them away again. Something named Smedge.

Wyatt pulled back a weak spot in the fence, and I slipped through first. He followed. The fence fell back into place with a soft clang. Air moved in a constant swirl, pushed by the traffic overhead, kicking up dirt particles and grit. I stopped at the base of the angled concrete and stomped my foot on the ground.

"Smedge?" I said. "Hey, Dirt Face, it's Stony."

"Stony?" Wyatt asked.

"Nickname."

"I figured." He did a complete three-sixty, taking stock of our surroundings. "Are you sure he's going to recognize you before he decides to pound on us with a big, gravelly fist?"

"Bridge trolls are blind, remember?" I stomped my foot again. "They don't rely on five senses like humans. He'll know me."

Sure enough, the solid concrete began to vibrate. Slowly at first, like the gentlest shiver. Then it built to a roar, and what was once solid began to run like quicksand. It drew inward, gathering like a miniature tornado beneath the bridge. I raised my hand against the wind, as every bit of dirt was drawn toward its center.

An arm reached out from its whirling vortex, a hand uncurling and dividing into four fingers. Those fingers splayed against the ground by our feet. Wyatt stepped back, but I stood my ground. A second arm joined the first, and then a head pulled out, forming from the dirt and sand and stone, as large as my entire body, with pronounced eyes that couldn't see and a mouth that couldn't taste. A neck and shoulders grew last, until Smedge the bridge troll appeared to have pulled himself out of a giant hole in the ground, only to lounge beneath the bridge, perfectly at ease.

Sounds rumbled deep within his throat, as he remembered how to communicate with other, more verbal species. Bridge trolls were part of the earth itself and communicated through tremors and vibrations of the crust and core, rather than of wind through the larynx. Some of the largest earthquakes in recorded history were because of troll wars—something no one taught kids in geology class.

"Him," Smedge ground out. His voice came across like sandpaper against metal—harsh and unpleasant. *"Not . . . welcome."*

"I'll make sure he behaves," I said. "Smedge, do you remember me? It's Stony."

Sandy eyes made a show of looking at me, but I knew better. Air circled me like a cyclone, caressing my skin with fine particles of sand. He was smelling me in his own way, making sure I was telling the truth. I only hoped his unusual senses could "see" past my new appearance and identify his friend.

"Yes, Stony," Smedge said. *"Told . . . dead . . . but not."*

"No, I'm not, but that's a really long story. I don't have a lot of time, and we need your help."

"What I do?"

I deferred to Wyatt. I hadn't asked him why he needed to speak with Smedge, so I couldn't ask the question for him.

"Do you know a sprite named Amalie?" Wyatt asked.

My lips parted. That was his question? Amalie was a Fey Council Elder, ruler of the Five Sprite Guilds. A queen bee to thousands of worker bees was the only way to describe the sprite ranks. Each Guild had a ranking Master, each responsible to Amalie for the safety of the sprites under their care. We'd never met, but I had seen her from a distance. Tall and regal, with the looks of a model and curves of a porn star, she was nothing like what the word "sprite" implied. Her bodyguard, Jaron, had the build of a weight lifter. The only detail that betrayed them as nonhuman was the way their eyes glowed. Bright and fierce, like cobalt embers.

"What does she have to do with this?" I whispered.

He shook his head—a curt warning not to question him. I narrowed my eyes, but complied, and imagined how pretty he'd look with a black eye.

"Powerful," Smedge said. *"Building."*

"What's she building?" Wyatt asked.

"Power. More power. Cons...cons..." He growled, unable to articulate the word.

"Consolidate?" I offered.

The gravel head nodded.

"Why?" Wyatt took a step forward, rippling with tension.

"Compete. Win. Power."

"Does this have something to do with our final job?" I asked Wyatt. "That thing I was looking into between the goblins and the Bloods? Are sprites involved, too?"

"Maybe," he said. "Amalie was there the night we found you, Evy. Everyone who was there is a suspect."

"Taking sides," Smedge said. *"All. You must."*

"Humans must?" I asked.

Another grinding nod.

"Are the trolls taking sides?"

He growled and stopped moving. The silence stretched out for half a minute. A car honked above us, but Smedge remained frozen in place—a concrete statue of half a man, protruding from beneath a bridge.

"Soon," he rumbled, the sudden sound startling me.

So even the trolls, notorious for walking the center line of any interspecies conflict, were taking sides. Sides in a battle that no one had told us human beings about, and that sounded more and more like a power play on someone's part. Power plays were not uncommon from goblins. Bloods hated us, but rarely made direct attacks. Sprites were either working with or against them, and trolls were lined up to pick teams.

"We have to find out who else is taking sides," I said. "Could the Fey Council have anything to do with this?"

Wyatt ran his fingers through his short, black hair. "I don't know, but none of the Triads were talking about it as of yesterday. It could be rogues pulling all the strings."

"Maybe. Amalie may lead the sprites, but she still answers to the other Fey rulers. Gnomes, faeries, pixies, dryads, and sylphs need to be consulted before a Fey decision is handed down."

Wyatt stared.

I frowned. "What? I pay attention when you talk. Mostly. But why was Amalie there during my rescue?"

"Because one of her sprite guards found you and led us there."

"No safety."

I had forgotten about the Volkswagen-sized stone head in front of me. Smedge settled deeper into the concrete foundation, creating a heavy rumble beneath our feet. Trolls possess notoriously short attention spans, and our audience was almost over.

"No safety where? Here?" Wyatt asked.

"Coming. Pounding. Go."

It was all the encouragement I needed. "Thank you, Smedge."

"Stony friend. Stay well."

"I will."

With a sound like fracturing wood, Smedge withdrew into the underside of the bridge until nothing remained but smooth concrete. We slipped back out through the fence's hole, but I faltered halfway across the street, attacked by the niggling sense of being watched. Wyatt stopped and looked at me.

A howl, inhuman and nearby, shattered the rumble of traffic. It bounced beneath the bridge, echoing long after its source had stopped. A hulking shape bounded into the center of the road on all fours, one hundred feet from our position. It came to a graceful stop and arched its back, slowly standing upright, its back legs curved and grotesque. They wobbled with the effort, but the creature maintained its balance. Thin, black fur covered its legs and torso, but its chest of roped muscle was bare, smooth, shiny, and white-skinned. Its similarly colored arms were just as well muscled, with long claws on its front paws and deep elbow joints perfect for running on four feet. A long, black-tipped nose jutted out above a too-wide mouth. Shimmering yellow eyes blazed with fury and the sheer love of the hunt. Pointed ears turned toward us, listening, covered with the same black hair that extended across its head and down its neck.

It opened its mouth, baring double rows of razor teeth and pointed canines. I watched the monster flex its jaw, a steel trap ready for the kill. My stomach knotted. I'd never seen anything like it, let alone fought one, and it truly was a hellhound from my nightmares. I saw the earmarks of at least two species in it. It had to be Wyatt's rumored hybrid.

In my periphery, Wyatt's left hand crept across his waist toward the shoulder holster. The hound's eyes shifted to Wyatt, and it snarled. The hair along its neck bristled.

"Don't," I said, barely moving my lips. If the thing had vampire reflexes to go with its teeth, it could be on him and tearing his throat out before Wyatt could pull the trigger. "When I say so, get in the car."

"Evy—"

"Argue, and he eats you for lunch."

"Fine, but I can't resurrect you twice."

"You won't have to."

The butterfly knife would take too long to retrieve and open. The hound shifted its eyes back to me. It drew a lazy tongue across its fangs. The creature's intense gaze sent a worm of fear down my spine. Adrenaline surged. Every sense felt sharper, keener. It growled again. I tensed and rose up on the balls of my feet.

"Now!"

Wyatt pivoted and raced for the car. I bolted three steps to the right, using my body as a barrier between him and the hound, and dropped down into a one-kneed crouch. My fingers found the serrated knife's handle, wrapped around it, and pulled.

Falling back to four legs, the hound moved, in a blur of fur and teeth and stink as I raised my left arm in a vain attempt to shield myself. The creature bit and held tight, rending skin and muscle to the bone. Blood spurted into my eyes, coloring the world crimson. An agonized scream died in my throat as the horrific wound went instantly numb. I lunged forward with my right hand and buried the serrated knife in the hound's soft belly. I pulled upward, slicing its abdomen like a fisherman gutting his catch.

Gunshots popped. One, two, three, four in a row. The hound screamed, inhuman and guttural. Thick, swampy blood poured down my arms, into my mouth. It tasted like ash. The teeth released my arm. Bladelike claws swiped across my exposed thigh as the hound fell, shredding skin. Its sheer bulk toppled me. I hit the pavement on my back, buried beneath blood and fur and muscle.

My thigh and arm shrieked, the hound's blood like acid on the open wounds.

"Evy?" Wyatt shouted.

"It's dead," I said, screaming to be heard beneath my prison. "Get this fucking thing off me!"

A lot of tugging from him and pushing from me levered the hound's corpse—already decaying—enough for me to slide out. I crabbed backward, getting clear of it. No amount of sputtering or deep breathing would dislodge the nauseating stench of its blood from my nose. Head to toe, I was covered in a slimy mixture of my own blood and its, painting me red and black.

I spat into the road, desperate to keep from up-chucking all over the street. Wyatt squatted in front of me, eyes wide. He wasn't hurt—small favors.

He lifted my left arm up by the elbow, avoiding the gaping flesh. I looked away, sickened by the sight of it. White hot pain lanced through the shredded muscle and bruised bone. My head spun. I wanted to lie down.

"Hell, Evy," he said. "That's going to need more than just stitches."

"Do you have something to wrap it in? We need to get off the road before another one shows up."

He stood and looked at the car. I didn't care if he used a blanket or a greasy rag, as long as I didn't have to look at that arm. He bolted to the car and yanked open the rear door. He rummaged in the backseat until he found what he wanted. The shoulder holster came off, and he tossed it inside. He returned to me with a bottle of water and nothing else.

He crouched down as he unscrewed the bottle cap. "Hold your arm out and try not to punch me when I do this."

I did as asked, hissing through clenched teeth when he poured the water over my arm. The pain was indescribable, but it washed away the hound blood irritant until only my red, human blood oozed from the torn flesh. Wyatt put the half-empty bottle down and began unbuttoning his shirt.

"You just got that," was my meager protest.

"I'll get another."

I decided to focus on his abdominal bruises while he ripped the shirt down the middle. Something thin and hard had made those, and they were too precise to have been an accident. I battled away the pain-induced mental image of a faerie one-third his size whacking Wyatt with a pencil. Really not funny. The makeshift bandage from earlier was still there, relatively un-bloody. One half of the shirt went around my arm, and I hissed as he cinched it tight. The dark material darkened further. My vision blurred.

He wrapped the other half around my thigh. It hurt less. Those twin gashes were superficial, less serious. Strong arms curled beneath my armpits and lifted. I tried to stand, slipped, and fell back against his chest. He grunted—probably because I stank to high hell. I stepped on his feet three times on the trip back to the car.

"Where are we going now?" I muttered, eyeing the backseat. It looked so comfortable. Nice to lie down on.

"My place." He put his hand on my head and guided me into the car. Like a cop arresting a suspect. So nice he didn't want me to bop my head.

Still, his place sounded like a bad idea. "They know where you live, dummy."

"I have a new place, dummy." He slammed the door shut.

I settled into the backseat, tempted to stretch out and take a long nap. My entire borrowed body felt numb, worn to the bone. My head thumped against the seat as Wyatt peeled onto the road. I closed my eyes, appreciating the new position.

"Evy?" Wyatt asked, his voice distant. Muffled. "Stay awake, you hear me?"

"Wanna sleep," I said. At least, I thought so.

Even as the rumble of the car rocked me to slumber land, I felt the lancing pain in my forearm and thigh turn to an intense itch and hoped it was a good sign.

Chapter Six

58:01

The warm, pungent aroma of frying bacon roused me from darkness. I peeled apart sticky eyelids and took quick stock of my new—and exceedingly unfamiliar—surroundings. I was on a bed in one corner of a studio apartment. At the foot, an open door peeked into a tiny bathroom. Beyond it was the living space. A small sofa shared room with a fridge, stove, and a freestanding cabinet. The front door was directly opposite the bed, secured with two dead bolts and a chain.

Wyatt hovered over the stove—the source of the bacon smell. He'd changed clothes again, this time into black jeans and a black T-shirt, and seemed oblivious to my presence. Two things felt immediately out of place: the stink of the hound's blood was missing, and I no longer felt funky and damp. In fact, I felt downright clean.

My left arm was still blessedly numb, wrapped up in white gauze and medical tape. I flexed the muscles in my left thigh and felt the familiar twinge of healing flesh. My hair was damp, as was the pillow behind my head. A green sheet came up to my waist, covering the lower half of my body. I was dressed in a large T-shirt. I clenched my right hand around the top sheet that covered me. Annoyance flushed through my chest, heating my cheeks. Not only had Wyatt undressed me, he had apparently bathed me, as well.

Son of a goblin's bitch!

I sat up, squeaking the bedsprings, and was struck by a wave of dizziness. My vision grayed out. It passed, and I blinked into a pair of familiar, coal-black eyes.

I lashed out by instinct, whacking my open palm across Wyatt's cheek. His head snapped sideways, and he stumbled back from the bed, his hand rising to his face.

"What was that for?" he asked.

"For seeing me naked." Considering everything he'd done for me, it was a ridiculous thing to say. He could have dumped me in the tub fully clothed, turned on the shower, and left me there to wake up and do it myself.

"It wasn't exactly an erotic experience for me, Evy. You are damned hard to carry up six flights of stairs when you're covered in slimy goo, you know. I could have left you in the car."

Busted. "I'm sorry."

He shrugged one shoulder. "I've had worse from a girl than a slap on the face." A half smile quirked the corner of his mouth. "And if it helps, I'll swear on my life that I didn't cop a feel while you were unconscious. You're healing on your own now." Back to the stove and the crisping bacon. "The arm should be good as new in a few hours. It's pretty amazing, actually."

I swung my legs off the side of the bed. The oversized

T-shirt barely hung to mid thigh, but it was modest enough. And it wasn't like Wyatt would care if I started skipping around the apartment in my underwear, since the sight of my naked flesh didn't seem to trigger anything in him but his inner medic. I stood up, sans dizziness this time, and put weight on my left leg. The bandaged cuts twinged, but did not pull or scream.

"Well, I guess this means one bit of good news," I said.

"What's that?" He forked slices of the bacon and put them on a paper plate.

"I can't be permanently wounded until my seventy-two hours are up." I observed the room, but didn't see a clock. Or windows. "What time is it anyway?"

He turned his wrist and consulted his watch. "A little after six."

"At night?"

"In the morning."

Hell, I'd been unconscious for almost twelve hours. A good chunk of time down the drain.

"Have a seat," he said. "I've got breakfast ready. We have a lot of work to do today."

"No kidding." I plopped down at the small, plastic dinette set against the wall by the front door. The chair was hard and the table's surface covered in scratch marks, but it was clean. No signs of ants or roaches. The wall behind me had a rectangle the size of a movie poster tacked to it, something I'd earlier mistaken for bad artwork. Close up, I identified thin rows of heavy rope, frayed over time. Bits of it were scattered on the floor. It looked like a scratching post.

Chalice's cross necklace lay next to my fork. I put it back on, unsure why I wanted to keep it close.

"So whose place is this?" I asked.

Two slices of bread popped out of a toaster. Wyatt added those to his plate of food. "A were-cat who owed me a favor. Do you want me to butter your toast?"

I blinked, realizing too late that it was a real question, not some clever double entendre. "Um, no, I can do it."

He started bringing things over to the table—a tub of whipped butter and a knife, a glass of milk, and finally the plate of bacon, toast, and sliced apples. I was amazed at how domestic the scene felt. And out of place. I rarely saw this side of Wyatt—the side that nurtured, that showed small cracks in his professional veneer. I was used to his sarcasm and teasing.

"Aren't you eating?" I asked when he sat down without a plate of his own.

"I already did."

I took him at his word and started buttering a slice of toast. The food smelled wonderful, and my stomach grumbled in anticipation of being fed. "So roughly fourteen hours of my afterlife are gone," I said, folding a few slices of bacon in the buttery toast. "Any ideas on how to spend the remaining fifty-eight?"

"A few."

Butter and grease dribbled down my chin. The flavors of the bread and bacon burst against my tongue. I chewed slowly, savoring each morsel.

"Care to share?" I asked, delving into bite number two.

He made a face—probably of disgust, but I was

enjoying my breakfast too much to give it any thought—and threw a paper napkin at me.

I snatched it off the table and wiped my chin. "So? Ideas?"

"That depends. You remember anything new?"

I stopped, an apple slice halfway to my mouth. A dark void still loomed over part of my memory. I didn't remember anything new. I don't think I even dreamed last night. "No."

"Really?"

"It's memory loss, Wyatt. It's not like flipping a switch."

"Never is with women."

I threw a piece of apple at him, which he easily deflected. "That's a horrible thing to say."

"And yet somehow untrue?"

"No, but it's still a shitty thing to say."

"We're under the wire here, Evy. I don't have the time or patience to be polite."

"Then be helpful. This is my life—afterlife, whatever. I'm the one who will be dead again in two and a half days, not you."

Wyatt froze, going completely still, like someone had hit the Pause button on a DVR. Seconds ticked by. He stood up, each movement precise and measured, pushed his chair in, and strode to the bathroom.

"Wyatt, I'm sorry."

Nothing. He went into the bathroom. The door slammed shut with a wall-rattling bang. No single swear word in my rather lengthy vocabulary seemed appropriate, so a slow string of them tumbled out of my mouth.

I had forgotten that Wyatt had negotiated for my

resurrection. The price he had paid remained a secret, but I could guess at its cost. He'd put his neck on the line by going against the Triads and the Council. He had saved my life with the hound. Hell, he even cooked me breakfast. And had I ever even said "thank you"?

Breakfast no longer seemed as wonderful, but I forced it down. I needed the energy, especially if we ran into another hound or a goblin patrol. No sounds came from the bathroom, not even angry stomping or pounding. He must be superpissed if he couldn't even vent his rage.

Wyatt had the physical training and temperament (read: quick to anger) to be a Hunter, not to mention the added advantage of his Gift. The only time I dared ask why he was a Handler instead of a Hunter, he assigned me to a two-day stakeout in the dead of winter. I didn't ask again.

I finished my breakfast, polished off the rest of the milk carton, and scarfed two slices of untoasted bread, but still there was no sound from the bathroom. I washed the dishes in the spotless sink and placed them in a sparkling metal dish rack to dry. The entire kitchen area was unnaturally tidy—in my rather messy experience—for a male were-cat living alone.

Still nothing from the bathroom, even as more minutes passed. Concern overruled my better judgment. I crossed the small apartment and banged my fist against the bathroom door.

"I'm not dead in here," came the reply.

"Say it to my face, then."

The door pulled open. I stepped back, startled. Wyatt stood with one hand on the knob, the other limp by his side. No tears, no redness, still no real emotion cracking through on his face. Just a study of calm.

"I'm fine," he said, brushing past me. He stopped in the center of the apartment, observing the cleaned-up kitchen. "I didn't know you were so domestic."

"Neither did I." I put my hand on his forearm, surprised to find his skin warm, almost feverish. "Wyatt, I am sorry."

He stepped away, withdrawing from my touch. "There's one of those plastic storage things under the bed. Dylan's girlfriend stays over and keeps stuff here, so something may fit."

I ducked around him, getting directly in his path, forcing him to look at me. "Thank you," I said. "For all of this. You keep saving my life and all I can do is insult you."

"You gotta go with your gifts."

I stared until I saw the glimmer of amusement in his eyes. "I really am sorry."

"I know, and it's really okay. I think I'd be angry, too, if someone disrupted my eternal rest because they had a question."

I laughed, and so did he. It felt great.

* * *

Dylan's girlfriend wore Petite; I now wore Tall. Her jeans fit at the waist, but rode up to mid shin like Capri pants. The gashes in my leg had healed completely by the time I dressed, so those bandages came off. The light, six-inch scars would probably fade in a few hours. My arm, on the other hand, itched like a bitch. I refused to look at the wound until that damnable itching stopped, but Wyatt peeked and said it was healing well. Bully for me.

The storage drawer only had two nice, button-up blouses in it. I grabbed the royal blue one, rolled up the sleeves, hooked the center three buttons, and tied the tails just above my waist. Not ideal, but better.

We still hadn't addressed the "What next?" issue. My instinct was to follow up on Amalie, since she was our only real lead. Smedge had said she was consolidating her power within the Fey community, in preparation for something big. The sprites were powerful and did not startle easily. They also didn't overreact to potential bad news. Much like the logically thinking vampires, they waited for said news and then reacted appropriately. The only major hitch: the Fey didn't live in the city. Unlike their Dreg counterparts, they preferred the solitude of the northern mountains.

"So let's go over this again," I said, joining Wyatt on the apartment's small sofa. "I met you the night of the thirteenth, right after the Triads attacked Sunset Terrace. I wanted to turn myself in, but you talked me out of it."

"Right so far. One of my informants told me of the alliance forming between goblins and Bloods. I wanted to check it out. You agreed."

"Where did I go?"

"What do you mean?"

"I was a Hunter, Wyatt. The goblins and Bloods wouldn't have just told me about their dastardly plan, and I didn't know any of them socially. After we met up, did I say where I was going next? What was my plan?"

His mouth puckered and his eyebrows furrowed.

"You said you were going uptown to Fourth Street, but wouldn't give me details."

My lips parted. I only knew one person uptown. "I must have gone to see Max. If he hasn't migrated yet, he could still be there."

"Max?"

"He's a gargoyle that lives on the library." I bounced to my feet. "Gargoyles never forget, so he'll be able to tell me what we talked about. Clues, Wyatt. Come on, let's go get them."

He grinned and, for a moment, seemed eager for the hunt. More like his old self. He stood up. "All right, then, let's go see about a gargoyle."

Chapter Seven

56:40

I call him Max because gargoyle language has no direct translation into English. Or any human language, for that matter. Names don't translate. Like birds, the sounds they emit change in pitch and pattern to communicate. Few gargoyles bother to learn the intricacies of human speech; fewer humans learn theirs.

This season, Max was perched on top of the Fourth Street Public Library. Most of his people preferred downtown locations closer to the other Dreg populations. He preferred uptown. Birds flocked there in spring and summer, because of the lower threat. Pigeons were a gargoyle delicacy and, for some inexplicable reason, pigeons love libraries.

Wyatt parked on a meterless side street and we hoofed it three blocks back to the library. Its impressive stone steps rose up like the front of a Greek theater, and the four-story building was just as impressive. A statue of a lion guarded the front entrance, clasping a sign in its marble claws that said: "Enter All Ye Who Seek Knowledge."

Fit us to a tee.

Fortunately for us, the library opened early, and we were among the first to go inside. An elderly woman with reading glasses attached to her head by a gold chain gazed at us from the front desk. I smiled, and she smiled back. The familiar scents of leather and old books filled the main foyer.

I strode toward the staircase and bounded up to the third floor. Wyatt followed at a slower pace, constantly tossing furtive looks over his shoulder even though we were pretty much alone. None of the librarians paid us any mind. On the third-floor landing, the corridor branched left into the fiction room. Directly ahead, the marble steps became a metal spiral that continued upward. A red velvet rope hung across, sporting a sign that announced: "Employees Only."

After double-checking that we were still alone, I stepped over the rope and continued up. Our footsteps echoed in the enclosed space, and it seemed to get smaller the higher we went. At the next landing we were presented with two doors—one marked PRIVATE, and the other ROOF ACCESS. We picked door number two and went up again.

I pushed open the exit door. Bright morning sunlight glared into my eyes. Facing east, the sun sat above the city's horizon like an orange ball of flame. A cool breeze tickled my cheeks. I inhaled the odors of gasoline and exhaust and asphalt—the scent of my city.

Wyatt touched my elbow; I moved out of the way.

The exterior of the door was painted to match the exterior stone, which rose up like a castle turret to create a faked fifth floor. It was all alcoves and empty space inside, the perfect resting place for a gargoyle.

A gravel path surrounded the hollow upper section. It was the only barrier between the building and a four-story drop to the asphalt below.

We crunched across the gravel and turned the corner to the north wall. One of the window insets had been smashed in, allowing a four-foot-wide access to the shadowy interior.

"Think he's home?" Wyatt asked.

"Should be," I said. "It's well after sunrise, and Max is more allergic than most. Just talking about the sun makes his skin crackle."

A common misconception about gargoyles: they don't turn to stone during the day and fly freely at night as some myths suggest. A stone gargoyle is a dead one. Like their vampire cousins, gargoyles are highly allergic to direct sunlight. Exposure dries out their skin and turns it slowly to stone. Five minutes or more of direct sunlight changes them completely. A difference in genetics makes the vampire less stable, easier to shatter into dust. Gargoyles, on the other hand, are solid.

Ever since the first stone gargoyles were discovered and placed on churches and cathedrals, humans have been creating their own, modeling them after cats and dogs and every other animal imaginable. Real gargoyles look more like squared-off humans, with block heads, fangs, wide mouths, long front arms, and short wings. How they manage to fly with those little wings is beyond me, but they do.

"Is he going to recognize you like Smedge did?" Wyatt asked.

"I hope so. I don't feel like taking a flying leap off this building if he gets testy."

"Ditto."

I climbed through first, eyes adjusting quickly to the dim interior. The faint, sweet odor of rot hit me first, but not strong enough to create a sense of dread. Max liked cleanliness in his nest. Even without looking, I knew a pile of bird bones was heaped in the left corner of the man-made cave—mostly pigeon bones, but Max would settle for a swallow or robin if nothing else presented itself.

The far right corner was cast in deep shadow, farthest from the entrance. Our bodies blocked the thin shafts of sunlight, creating a prison-bar pattern on the stone floor. Something shifted in the shadow, a sound like sandpaper on metal. A deep growl filled the space, vibrating in my chest. The short hairs on the back of my neck prickled.

"Max?" I said. "It's Evangeline Stone and Wyatt Truman."

Snuffling, and then a thick baritone, full of clicks and rasps, asked, "Why the new look, Evangeline?"

"I died and rose again. We just had a few minor hitches. You gonna come out and say hello?"

He withdrew from the shadows, lumbering forward on thick haunches. His back was curved slightly, thanks to the weight of his massive, muscular forearms. His head was almost perfectly squared, and his mouth nearly as wide as his entire face. Two thick fangs hung down over his lower lip. A sharp brow ridge accentuated his large, luminous eyes. Gargoyles had no hair, only pointed ears and a smooth head.

Max walked forward, into the dim light. Behind me, Wyatt shifted, becoming defensive. I reached back, found his arm, and squeezed. He stilled, but tension rippled beneath his shirt. I didn't blame him. Most people freaked at the sight of a seven-foot-tall gargoyle.

"Hello," Max said. "I had heard through the Clans that you died, Evangeline. I am pleased you have risen and shall rejoice in it."

"Don't rejoice too much, it's just temporary," I said. "I have a puzzle to solve, and I was hoping you'd be able to give me a few of the pieces."

"You have only to ask for my assistance, and you shall receive it. You know this, as you have come to me many times."

Very true. Outside of Danika and my Triad, Max was the closest thing I'd known to a friend, and I often asked him for advice. "I came to you a week ago," I said. "Why?"

"You do not remember?"

"No, there was a hiccup in my resurrection. I can't remember the very important information that I was brought back to reveal."

Never play poker with a gargoyle. They epitomize the term "stone-faced," and that comes pun-free. His impassive face loomed above me for several seconds, betraying nothing, until he finally said, "We have not spoken directly in two weeks, Evangeline. If you came uptown a week ago, you either found me not at home or not at all."

My mouth fell open, hope fleeing with it. "Seriously?"

"I am serious. We do not understand your humor."

"Where were you last Wednesday night, going into Thursday?" Wyatt asked, stepping up to my side.

Gargoyle poker face strikes again. "Hunting," he said. "I am rarely at home during the nighttime hours;

Evangeline knows this. She was foolish to think she would find me here that night."

"I would have waited for you to come back," I said. Flames of annoyance sparked my temper, frustration fanning it into a low burn. "I would have waited if what I had to ask you was that important, and damnit, it was. Wyatt is the last person that I remember seeing before my memory blanks, and if he says I came uptown to Fourth Street, I was coming to see you."

"I do not doubt the intention, only the outcome. Perhaps your journey was interrupted by other forces." Max's gaze flickered to Wyatt. "If you did, indeed, come in this direction."

"What the hell is that supposed to mean?" Wyatt asked.

I reached out and placed a calming hand on Wyatt's chest. His heart thrummed against my hand, beating furiously with his anger. "I trust Wyatt," I said to Max. "If he says I came here, then I did. Or I tried to, and didn't get that far. But since I obviously didn't, and we have you here now, what have you heard about a pact being made between goblins and Bloods?"

Something flickered in his stony face. I couldn't quite nail it. Surprise, maybe, or dismay. My words had finally made an impact.

"Such a pact would be devastating to humans," Max said.

"You think so?" I deadpanned. Then, remembering the lack-of-humor thing, I added, "Yes, it would be. Very devastating, and that's apparently what I was investigating when I was kidnapped and tortured to death. Is there anything you've heard?"

"Vampires and goblins do not work together."

"Traditionally, no," Wyatt said. "But it's been a week for trying new things, hasn't it? Like answering a simple question."

Max's heavy brow furrowed, a sure sign of deep thought. "Please believe that I wish to help."

"I know you do," I said.

Wyatt took a step forward, fists clenched by his sides. "Then try answering the question."

"Wyatt." I reached for his arm, but drew away, stung. Energy sparked around him like static electricity in a wool sweater. I'd never felt such a burst of power from him before.

"What do you know about an alliance between Bloods and goblins?" Wyatt asked, his voice adopting that low, measured tone he reserved for the moment before attack. The residual energy forced Max backward two steps. Wyatt was preparing to use his Gift. Brute force against a gargoyle was dumb, so what the hell was he going to summon?

I backed off and let him work. I trusted Max, but he was still a Dreg. I trusted Wyatt more.

Max growled—a scarier sound than any angry dog has ever uttered. "The full measure of my existence is a vast ocean to the small pond of yours, Wyatt Truman. I know much, and yet there are things I am unable to reveal. Things that will come with the recovery of Evangeline's memories."

My hand jerked. Was that an admission of guilt? Some ass-backwards way of saying he did know something, but couldn't tell me? I gaped, finally seeing Max as he truly was. No longer a trusted confidant, but as another Dreg who deserved my suspicion and skepticism.

"Did you see me the night I disappeared?" I asked.

Max continued to watch Wyatt. "We did not speak that night."

"That's not an answer."

"It is the only answer I have, Evangeline. I am sorry."

Wyatt raised his right hand and held it palm-up, level with his eyes. Light sparked above his palm, at first just a glimmer. It grew, coalescing into a baseball-sized sun that radiated heat and glowed yellow-orange. Max retreated to the deep corner of his nest, out of the arc of the orb's light. Awed by the unexpected reaction from the gargoyle, I studied the offending object, trying to figure out what had frightened Max into the corner. I felt the heat, both from the orb and Wyatt. Felt the enormity of what he'd done.

Wyatt had summoned sunlight.

He stepped toward Max, increasing the power of the sun orb. Max roared, the sound shaking the stone walls around us. A soft snap-crackle sound filled the room, along with the odor of ozone.

"You will kill me and still know nothing," Max said.

"I don't want to kill you," Wyatt said, taking another step closer. "I just want to know what you know, so unless you want the world's worst sunburn, I suggest you spill it."

"I can reveal nothing to you or your species. No threat can change that fact."

"Really?"

The sunlight grew brighter, the snap-crackle more

pronounced, like someone walking across a floor littered with peanut shells. A low whine followed—the
two sounds linking and creating a symphony of Max's
pain. More than the effect on Max, however, I was
stunned by the display of power from Wyatt. A few
times in the past, I had witnessed him summoning
small objects, weapons, sometimes even a spark of
flame when he needed a match. But never the power
of the sun itself, concentrated and perfectly under his
control.

Ozone continued to fill the room, nauseating me.
Max did not move again from his corner. Standing
straight and tall, he did not flinch from the threat or
his impending death, because I had no doubt that
Wyatt would turn him completely to stone.

"He won't tell, Wyatt," I said. "He can't."

Wyatt flinched, but did not look away from Max.

I tried again. "He's a gargoyle. His word is his
bond. Once he gives his word in a promise, he can't
break it. Whatever he knows, he's promised someone
not to tell us."

No one spoke; no one moved. Wyatt's fury at
Max bubbled just beneath the surface, but Max was
only reacting according to his nature. For that single
fault, I couldn't let him die. He had been a loyal friend
in my old life, and for that he deserved mercy. I circled
around in front of Wyatt, blocking his path to Max.

Our eyes locked over the hot glow of the sun
sphere. Orange light reflected in Wyatt's gaze, illumi-
nating the black depths I knew so well. Tangled with the
light was something else, something more sinister—a
deep-seated desire for vengeance at any cost. Hatred
of certain Dregs projected to all of them without

reason or direction. Sweat beaded on his forehead and red tinged his nostrils—sure signs of his Gift's physical toll.

"Don't kill him," I said. "Please."

Wyatt closed his fist. The sun orb disappeared, the residual warmth fleeing a split second later. The orange light remained in his eyes for a brief moment, flickering like living flame, before extinguishing.

With that light went the careful control Wyatt had erected over his body. He swayed like tall grass in a breeze. Sweat ran in thin rivulets down his cheeks.

"Wyatt?"

"I'm fine," he said, the hitch in his voice indicating he was anything but. He wiped his hand under his nose, smearing blood on his fingers. Even in the bad light, I could tell he'd gone pale. He glared and snapped, "I said I'm fine."

I almost called him on it, but Wyatt would never admit to the pain he was in. Especially in front of Max, who hadn't moved, and any damage done was hidden by shadows. Only his face was visible, and it revealed nothing.

"Is there anything you can tell us, Max? Anything at all?" I asked.

"Only that if you return, I will not be here," he said. "A war is coming, Evangeline. I hope you choose the correct side."

The chilling words buried in my heart like a blade. "Max, if we meet again in this life, will it be as enemies?"

"We will not meet again." He spoke with such finality that my heart broke a little. There is an old joke about not making friends with your food. As a

Hunter, I never should have allowed my friendship with Max. Gentle or vicious, kind or cruel, at the end of the day—or the world, as events were slowly pointing toward—he was still a Dreg. He had betrayed me.

Wyatt touched my shoulder. "Let's go, Evy. We're done here."

I let him guide me back to the exit, toward the bright morning sunlight.

"Trust no one, Evangeline," Max said. "Not even your own people."

The warning rang in my head as I climbed back out to the gravel path. Traffic rumbled and honked below, going about its morning routine, oblivious to the goings-on high above. Wyatt shadowed me, as pale in sunlight as I'd suspected in the dark. He moved slowly, carefully, like an old man afraid of falling and breaking a hip. He caught me checking and glared, his point clear.

Ignoring him, I led the way back to the stairwell and down into the bowels of the library.

At the bottom of the service stairwell, I reached for the utility door with trembling fingers. My knees wobbled. The enclosed space tilted. I grabbed for the wall, but my legs turned to jelly. Trembling arms looped around my waist, and we sank down to the steps. Wyatt engulfed me with his arms, holding me warm and safe. Chills racked my body. Gooseflesh broke out over my arms and chest. I leaned against him, grateful for the support and hating myself for the sudden weakness.

His breath was hot against my ear, whispering words I couldn't hear over the roar in my head. Tears stung my eyes. I blinked rapidly and bit down on the inside of my cheek to chase them away. Freaking out right now was simply not an option. We still had too much work to do, and the clock never stopped, ticking away my last hours on Earth with unflinching steadiness.

"I'm sorry," I whispered.

"For what?"

"This."

"I think you're entitled, Evy." One of his hands found mine, and our fingers curled together. "I can't imagine being where you are now. Everything you knew has turned on its head, and you're doing your best to cope with it."

"I keep hoping I'll wake up and be grateful that it's all just a nightmare. A great big, freakish nightmare."

"I wish it was."

He squeezed my hand, and my stomach fluttered. As urgent as our job was, and as much as I knew we had to go find the next clue, I was perfectly content to sit there for a while. I was safe in Wyatt's arms, protected by someone as strong as me—though perhaps more powerful; I'd just seen him harness the sun.

Gentle fingers brushed a lock of hair away from my cheek and tucked it behind my ear. He rested his chin on my shoulder, seemingly as at ease as I was in our impromptu embrace. I could see his profile in my peripheral vision. His brow was knotted, his lips pursed. I smelled the faint odors of coffee and sweat, and a more basic scent. One I couldn't readily put my finger on. The basic scent of a man, perhaps? It was feral, strong, and heady.

And arousing.

I closed my eyes, falling into the scent of him. I remembered the taste of him—but how? We never had a physical relationship. He was my boss, not my lover. So why did I remember the gentle bruising force of his kisses, the hard knots of muscle on his back and shoulders? I shouldn't know those things.

Until perfectly rendered memories sped through my conscious mind, finally released from their prison. Not everything, but enough. My eyes flew open.

Wyatt tensed. "What is it, Evy?"

I clutched his hand tighter, pulling strength from him and feeling no shock or shame at what I now knew had happened. Only measured relief. "I remember something," I said. "I remember us."

Chapter Eight

May 11th

The empty boathouse reeks of tepid seawater and day-old fish—sure signs that multiple goblins only recently vacated the premises, since neither fish nor boat have seen its cobwebbed interior in at least a decade. It's a smell I know, specific to goblins, and as always, it makes my stomach churn.

Ash steps out from behind a pile of moldy sails, her flashlight cutting patterns in the dust and grime. "So much for our hot tip," she says.

"You need better sources," I reply.

"I haven't heard your troll offer up anything lately."

I shrug, in no mood to play Who Has the Better Snitch? The goblins are no longer here, but this stretch of the Black River docks is notorious for drawing the after-dark crowd. Something worse may be along soon, and we're one man down. Jesse split an hour ago to swing by Wyatt's apartment. Our Handler has been out of contact all damned day—not normal behavior for him. Not at all.

Jesse should have reported—

Ash's cell phone chirps. She fishes it out of her pocket and checks the screen. "It's Jesse."

Think of the devil and he calls.

She frowns, then types in a text message. Something chimes back. She puts the phone away. "He needs us at the Corcoran train bridge ASAP."

"Did he say why?"

Her almond eyes crinkle with concern. "The message said he'd found Wyatt."

My stomach bottoms out. I'm sprinting for the car, beating back fear with a mental stick. We're nearly a mile away on the wrong side of the river, and the drive over is interminable. Ash is quiet, stoic, so composed next to my constant fidgeting. The Korean American yin to my Barbie-girl yang. I'm grateful for her centeredness; it means I don't have to drive.

It occurs to me to call Jesse and demand to know exactly what he's found, only I don't really want to know. Triads survive the death of a Hunter; few survive intact and effective after the loss of a Handler. Wyatt is our glue. He has to be fine.

The train bridge is a black smudge against the navy night sky, a wrought-iron overpass that towers above two intersecting alleys and half a dozen abandoned construction sites. Corcoran Place is a known Dreg neighborhood—a trashy section of downtown with no actual stops along the train route. No one goes there on purpose. Except us.

Jesse is leaning against one of the iron pylons as we approach. He stands straight and jogs over to meet our car. Ash parks in the quiet alley, and I am tumbling out before the engine is off.

"Where is he?" I demand, circling to the front of the car.

"Where's who?" Jesse asks, thick eyebrows knotting quizzically. He looks over my head as Ash's car door slams shut. "What's going on? You paged me half an hour ago to meet here. Did you stop for kimchi on the way?"

Ash snorts. "Bite me, taco boy."

I reach up and ball my fist around the front of his shirt. "Where the fuck's Wyatt?"

"Hell if I know," he says. "He wasn't home."

Ash appears by my side and gently unhooks my hand from Jesse's shirt. "Then why'd you text that you'd found him?" she asks.

Jesse blinks. "I didn't text you."

The knot in my stomach pulls tighter. "You didn't ask us to come here?" I dread his reply.

"I thought you paged me."

"Shit."

As if my angry curse is their cue, a swarm of Halfies descend from the shadows—from beneath abandoned cars, between pylons, seemingly out of thin air. One leaps onto the hood of the car. I count thirteen, all moving with trained ease, as a fighting unit. Not something I associate with wild packs of half-Bloods.

Three against thirteen—bad odds.

We create a triangle, backs to one another as the Halfies close in their circle. My gun is holstered around my ankle, along with my two favorite hunting knives. A dog whistle is on a cord around my neck, hidden beneath my T-shirt.

My knot of fear loosens. Adrenaline surges. Good

or bad odds aside, this is what we live for. They won't get us without one hell of a fight.

Only they aren't attacking.

This just won't do. "Hey, Jesse," I say loudly, "know what's uglier than a dead half-Blood?"

He grunts. "What's that?"

I look right at the spike-haired Halfie on the car hood. "A live one."

It launches at me. Without the superior speed and agility of a full-Blood, the attack is awkwardly managed, but it signals the others to converge. I drop to one knee, pull my gun, and blast an anticoag round right into Spike's throat. Blood sprays my arms and face, heavy, and stinking of old coins. I surge to my feet, replacing gun with knives, and seek another victim.

Ash spins between a clot of Halfies, taking down two with precision kicks to the temple. The self-proclaimed love child of an international jujitsu champion, she makes martial arts look easy. I envy that. My own moves are powerful, but always feel forced, unbalanced.

Jesse, on the other hand, swings his double-blade ax through the onslaught like a lumberjack.

My feet are swept out from under me, and I hit the pavement hard on my back. A Halfie is on top of me, hands clawing at my neck. It rips the corded dog whistle away. I swing a blade at its throat, but it leaps away, whistle in hand, before I can connect. I'm back on my feet and in the fray before one of the others can take advantage of my prone position.

The Halfies' numbers are quickly cut in two, but they are infuriating me with their collective attacks on my partners. Again and again, I pull them off or kick them away.

What? I'm not worth the effort of trying to kill?

A Halfie with dyed blue hair knocks Ash to the ground and straddles her stomach. I drop a knife, grab my gun, and blow the blue head out sideways. Someone stumbles into me. I lose my balance and roll, coming back up on my knees to the sound of Jesse's surprised shout.

Barely tall enough to hold him, a Halfie has Jesse's right arm twisted up behind his back and the other across Jesse's chest. My heart nearly stops when fangs sink deeply into Jesse's neck. I meet my friend's shocked gaze, coffee brown eyes wide with shock, narrow mouth puckered into an O, blood draining from his face. And his neck, as the Halfie feeds.

Like a mosquito bite, the bite of a Blood requires an exchange of numbing saliva. Those not lucky enough to be drained to death become infected and eventually turn into the rogue half-Bloods that wreak havoc on the fragile peace between the races.

"No!"

I'm uncertain if it's me or Ash screaming, only that we are both moving. She reaches him as the feeding Halfie lets go, her blade immediately burying between its eyes. Jesse hits his knees, eyes glazing over. A Halfie sporting a letterman's jacket reaches for Ash; I tackle the beast, snapping its neck on our third tumble across the pavement.

I turn back. Ash is on her knees in front of Jesse, trying to look at the wound. Babbling that we can help, tears in her voice. I try to stand, and the world slows down.

A flash of silver in Jesse's hand matches a new gleam in his eyes. Ash looks for me over her shoulder. I shriek at her, incomprehensible. Jesse buries a switchblade in Ash's throat. Blood gurgles from her mouth and dribbles down her chin. Eyes that can simultaneously laugh and hate stare at me in shock, and then the life in them dies.

As Ash dies.

I'm cold. I can't scream. It's all wrong. This hasn't just happened. It's impossible.

The four remaining Halfies seem to melt back into the shadows, leaving me with my partners. One dead, one infected, both of them lost to me.

Jesse stands, his eyes glinting in the orange light cast by street lamps. Soon his hair will turn mottled white and his fangs will grow in. He's one of them now, one of the things I hunt and destroy. He looks at me, then at the body by his feet. Back up to me, and I see something I do not expect: confusion.

"I think I did a bad thing," he says. "But her blood smelled so sweet, Evy. It still does."

A high-pitched whimper rips from my throat. Trembling from head to toe, I take two steps forward, closer to him and the place where I dropped my gun.

He narrows his eyes at me. "You smell sweet. So sweet and pure."

If he smells purity in me, he needs to get his nose checked. This monster in front of me isn't my Jesse. It isn't the man I'd once confessed my worst sins to over a bottle of tequila, a bowl of lemons, and a shaker of salt. It only looks like him. In my head, I scream for Wyatt to guide me. I know what must be done; I just don't know if I can do it.

Jesse advances, licking his lips. I retreat. I have one knife, clutched so tight in my left hand that my knuckles scream.

"You know what I'm going to enjoy?" he asks, no longer advancing.

I eye the gun, on the ground just behind him. Five feet from me. "What's that?"

"The look on Truman's face when we knock on his door."

"What makes you think I'm going to go anywhere with you?"

He grins and it's terrible. He runs the tip of his tongue over the small points on his developing canines. "Because all it takes is one little bite."

"Try it," I growl.

He charges. I drop, tuck, and roll. On my knees and gun in hand, I spin, aim, and fire. He hasn't managed to turn. My shot hits him squarely in the back, through his heart. He falls, head cracking off the pavement, and is still.

I crouch in the street, body trembling so hard I bite my tongue and draw blood. How am I ever going to explain this? Will Wyatt forgive me for what I've done? Will I ever forgive myself?

Do I want to?

I have no answers. I cannot think. I need help. I don't want to leave him, but my phone is broken. I feel the pieces shifting in my pocket. I can't bring myself to search the two bodies nearby. Bodies I can't bear to look at, much less touch.

Numb, exhausted, and bordering on hysterical, I jog off and leave my family behind. The Triads will help. They have to.

* * *

Two days later, I welcome death. I will place a welcome mat for it, if such a thing is possible. I have paid a high price for my own selfish nature, and will never stop paying—not until I am allowed final rest.

I crouch in a dark alley, listening to the screech of fire engine sirens. The hulking vehicles tear down the street toward the blazing apartment building, red lights flashing, announcing their presence to the sleeping neighborhood. They will arrive too late.

Danika is dead. The Owlkins are obliterated, massacred by people I once considered friends. Murdered in their homes, punished for their silence, for their loyalty and unflinching desire to protect me—not even one of their own. I ran to them for protection after my own people betrayed me. Their deaths are my fault, and I know I will burn for it.

But not until my betrayers join me in Hell.

My route takes me deeper into the alley, to the service street that runs behind the buildings. I stay close to the shadows, ignoring the stench of rotting garbage. The air is heavy, already hot for May, and presses down like a blanket. Something hisses, but it isn't a stray cat. It is something else, telling me to keep my distance. I do.

Keeping low, faster now. Two blocks farther and I break into a dead run. Pushed by fear and guilt, I draw energy from a tapped well, and surge forward. At the end of the block, I dash across a busy intersection. A car horn honks. Leaping over a low stone wall with unfailing grace, I hit and roll and run. On through a dark park, its rusty merry-go-round tilted and broken.

Swings dangle from fractured chains. The slide is warped, the monkey bars covered in grime.

A trio of gremlins, no taller than my leg, scatter as I pass. I ignore them, unconcerned with their business tonight. The Dregs get a free pass, and I have no time to enjoy their confusion. Tonight, I have no beef with the nonhumans of the world. My enemy is the Metro Police Department. In one day, I have gone from their star Hunter to a wanted fugitive accused of murder.

They never gave me a chance to explain how my partners died.

At the far end of the overgrown park, I jump another stone fence. I land in a puddle, spraying tepid water over my shoes and black jeans. So much for not leaving tracks. I briefly consider disposing of the soaked sneakers, but I can't run around the city barefoot.

Once again on a residential sidewalk within eyesight of dozens of apartment windows, I reduce my speed to a fast walk. It's a good chance to catch my breath, to consider my options. I could just keep running and never look back, get out of this damned city and away from the Dregs. Find a place somewhere else, without the sharply delineated lines. No Triads. No Handlers. Just ordinary people.

But I can't do that. Leaving means no justice for the Owlkins. It means no justice for Jesse and Ash, no justice for myself. And what of Wyatt? I haven't seen him in two days. With two of his Hunters dead and a third on the run, what happens to him? Will the brass have him neutralized?

"My first loyalty is to you three," Wyatt told us once. "It always will be."

At the end of this block, I dart into a pay phone booth. I dig into my pocket for change. A few coins are all that I possess now, and I drop most of them into the slot. I dial a number as familiar as my own birth date and wait. A computerized buzzer ticks off the rings on his end of the line.

"Be there. Come on, Wyatt. Answer your phone."

The line clicks, and a familiar voice asks, "Yes?"

"It's me."

Silence.

"Don't come here, Evy," he says. "The brass knows what you did. I can't help you."

The words hurt. My teeth dig into my lower lip to drown out that pain with another. "They killed the Owlkins. Do you hear me, Wyatt? They slaughtered an innocent Clan."

"It's a dead end, Evy, I can't help you. You have to go down this road by yourself, I'm sorry." Click goes the line.

I drop the phone back into its cradle, hope daring to peek through the cloud of fear wrapped around my heart. If I am right, it's a code. Dead Man's Street—the dirt road that runs down by the Black River and the railroad tracks. He is telling me to meet him there; he has to be.

Believing it because I have no choice, I turn and head south. Without transportation, the trip will take at least an hour. I can't risk the main city streets. Spies are everywhere, and they sell their information cheap. I stick to the shadows, drum up my courage, and run.

* * *

I crouch beneath an abandoned boxcar. It smells of human waste and rotting wood. The odors of oil and smoke join it, tinged with engine grease. The tracks around me are silent. Nothing disturbs the quiet of the moonlit train yard, save the occasional car that drives across the Wharton Street Bridge above, casting intermittent beams of light. I have been waiting for close to an hour, timed only by the ringing of a church bell on the other side of the river.

He isn't going to show. I've fooled myself into thinking I still had one ally. My hands tremble, rocked by fear, inevitability, hatred. The tracks look like a nice place to throw myself the next time a train passes this way.

Gravel crunches. I peer out from the shadows of the boxcar. The sound draws closer, light steps trying to disguise themselves and failing. A figure emerges a hundred feet away, coming around the corner of a loading platform. He stops, waits. My heart soars, relief punching me in the stomach. Wyatt gazes around the train yard, moonlight glinting off his black hair. It accents the ever-present shadow on his face that no razor seems to touch.

I don't move. Not even relief overpowers my ingrained sense of survival. I am a Hunter. I won't move until I'm sure of my surroundings. It can still be a trap.

Wyatt steps farther into the yard and begins to unbutton his shirt. I stare. He shrugs out of the shirt, holds it at arm's length, and turns in a slow circle. Exposed. Unwired. Asking me to trust him. I let out a breath. He puts the shirt back on, looking everywhere at once. Taking it all in.

Satisfied, I crawl out of my hiding place. He spots me and gapes. I realize I must be a mess, with blood on my clothes and in my hair, ash and soot adding gray to the red. He takes a step forward; stops. I wave him over. He comes.

I climb up into the boxcar, preferring its grimy, cobwebbed interior to crouching beneath it. Wyatt appears in the doorway, backlit by moonlight. I offer a hand and pull him up. His hand is so warm; I don't want to let go. He surprises me by tugging me into a tight hug. My arms come up around his waist.

"I'm so glad you understood me," he says. "Are you okay?"

Stupid question. "I'm pretty fucking far from okay, Wyatt. The Triads, the people I worked with for four years, won't listen to me anymore. Why won't they let me explain what happened?"

He disentangles himself, holds me at arm's length. Black eyes seem to see right through me. "You know they won't, Evy. They don't give second chances. You've been marked as a threat. They won't stop sending Triads after you until you're dead."

"You think I don't know that?" I pull out of his arms and withdraw to the shadows of the boxcar. Dark and rot press in on me. "I've thought about turning myself in. Hell, I even thought about a spectacular leap off the bridge up there, because it seems easier than this. I don't have anyone."

"You've got me."

The statement of singular fact unnerves me. I don't deserve his loyalty, even though every fiber of my being craves it. Craves knowing I'm not alone in this battle. "If the Council finds out you're helping me, they'll kill you, too."

"They can try, but they won't."

That certainty does nothing to settle my nerves. "You don't know that, Wyatt."

"Yes, I do." He steps forward, hints of light casting odd, angular shadows on his expressive face. Faith and concern war there, and his eyes sparkle with life. Wonder fills his smile. "Elder Tovin told me so. We get a happy ending, Evangeline Stone."

"Elder Tovin?" A tremor steals down from my scalp to my toes. Among the oldest and wisest of the nonhumans in the city, Tovin is rumored to be an elf prince banished Upside by his people for choosing a bride outside of his race. He's also rumored to live in a mushroom, eat cats for breakfast, and fly during full moons. No human I've met prior to Wyatt has ever seen him, or any other elf. Neither Fey nor Dreg, elves have six-hundred-year life spans. Tovin has supposedly spent the last four centuries among humans.

"That's where I was that night, Evy. He asked me to come see him. Said he had important information for me. When Tovin summons, you go."

That night. The night I killed Jesse. The one night, out of all other nights, I truly needed Wyatt's wisdom, and he'd spent it conferring with an elf. I had wondered, needed to know, and now I did. My fists ball, nails digging into palms.

"Happy ending?" I snarl. "He saw a happy ending, but he didn't see how much I needed you by my side? Maybe everything wouldn't be so fucked up right now if you'd been there."

He flinches, but stays fast. "This is the path, Evy."

"Don't give me that destiny bullshit. You know I don't buy it."

"And you know I do, so one of us is going to look pretty stupid when this is over."

"I think one of us already does, because if this is what destiny had in mind, you can tell her to eat me. People like us don't get happy endings."

Anger flickers across his face. "They do, if they work hard enough. We can fix this. You don't have to spend the rest of your life looking over your shoulder."

"The Department won't hear me out, and you know it."

Getting the hell out of Dodge seems like the only viable solution. There is nothing to be fixed, only endured. It won't be long before the brass starts itching for results and reports me to the regular police. Once that happens, when both the public and private faces of law enforcement are after me, it's over. I'll have nowhere left to turn.

The one thing I still don't understand is the timing. How in hell did the brass have a Neutralize order on me within minutes of my leaving the scene of my supposed crime? Not hours, minutes.

"Who reported it?" I ask.

"Reported what?"

"Who reported what happened at Corcoran? Who told the brass it was murder and set me up?"

"I don't know, Evy. Communication with the brass is one-way, remember?"

Right. Three unknown and unnamed officers in the high ranks of the Metro Police Department, who sit on their fucking Mount Olympus with representatives from the Fey Council breathing down their necks as they pull our strings. With a snap of their collective fingers, and on someone else's word, they ordered nine other Triads to turn on one of their own. Because the brass knew they would. Handlers are well trained to follow orders. To respond to imperatives from the brass like Pavlov's dogs to that damned bell.

Thank God Wyatt is finally deaf to its tune.

"One-way, right," I say. "So I guess that makes pleading my case an example of words falling on deaf ears?"

"They might listen if you bring them something they can use. Something valuable."

"Like what? The head of a gorgon?"

"I was thinking something a little less mythical, and a bit more tangible. Information."

He is ignoring every single sarcastic retort, stuck on some imaginary idea of forgiveness and a fairy tale ending. I'm doomed, and he knows it. Still, a small part of me wants to believe him. To believe that there is a chance I can come out of this with my skin intact.

"What sort of information?"

"Tovin told me something else, the reason he summoned me, but we shouldn't talk about it here," Wyatt says. "You never know who's listening. I have a hotel room not far from here. It's under a protective barrier, so no one will find us. We'll talk about it there."

It can still be a trap. At least here, in this dirty boxcar, we are on familiar territory. I've hunted and killed here. I know all of the hiding places. But I trust Wyatt, because nothing he's said sounds like a lie. He's smart and skillful, but he's never been good at lying to me.

"Fine, let's go," I say.

*   *   *

We don't speak during the ten-minute walk to the West Inn, a two-story motel with bad parking lot lights and dirty windows. It's quiet, private; the sort of place we need. It's nestled just on the edge of Mercy's Lot, surrounded by strip malls and consignment shops.

We reach the motel in the middle of the night. Foot traffic is nonexistent, but I still pause before crossing the street. No cars, no signs of life, just gentle quiet, practically unheard of in a city our size. Wyatt crosses first, palming his room key. He has a room on the very end, closest to the street and farthest from the office. I eye all possible exit points and escape routes—one front window, a path across the parking lot or to the sidewalk, no direct access to the second level or roof—before following.

I expect attack at any moment and am relieved to reach the door safely. My skin tingles as I cross the threshold and pass through the protection barrier. He closes the door, turns the lock.

The room is small, barely large enough to accommodate a pair of full beds. A plastic table and chairs are pushed to the front corner, nearest the single window. Hideous striped drapes are drawn shut, blocking out roving eyes and neon streetlights. Rumpled clothes lay in a pile by the bathroom door. Toiletries cover the vanity area.

"You've been here awhile," I say.

"A few days. Even before I talked to Tovin, I was worried. Worried that something was going down. I wasn't sure who to trust. I didn't want to be anywhere I could be found."

Not even by me. I spy an electric water kettle on the room's cheap bureau, and next to it a box of instant cocoa packets. A smile steals across my lips before I can stop it. I want to be angry with him, but all I am now is tired. And smelly. Coated in sweat and ash and blood.

As if reading my mind, he says, "There are fresh towels in the bathroom, Evy. Go clean up and then we'll talk."

I want to argue, to get the inevitable taunts and blame-tossing out of the way first. Instead, I brush past him, eyes on the bathroom door. I can do a better job of ripping him a new asshole when I don't feel quite so much like death on a cracker.

*   *   *

An hour later, I sprawl on one of the beds in a borrowed T-shirt, and feel more or less human again. More or less, because I never have felt completely human.

Hunters are recruited for many reasons. Most often, it's because we're smart, strong, and we like violence. It's also a better alternative to jail. The recruiters see potential for strength, cunning, and obedience. We are generally orphans, usually unwanted, and always unmissed, taught to think only about the next kill. To follow one leader and trust in groups of three—our Triad.

They had hit the mother lode with me: orphaned at the age of ten, and in foster care until my arrest at the tender age of fourteen. I celebrated my eighteenth birthday with a breaking-and-entering bust that brought me to the attention of the Metro Police. I led them on a merry chase through Mercy's Lot while resisting arrest, and accepted a one-way ticket to Boot Camp in lieu of jail time. Anything was better than jail.

At least, I used to think so.

Jesse and Ash had lost their senior teammate a week before I was assigned to Wyatt. They took to me faster than he did. He said at least once a week that I didn't have what it took to be a Hunter. Times have changed.

Wyatt hands me a steaming porcelain mug. I inhale the rich scent of the cocoa, soothed by the gentle aroma of chocolate. The hot mug burns my fingertips, but it is a welcome pain. I sip. It scorches down my throat and warms my belly.

He sits on the edge of the bed, intent on me. "Tell me about it, Evy."

"About what?" I ask, playing obtuse. Buying time to summon the words. He is silent, not playing along this time. I clutch the mug in both hands. My skin heats.

So I do. When I get to the part about Jesse's death, Wyatt slides up the bed until he can touch my arm. I don't draw away. I find a tiny measure of comfort in his touch, his warmth. He brushes my tears away with his hand. He offers what I needed two nights ago— unconditional love. Acceptance of tragedy and the promise of hope. I put the mug down on the room's single nightstand and surge into his arms, burying my face in his shoulder. He holds me, hands stroking my back, his voice soft and murmuring empty words.

"They didn't tell me," he says. "The brass said nothing about Jesse being turned, just shot in the back."

"What about the Halfies?" I ask, lifting my head. "Their bodies wouldn't have had time to decompose."

Wyatt shakes his head. "None were found, just Jesse and Ash. Someone set you up, Evy. Someone who wanted all three of you dead."

I rest my head on his chest, drawing strength from him. His arms tighten around my waist. His heart, thudding so close to my ear, speeds up. He shifts. I remember his words from an hour ago: a happy ending for us. What sort of happy ending had Tovin seen? I love Wyatt, as much as any person possibly can, but not in a romantic way. I never had those feelings for him, and I don't have them now.

I close my eyes, but all I see is the fight that killed my partners. My friends. I see how fiercely they pile onto Jesse during those first moments. I see Ash, black hair a blur as she becomes the warrior I have always longed to be. The fight is so well coordinated, unexpectedly so for Halfies. They move in packs and fight dirty. This is more planned, more focused—just not on me.

My eyes snap open. I must be remembering it wrong. But as I replay the battle from first blow to last, I keep reaching the same conclusion. After my initial taunt, none of them made a move on me. And the remaining Halfies scattered when Ash fell, and I was the last human standing.

Fucking impossible.

No, I am just tired and way beyond stressed. That line of thinking screams "inside job," and I'm just not going there. Not until I can think straight again. "I don't understand, Wyatt," I whisper. "Do the Triads—?"

"Right now, I don't trust the Triads. Or the Council, for that matter. There's no way to know if one of them is in on this yet. But we could get them to listen to you."

"You mentioned that before. About information?"

He releases me, and I miss his embrace. I feel cold without it. He paces to the other side of the room, hands balling into fists. I can almost see imaginary wheels turning in his head. "Tovin has been hearing rumors for a few days now, mostly through informants and the gossip train, about a possible alliance developing between the goblin Queens and one of the Blood Families. And now I've started hearing them, too."

My heart hammers. A chill worms down my spine, stirring up the sudden urge to vomit. "That's not possible. Goblins and Bloods hate each other."

"Normally, they do, but they hate humans and the Fey even more. An alliance like that would be a disaster to us and the Fey Council, and to everything we've managed to build over the last decade. It would force the other races to take sides, and not all of them would side with us."

"How reliable is your intel?"

"No one jokes about something like that, Evy. If they're hearing it, it's happening. The question now becomes when, and why? If we can get a bead on those things, find something to give the Council that can prepare them for the possibility of a species war, it could go a long way toward getting the brass to listen to your side of the story. Right now, we're under orders to shoot you on sight."

I shudder. "Guess I'm lucky you found me first."

"I'll protect you, Evy." He returns to the bed, sits

down in front of me. "I promised I would, and I will. We'll figure this all out together."

His hands cup my cheeks and force me to look into eyes that seem to see right through me, right into my heart and soul. So protective and loving. I crave those things. If only they can be enough to make me believe in his promised happy ending.

His breath is sweet, like chocolate, and warm on my face. I feel every callus on his fingertips, every rough patch of skin on his palms. His thumb gently strokes across my cheek—a featherlight touch. The world is more vivid, if only for a moment.

Wyatt's mouth captures mine, and the world goes away. I have nothing to lose, and he has everything to gain. He wants this. I don't know if I do or not, but I submit. Instinct takes over. I reach for him.

Hands caress flesh. Clothing falls away, replaced by touches and kisses. I taste his sweat; he tastes mine. Our bodies are one—stroking, taking, needing. Time is nothing. The world means nothing. We take pleasure in each other, finding elusive comfort in this sudden intimacy.

It is over too soon. He holds me close, my back to his chest, still breathing hard against my neck. My body trembles, as much from the pleasure he has given me as from the fear of facing tomorrow. Everything has changed. There is no going back.

"I love you, Evy," Wyatt whispers.

I do not reply.

Chapter Nine

56:06

Certain my death would come soon and on swift feet, I had felt no shame in allowing the seduction. Not that night. The shame consumed me a week later as I sat on the bottom stair of a dank library service stairwell. My body had lied to Wyatt, faking love when all it craved was sensation. Touch. One last hurrah before I died.

A perfect moment for both of us, if he'd let me stay dead.

"I'm sorry, Wyatt." My voice echoed, harsh and piercing. I longed to pull out of his arms, put as much distance between us as possible, but found myself immobilized. Not by his embrace, but by my own emotions. I had felt alive during those intimate moments. Alive and wanted and necessary, able to face anything the Dregs threw at me. In that dank library stairwell, I wallowed in shame.

"Sorry for what?" Wyatt asked.

"I shouldn't have slept with you."

A ripple went through his body, and I felt it keenly.

Not quite a shiver, but close. I wanted to take back those hurtful words, erase them from his memory. I saved him the trouble of pushing me away and stood up, untangling his arms from my waist. Two steps took me to the stairwell door. I pulled the knob. His hand slammed against the door and pushed it closed again. I yelped.

"Don't run from me, Evy," he said.

He grabbed my wrist. Instinct kicked in. I twisted my hand around, stepped to the left, and reversed the grip. Drew his arm up and behind his back, effectively pinning him face-first to the door. My free hand squeezed his shoulder. I'd snapped necks from this position, killed dozens of Halfies with a single, pointed blow through the heart. I didn't want to hurt Wyatt. Far from it. I just needed room to think.

"Don't do that," I hissed into his ear. "Ever."

"I'm sorry."

I let go and moved to the other side of the tiny space. He stood still for a moment, then slowly turned around. His jaw was clenched, his mouth drawn into a straight line. The sight of him, so grim and desperate, deflated my anger.

"This was Tovin's idea of a happy ending?" I asked. "Me dying, you putting yourself on the line to bring me back, and for what? To stop a war in a world that doesn't want us here? That wouldn't give a rat's ass if we both keeled over and died? Is that what we're fighting for?"

Wyatt shook his head. "No, I'm not fighting for this world. I'm fighting for you, because against my better judgment, Evangeline, I fell in love with you. With your sparkle and energy and wit. With the way you used to cut your own hair, even though it was never straight or even. With the look on your face when you drank hot chocolate. For everything you put into doing your job and never got back from it."

His words cut like glass, right through a tough exterior I'd spent years erecting. I wanted to melt into the floor. Hide from his emotional soul-baring. Put the genie back in the bottle and pretend it had never come out.

But he wasn't letting that happen. "I love you," he said. "I didn't know if you loved me, and now I don't think you did. But that's okay, because I never asked you to. Everything I did was my choice, and mine alone." He started to add more, then stopped, searching for the right words.

"I'm not who I was before, Wyatt." I was of two minds about his confession. The old part of me wanted to derail his lovefest right then and there. The new me—the part of Chalice Frost that remained alive and attracted to Wyatt, the part that felt the invisible power tethering Wyatt to the magic of the Fey—rebelled. So many things warred against the me who wanted to let myself care again.

"You may look different, but you're still you," he said. "I wasn't in love with your blond hair and blue eyes, Evy. It's what's inside that makes you who you are."

"It isn't enough if you're not attracted to someone, too."

His eyes narrowed. They roved up and down my borrowed body. I shrank under his scrutiny, unused to such a blatant perusal. "You're right," he said after a few seconds of silence. "I suppose I was a fool for thinking otherwise."

Was that an insult? He quirked one eyebrow, tele-graphing disappointment, disinterest. I bristled, fists balling by my sides. I covered the distance between us in two measured steps, intent on smacking him across the face.

He reached up, wrapped both hands around my neck, and kissed me so hard our teeth clashed. I responded, mouth and body surging against his. Hands tangled in my hair, roamed down my neck, across my shoulders. Our tongues danced, teasing and tasting.

I wanted to stop; I also wanted him. Unlike our first time, when I invited him into my body for his own pleasure, I now wanted him for mine—if it was really mine at all. My skin burned where he touched. I craved his scent, his taste, in a way I couldn't explain. Could barely control.

I broke the dizzying kiss and stepped back. I couldn't help noticing the slight bulge in his pants, or the curious glimmer in his eyes. I didn't know what was me, what was memory, and what was Chalice. Too many people's emotions in one head. And now wasn't the time.

"I do love you, Wyatt," I said. "I always have, but not romantically. I'm sorry if I made you think otherwise."

"And now?"

"Now?" How much of love was physical attraction? I didn't know, but my lips still burned from his kisses. My heart beat faster at the sight of him, red-cheeked and out of breath. I remembered how it felt to have him inside of me and something new—and entirely Chalice—wanted him there again. "Now? The things I crave aren't appropriate for a public library."

"What's changed?"

Everything. Me, him, the world. We weren't the same people we'd been, even five minutes ago. As my memories returned, I would continue to evolve. Into someone who battled against foreign desire and fought for duty above self. One who would be dead again in fifty-something hours. One who would leave him again.

"Evy?"

He stood toe-to-toe, drilling me with his intense gaze. I looked down, unable to drum up any of my previous levity. All I felt was consuming sadness—heavy, palpable, and suffocating.

"We should go," I said. "We're running out of time."

I opened the service door and fled into the bright third-floor corridor. Wyatt followed at a distance, and we did not speak again until we returned to his car.

* * *

"Chalice!"

The stranger's voice bounced off the building behind me. I froze in place, fingers brushing the door handle. On the other side of the car, Wyatt tensed. We both turned in the direction of the library.

A boy in his late teens jogged down the sidewalk, his long brown hair flowing behind in tangled strands. He wore baggy jeans and moved with all of the grace of a newborn foal. He stumbled once, but kept going, intent on me.

"Hey, Chal," he said, putting on the brakes. He almost overshot me.

"Hey," I replied, not a clue who the kid was. Damn Chalice for having friends.

"What happened to you yesterday?" He had a high, nasally voice that, I imagined, became quite irritating after long-term exposure. "Dude, Baxter was furious when you didn't show, and then he got all worried, 'cause you're never late." He eyed the bandage on my forearm. "You okay?"

"Yeah, I am now," I said, holding up my arm. Lies tumbled out of my mouth. "Grease fire in my apartment. My, um, brother, Wyatt, over there was visiting, and he wanted to make stir-fry. He sloshed the oil and it got me, but then I had a bad reaction to painkillers at the hospital or I would have called. Tell . . . uh . . ." What name had he said? "Tell Baxter I'm sorry."

The kid cocked his head to the left, analyzing one of those sentences. With my luck, Chalice was an only child and everyone knew it. He'd call me on it, and I'd have to fudge another lie.

"Tell Baxter yourself, Chal; he'll be there when you go on-shift tonight," he finally said.

I bit the inside of my cheek to stifle relieved laughter. Yeah, that was going to happen. "Right, sure. Look, I hate to be rude, but I really have to go."

"Yeah, okay." He shrugged one shoulder, seeming unbothered by my abrupt dismissal. He looked across the car and offered Wyatt a half-assed salute. "Dude, your sister's awesome." He turned and continued his wobble-legged journey down the street.

After he managed to put about twenty feet of distance between us, I turned and placed my palms flat against the top of the car. "That was somewhat surreal."

"Brother?" Wyatt asked, still ghostly pale from

his summoning exertion, but seeming less likely to be bowled over by a strong wind.

"It slipped out. At least I didn't say that I missed my shift because I was dead and hadn't made my four o'clock resurrection appointment yet."

"His expression would have been priceless."

"Why couldn't I have woken up in the body of a homeless person that nobody knew? This has the potential to become very, very complicated."

"I think we've passed that mile marker already. You said you met Chalice's roommate. Now we know she has a job somewhere, so people are bound to recognize her."

"Not to mention the suicide report that some city cop has probably filed away with Chalice's photo in it."

He blew air through his lips, eyebrows scrunching. "We need to make you disappear, Evy. Get Chalice Frost erased from the system."

"You're thinking of this now?"

"I've been a little distracted by other details, like tracking you down and tending to your self-healing wounds. If you'd come back where you were supposed to, it wouldn't be an issue."

I rolled my eyes.

He mimicked me, and then said, "We need to get this done so we can keep focusing on your memory."

He was right. Hoping that Chalice Frost's former life wouldn't become a problem had been idiotic. We should have dealt with it right away. Time to correct a mistake. I just didn't know what to do about Alex Forrester, but knocking him out cold and locking him in a closet for the next two days sounded promising.

I opened the door and climbed into the passenger seat. "So how do we do this?"

Wyatt turned the key and the car engine roared to life. "I need to stop by a bakery."

I stared.

He winked. "Trust me."

Chapter Ten

I balanced the bakery box in both hands, careful to not drop and ruin the expensive treat inside as I ascended the rickety metal staircase. Wyatt led the way up, taking the steps two at a time. The interior of the service stairwell smelled of forgetfulness and disuse.

We had returned to downtown. Wyatt had left me in the running car while he ran into a bakery and, moments later, returned with a white box. I hadn't opened it, but a sticker on the side said "CSCK—Cherry Top." Given the shape and weight of the box, I silently translated that into "Cheesecake—Cherry Topping." I had kept my questions to myself, even when Wyatt drove us back toward Mercy's Lot.

Halfway there, he had said, "You know, you're showing amazing restraint."

"With what? The cheesecake?"

A tiny smile. "No, with not asking me about the night you died. And who else was in the room."

"You'll tell me when I need to know something."

"Fair enough."

After reaching the outskirts of Mercy's Lot, he had parked in front of an abandoned potato chip factory and said we needed to head to the top level.

Six flights up I smelled it. Faint at first, and then gradually stronger—the eye-watering stench of fermented sugar. I felt like I was walking into a distillery, and that clued me in as to who we were visiting.

Gremlins are the cockroaches of Dregs. They live short lives in the dark (eight days is the record), reproduce like bunnies, and are hard to kill. They are also hermaphroditic. On the fourth day of their lives they produce and fertilize litters of twelve, which are fully grown within twenty-four hours. Gremlins are as notorious for causing havoc with machinery as they are for having a sweet tooth. Existing almost entirely on a sugar-based diet, their waste created the alcoholic smell that permeated the upper floors of the factory.

I'm still waiting for some brave soul to start marketing Gremlin Piss Schnapps.

Flexible as putty and ugly as sin, the eighteen-inch-tall creatures didn't fear the Triads. Instead of death and destruction, they specialized in causing trouble and occasional mayhem. We had no reason to hunt them. Their only natural enemies were gargoyles—as a crunchy snack or sport hunting, I didn't know—and their own brief life spans.

On the seventh level, I began to hear the scuffling sounds of small feet racing back and forth. They knew we were there; it was only a matter of seconds before they sent an emissary. Gremlins did not speak to outsiders en masse. They rarely showed their full strength, and given the size of the factory (and the stink), there could easily be thousands of gremlins breeding in the shadows.

We reached the eighth floor. A reinforced fire door blocked the top of the stairwell. Wyatt banged his open palm against it.

"Ballengee be blessed," he shouted. His voice bounced off the enclosed space, and I clutched the bakery box closer. More scuffling preceded a single set of footsteps.

A lock turned on the other side of the door. Wyatt pushed. The tiny creature scrambled away and disappeared. I followed Wyatt into a haze of odor so thick my eyes watered. It felt heavy against my skin, like a fog of liquor fumes. I held my breath, but it did no good. The stink was everywhere, seeping into my pores, so strong I could taste it.

We stood on the upper balcony of a catwalk that overlooked a cavernous production area. To my left was a row of offices, the doors gone and glass broken out of every window. The open area below caught my immediate interest. Hundreds of gremlins scurried about on those multilevel floors. Dozens of nests, made of cardboard and shredded debris, dotted nearly every available space. The din of their chatter and daily activity sounded like faint machine-gun fire—constant and sharp. Huge metal vats (likely old deep fryers) were filled with pools of amber liquid.

"They certainly took the term, 'piss pot' to a literal level," Wyatt said.

I snorted, but could not drum up laughter. The sight of so many Dregs in one place startled me. I had never seen such a gathering, nor been invited into the heart of this community. Whatever "Ballengee be blessed" meant, it worked to gain their trust.

"Why for come you?"

The tiny voice startled me. I spun around and nearly dropped the cheesecake. Barely twenty inches tall, an elderly gremlin gazed at us from the floor. Its long, apish arms and knob-kneed legs were wrinkled, with yellowish skin that seemed transparent in places. A round, distended belly hung low. Tall, rabbitlike ears stuck out from its oval-shaped head at perfect right angles, accented by tufts of green fur. More green fur covered the top of its flat head. The gremlin smiled, revealing two rows of tiny teeth in a mouth that seemed too small for the width of its head. Red eyes blinked, shifting from me to Wyatt.

"I would like to buy a favor," Wyatt said.

The gremlin tilted its head, a very thoughtful (and human) gesture. "Payment?"

Wyatt nudged me. I opened the top of the box and squatted down. The gremlin peered into the box. A whistle of delight turned into a shriek, and it rubbed clawed hands together. I pulled the box away before the little critter could drool all over it.

"Favor?" it asked.

"A computer wipe," Wyatt replied. "I need all traces and records for the name Chalice Frost erased. Every data source, every police file, all of it. After today, she doesn't exist. We need paper copies of everything dropped at this address."

"Chalice Frost," it repeated. The tinny voice did not match its horrific appearance. It seemed better suited to a tiny human being than a creature of nightmare. It took a slip of paper from Wyatt. "Will done be. All is that?"

"That's all, and I need it done in two hours."

"Less."

"Good."

The gremlin extended its clawed hands toward me. I looked at Wyatt; he gestured toward the bakery box. I handed it over. The small creature grabbed it and hobbled off, probably to gorge its latest brood.

"That's it?" I asked.

"Yes, that's it," Wyatt said.

"How do you know it will keep its part of the deal?"

"How did you know before that Max wouldn't spill his guts?"

"Point taken."

Gremlins don't understand deception. It's a very human trait. For many of the Dregs, especially those who are more animal than others, things simply are. Gremlins need food. In return for food they don't have to steal themselves, they will grant a favor. It doesn't even occur to them to not hold up their end.

I followed him across the balcony, back toward the stairwell. "Too bad human beings aren't more like gremlins," I said. "Then we probably wouldn't be in this mess."

"I hear that."

"So Chalice is almost taken care of." My voice echoed around us, and I reminded myself to whisper. "What's our next step, O Great Mastermind? Max was a dead end. Any other suspects on the list of people present the night I died?"

Wyatt stopped on the steps; I grabbed the rail to

halt my own forward movement and avoid knocking him down to the next landing. He tugged back the sleeve of his shirt, twisting his wrist to check his watch. The glowing face lit up with the time—barely after ten. I watched the seconds click by, ticking away the last few days of my life. One, two, three seconds that I would never get back.

"I think it's been long enough," he said, breaking the silence.

"Long enough for what?"

He turned his head and looked up at me. Something hard and angry flickered in his eyes. "To talk to Rufus."

* * *

Rufus St. James was Wyatt's mirror opposite. Another well-known Handler, Rufus exuded the patience and understanding of a wizened gnome lord, and was slower to anger than any human being I'd ever met. His Triad was as elusive as mine had been infamous, preferring stealth and secrecy to a reputation as swift dealers of punishment. Probably why they were still alive, and we were all (technically) dead.

Wyatt took us to the east side of Mercy's Lot, far beyond the last of the apartment buildings and row homes. I considered asking where the hell we were meeting Rufus, but the hard line of Wyatt's jaw (he was going to break his teeth one of these days) kept me silent. His path took us to the weedy parking lot of an abandoned fast-food restaurant. An empty strip mall occupied the other half of the lot, every storefront covered with graffiti. The sounds of the city seemed so far away from this ghostly part of town. Oddly stronger, though, were the lingering threads of static that still tickled the edges of my senses.

He parked around back, careful to obscure his car from passing motorists. Judging by the potholes we'd hit, I doubted many people ventured into this area, especially after dark. It felt like the perfect Halfie feeding ground.

A brand-new padlock secured the rear exit of the restaurant. Wyatt produced a key and let us inside. Faint odors of stale grease and humid air made me sneeze. I followed Wyatt through a dusty, grimy kitchen, toward a huge, walk-in refrigerator.

"Why are we meeting Rufus here?" I finally ventured to ask.

Wyatt looked at me over his shoulder. "Because this is where I put him."

I gaped at the refrigerator, noticing for the first time that the temperature controls were set to forty degrees Fahrenheit. Wyatt had kidnapped a fellow Handler and held him in an industrial fridge? More than unexpected, the realization was downright horrifying.

Hear that, Chalice? This is the guy you're so keen to sleep with.

Wyatt tugged the handle. The door squealed open. Cold air wafted around my ankles, sending gooseflesh tickling across the backs of my legs. I didn't want to look, but felt compelled to follow. If Wyatt had Rufus locked up in a fridge, he had a good reason for it. I refused to believe that Wyatt had completely lost his grip on reality.

Rufus sat in the center of the room, legs tucked

oddly beneath him so that his ass rested on his shoes rather than the cold floor. He wore jeans and a T-shirt, and held both arms tightly around his waist. His pale skin was nearly translucent, contrasting harshly with his strawberry blond hair. Freckles dotted his face and neck like pockmarks. He shivered so continuously, he appeared to vibrate. I saw no chains, no restraints holding him in place. Bright hazel eyes glared first at Wyatt, then at me.

I didn't dare speak. Rufus didn't seem to have the strength. For a moment, the gentle thrum of the refrigerator was the only sound in the room.

"Ready to talk now?" Wyatt asked. "Or do you need a few more hours to chill?"

The pun fell flat, and I could have punched him for even uttering it. Rufus ignored him, his attention still on me, trying to puzzle me out. Unlike Wyatt, Rufus was a powerless Handler, known more for his extreme intelligence and tactical mind. He was measuring his chances, observing his situation. Considering the latest unknown variable: me.

"You're a fool, Wyatt," Rufus said at last. "Born one, and you'll die one."

Starting out with a verbal challenge—not good. I expected Wyatt to usher me back out of the fridge and slam the door, giving Rufus more time to "chill." Instead, he asked, "How's that?"

"For believing Tovin." Wyatt arched his eyebrows, the only indication that Rufus's words surprised him. "For your insistence in holding on to the naïve idea that people like us get happy endings. How can you think for a second you'll get away with what you've done?"

"It's not about happiness anymore, Rufus. Right now it's about justice for Evy, and stopping what's about to happen."

"Ah yes, the infamous deal between goblins and Bloods. Why is it no one else has heard of this? Why isn't the brass all over it, Wyatt? You're putting yourself up against a dozen other races, and for what? There's no cause; no effect. It's all in your head."

"Is that what they're saying? Poor Truman has lost his mind, so let's bring him in for the public's safety?"

"No, for your safety. Everyone knows you're powerful, and now they think you're insane. The old Wyatt Truman would never have tortured a friend for answers that don't exist. The old Wyatt Truman wouldn't have made a freewill deal to resurrect a wanted murderer just to further his fantasy of redemption."

Wyatt lunged. I blocked him and was nearly bowled over for my efforts. I pressed my hands against Wyatt's shoulders, holding him still. Fury flickered in his eyes, bright as fire and just as dangerous. I held my ground, my own temper peaking.

A freewill deal.

I'd questioned the bruises on Wyatt's abdomen, as well as his simmering anger, in the were-cat's apartment when I questioned his investment. Magic isn't cheap, and it's often dangerous. Because it breaks that tenuous barrier between life and death, I'd been unable to imagine the price Wyatt had paid to bring me back. Nothing seemed like enough, and I had never pondered such a huge sacrifice.

A freewill deal is exactly how it sounds—the willing trade of one's free will in exchange for magic. Only the most powerful mages in any species can perform such a bargain, resolve tested by the beating and contract signed with blood. Wyatt had traded his free will in order to give me three more days.

"I'm the one who will be dead again in two and a half days, not you." In some ways, he *would* die. He would be subject to the will of his master for the rest of his natural life. Way longer than my three days. All for what was in my head.

No pressure.

"Wyatt, don't," I said.

The tone of my voice drained away some of his fight, and Wyatt took two steps backward, hands fisted by his sides. I pivoted and looked down. Rufus gazed at me, eyebrows knitted together, lips slightly parted. His eyes darted back and forth, studying me. Understanding what he'd just seen.

"Who are you?" Rufus asked.

"A wanted murderer," I said. "Nice to see you again, Rufie. How's Tully? Still addicted to sunflower seeds?"

His mouth curled into a silent O. "Evangeline?"

"In someone else's flesh."

Rufus closed his eyes and, if possible, went paler. When he again looked at me, grief and resignation warred for dominance. "I'm so sorry, Evy, that he pulled you into this fantasy. He should have let you rest in peace."

"Yesterday, I might have agreed with you, Rufus, but today? Not so much. Wyatt isn't crazy. Something is happening; we heard it this morning from a gargoyle. The races are choosing sides, and something's about to blow."

I crouched in front of him, trying hard not to shiver in the chilly room. "Now, I'm thinking one of two things is happening here. Either the brass know what's coming down and are trying to cover it up by making an example of me and Wyatt, or—are you ready for this?—someone in the Fey Council is keeping us in the dark. They aren't talking to your bosses, so nothing comes down to you. The Triads stay running in circles, hunting one another, while something else much more sinister takes place right under our noses."

Rufus sneezed, and a tremor racked his body. "Why did you kill your partners?"

I blew air between my teeth, creating a frustrated whistle. "I didn't; not really." I explained it again, as it had happened. The mere fact that Jesse had been turned before death shocked Rufus as much as it had shocked Wyatt. Nothing like a dose of truthfulness to wake you up to reality.

I sensed warmth behind me. Wyatt stood to my right side, so close I felt his heat. Tension vibrated from his body. Rufus shifted his attention between us, coming to some sort of silent decision, weighing my words against Wyatt's actions.

"Why would they lie?" Rufus asked. "About Jesse, I mean."

"Like she said," Wyatt replied. "To keep the Triads off balance and hunting one another, instead of sniffing around what's really going on. If the attack on my Triad was a setup from the get-go, we've all been played for fools. You and Baylor and Kismet have been so wrapped up in hunting—first for Evy, and then for me—that you haven't had time to notice anything else happening."

"Like a consolidation of power?"

"Precisely."

It made a horrifying kind of sense. Handlers had a free hand to run their Triads as they saw fit, doling out assignments and keeping tabs on the activities of their Hunters, but even the Handlers had bosses (the brass) to report to—three officers in the upper echelons of the Metro Police Department, whose identities were carefully guarded. Especially from the regular police department.

Triads are isolated, only allies to one another. The real cops can't help us; normal people barely notice us. Turn us against one another and we fall apart; change the status quo and the center can't hold. As Triad Handlers, if Rufus, Baylor, and Kismet received a Neutralize order from the brass, they followed it. No questions. Just action.

"We need to find out who got rid of the bodies," I said.

Rufus blinked. "Which bodies?"

"All of the Halfies that Ash, Jesse, and I killed that night. The ones that support my version of events." I swallowed against a lump in my throat. "I had to leave them to call for backup, but I was blindsided by Kismet's team before I could get back to the site. They already had orders to Neutralize me for murdering my teammates. Less than ten minutes after they died, I was wanted."

"So someone set you up," Rufus said.

It was exactly what Wyatt had said a week ago. Someone on the inside knew how to get us to that train bridge, and how to get nine other Triads to turn against me. To focus all of their energies on finding and Neutralizing me, instead of paying attention to the Dregs.

"Yeah, someone set me up."

"It doesn't make sense," Rufus said, shaking his head.

"Of course it does," Wyatt snapped. "It makes perfect sense. And it was also a terrific excuse to massacre the Owlkins, one of the largest Clans that sympathized with our species. We've been chasing our own asses for the last ten days, while the Bloods and goblins have been amassing power."

I crouched, getting eye level with Rufus. He didn't look away. "Rufus, I need your help," I said. "I don't have all of my memories back. I don't remember the final three days of my—Evangeline's—life, or anything that happened while I was captured. We need to piece this together, and we can't do it alone. We've only got two days to prove that Wyatt isn't nuts, that I'm not a traitor, and that there *is* some sort of plot against humanity brewing in the Dreg world."

His hazel eyes captured mine for a moment, as though attempting to see past Chalice's plain brown irises and into my soul. To see the person I'd once been, who lurked deep inside of the shell of a woman he didn't recognize.

"On one condition," he said.

"What's that?"

He glared over my shoulder. "Hot coffee and a blanket."

Chapter Eleven

54:15

"Where's your team?" I waited until we were back in Wyatt's car, with Rufus wrapped up in a blanket from the trunk, and us well on our way to get some drive-thru coffee, before asking the question foremost on my mind. I twisted around in the front passenger seat to face him.

"No idea," Rufus said. He'd taken on a bit of color since we helped him limp out of the refrigerator. "I've been locked up for the last thirty-odd hours, so they could be anywhere in the city, probably looking for me. My kids are loyal, too."

The last was directed at Wyatt, but he kept his concentration on driving.

"Could you convince them to help us?" I asked.

Rufus shook his head. "I'm still not convinced *I'm* going to help you, so how about one step at a time? You really don't remember anything between telling Wyatt that you were going uptown, then waking up in a new body?"

"I really don't, and I wish people would stop

second-guessing that. Do you think I like not knowing where I was or what happened to me?"

Wyatt grunted. Okay, so he knew what had happened to me, but I still couldn't bring myself to ask for those details. Instinctual revulsion at those goblins had been enough to hint at the torture they'd inflicted; I didn't need it drawn out in pictures. And yet I knew that my desire to remember everything for myself was costing us precious time. Time we couldn't afford to waste.

"Okay, you guys know what happened the night I was found," I said. "Since I can't seem to get it together, tell me your side of what happened. Who was there? Who said what? Maybe it will jog something."

"I got the page in the afternoon and called in, like usual," Rufus said. "The message said you'd been found, and that my team was needed on the scene. When we arrived, Wyatt, Amalie, and her guard, Jaron, were already there. So was Tybalt, but no one else from Kismet's Triad. Kis told me later that the others were on patrol down by the docks and couldn't get there in time. That's everyone."

"One of your team was missing," Wyatt said. A small amount of accusation tinged his words.

Rufus flared his nostrils. "Tully and Wormer were there. Nadia didn't respond right away."

I knew the three by name and by the occasional joint operation. We'd met maybe half a dozen times in our careers, which wasn't unusual in our line of work. Death followed us around, so it was better to maintain a distance. Befriend only your two Triad partners, and keep everyone else at arm's length.

And Tybalt . . . I think I punched him in the face once.

"It was a train station on the old track," Rufus said. "Part of the abandoned passenger line that followed the river over the Anjean tributary and into the East Side. No one was guarding it, so they must have heard us coming. . . ."

"Or been tipped off," Wyatt added.

Rufus quirked an eyebrow at the back of Wyatt's head. "Would you like to do the telling here?"

Wyatt raised a dismissive hand, attention never wavering from the road in front of him.

"We found you downstairs in some sort of basement," Rufus continued. "Old offices or storage or something. Amalie could still sense the immediate presence of others, so I sent Wormer and Tully out on recon, just to make sure we were alone. You were . . ." His mouth twitched, eyebrows knitted, as if he couldn't quite reconcile his memory with the woman watching him from behind a stranger's face. "You were dying. Wyatt went nuts when he saw you."

Bright spots of color flared on Wyatt's cheeks. His jaw clenched, knuckles stretching white against the steering wheel. In this new body that desired him and its short-term lease on life that practically begged me to do some stupid things with it, I liked the idea of him going crazy protective. Just not with so much at stake.

"Tybalt tried to keep him back, but we couldn't . . . Help didn't get there in time. You never said a word."

"But I was conscious?" I asked.

"Conscious, but I don't know if you were lucid. You tried to talk, but nothing came out."

"Regardless, I saw the people in the room. You, Wyatt, Jaron, Amalie, and Tybalt." Wyatt was convinced I'd been afraid to speak in front of someone present that night. Afraid to speak in front of either a respected Council sprite, her aide, a fellow Hunter, or a Handler. None of those thoughts was comforting.

Wyatt loosed his grip on one side of the wheel and reached across the seat. He gently squeezed my knee— a show of support, or an effort to keep me from voicing my thoughts, I don't know. Either way, I kept those fears to myself.

"Where is Tybalt now?" I asked instead.

"Probably on a routine patrol," Rufus said. "Kismet's Triad has kept tabs on the east side of town by the tributary. My team was the only one dispatched to locate Wyatt; everyone else is on regular duty."

"Locate?" Wyatt snorted. "You would have put a bullet in the back of my head, if you'd had the chance."

"Bullshit, Truman. Our orders were to bring you in, not kill you."

"Yeah, leave that job to your bosses."

"They're your bosses, too."

"Not anymore." He glanced up into the rearview mirror. "In case you hadn't noticed, I don't exactly work for the brass anymore. I have a funny feeling my credentials have been revoked. Being labeled a danger to myself and society can do that."

"I was doing my job."

"So was I."

The testosterone levels in the car were reaching a dangerous high, and I swallowed a sarcastic comment about bringing out rulers. It wouldn't help diffuse the situation, because I was staring at a pair of alpha males. Both wanted to prove their point, but at the moment, I didn't care who was the bigger man. I needed their collective attention.

"Hey!" I said. "Dead person here, working on a strict timetable. Can we concentrate, please, and save the shit-slinging for my after-afterlife?"

"Evy—" Wyatt started.

I spun in my seat, pointing one finger at him like a teacher berating a belligerent child. "And don't think I'm ignoring what he said about a freewill deal, Truman. We'll be talking about that at a later time."

He clammed up and steered the car into the parking lot of a Burger Palace. The ancient chain never installed drive-thru windows. They were notable for being the only place in town to offer a five-alarm chili cheeseburger and guarantee a refund if you ate the whole thing. Jesse did it once, and then spent the entire next day vomiting it all back up.

"I'll get the coffee," Wyatt said. "Anyone want food?"

"Turkey burger with everything, and a side salad," Rufus said.

I bit my lower lip to hold back laughter. Interesting choice after being locked up for a day and a half. Wyatt looked at me, but I shook my head. Watching Wyatt disappear inside of the Burger Palace's redbrick walls, I felt an unfamiliar sense of separation. Since that moment we met outside of the pay phone booth, we had not been more than ten feet apart.

I grasped the door handle, overcome by the urge to follow him, to maintain that physical proximity. Keep him close where I could protect him.

I was being foolish. He'd be back in five minutes with coffee and food and a smile for me. And probably a frustrated glare for Rufus, who kept staring at me like I was a particularly fascinating museum exhibit. I picked at the corner of my bandage. The itching had stopped. It finally seemed safe to look.

"What's it like?" he asked.

"What's what like?"

"New life."

Good fucking question. "Kind of like looking through a camera lens. Everything is sharp and in focus, but doesn't feel quite real. My body is taller, and Chalice has a lot more hair."

"Chalice?"

"Frost." It still felt odd to say her name like she was an individual. More and more, we were becoming the same person. One unique identity, rather than two sharing one space.

"Did you know beforehand?"

I blinked. He really needed to quit with the cryptic questions. "Know what, Rufus?"

"About the supposed union between Bloods and goblins. This thing that has Wyatt so hell-bent on breaking every single rule."

Oh, that. Yes. "No," I said.

"But you are absolutely certain now that he's right about this secret alliance? No doubt in your mind?"

I had doubts about a lot of things, none of which would go away until the last of my memories returned. The only thing I didn't doubt was Wyatt, because he'd given me no cause.

"I think Wyatt believes in this enough for both of us," I said. "He believed enough to give up his free will in exchange for my help. I'm not the only one on this three-day timetable, and until my memory returns and I know it, too, he'll know for me. Someone set me up for murder, Rufus, and until I find out who, Wyatt is the only person I still trust."

"Not even me?" It was matter-of-fact, a question with no hint of anger or surprise. Just curiosity.

"Not even you." Maybe Chalice's roommate. He seemed nice and completely oblivious to Dreg dealings. Not that I had any reason to contact him again before the clock ran out.

He blew hard through his teeth. "I feel like I need to apologize to you."

"For what?"

"For my part in what happened to the Owlkins. I know you were friendly with them, and I'm sorry." I closed my eyes, silently begging him to shut up. He said it anyway: "My team led the assault."

Fists clenched in my lap, I tried to keep from flying at him. "You were following orders."

"That doesn't help me sleep at night."

"Good."

I glanced at the restaurant's side door. A young couple bounced out, each carrying a supersized soda cup and matching silly grins. Still no sign of Wyatt. Rufus fidgeted in the backseat. His eyebrows were knitted, his mouth drawn into a tight line. If I hadn't known better, I'd have guessed he was having a bowel movement.

"You okay?"

He flinched and didn't look at me. "I need to use the facilities."

I knew it. "Go ahead. I'll make sure Wyatt doesn't drive off without you."

I smiled. He didn't.

Rufus slid out of the backseat, letting the blanket fall to the cracked vinyl in a puddle of blue terry. He slammed the door and limped past me, around to the front of the car—the roundabout way of getting to the building next door. He stopped in front of the bumper, hands thrust deep into the pockets of his jeans. He stood there.

The short hairs on the back of my neck prickled. Warning lights flashed in my mind. I looked around, getting a three-sixty of the parking lot and all access points. Our side was against a slat-wood fence, ten feet tall and bordered by bushes and parking spaces. The back of the lot bordered the rear of a rotting apartment building, rusty fire escapes practically falling off the brick, and no street access. The opposite side of the restaurant—which I couldn't see from there but vaguely recalled from driving in—was another stone barrier, the freestanding wall of a rubbled strip mall. It was a box canyon.

I opened my door, snagged the knife from my ankle sheath, and lunged, knocking Rufus backward and pinning him beneath me. His head cracked off the blacktop. He yelped.

"You son of a bitch." I pressed the serrated blade to his throat. "How long have they been tracking us?"

"I don't know," Rufus gasped, eyes wide and wild. He didn't fight back. "Probably since I got out of that damned fridge. The brass is tabbing all of us, Evy. They'll be here any minute. You need to run."

I blinked and pressed the knife harder, drawing

a speck of blood. "Run right into a fucking trap that
your pals set up for me? No thanks."

"Before they get here. I believe you now, and I
didn't before, I'm sorry. I can still help, but you need
to get away right now."

I looked over the hood of the car. Two black sedans were in the opposite-turn lane, and as I stared,
the first turned left into the parking lot entrance. It
crept forward, tinted windows glaring with specks of
sunlight. "Goddammit."

"Hit me. Hit me and run. There's a pay phone on
the corner of West Elm and Tierney. Be there at dusk
and I'll call you."

"Wyatt." I lunged toward the restaurant, but
Rufus grabbed my wrist. I stumbled sideways, nearly
falling on top of him.

"I'll help you get him back, Evy, but right now hit
me and go!"

I did, without further thought or hesitation.
Fingers numb and wrist aching, I bolted. Across the
rocky pavement, toward the back of the lot, eyes on
the lowest rung of the fire escape. My heart was thundering in my ears, and adrenaline surged through my
veins.

Voices shouted. Gunshots pinged the blacktop by
my feet. Something grazed my ankle with liquid fire.
Each step was agony, but no other shots connected.
One foot on a trash can lid vaulted me up to the fourth
rung of the rusty escape ladder. Up I went, scrambling
for each purchase. At the first landing, a peppering of
gunfire shattered the nearest window. I hurled myself
through, tucking into a tumble. I hit rough carpet, and
glass dug into my arms and shoulders.

I sprang up into a crouch, in the middle of a dim living room, ripe with the odors of last night's binge. Empty bottles and paper wrappers littered the floor and tables. A trash can was piled high with garbage of every variety. But no one came running at the sound of my inauspicious entry.

The ceiling exploded bits of plaster as more bullets flew in from the destroyed window. I ran toward the front door, leaping awkwardly over an upholstered ottoman and almost tripping over my own feet. Chalice's feet. Why couldn't I have been resurrected into a ballet dancer? I fumbled with the door's chain—on, so someone had to be home—and turned the dead bolt.

"What the blue f—?" A man's voice turned into a startled yelp, punctuated by a thud. I didn't stop, didn't turn, simply yanked open the front door and ran.

A long, bare cement block corridor greeted me. I spotted a red "Exit" sign and jerked left, heading toward the fire door. I slammed through it and hit the cement stairs at a dead run, down two at a time, adrenaline feeding me more speed than felt natural. My ankle was numb, probably leaving a trail of blood for anyone with two eyes to follow, but I couldn't stop to wrap it. I had to keep going. To get away before they had me cornered.

I burst through the first-floor door and emerged in a dimly lit lobby. An elderly woman stared at me over her cane. Her mouth dropped open, and a thoroughly gummed cigar fell to the threadbare carpet. I tore past her, toward bright sunlight and a pair of double glass doors. Past a row of metal mailboxes and a closed door with "Manager" printed in choppy block letters. Back outside into warm spring air.

And the wail of police sirens.

The west wall of the apartment building butted up against a grubby mom-and-pop grocery. The windows were papered with ads dated two years ago, but still advertising "Fresh! And Cheap!" produce. I stopped on the cracked sidewalk, under the protection of a red vinyl canopy, and tried to catch my breath. Calm my heart. Think straight.

My teeth ached, and I finally noticed that at some point during my flight, I'd bitten down on the handle of my serrated knife—probably right before I climbed the fire escape—and it was still clenched in my teeth. I slipped it back into its sheath, and then checked my other ankle. My shoe was soaked, but the graze had stopped bleeding, leaving behind an angry red gash. A quick sidewalk check revealed no trail.

The sirens grew louder, bouncing over from the opposite block. Distant reminders that I'd left Wyatt behind. Alone.

A figure emerged from the apartment's lobby door, but he looked the other way first. I ducked into the grocery store, assaulted by frigid air and the yeasty odor of bread. Two ancient checkout counters marked the front of the shop. I smiled at the clerk—a bland girl no older than sixteen. She smiled and returned to her magazine.

I slipped down the first aisle, making tracks to the back room. Two rows over, I spotted a swinging "Employees Only" door. A bell jingled at the front of the store. My stomach churned. I pushed through, urged onward by fear and a feral need to avoid capture. I couldn't help Wyatt if I were in matching handcuffs, or dead for the second time.

The stockroom reeked of rotting vegetables and stale water, thick and nauseating. But I ignored the stench and navigated a path past a small office—hearing the sounds of heavy breathing, which told me where the rest of the staff was—to another door. This one was next to a loading dock. The wires on the emergency handle were cut. The employees probably used it regularly. A tentative nudge proved me correct. I pushed it open far enough to get a peek into the back lot.

The loading dock was blocked off by three metal Dumpsters. A ten-foot chain fence, topped by razor wire, separated the narrow alley from the lot behind it. The Burger Palace was on my right, catty-corner from my position, line of sight obscured. I ducked outside, staying as close to the trash cans as I could manage without vomiting from the odor of rotting meat and produce. Then I ducked past them to the fence.

Between the scratchy branches of two unruly bushes, I could see part of the parking lot. Wyatt's car was still in its spot, flanked by the two black sedans, all four doors thrown open. Two men about my (former) age were searching it—Hunters I vaguely recognized, mostly from instinct. The way they moved, analyzed, and searched for clues was instinctual, calculated, and deadly.

Rufus sat on the curb, holding an ice pack against his jaw. A man in a smart suit—a Handler named Willemy, if I recalled correctly—crouched in front of him, his hands moving in circles as he talked. Rufus kept shaking his head, saying little.

The one person I needed to see was missing. He could be in one of those tinted sedans, bound and ready for transport elsewhere. Would he have resisted and forced them to take desperate action? No, he wouldn't risk getting himself killed. Not now. I just needed to see it with my own eyes.

A telephone rang. Willemy fished in his jacket pocket and retrieved his cell. His drooping frown morphed into sheer delight. He snapped the phone shut and said something to Rufus, who nodded, silent. I squinted at him. From that distance, I couldn't tell if he was out of sorts from my punch, or if he was just a good actor. Willemy seemed finished with him for the time being. He stood up and faced the restaurant.

The side door swung open. Nadia Stanislavski and Philip Tully emerged, one on either side of Wyatt. His hands were cuffed behind his back, and he walked straight. No limping or dragging, no marks that I could see. Sharp pain lanced through my palm; I loosened my fist, releasing nails from indented flesh.

They led him toward the closest sedan. He looked straight ahead, giving nothing. If he expected me to be there somewhere, waiting for him, watching in the wings, he gave no indication. He would have yelled and cursed had he known I was crouching in the bushes instead of putting miles between us. I wanted to let him know I was there, to give some suggestion of my presence, but I remained a silent spectator, watching as they ushered him into the car and slammed the door.

Nadia slid into the front seat of Wyatt's car. Rufus climbed in next to her. She followed the black sedan out of the parking lot, taking Wyatt away. One car remained behind, as did Tully. He was perched on the hood, waiting for . . . who? The person who'd chased after me, most likely. If the entire Triad had come after its Handler, that meant Wormer was tracking me. Or had already lost me; I couldn't be sure. There were damn few things I could be certain of at that particular moment in time.

My neck prickled. I held my breath. Soft leather soles whispered across the parking lot's cracked blacktop, kicked the occasional pebble, and came to rest close by my position. I didn't turn to look. Looking might rustle the bushes that protected me. A cramp lanced through my thigh. I bit my tongue, trying to distract myself from the agony I couldn't acknowledge. I needed to breathe.

The footsteps moved past me. I let out a shaky breath, then inhaled slowly. My burning lungs wanted to cough. The cramp intensified; tears sparked in my eyes.

Something beeped. Fabric rustled. A man's voice said, "Yeah?"

Over the phone, someone replied, "You find her yet?"

From the corner of my eye, I saw Tully standing by the sedan with a phone pressed to his ear.

"No. Whoever she is, she's fast," James Wormer said.

"Bring it in, then. We need to get back. I want to be there when they question that asshole."

Wormer snickered, and the sound sent shivers up my spine. "I'm on my way. After what he did to Rufus, I want to hear that crazy fucker scream."

I closed my eyes, concentrating on the exquisite agony in my leg—using it to stay grounded and ignore my urge to leap out of the bushes and pound Wormer's face into the pavement. Seconds ticked away. Car engines rumbled. Horns honked. Two doors slammed. I looked again. The sedan was driving toward the parking lot exit.

Briefly, I considered chasing it, but once the car made it to the road, I'd have no chance of following. Handlers and Triads didn't have one specific meeting place—no clubhouse or police barracks or underground vault. Except for Boot Camp, which enjoyed a quiet corner of the forest south of the city, secured facilities for questioning and detaining Dregs changed on a monthly basis. They could question Wyatt anywhere in the city.

I had no Handler, no car, and no clue as to my next move. I climbed out of the bushes and stretched my aching leg. Long hours before dusk stretched out in front of me, but I couldn't wait. I had to do something. Just not alone.

Evangeline Stone had no remaining allies. Chalice Frost had one person in her life who just might drop everything and help—if I could convince him I wasn't nuts.

Chapter Twelve

53:25

Hitching a ride across town is not recommended, unless you know you can fight off a potential attacker. Confident in my knowledge of fighting skills—although not so confident in my ability to get Chalice's body to do what I needed—I accepted the first ride I received and made it back to Parkside East in less than thirty minutes.

No little girls followed me into the elevator. The entire building seemed deserted in the middle of the day. As I fished Chalice's keys out of my borrowed pants, my hands began to shake. I had no particular reason for nerves, but I also had no reason to think Alex Forrester was even home. This could very well turn into a gigantic waste of time.

I turned the key, but the dead bolt was not secured. I wrapped tentative fingers around the doorknob, but it was yanked out of my hand. I took a startled step backward. Alex stood in the open doorway, his wide blue eyes drilling holes into me. I squirmed under the

intensity of his stare as relief, anger, and confusion—
all meant for someone else—flashed across his face.

His lips twitched, but he seemed incapable of speaking, so I helped him out. "I said I'd come back."

He nodded, his attention dropping to my bandaged arm, and then lower to my blood-soaked shoe. He frowned. "You're hurt, Chal."

"It's just a flesh wound," I said, shrugging one shoulder. "Can I come in?"

"Of course."

I stepped around him, pausing in the entry long enough to take off the dirty sneakers. No sense in tracking blood and gunk all over the carpet. He closed the door and walked across the living room, right into the bathroom. For the briefest moment, I thought of Wyatt, of sending him stalking into the bathroom that morning after a careless comment.

Alex returned a moment later with a white first aid kit. "Sit down and let me take a look at that."

I perched on the very edge of the sofa. It wasn't my home, not really. I didn't know this place, even though evidence of Chalice was all over the room, in the décor and the photographs and the titles of the romantic comedies that lined one shelf near the television.

Alex sat down on the coffee table, directly across from me, and opened up the kit. He removed several bottles, a package of gauze, and a roll of white medical tape—precise movements that betrayed practice. I presented my ankle to him. His hands were cool, almost cold, the fingertips gently callused. He turned my foot to get a better view.

Lips pursed, he stared at the wound. "Weird," he muttered.

Don't let him know it's from a gunshot. "What's weird?"

"The blood on your shoe is fresh, but the wound's already healing." He reached for a cotton ball and soaked it in alcohol. "What's going on, Chalice?"

"That's the question, isn't it?"

"You're lucky it didn't get infected." He cleaned the dried blood from my skin. The alcohol was cold; my leg tingled. He tossed the cotton and took out a bottle of antibiotic ointment. With a second cotton ball, he spread some over the cleaned area. "Where have you been?"

"Taking care of things that needed attention."

"When you didn't come home last night, I thought I'd imagined you. So I called the morgue, and they said one of their lab techs was under sedation after she almost autopsied a living person." He exhaled sharply and reached for a gauze pad. "How could I have missed that? Some med student I am."

I felt an odd instinct to protect him from the truth, but to also give him the benefit of knowing he hadn't missed anything. He was second-guessing his medical skills, but not because he'd missed anything; because of magic. "If it helps," I said, pretty certain it wouldn't, "a handful of E.R. doctors and a coroner all missed it, too."

He paused in pressing a length of medical tape against the gauze pad. "Not that, Chal." He met my gaze, and I almost fell into the depth of anguish I saw in them. "I meant your suicide attempt. How depressed you'd been about finals, and your stress at work. I was so busy with classes that I didn't take the time to notice. You're my best friend in the world, and half the time I couldn't even see you."

Oh great. Now I get to crush his spirit and tell him, "No, sorry, you did let your friend die." I get to break him all over again.

He applied the tape, then reached for my left arm. I flinched and pulled away. More hurt flared in his eyes. I didn't know how to explain why a healing dog bite resided where a knife gash should have been.

"Say something," he demanded.

I blinked. "What would you like me to say, Alex?"

He stilled. Wrong answer, apparently. With careful, calculated movements, he stood up. Backed around the coffee table, toward an upholstered chair, unwilling to startle.

"Chalice, what was the last thing we did together the night before you cut your wrist?" His voice was hollow, almost afraid. He knew something was wrong. Instinct contradicted his senses, and he was smart enough to trust the former.

Now or never. I just hoped he took it well.

"I don't know, Alex," I said, still sitting, making no move to approach. "This is really hard to explain, but try to keep an open mind." I took a deep breath. Exhaled. "I'm not Chalice."

His lips puckered like he'd eaten a lemon. Hands braced on his hips, he said, "Sorry. What?"

"Look, you seem like a terrific guy and a very loyal friend, so I hate doing this to you. But Alex, Chalice did die. You found her and called an ambulance. She was pronounced dead and sent to the morgue. None of it was imagined, nothing was a mistake. Well, except the whole suicide thing, in my opinion, but who am I to judge her?"

He backed up a few more steps. The backs of his knees hit the chair. He sat down hard, never breaking eye contact. Something else began to cloud his expression. Something angry, almost sinister. "This isn't funny," he snapped.

"I know."

"Look, I get that you were depressed, and I'm sorry for my part in what you did—"

"Christ, Alex, I didn't kill myself, okay? My name isn't Chalice Frost, and I am not your friend. I mean, I would like to be, but I'm not her."

He nodded. "Near-death experiences change people. . . ."

Okay, he was so not getting it. I dug under the tape binding my arm and ripped the old gauze away. The flesh was bumpy and angry red, but healing, with no signs of the suicide scar.

"Fine, doctor-in-training. Explain this."

He gaped. "What did that?"

"Last night, an hour after I left here, I was attacked by a creature I hope you never meet in a dark alley. It was about seven feet tall when it stood upright, had sharp-ass teeth, and it took a chunk out of my arm. But since I'm just borrowing Chalice's body for a limited time period, I started to heal. That's why the other scar is gone, and why the wound on my ankle—a bullet graze I got less than an hour ago—is partially healed already."

I leaned a little closer, still displaying my arm. "That's what did that."

Alex leaned back, deflated. His face went slack, pale. "I think I'm going to be sick."

"Don't do that." I smiled, hoping to keep him calm. "If you get sick, then I'll get sick, and pretty soon we'll be barfing all over each other."

The barest hint of a smile ghosted across his lips. "You don't talk like her."

"That's because I'm not."

"You're wearing the necklace I gave her for Christmas last year."

I touched the silver cross. "I can take it off."

"No." He leaned forward, scrubbed his hands across his face, up into his hair, and back down again. Rubbing the words in, getting them to stick. After a moment he stilled, with his chin resting in the palms of his hands.

"Okay, let's pretend for a minute that you're not really Chalice," he said. "And that this isn't some grief-induced hallucination. Who exactly are you?"

"The truth?"

"Yes."

This would be interesting. "My name is Evangeline Stone. I have lived in the city my entire life, and for the last four years, I have been employed by a secret unit of the Metro Police Department as a Dreg Bounty Hunter."

His eyebrows arched comically high. "A what hunter?"

"Dreg Hunter."

"It that like slang for criminal?"

"It's a derogatory catchall for the dozen or so species of creatures that secretly live here in the city. Mostly goblins, gremlins, trolls, gargoyles, vampires, and weres. My boss is called a Handler, and I work in a three-person Bounty Hunter squad called a Triad. We hunt rogue elements, carry out special warrants, try to keep some species from killing one another and wreaking havoc in the process, and dole out punishment when lines are crossed.

"My boss's bosses are three anonymous, high-ranking police officers, who work in tandem with the Fey Council—that would be faeries, sprites, gnomes, pixies, and sylphs—to keep the peace and prevent the Dregs from killing everyone on the planet. Kind of like the Mafia, but shorter and with magic and pointy ears."

I stopped. Alex stared. And stared. He blinked once. His jaw twitched. Water dripped from a faucet somewhere—the only sound in the room. He stood up, and I tensed, trying to anticipate his reaction. I expected a verbal attack, maybe even a physical one. Instead, he wandered into the kitchen, as though he'd just offered to retrieve refreshments. He went straight to the refrigerator, where he opened the door and ducked down.

A drawer squeaked. Bottles rattled. He stood straight, let the door slam shut, and twisted the cap off a bottle of beer. One, two, three, four long pulls. He held up the bottle, studying the label like he'd never seen it before today. Then he took one more deep swallow and returned to his chair, the bottle still in his hand.

"Well, either you've gone completely insane," he said, sinking into the upholstery, "or I have."

"We are both very much sane, Alex. Most people don't know about the Dreg population. They're good at staying out of sight, and we're good at covering up after them. Remember the downtown blackout two years ago?"

"A power grid blew."

I shook my head. "Gremlin revolt. They did it because the Council demanded work without proper compensation. So they demonstrated their power, which put pressure on the Council from several sides, including humans. One power failure can be explained, but not the entire city. The gremlins got what they wanted."

"A gremlin labor strike?"

"Yep."

He downed the rest of the beer and deposited the bottle on the coffee table with a clunk. Twin smudges of color darkened his cheeks. "Gremlins." He turned the two-syllable word into four, testing its sound and texture. "Vampires are real?"

"Very real, but more *Lost Boys* than Bram Stoker, and it's forbidden to turn humans. The change is actually a physical reaction to a parasite present in a vampire's saliva and—never mind; that's a long story. At any rate, bite survivors are considered inferior half-breeds, and are hard to control. Not human and never fully vampire."

"Okay, that was way too much information."

"You need to know this stuff, Alex."

"Why?" He leapt to his feet and stormed to the other side of the living room. He planted himself in front of the patio doors, casting his shape into a back-lit shadow. "Why the hell did you come back here if you're not Chalice? Why are you dragging me into this crazy fantasy world you live in?"

I stood up with measured movement, taking care to not startle him. My good humor and sympathy were quickly disappearing, replaced by frustration. "Because I need your help, Alex, and I don't have anyone else I can trust."

"What about your team?"

"They're dead."

"Your boss?"

My heartbeat quickened. "He's why I need your help. He's been captured."

"By whom?"

"The people he used to work for."

Alex tilted his head to the left. "Wait a minute; you said he worked for the police. He's been captured by the cops? As in arrested?"

More complications. I blew hard through my teeth. "Yes and no. It's more complicated than that."

"I don't see how. He was arrested for a reason, right? So does that make you the good guy or the bad guy in this little melodrama?"

"Depends on your point of view, I guess." I launched into the rest of my story, starting with the setup at the train yards and ending with the night I was kidnapped. It was all I knew for certain, and I hoped it told him that I wasn't the villain. But I certainly wasn't an innocent bystander, either. There was no black and white in my situation. Only varying shades of gray.

Alex listened attentively, giving no hint of his inner thoughts. He remained quiet for a full minute after I finished. "Okay," he said. "Let's say I believe everything you've told me so far and that I don't think you're off your rocker. Here's the sixty-four-thousand-dollar question."

"Why am I, Evy Stone, in Chalice Frost's body?"

"Yeah, that would be the one."

A completely reasonable question that I felt somehow compelled to answer. Not only because I needed his help, but because I felt connected to him, on some basic level that may have been a carryover from being in Chalice. They had been friends. I needed him to believe me.

"I don't remember anything after five nights ago," I said. "The night I set out to prove I'd been set up, I was kidnapped. I was taken to an abandoned train station and tortured for two and a half days, and I eventually died. I was dead for three days, until a dear friend paid a terrible price to bring me back. He traded for a Fey spell that required a freshly dead body for my soul to inhabit. Only something went wrong. I went into the wrong body and without my complete memory, and now I can't remember what I was too afraid to tell him before I died. Until I remember what I've forgotten, I can't clear us."

"Why bother?"

I balled my fists. "Why bother what? Saving him?"

"No, I understand that. Why bother trying to clear yourselves in the first place when it's easier just to run?"

Running had never been an option. Not even that first night, fresh from the deaths of Jesse and Ash and the unexpected betrayal of my former allies. "This is my life, Alex. It's all I've known since I was a teenager. It never occurred to either of us to not fight this. Besides, there's more at stake than just our lives. Although right now, saving Wyatt's life is all I care about." I walked toward Alex, and he didn't flinch.

"His name is Wyatt Truman. He was my Handler and my . . ." My what? Lover? Not exactly. I stopped an arm's length away. Tears prickled my eyes. "I have to save him."

Alex lifted his right arm. His fingers stopped inches from my face. I remained still, allowing him his exploration. Tentative fingertips traced the line of my jaw, from ear to chin. Proving I was real, that he wasn't imagining it all. Touching the face of a woman he'd seen die. Knowing that a stranger lived in her shell and that the woman he cared about was never coming home. Was he convinced? Or simply contemplating escape?

His touch dropped to my shoulder, down my arm, until he finally grasped my hand. He squeezed it; I squeezed back.

"Evy, huh?" he said.

"Assuming you believe me and we're not both crazy."

He smiled.

Shadows darted past the patio doors, too fast to count. I yanked hard on Alex's hand. He yelped and tripped and fell to the carpeted floor. I dropped to my knees and covered his head with my hands.

Above us, glass and wood exploded in a shower of tinkling shards.

Chapter Thirteen

53:02

Heavy boots landed near my head, crushing broken glass into the thick carpet. I lunged upward and drove my balled fist into the intruder's groin. Hard bone met delicate flesh, which gave way under the blow. The man howled and doubled forward. I thrust upward. Knuckles connected solidly with his chin. For a split instant, I looked into Tully's shocked eyes, and then he was toppling backward.

I rose into a crouching position and spun toward scuffling sounds. Alex and Wormer were on the ground, wrestling for control of a revolver. Wormer had used his advantage in bulk to roll Alex onto his back. The gun shifted above their heads. Someone squeezed off a wild shot that took out a vase on the counter. Glass shattered and pinged.

I grabbed the closest weapon within reach—an iron candlestick sporting a half-melted red pillar—and swung. It connected with the side of Wormer's head. He grunted and lost control of the gun to Alex. It was more of a glancing blow than the knockout I'd hoped for, but it did its job. Alex gripped the gun by the barrel, eyes wide, like he couldn't believe he wasn't dead.

"Get off him, asshole." I shoved Wormer with my foot, and he fell sideways. The bloody footprint left behind on his shirt surprised me. I didn't even feel the glass.

I readied the candlestick again, hoping to deliver a coma-inducing blow.

"Watch out!" Alex shouted.

Too late. Something hit my neck, sharp as a knife thrust. Lightning exploded behind my eyes, and every nerve ending was on fire. My heart raced, and I could barely breathe fast enough to compensate. I lost muscle control and fell to my knees. A hot flush broke across my skin. Then the agony ended as abruptly as it began, and all I felt was cold. I shrieked as I fell.

Broken glass cut into my right arm. I smelled sizzled flesh. A flash of something long and black entered the periphery of my vision. Cattle prod. Nice move. Didn't see that one coming.

"We're better trackers than you realize, little girl," Tully said.

Little girl? I rolled onto my back, hoping for a good opening, but he gave me none. He stood out of arm's (and foot's) reach, the cattle prod in his left hand and a revolver in the other. Pointed not at me, but past me. Over my shoulder, Alex was sitting up with both hands braced around the butt of his acquired gun, muzzle pointed at Tully. His hands trembled ever so slightly.

"Put it down," Tully said.

"Hell no," Alex replied, but without the necessary

force. His fear was betraying him. "You broke into my apartment. You're intruders. I can shoot you."

Tully's nostrils flared; he didn't like the threat. "My superiors know where I am. If I don't check in on time, they come here looking for me. You don't want that."

"He's not kidding," I said. My hand investigated my neck and found a quarter-sized burn.

The gun's aim didn't move, but I came under Tully's scrutiny. "We know you're helping a fugitive named Wyatt Truman. Why? Who are you?"

He didn't know me, which meant the brass didn't know about my resurrection. I didn't know how Wyatt kept it secret, but he had. Advantage one for my team. Behind Alex, Wormer groaned. He seemed to be struggling to sit up. Maybe I'd whacked him good after all.

"Where'd they take Wyatt?" I asked.

Tully's nostrils flared. "Do you really think you're in a position to ask me questions, lady?"

"Yes."

He fired. I felt the heat of the bullet as it passed by my cheek. Behind me, Alex cried out. I twisted around, coming up on my hands and knees, stomach knotting as I prepared for the worst. Alex lay on his side, one hand pressed against his right temple. Blood oozed between his fingers, but he was very much alive. Alive, aware, and swearing colorfully enough to make even me blush.

I lunged for the gun he'd abandoned. More lightning, this time in my lower back. Cursing my own idiocy, I collapsed by Alex's feet. My stomach muscles spasmed. Bile scorched the back of my throat and left a sour taste in my mouth. An unexpected whimper tore from between clenched teeth.

The jolt ceased. I didn't move, choosing instead to simply breathe. Stupid; goddamn stupid.

"Still think you're the one asking questions?"

A sardonic retort formed in my mouth, but thankfully died a quick death before I could utter it. I needed my wits about me, not volts of electricity coursing through my body. "No," I hissed. "You're in charge."

"Good girl."

I drew my knees up to my chest and rolled, hoping to sit up. A sharp kick to the middle of my back felled me again. I took the hint and stayed low, choosing to roll onto my back and prop up on my elbows. I disliked the prone position, but at least I could glare right into Tully's eyes. It also gave me a better view of the room.

Pale, but very much alive, Alex scooted closer to me. Blood stained the side of his face, neck, and shirt collar. Wormer loomed above us, once again in charge of his own firearm, and apparently very much in favor of using it.

"Now," Tully said, "let's try answering my questions. Who are you?"

Smug. I hated that. Self-preservation took a backseat to annoyance. "I'm the thing that the shadows fear."

Confusion creased his forehead. It was a line Triad members used jokingly amongst ourselves. We hunted the creatures that haunted others' nightmares. Tully seemed to understand the reference. I could see imaginary wheels turning in his mind.

"Truman tell you to say that?" Tully asked.

The burn on my neck began to itch. If I was lucky, it would heal fast and freak Tully out just a little bit. "Wyatt didn't tell me to say anything. He never expected us to be separated."

"That right?" Tully circled to my left, positioning himself closer to Alex and farther from me. The cattle prod bounced in his hand. "Don't make me ask your name again."

"You wouldn't believe me if I told you."

"Try me."

I quirked an eyebrow. "I'm disappointed in your partner, Wormer," I said, tossing the silent Hunter an over-the-shoulder look. "He doesn't recognize me. That hurts my feelings, Tully; it really does."

They exchanged looks, sharing their confusion. Time ticked onward. They couldn't stay and question us for very long. The scuffle and gunshots should have aroused the neighbors. Surely someone in the building would know to call the police and report suspicious activity.

"Her name's Chalice," Alex said. "She works in a coffee shop. We're not who you think."

"You're not?" Wormer said. "Guess we'll just have to kill you, then."

"Cut it out," Tully admonished. "We don't kill humans, and you know it."

Tactical slip. Wyatt would have reamed me a new one for saying that in front of a civilian. Admitting to not killing humans blatantly said that you killed something else.

Tully studied me, still trying hard to see past the unfamiliar exterior to the person hiding inside. "We'll take them with us. We can't break her here; we've already made too much noise."

"No, leave her here," Alex said. "I know things; you want me. Not her."

Wormer nudged the back of Alex's head with the muzzle of his gun. "What things do you know?"

Alex glared at Tully, but wouldn't meet my eyes. "I know that the downtown power outage two years ago was caused by gremlins, and not what the public was told."

My mouth fell open, but the pair of Hunters misinterpreted my annoyance as shock. Tully crouched down, putting himself at eye level with Alex. Still out of my range, though. The candlestick lay nearby, within arm's reach.

"Who told you that?" Tully asked.

"I'll tell you everything," Alex said. "Just leave Chalice here. She doesn't know anything."

"Oh hell no," I said. "Alex, I know you feel terrible about Chalice, but trying to be a hero and save me isn't the way to atone for it. She wouldn't want you to get yourself killed."

Tully pointed the gun at me. "I thought you were Chalice."

"And I thought you were an asshole. Too bad only one of us is right."

Tully swung the cattle prod toward my left arm. At the last moment, I blocked it and kicked him square in the groin. The second direct hit in five minutes sent him to the ground like an anvil. I twisted the cattle prod out of his grasp with the intent of using it on Wormer. Turned out I didn't need it.

Alex had grabbed the abandoned candlestick and

cracked it across Wormer's jaw. The trigger-happy Hunter squeezed off a round that shattered the room's only other window before he slumped to the floor. Satisfied, I shoved the tip of the cattle prod into the hollow below Tully's Adam's apple. He gurgled and twitched. When I pulled it away, he lay still.

I watched and waited, expecting a miraculous recovery and second attack. It never came.

"Oh my God," Alex said.

"You okay?"

"I'll live." He dropped the candlestick. It cracked against bits of glass. Still sporting a frightening pallor, he studied me with the eyes of a trapped deer. "You're bleeding."

"So are you."

We helped each other stand and wade through the sea of broken glass. The sole of my cut foot stung and left prints on the carpet. My trail followed us back to the sofa, a safe distance from our disabled attackers. Alex sank into the cushion. His slight tremble turned to full-on shaking.

"Who were they?" he asked, the tremor reaching his voice.

"People I used to work with, others like me, only in the bodies they were born in. I'm so sorry; I don't know how they followed me. I thought I was careful."

"And you're sure that you're the good guy?"

"I know I didn't do what they're accusing me of doing."

"Murder?"

"Right."

He hung his head. I pawed through the first aid

kit. Found more gauze and a small bottle of peroxide. I sat down on his right side.

"I need to clean you up so we can get out of here," I said.

"And go where? This is my home. Where am I supposed to go?"

"Look, you can call the police, only I won't be here when they arrive. And good luck trying to explain how you took out a pair of intruders on your own, not to mention the bloody footprints I've left all over the place."

I dabbed at the drying blood with a peroxide-soaked cotton ball. He hissed and pulled away from my touch. I grabbed his chin and held him still.

"This isn't going to go away, Alex. As much as I know you want to curl up in bed and wake up last week, with Chalice alive and your life not in shambles, it's not going to happen. This is reality, pal."

"So says the reincarnated dog hunter."

"Dreg."

"I know." Heartache tinged his words. He grasped my hand, pulled it away from his chin, and squeezed. His liquid blue eyes held steely determination. Bright spots of color had flared in his cheeks. "I believe you, Evangeline Stone. So what's our next move?"

"We clean up and change. Tie them up, gather whatever cash you've got around, then get back to the east side of the river."

"Why the east side?"

"Because that's where Wyatt is."

His nostrils flared—an odd reaction. "And we need to save Wyatt, correct?"

"Very correct."

"Do you have a plan for that?"

"Working on it." I released his hand and continued cleaning his face. "Now hold still so I can get this done."

* * *

The response time for reported gunshots was idiotically slow. We were in Alex's Jeep, emerging from the underground parking garage and into daylight, before I heard the first siren. He turned north and chose a roundabout way back to the Wharton Street Bridge. It took us deeper into the heart of Parkside East, past high-rise apartment buildings and the first hints of residential houses.

The bullet graze had oozed through the bandage, which barely covered swollen skin. His eye would blacken eventually. During the five minutes it took to fill a backpack with supplies, lash our houseguests to the dining room furniture, and put on a fresh shirt, he'd lost the deer-in-headlights look, and adopted the attitude that must make him a good med student—stern rationality in the face of insurmountable odds.

I just kept an eye out, waiting for hints of a mental breakdown. God knew he was due.

The burns no longer itched, and my skin was as smooth as it had been before the attack. The dozen or so glass cuts on my arms were also healing. I'd shed my borrowed clothes and slipped into fresh jeans and a T-shirt. The change made me feel mostly human again. The only thing I couldn't help was the blood-stained sneakers. It was that or leather sandals—not great for kicking and running.

"Where are we going?" Alex asked.

"Back downtown, eventually."

He turned down another residential street, lined with trees that sported dog-proof fences, sidewalks without cracks or weeds, and houses that cost more than an entire block of Mercy's Lot real estate. I felt intimidated by the wealth. While Chalice and Alex belonged in such a high-class area, I did not. I grew up in the city; I felt out of place in the suburbs.

"How long have you lived here?" I asked.

"About six years. St. Eustachius has one of the best orthopedic centers in the country, and that's what I wanted to do."

"Wanted?"

He shrugged one shoulder. "Something tells me I'm not making it to class tonight."

"I'm sorry."

"It's not . . ."

"It's not what?"

Another right turn angled us south, back toward the river and bridge. He gripped the steering wheel, seeming to debate his reply. "I was going to say it's not your fault, but in a way, it is. It's just not your fault on purpose, if that makes sense."

"It does."

It wasn't as if I'd chosen Chalice's body. But everything that I'd done since waking up in it—including taking my shitfest into the middle of Alex's mundane life—was most definitely my fault. He was missing class. He was being chased by the Triads. Glass and blood and two men tied up with Lycra exercise pants decorated an apartment to which he couldn't return.

"You're right, Alex," I said. "This is my fault. I

want to tell you that when it's over, your life will go back to normal, but I can't. I can't promise you anything."

"Then how about we make a deal? I'll help you to get Wyatt away from the people holding him and if, by some miracle, we manage to survive it, you two disappear. Just get out of the city and forget this thing about clearing your name."

The pleading tone of his voice hurt, but it wasn't a deal I could make. And it had little to do with my tarnished name.

"I'm sorry, Alex, but I can't agree to that, and it's not because I don't want to now. I have two much bigger reasons why I can't leave town, and foremost is the alliance. You cannot imagine how devastating a united uprising would be to humanity. If the goblins and the vampires go against us, other races will divide, and not everyone will be on our side. It would be like the United States standing alone in a world war against the entire eastern hemisphere. We would lose, and we would become no better than the domesticated animals we keep as pets and food and labor. Exposing this truce before it happens . . . I have to try. Do you understand?"

"I'm trying to," he said after a prolonged silence. The Wharton Street Bridge loomed in the distance, gray and stark. "It's a little difficult to accept the idea of goblins running around the city, much less war-mongering with vampires."

"I know it's not as exciting as dissecting a cadaver for anatomy class, but bear with me."

That elicited a tentative smile. "What's the other reason? You said you had two."

I considered asking him to pull over, not knowing how he'd react. And the last thing we needed was a fender bender. "Because I'm running on borrowed time. Resurrection is temporarily stable at the best of times, but it's not permanent. I'm only borrowing Chalice. I had seventy-two hours from the moment I woke up yesterday afternoon at quarter after four. That's all I get."

He stopped behind an idling Honda. Opposing traffic flowed across the bridge while we waited to make a left turn. He shifted his upper body to face me more directly. I didn't see the expected surprise—only sadness. "Why so short?"

"Like I said, the magic is unstable." I chewed on my lower lip. "Anytime magic is used, it upsets the natural balance of things. Usually it's self-correcting, but this is different. I died three days ago because I was meant to die. It was my time, no matter what Tovin said."

"Who's Tovin?" Alex asked.

I waved one hand in the air. "Never mind, because that's not the point. It happened because it was supposed to happen, but when Wyatt brought me back, it upset the balance. Everything I do, everyone I interact with, is affected by my presence. There are consequences, and they compound with every extra hour I'm alive."

"What sort of consequences?"

A car honked. The Honda had made its left. Alex hit the gas. We shot forward and barely managed our turn before the light changed back to red. Up onto the bridge, and toward the heart of downtown and Mercy's Lot.

"What sort of consequences, Evy?"

"You, Alex. You should be busy planning a funeral right now, and while that's depressing and terrible, it's a far cry from being on a Triad hit list. You never would have been dragged into this if I'd stayed dead."

"So what happens when your time limit is up? What happens at four o'clock, the day after tomorrow?"

"You get to bury Chalice. And I go back to being dead. Heaven or Hell or limbo, I don't know, but I go back and the world turns without me."

"Wyatt?"

A chill wormed down my spine. "He made a free-will deal with an Elder."

"What's that mean?"

"It means that when I die again, Wyatt loses his free will to an elf named Tovin."

"I still don't—"

"In some ways, he'll be no better than dead. Does that simplify it? Imagine losing your ability to make decisions; to take a piss without permission; to fucking love someone."

Alex had paled considerably during my mini rant. "For how long?"

"Forever. There's no statute of limitations on this particular brand of magic bargain."

On the other side of the bridge, I directed him to go south. The background static, all but gone while in Parkside East, tickled the back of my mind. I concentrated on it, somehow comforted by its presence. Like an invisible security blanket.

We managed three more blocks before Alex spoke

again. "You said you lost part of your memory, right?" he asked.

"The final three days of my life, yes."

"Have you tried hypnosis?"

"Are you serious?"

"Chalice believed in it."

"I'm not her."

He flinched. I regretted the barb. I wasn't Chalice, but I didn't have to be insensitive to his suggestions. I believed that all manner of creatures roamed the earth and that we were on the brink of a species apocalypse, but I couldn't bring myself to believe in something as small as hypnosis? Tragic.

"Have you ever seen it work?" I asked.

"At a carnival once."

I snorted. "Not exactly a ringing endorsement."

"What have you got to lose?"

Respect? I bit my tongue. Being around Alex encouraged me to curb the more serious side of my sarcastic nature. It was as inexplicable as it was annoying. But he seemed so gentle—pain-induced cussing aside—that I hesitated to bring out the big guns.

"This isn't a crystal ball psychic, right?" I asked. "Just a hypnotist?"

"Sure, yeah. How about your shrink?"

"My what?"

"Sorry, Chalice's therapist. She was going to counseling for a while. She never told me what for, and I was too self-absorbed to ask, but the lithium prescription kind of gave it away."

Depression. Yikes. But the shrink gave me an in that—

Shit. The gremlins. "I don't think that will work."

"Why not?"

I explained. He pulled his lips into a taut grimace. I patted his knee. "Sorry you asked?"

"A little bit, but even if there's no record of her being a patient, the doctor will remember her."

"Yeah, but we don't have time to make an appointment. I've only got two days. I like the idea, but let's table it for a while. I need to concentrate."

"On Wyatt?"

Was I wearing a sign? "Yeah, sorry."

"Don't be sorry, Evy. He's important to you." Jealousy dripped from his words. His brain still had a difficult time distinguishing me (Evy) from the body that I inhabited. The befuddlement tempted me to just ditch him at the next block, but that was a death sentence. As soon as Tully and Wormer were found, Alex Forrester would be a wanted man.

Just like me.

But he was correct—Wyatt was important to me, and not just because of the investigation or our past. My resurrection bound me to him in a way I still didn't understand. Since the moment he entered that burger joint, I had missed him. Physically missed his presence, like an amputee misses a leg or an arm. He was gone, and I was incomplete.

"He's more than that," I said.

"I figured."

"What's that supposed to mean?"

He looked straight ahead, eyes on the traffic in front of him. "I've heard women talk about guys like that, with that tone."

"We have a tone?"

"Forget it."

"Oh no." I turned sideways in the seat, giving my full attention, and he squirmed. "What tone?"

"You're like a dog with a bone, that's all."

"You should see me when I really want information from someone." I cracked my knuckles for effect; he winced.

"I just . . ." His fingers flexed around the steering wheel. "I mean, I've never even met the guy and I'm a little jealous. Just ignore me for a while, okay?" Humor speckled his words, so I let it go. "Where are we going again?"

"Lincoln Street Bridge. I need to check on a friend."

He nodded and moved into the right-turn lane. "Lincoln Street it is."

Chapter Fourteen

52:17

A coat of fresh, black tar covered the underside of Smedge's bridge. Every available cement surface was coated with the oily substance that prevented bridge trolls from rising. Smedge had been forced to relocate. The city had a plethora of bridges—footbridges, overpasses, train bridges—and an almost equal number of trolls. Finding another home would be difficult. Until he surfaced and sent word, I had no way of contacting my last Dreg ally.

Alex remained in the car with the engine running while I inspected the area. He hadn't argued, and I appreciated his growing trust. The footprints in the dust were inconclusive. Average shoe sizes, bipedal, and at least four different people. They left nothing behind. Even the body of the hound I'd killed the day before was gone, every drop of blood washed away. Someone was being careful. Too careful.

I climbed back into the passenger seat and stared at the dashboard, willing an idea to come to me. Something more productive than sitting around and waiting for dusk and the promised phone call from Rufus.

Staking out the phone booth was a good idea. That prevented someone else from getting there first and laying a trap—assuming he even called. I wanted to trust Rufus; his Triad was merely reacting to the information at hand. Their leader had been kidnapped. They needed to get him back at any cost. I understood that sort of blind devotion.

"Your friend's not here?" Alex asked.

"No, he's not."

"So what now?"

It was time to do the one thing I'd been avoiding— go to the place I didn't want to venture without Wyatt by my side. It could jog my memory, and I wanted Wyatt there when it did. He would understand without my giving him the details. Alex—bless his innocent little heart—needed everything painted in broad strokes. But as much as I hated going, I couldn't just sit on my ass for four hours until the sun set.

"We go farther south," I said. "Over the Anjean River, and follow the train tracks to the East Side."

"What's over there?" Alex asked, shifting the gear back into Drive.

"An abandoned train station. That's where I died."

*　*　*

"So how does one become a Dreg Hunter, exactly?" Alex asked.

Neither of us had spoken in the ten minutes it took to reach the East Side, and his question came without preamble. I could only imagine what was going on in his head. "We recruit, same as anyone else."

"Not quite like anyone else. You can't exactly set up a booth on Career Day."

I snickered. "We tend to do our recruiting at juvenile detention centers and orphanages."

"Seriously?" His hands gripped the steering wheel a little tighter.

"As a vampire bite. Though the recruiters don't wear suits or ask for references. They want kids who are looking for direction, kids they can train to kill."

"You say that like it's normal."

"Normal's relative. When Bastian recruited me, I was barely eighteen, and my biggest goal at the time was avoiding an adult prison sentence for B&E."

"Whose house did you break into?"

"The guy who ran the McManus Juvenile Detention Center. The one I was in for most of my teenage years."

"Why'd you break into his house?"

"So I could beat the shit out of him. Payback for beating the shit out of me a couple of times."

The steering wheel creaked; his knuckles were white. He stared at the road ahead, shoulders tense. "And orphans?"

"No one's there to miss us when we die."

"Someone obviously cared when you died."

"I meant at Boot Camp."

"What's that?"

I blew hard through my teeth, glad we were nearly to the train station so the conversation could end. "They don't just put a knife in our hands and tell us to kill, Alex. We have to survive Boot Camp first. The ones who live become the Hunters."

"And this is legal?"

"Probably not, but it's necessary. Why do you think you've never heard of us before today?"

"What about Wyatt?"

"He's definitely heard of us before today."

"He's your Handler, right?" Alex asked, exasperation leaking into his words. "Do they do Boot Camp?"

My lips parted. It was a question that, in four years, I'd never actually pondered. Handlers knew what they were doing; it wasn't my job to ask how they learned it. "I'm sure they've got their own training requirements. Think of Hunters as the prizefighters and Handlers as their coaches."

"Some of the best coaches are former players."

I shrugged. "If any of the Handlers are former Hunters, no one talks about it. We do our job, we save lives, end of story."

"Okay."

Trees green with spring leaves surrounded the station. It felt desolate and lonely, the perfect place for a kidnapping. Ten-foot-tall chain-link fencing lined the perimeter, but the lock had long since vanished. Alex drove through the empty parking lot, cracked and overgrown with grass and dandelions. Space lines had faded away, leaving behind a sea of grayed asphalt and little else.

The station itself was two stories tall—an old-fashioned gabled style with peeling red walls and white trim. Boards covered windows long devoid of glass. Childish graffiti marked dozens of teenage dares and initiations. The platform on the rear, facing the tracks, was warped and defaced and probably rotting in a dozen places. It smelled of fuel and decay.

Alex parked close to the building. He turned off the engine and reached for the door handle. I put a hand on his arm.

"Give me five minutes," I said. "If I don't come out, I want you to drive away like a bat out of Hell. Do you understand?"

He seemed poised to argue the point. Instead, he nodded.

I took a tire iron—the closest thing I had to a weapon—out the trunk. Avoiding the platform and its potential fall hazards, I entered through the front. The door sported a brand-new padlock. It hung loosely on the hinge. I brushed a finger across its surface—no dust. Someone was there. My heart thudded; I willed it to slow. I wanted to warn Alex away, but curiosity drew me inside.

The knob turned without squeak or protest. The hinges were oiled. The thick odors of dust surprised me. My nose twitched. I pinched it to force back a sneeze.

The lobby was empty, illuminated by gaps in the boarded windows. The dusty floor sported a trail of footprints and smudges, all leading past the rows of glass ticket booths to a rear door marked PERSONNEL. I tiptoed toward it, following the trail, silent as the dead. Wood creaked, but not under my feet. Somewhere lower.

At the door, I stopped to listen. No voices, no footsteps. My hand ached, and I flexed my grip on the tire iron. It helped, but my heart still pounded like machine-gun fire. I wanted Wyatt—his gun, his courage, and his powers. I was weak in Chalice's body, and I despised myself for it, but I had to press onward. If I quit or failed, Wyatt could die. No matter what Tovin demanded of him later, I couldn't be responsible for his death. No one else I cared about was going to die before me.

The doorknob gave the tiniest squeak, which the hinges echoed. On the right were ticket windows long empty and relieved of their glass inserts. To the left was a staircase that descended into a distant light source. The old, grayed wood looked loud and dangerous, but I had no other way down. Progressing one foot at a time, I went down three steps before one creaked.

I froze. No movement below. No shouts or alerts. I was quickly running out my five-minute clock and had to keep going. Down three more. A narrow, dimly lit hallway came into view. Two bare bulbs hung from broken fixtures, set ten feet apart.

No sense of déjà vu overwhelmed me. No feeling of familiarity filled me or twisted my guts. Rufus said this was where I was kept, but I didn't remember it— likely because I hadn't been conscious during the trip down, and I'd certainly been dead during the trip back up. I needed to find the room I was held in.

The air shifted. I sensed it too late to duck properly. The cool body slammed into my shoulders instead of my back. I tucked and twisted and sent the body sailing over me. It hit the paneled wall with a rattling thud and a pained screech. I remained crouched, braced by my left hand, tire iron in the right, while the vampire righted itself with preternatural ease and flipped to its feet.

At first glance, vampire males are often difficult to distinguish from females—the same white-blond hair; the same pale, angular features; the same lithe, flat-chested figures—but this one was definitely female. Her violet eyes flashed. She bared brilliant white fangs. A feral growl bubbled up from her throat. She watched, but didn't attack.

"Who are you?" she asked.

"The welcome wagon," I said. "We heard the place had new tenants, and wanted to drop off a fruit basket."

She sneered. "You are not afraid."

"I used to kill things like you for a living."

"Used to?"

"I lost my license."

"Or your nerve."

I laughed; I'd lost more than my nerve. She stood up straight, paying no attention to the weapon in my hand. Her nose twitched. Muscles rippled beneath pale, stretched skin. She was trained, probably a soldier out doing a little recon. Vampires are notoriously tall and skinny, rarely shorter than five foot ten, but this one put her own kind to shame. She clocked in at six foot two easy, and towered over my still-crouched position. Like a fashion model, she reeked of malnourishment and starvation.

Not surprising when all you ate was blood.

"You are not human," she said.

"Now, that's not nice." I swung the tire iron.

She ducked. Her fist slammed into my midsection. I used the sudden change in momentum to bring the iron down in the opposite direction. It cracked against her ribs even as I fell to my knees, gasping for air. She retreated, snarling.

"Who are you?" she asked again.

I glared at her, still on my hands and knees. "I'm annoyed. Who are you?"

"I am impatient."

"Nice to meet you, Impatient."

Her purple eyes roved over my body, examining me. She inhaled deeply, nostrils flaring. "What is your business here?"

"House hunting. Is this place for rent?"

She bared her fangs. "Can you not provide a serious response, child? I could kill you where you crouch."

I drew up to my full height—not very impressive next to her—and held the tire iron back like a baseball bat. Ready to swing for home the moment she moved. "I dare you. What are you doing here? This isn't your part of town."

"I suspect my purpose is the same as yours—to discover the identities of those who would spread lies of an alliance between goblins and vampires, and to stop them."

My jaw dropped. I couldn't help it. Behind her formal tone, I heard sincerity. A small spark of hope flared to life.

"You're against the alliance?" I asked.

She tilted her chin. "I and most of my kind see no benefit in it, in the long term, and know nothing of its purported existence. Goblins are a disagreeable sort—disgusting, destructive, and incapable of forming a productive society. Many vampires share their view of humanity, but I would prefer to live alongside

your kind than theirs. We would lose more by align-
ing ourselves with goblins than we could ever hope to
gain."

"Do your leaders share this opinion?"

Something flickered in her eyes—curiosity? "None
of the Families speak of it openly, child, because it is
not happening. I heard the rumors from an underling,
but we do not act upon rumor, only upon facts. I fed
the rumors to a human informant, and he was supposed to investigate the allegations, but I have since
lost contact."

Alarm bells wailed through my head. "What was
your informant's name?" I asked.

"He asks me to call him—"

"Evangeline!"

I spun toward the stairs, nearly tangling my ankles in my haste. Behind me, the vampiress snarled.
Footsteps thundered down, followed moments later by
the rest of Alex. He froze on the bottom step, hand on
the narrow railing, attention fixed over my shoulder.

"I'm fine," I said to him, keeping myself between
the two. "He's a friend, Impatient. He's not a threat."

She made a show of sniffing the air. "No, I suppose he is not. And my name is Isleen."

"Evy. He's Alex."

"What's going on?" Alex asked.

"Potential ally," I said. To Isleen: "You were saying he asked you to call him what?"

"Truman," Isleen said. "That was the name he
gave me."

Wyatt. He hadn't told me who his informant was,
the person who'd told him about the potential alliance. Turned out it was someone with pretty good in-

tel and a direct link to the upper echelons of vampire power. An alliance that had once felt like only a possibility now inched closer to terrifying reality.

"You know him," she said when I didn't speak.

I really had to learn to control my facial expressions. "Yes, I do. He's been captured by the Triads. They're holding him for questioning, but I have a contact on the inside who can help us break him out."

"To what benefit?"

"To save his life?"

Isleen inclined her head, a subtle gesture that dripped with condescension. "Will his help be beneficial to our cause?"

Our cause? My wrist ached. I loosened my grip on the tire iron, allowing circulation back into my hand. "What the fuck do you think? Yes, he will be beneficial to our fucking cause."

"That is all I was asking. Do not get upset."

"Lady, you haven't seen me upset."

"You are as loyal as he said."

I stared, my temper teetering on DefCon Five. "You know who I am?"

"At first I was uncertain, but now I am not. He spoke of you, Evangeline, although I imagined you younger."

"And blonder?"

"Pardon?"

"Long story, and it has everything to do with why I'm here."

Her eyes asked the silent question, but I hesitated. I hadn't the stamina to repeat my sordid tale twice in one day. Besides, I still wasn't certain that I trusted her. Vampires are, by nature, very self-centered. Their goal is always the betterment of their people, and if other species are trampled along the way, so be it. Deceptive and willing to play you like a fiddle for their own purposes, they still possessed one quality that many humans did not: an unwillingness to lie.

Still, I saw little distinction between deceiving and lying, but vampires saw an ocean of difference. How could they be proud of a culture that embraced duplicity?

Isleen watched me with cool disinterest. She pretty much ignored Alex. Both scored her faith points, but instinct kept me from trusting her. Her people were part of this rumored alliance, whether she liked it or not. And Wyatt and I weren't exactly low-profile players in the Triads. I had to be sure.

"What does Truman look like?" I asked.

"Taller than him," she replied, nodding in Alex's general direction. "Black hair, dark eyes, I believe what you call a Mediterranean look. Greek, perhaps? A soft voice that deepens when he is angry."

So far so good. "What about the scar?"

"Scar?"

"Yeah, the scar on his face."

She remained motionless. If she'd been up close and personal with Wyatt like she said, if she knew him at all, then she'd know—

"He does not have a scar on his face. None that was ever visible to me."

"Good."

I walked past her, toward the other doors that lined the corridor. Interview time was over. I needed to do what I'd come here to do. I passed several doors and stopped in front of one that sported a broken padlock. The door's nameplate had been ripped off and a black X had been drawn in paint. No, not paint. I touched it, and a soft fleck came off on my fingertip. Dried blood. I jiggled the knob; it wasn't locked.

"I would not, Evangeline," Isleen said. She stood next to me without seeming to move. Alex hadn't twitched from his place by the stairs.

"Why not?" I asked.

"Death is in that room. Something wicked and depraved happened there. It is quite overwhelming."

Fear traced lines across my back with icy fingers as I realized which door I had been drawn to. I had died in this room. Going inside might jog loose the rest of my missing memories. But faced with that possibility, I hesitated. Some things were better left buried; others had to be dug up again, no matter how painful. Which was this?

Beyond my hesitation, one simple thought rose to the surface: Wyatt needed me. I had to do everything in my power to save him. He brought me back, gave up his free will, so I could tell him what happened in that room. Not going in failed him, made his sacrifice for nothing. No.

"I have to go in," I said, as much for Isleen as myself. "I have to see it."

She retreated a step. I turned the copper knob. It didn't squeal. The door creaked open. Warm, humid air crept out, bringing with it the heavy odor of death. Metallic, sweet, and thick, it was a physical entity that forced me backward. I released the knob, but the door continued to swing into inky blackness.

Just inside, my fingers found a switch. Dim, garish light from a single, naked bulb flooded the room.

Dried blood spackled every surface. Barely larger than a coat closet, the room's wood-paneled walls sported haphazard sprays and streaks, with no discernible dispersal patterns. A stained and ripped mattress lay on the cement floor. Two lengths of chain were bolted to the wall above one end of the mattress, each ending in a pair of unlocked handcuffs. A set of rusty shackles, like something from a bondage film, lay on the floor by the opposite end of the mattress.

It was the source of the smell, of the dread, and of the sense of death. My death. My blood.

"Oh my God."

Shit. "Alex, don't come in here."

Too late. He bolted back into the hall before he threw up. I ignored the retching. I couldn't lose it, too. This was what I'd come to see. It's what I had to remember. How had I gotten there? What had I learned that was so goddamn important?

I tried breathing through my mouth, but could still taste the stench. It permeated the room, the air, my senses, my skin—everything. I thought about Max and going to see him the night I left Wyatt's bed, so certain that Max could help me, give me something on an alliance that was—at that time—only a rumor. Tell me if it was fact or fiction.

I took another step inside, less than a foot from the torn and defiled mattress. I studied the bloodstains. Most were centered, and imagination, not memory, told me its source. My stomach tightened, forcing bile into my throat. More blood dotted the head, near the dirty handcuffs. Footprints smeared it in unremarkable patterns on the concrete floor, but left no discernible shapes or sizes, just shadows of many feet. Had

Wyatt knelt there? Held my hand? Watched me gasp for air and finally die?

The handcuffs had bound my wrists, the shackles my ankles, and had held me prisoner for almost three days. Most of the blood spilled was mine, but I felt some semblance of satisfaction in knowing—because I knew how hard I would have fought—that some tiny amount belonged to my captors. I knew I had been tortured here, because Rufus said so. I knew I had died here, because Wyatt said so.

But I knew nothing about that room from my own memory. Nothing.

The room tilted. I was on my knees, arms around my waist, hugging myself tightly. My entire body trembled. Slowly, I was beginning to lose it. If seeing this hadn't shocked my memory into returning, would the next forty-eight hours really make a difference?

"Evy?" Alex was in front of me, crouched to eye level. He held my upper arms and shook me gently until I met his eyes. Twin blue puddles of concern shocked me out of my downward spiral. "Evy, are you here?"

I licked my lips, tasting death. "I'm here."

"Do you remember?"

Tears, hot and bitter, seared my eyes. I didn't blink, only stared. Sought answers in his eyes and found none. I was stronger than this. I inhaled and held it, imagined the oxygen was cleansing me, energizing me. Centering me so I could get on with the task ahead. In Alex's concern, I saw Wyatt—waiting for me, counting on me to rescue him and make it right. To do what he'd brought me here to do.

"No," I said on the exhale. "I tried and it didn't work."

"I do not know what memories you have lost," Isleen said, "but perhaps memory is not what drew you to this place. Perhaps it was fated that we meet."

"I don't believe in fate."

"No? Truman places great value in fate and fortune."

I thought of Tovin and the vision that had brought us to this point—Wyatt's blind adherence to that bright, happy future. It set all of these events into motion, and with only two days left, that future loomed on the edge of darkness. One gentle push and it would fall into the abyss, along with my life and his free will. So much suffering for nothing.

Using Alex for leverage, I stood up. He hovered, and I let him. Isleen stood casually in the doorway, outwardly unaffected by the sight or odor of the room. It surprised me, with wood surrounding her in all directions. Polished or not, it had to be discomfiting. Never mind her keen sense of smell.

No, her nostrils flared every few seconds, timed with the rise and fall of her chest. She sensed it; she was just good at hiding it.

I stood toe-to-toe with her, unintimidated by the eight inches she had on me. "Truman's blind devotion to the idea of fate is why his own people are trying to kill him."

She arched a slender eyebrow. "I thought his people were trying to kill him because he possesses information they do not wish to see made public."

"That's insane. They think he's a traitor. No human

would benefit from a vampire/goblin takeover. All of us would suffer."

"Except for the humans rewarded for seeing such a takeover to fruition."

The room suddenly seemed twenty degrees too cold, the walls too close. What she suggested was impossible. Goblins couldn't be trusted. No one with any sense made a deal with one and expected them to uphold their end. Not without a vampire to ensure it.

"This is insane," I snapped. "They took Wyatt because he kidnapped one of them and tortured him for information. They think he's turned rogue, that's all. You're making me see conspiracies where there aren't any. You don't have any proof."

"You are correct in this, Evangeline. I have only my suspicions and experience."

"Well, I've got my suspicions and experience, too, lady."

"Then I apologize for voicing my assumption, but my previous observation still stands. We were meant to meet, you and I. We are battling a common enemy, and we are running out of time."

"You think we should help each other out?"

"I do."

"Because you're happy with the status quo and don't want to see your people become a dominant species?"

"I do not wish to see the goblins become a dominant species. Vampires may not be dominant over humans, but we are still a superior race. Nothing changes that."

I snorted. "So how can you help me?"

"Have you ever heard of *Mo'n Rath*?"

"Punk band?"

"It is an ancient vampire ritual," she said, unflustered by my sarcasm. "We live long lives and, at times, we forget. The *Mo'n Rath* helps us recover forgotten memories. I have never attempted it with a human, but as I said before, you are not completely human. It may work."

Alex had suggested hypnosis. Isleen was suggesting a vampiric memory ritual. As much as I preferred waiting for what was behind Door Number Three, I had to do something. The memories weren't coming back on their own, so I had to go in and dig. Or let someone else do the digging.

And what was with her insistence that I was not completely human? Was it another side effect of the damned resurrection spell? If so, Wyatt was going to get an earful.

"Say we do this," I said. "What do you want out of the deal?"

"Simply to stop the alliance. And, of course, I get to slay the vampire traitors involved."

I looked at Alex. His expression was slightly glazed. It was familiar—the one he got when things started getting excessively weird. Sooner or later, he'd get used to it, but for now his innocence was refreshing. It reminded me what the Triads fought for—confidentiality. We kept the Dregs a controlled secret, and the rest of the world went about its merry way. Failure meant a lot more people walking around the city wearing expressions identical to his.

"You don't have to keep helping me, Alex," I said.

"Yeah, I do," he said.

"You could get out of the city, far away from all of this."

"I don't have anywhere else to go. Chalice was my family."

I brushed his cheek with the back of my hand, my heart swelling with gratitude.

"Touching," Isleen said, "but we should be going."

Leave it to a vampire to ruin a tender moment. I turned back to face Isleen. "Do you know someone who can perform this ritual? Someone trustworthy?"

"I do," she said. "Myself."

Chapter Fifteen

51:50

We left Alex's car by the train tracks. I had no intention of returning to the abandoned station, and by now the make and plate had been given out to every cop in the city with a working radio. Isleen led us to her stashed vehicle—late-model sports car with tinted windows. It looked like something a rich lawyer would drive.

She surprised me by walking across the weedy parking lot without any protection—no hat or gloves or even an umbrella. Vampires are highly allergic to direct sunlight. They burn like paper under a blowtorch—sizzling skin, smoke and odor, and mighty pain.

Yet Isleen walked with confidence radiating from her pale, lithe body. I kept pace, waiting for her to explode in a fiery ball under the harsh glare of the afternoon sun. Nothing, not even a flinch of discomfort. Next to me, Alex shot curious glances my way, but didn't ask. I was wondering the same thing.

Alex barely fit in the tiny sports car's backseat; it was designed more for looks than function. I scooted forward as far as my knees allowed. Isleen reached forward and turned the key in the ignition. Up close, I noticed the shimmer on her skin. Not sunscreen—there wasn't an SPF high enough to protect her particular skin type. Something else.

"Where?" I asked.

"South," she said. "There is a Sanctuary. Few know of it. It will be safe enough to let our guard down."

Says you. There were protected places in the city—buildings or just rooms considered sacred by Dregs. Magical hotspots, places where the magic of their world below (or above, or next to) bled into ours, sort of like hot springs. They were the invisible sources of the Fey's power and well guarded by them—and apparently, also by vampires. Places where the Gifted were born. Similar to churches or cathedrals; but very few of Dreg-kind respected human faith.

The major difference was that the Dregs didn't hang signs on their Sanctuaries, advertising their presence. For all I knew, hotel room 29 at the Holiday Inn Express could be one.

I rarely ventured into this part of the city. South of the East Side, but still on the opposite riverbank from Uptown, it was a blend of low-rent motels, abandoned storage facilities, car dealerships, and factories. The city seemed grayer there, less bright. Full of secrets in a way that even Mercy's Lot could not challenge. The side streets were quiet for midday and we zipped past block after block, moving farther south. We didn't speak. The radio stayed off.

Isleen turned left at a blinking light, taking us down a road with a self-storage center on one side of the street and a used-car lot advertising "Very Clean" cars on the other.

A shadow bolted out of the used-car lot, swifter than man or beast had any right to move, on a collision course with our car. Isleen yanked the wheel. I saw black fur and razor teeth an instant before the hound slammed into my door. Metal groaned. Glass crackled. Tires squealed as the car skidded sideways.

I banged into Isleen's shoulder. She kept control of the car, depressed the gas pedal, and we shot forward. The engine roared. So did the hound tracking us. I righted myself in what space I had. Half the door was smashed in, uncomfortably close.

"Evy?" Alex asked.

"I'm okay."

I twisted around in the bucket seat. The hound was trailing us, seeming unfazed by its headlong tumble into solid steel. It kept pace with its four muscled legs, each springing leap taking it as far as we could drive in the same span of time. And it was gaining.

"How did it track us in a car?" I asked.

"It was following me," Isleen said. "I killed another this morning. I may have failed to properly wash its kin's blood from my tires."

"You drove over it?"

"Through it, actually." The corners of her mouth quirked. It was almost a smile. "Hold on."

She said it too late and yanked the wheel hard left. I slammed shoulderfirst into the impacted door. Needles of pain danced up my arm, and I cried out. My back hit the dash. I slipped and found myself in the uncomfortable position of being stuck ass-down on the floor, with my feet in the air.

"Apologies," Isleen said.

"Is it still gaining?" I asked.

Alex peered out the rear window. "Yeah. What the hell is it?"

"No idea," I said, tugging myself up. No small feat, given the zigzagging pattern Isleen was making through traffic. And I couldn't imagine what passersby thought of the animal chasing our car down the street.

"It is a vampire and goblin crossbreed," Isleen explained. Her tone remained even, without a hint of the panic that was singeing my nerves at the very idea of such a combination. "The two species are not sexually compatible, but with the advent of genetic cloning, many things are possible."

"There's something else in there, too. I know goblins run faster on all fours, but this thing's got some beast in it."

"It is possible, but I do not know its exact origin, or how many more exist."

"Wyatt and I killed one, so that's at least three," I said, climbing back to a semisitting position on the front seat. "The miracle of modern science."

" 'A malady of modern science' is a more appropriate euphemism."

I couldn't argue with that. "Got any weapons?"

"In the glove compartment."

Naturally. I popped open the dash, expecting the customary assortment of registration papers, napkins, trash, maybe a parking ticket or two. Instead I was presented with a slim leather case containing the registration and insurance cards, and nothing else. I felt along the edge of the lining until my nails caught. I ripped it away and found three Glocks.

"Center weapon," Isleen said. "The bullets should be able to pierce the hound's hide."

The gun was too heavy in my hand—a foreign object I hated using. I flicked off the safety. One centered kick popped out the fractured door window, and we left it behind on the street. Isleen made another sharp turn. I held on to the door handle this time and managed to keep my bearings.

My head, shoulders, and arms went out the window. Air blasted my hair in front of my face, creating a curtain of brown that was difficult to see through. Missing my old, short hairstyle, I took aim at the snarling hound and fired.

The bullet struck its left foreleg. Murky blood and flesh exploded from the wound. The hound wailed its pain and fury, drawing back thin lips and fixing its wild eyes on me. I aimed for those eyes. Squeezed the trigger. The car hit a pothole and bounced, and the shot went wild. My ribs slammed against the door.

"Goddamnit," I said.

"Apologies," Isleen replied.

From Alex, I got, "Jesus, Evy, be careful."

Third bullet hit the same foreleg, a few inches higher. Blood trailed in a slick stream, but didn't slow it down. Give me a blade and an open field any day. Guns were just a pain in the ass.

"Stop missing," Isleen said.

"Would you like to do this?" I tried to get another bead on my target. The damn thing was learning, weaving now, making sure I couldn't get him in my sights. "Shit."

Isleen snorted—a surprising sound from her. "Hold on to something."

The car surged forward. I clutched the smashed door so I didn't fall out the window. We flew through an intersection to the tune of honking horns and screams. The hound leapt neatly over the hood of a braking sedan, hit the pavement, and was promptly struck head-on by a careening van. The van came to a sudden halt, but the hound's body rolled. It came to rest against a street sign on the far curb.

An ounce of hope was quickly shredded as the hound crawled back to its feet, seemingly unfazed by its collision. It continued to track us, oblivious to the shrieking pedestrians. Every scream echoed in my ears. It was the most blatant display by a Dreg I'd ever seen. No way the brass could explain this one away.

Of course, I'd said that about the gremlin strike and been wrong.

"Didn't work," I said to Isleen. "Got any more ideas?"

"Just one."

Brakes squealed. She spun the car, turning my side to face the street we'd just come down. I used the momentum to leap through the window. I tucked my head down and struck the pavement on my left shoulder, followed through with the roll, and came up unsteadily on my knees. Ungraceful by my standards, but probably the most acrobatic thing Chalice's body had ever managed.

The world spun, but I steadied fast. The odors of burnt rubber and oil stung my nostrils, sharp and cloying and immediate. Screams faded into the distance. My vision tunneled, focusing only on the rampaging hound, leaving bloody prints everywhere it stepped.

I raised the gun, using my left arm to steady it. A car horn honked somewhere, muffled and unimportant.

Down the sight of the revolver, I gazed at the hound. At its chest and hair, to the point where its heart should reside. Each step forward widened the target, but I didn't need a large field. I had him. I felt it. I squeezed the trigger.

A dark blur on a bicycle toppled over, shrieking in pain.

I screamed. The hound leapt over the flailing biker and landed in a crouch, ready to spring. Epithets poured from my mouth, streaming faster than I could properly articulate, my fury dripping out with each syllable. The hound pounced, its massive body on a collision course with mine. I tucked and rolled without waiting, counting on the hound's speed to carry its mass over me. Heavy feet hit the pavement. I came up and fired.

The back of the hound's head exploded, spattering the side of the car with bone and hair and gore. Its body jerked as it fell, still fighting out of instinct even though its brain was gone. It twitched once, twice, then lay still.

"Evangeline, we must go!" Isleen shouted from the car's interior.

Her commanding voice snapped me back. I stood, fist tight around the gun. Onlookers stared from the safety of sidewalk benches and parked cars, wide-eyed and openmouthed. Some were on their cell phones. No one made a move to help the young man on the bike, who clutched his bleeding thigh with both hands.

I'd shot an innocent.

As a Hunter, it was my duty to protect Joe Citizen.

Innocent bystanders were not to become victims of the Dregs and their violence. Yet I had brought that violence on someone by my own hands. I expected revulsion, but felt only pity. Pity that, while shot and in pain, this man would never know the extent of what had happened that day. Getting shot sucked, but being ripped to shreds by a rampaging hound from Hell was a fate far worse.

"Someone call an ambulance," I said, even as I heard the first faint sounds of sirens.

"Evangeline!"

"Evy, come on!"

Feet first, I slipped back into the car and into a spattering of dark blood. It was on the dash and the edge of the seat, the odor almost more than I could bear. Isleen sped away. I let myself fall back against the seat, still clutching the gun. The muzzle was hot; it scorched my chest. I didn't care. The heat felt good. The sirens faded.

Alex squeezed his broad shoulders between the seats. Worry clouded his gentle eyes. He touched my cheek, featherlight. Affectionate. "You okay?" he asked.

"No."

He took quick visual stock and seemed to realize I didn't mean physically. I wasn't injured. I just wasn't okay, either.

"You didn't shoot that man on purpose," he said.

"Doesn't matter. I still shot him."

"It was an unfortunate accident," Isleen said. "One you cannot afford to dwell on if you are to complete the task ahead. Much depends on our success. There will be time for self-pity at a later date."

"For you, maybe."

Alex winced. Isleen only tightened her fingers around the steering wheel. The leather cover creaked.

I recognized our new direction. She made another turn. A block away stood the fading, deteriorating skeleton of the Capital City Mall. Abandoned fifteen years ago when the new mall opened uptown in Briar's Ridge, Capital City had slowly rotted away. The vast parking lot was cracked and overgrown with grass and weeds. Time chipped away at the paint and tile walls, mottled glass doors, and rusted delivery bays. Graffiti adorned surfaces no longer repainted.

It was shaped like a U, with the main entrance on the front curve and anchored on both ends by former department stores. Isleen drove across the rear parking lot, and we entered the interior of the canyon, straight across pavement that had once been the patio of a diner, and into a wall.

At least, I thought it was a wall.

But it turned out to be an impressive illusion of a wall, because we drove right through it—down the mosaic tile corridor, past a row of boarded-up storefronts, and straight to the center of the mall. Skylights illuminated a dry fountain that hadn't run in years. Empty beds surrounded it, devoid of soil and no longer sustaining the dense foliage of yesteryear. It smelled of dust, dry and lonely, and something else I couldn't place. Something faint, hinting at power. It buzzed in the air, a gentle caress from an invisible hand. I felt the energy of Isleen's Sanctuary.

Alex and I climbed out on the driver's side. I'd had my fill of going in and out of car windows. My sneakers squeaked on the floor and echoed harshly in the oppressive silence. We followed Isleen past abandoned kiosks, benches that hadn't held someone's weight in over a decade, and stores long boarded up and forgotten.

The odor of the hound's blood followed us, absorbed in my clothes. I'd have to change soon or be stuck with the offending stench—not something I cared to live with. I'd been covered with it twice in twenty-four hours.

"Do you feel it, Evangeline?" Isleen asked. Somehow, her voice did not echo. It simply hung in the air.

"What should I be feeling?" I replied, even though I did feel it. There, yet intangible, like static electricity.

"You'll know."

"If it helps," Alex said quietly, "I don't feel anything."

"Nor should you," Isleen said.

He shrugged it off, taking no offense at the dig. The shell shock seemed to have worn off a bit, and he was taking in his surroundings, absorbing salient details, remembering. I reached out and curled my fingers around his. He squeezed back.

Isleen turned down a narrow service corridor, past a bank of pay phones that advertised local calls for a dime. A few more yards down, she stopped in front of a veneered door. I stared at the blue plaque pasted to the wall next to it.

"Are you serious?" I asked. "This is the Sanctuary?"

She nodded.

Alex blanched. "The women's bathroom?"

"We do not choose the locations," Isleen said. "However, once the Breaks are discovered, we do what we can to protect them. Why do you think this mall was rendered inoperable and closed down?"

"Bad Chinese at the food court?" I said.

A flutter of her eyelids was the closest Isleen got to rolling her eyes at me. She pushed the door open. I swallowed before following her inside, prepared for an onslaught of horrible smells and disgusting sights—rotting waste and stained floors, stale urine and broken mirrors.

Instead, the faintest hint of incense, tangy and bitter, tingled my nostrils. Candles adorned the polished sinks and counters, their light reflected by the spotless mirrors. Plush, forest green carpet covered the floor. The stalls had been removed. Three toilets were covered and resembled comfortable side chairs. The air was warm, but not oppressive. It felt inviting, almost invigorating. All-encompassing. My entire body tingled. I tried to ignore it, to dim the sensation lest I fly apart.

"I've never felt anything like it before," I said.

"This is the fanciest bathroom I've ever seen," Alex blurted out.

"It is a Sanctuary," Isleen said. Her voice adopted a sharp edge, revealing her protectiveness of the place. "It is no longer meant for its original purpose."

Alex held up his hands in surrender. "I meant no disrespect."

"I risk much by bringing you both here. The wrong person could do great damage with the location of a Break. Irreparable damage—"

"We aren't telling anyone, I swear," I said to stave off her speech. I knew the risks. I also knew I didn't trust anyone outside of that room, except for Wyatt. I sort of still trusted Rufus, but that could swing either way. It all depended on his phone call at dusk. Still nearly two hours away.

"A *Mo'n Rath* is a private ritual," Isleen said. "Do you wish your friend present?"

"I trust him."

Under Isleen's direction, I lay on my back in the middle of the plush carpet, arms at my sides, toes pointed up. The fibers were soft and smelled faintly of dust. Isleen knelt at my head. Cool fingers massaged my temples in gentle circles. Tension fled my body, replaced by relaxation and a vague sense of safety tempered by intangible power. I closed my eyes.

She placed her palms over my cheeks, thumbs still on my temples, skin unnaturally cool. She spoke words that I didn't know. They sounded vaguely Latin, peppered with garbled nonsense. My mind began to wander, and rather than fight, I let it. I was both there and elsewhere, drifting along like a leaf on the wind. Back through recent memory: the car chase, interrogating Rufus, my first meeting with Alex. Into impenetrable darkness that seemed to last forever.

Until it spit me back out into dim lamplight.

And Wyatt's warm, comforting embrace.

Chapter Sixteen

May 14th

Lights from the street cut intricate patterns across the threadbare carpet of the motel room, shifting from red to green to blue and back again, all in time with flashing neon signs. I cannot sleep. Too many thoughts plague me. Fear of what lies ahead, affection for the man next to me, uncertainty of our futures.

Wyatt's arms tighten around my middle. I tense, but he does not wake. He is dreaming, muttering. It may be a nightmare, but I allow him to sleep. If he wakes, he may want to talk. I don't. I have committed a grave error by sleeping with him. I gave him an attachment, and Handlers cannot function if they are too attached to their Triads. It is their job to order us into dangerous situations. Into certain death, if need be.

How can he do that after proclaiming he loves me?

I consider sneaking out, setting off on my mission without a good-bye. It is useless. He is no Hunter, but he will know when I get out of bed. There is no sneaking away from him. But I cannot continue to laze about. I still have to clear my name and find justice for my murdered teammates.

My fingers slip around Wyatt's. I draw his hand up to my mouth and kiss his knuckles. He stirs. His breathing quickens. He is awake.

"I have to go," I say without looking at him.

"I know." He kisses my bare shoulder. "Can I ask where you're going?"

"Uptown around Fourth Street. I know someone there who might be able to help with information."

"Who?"

"I'd rather not say."

I stand up, feeling no shame in my nudity as I search for my clothes. Wyatt sits, the blanket tight around his waist, and I am glad. I fear he will try to stop me or, worse, insist on going with me to see Max. He surprises me by doing neither. He simply watches while I dress and finger-comb my short hair back into order.

"You're sure this person can help?" he asks.

"Pretty sure."

I go to the sink and splash cool water on my face. The terry towel is rough as I pat my skin dry. I turn. Wyatt stands in front of me with a sheet bunched around his hips. Uncertainty etches lines around his eyes and brackets his mouth. I want to reassure him, to force that uncertainty away, but I don't. Wyatt believes in me. It is the only reason he isn't begging me to stay.

"The protection barrier on the motel will last two more days," Wyatt says. "Come back here when you've talked to your friend."

"I will." I check the digital clock on the nightstand.

The sun won't rise for a few hours, so I'll probably have to wait for Max to return. "I should be back before noon."

"If you find out something—"

"I'll call."

"Be careful."

"Do you really think you have to say that?"

"Yes."

I throw my arms around his shoulders and hug him before I can stop myself. His arms snake around my waist. The sheet whispers to the floor. I press my face into his shoulder, inhaling the scent of him—musk and cinnamon. Burning it into my memory. I know I may never see him again. I want to take this with me.

"I'll be careful," I say. "Don't do anything stupid while I'm gone."

He chuckles. I pull away before anything else is done or said. I have to get moving before sunrise. At the door, I pause and look back. He still stands with his back to me, but is watching me in the mirror. I wink. He smiles.

And then I go.

*   *   *

The library is closed, but I make easy work of scaling the back wall. A metal gutter pipe provides adequate handholds. I climb quickly on pure adrenaline, positive of assault at any moment. The rear alley is quiet, but that means little. Things always seem to go dead silent right before a sneak attack.

I swing over the edge of the wall. In the dim light, I find the cement path and avoid making noise on the gravel bed. The entrance to Max's lair is around the next corner. The sky is still black, but the barest hints of blue peek out over the eastern horizon.

Silent steps carry me down the path. I pause every few yards to listen and sniff the air. At the corner, I stop, alarmed by the faint sound of voices. Low and hushed; nearby. Too close to be coming from the street. I close in on the entrance to Max's home. Each step brings those muffled voices closer.

Max. I know his voice, so unique because he is a gargoyle. Not as unnatural as Smedge's, but just as stony. The second voice is female. The cadence surprises me, as does the familiar lilt to her words. She's a Blood.

I creep closer to the entrance and listen.

". . . a disaster for our two peoples," the Blood says. "You know I speak the truth; you cannot deny the implications."

"I deny nothing," Max replies. "But I also admit to nothing, Istral. If what you say is true, it is your problem, not mine."

"But it will become everyone's problem. Do you wish to be ruled by the goblin Queens?"

"No more than I wish to be ruled by humans, but that is how things are. If the balance of power changes, the gargoyles will adapt, as we have done for centuries."

"Your statement reeks of cowardice, dear cousin."

"Merely discretion. There is a reason my kind no longer adorns the spires of human cathedrals. We know when to not interfere in the affairs of others."

The conversation confuses me. This Istral is a vampire; her use of "cousin" confirms it. Why isn't she talking him into the Alliance, rather than against it? Unless even the Bloods are divided on the matter. I can use this.

"You are foolish to allow the actions of others to determine your fate," Istral says.

"Gargoyles have survived in Man's world for centuries longer than vampires, Istral. Don't discount our methods so quickly. You could learn from our experience."

"I would sooner stand in the sun without protection."

He's getting her riled up. Good old Max. Related or not, gargoyles and vampires don't get along under the best of circumstances. They have different temperaments and opposing viewpoints on the place of Dregs in Man's world.

"What is it?" There is alarm in Max's voice.

"Human female," Istral says with open distaste. Shit. "She has recently mated with one of her kind."

Okay, that's just gross. I should have showered, true, but "mated"? Who says that? I start backing up, uncertain of Istral's reaction if she catches me here. At the corner, something stings my ankle. I spot the dart. My leg is already numb. I fall on my left side, probably scraping skin on rock, but cannot feel it. Everything is numb. I can't blink, I can't speak. I can't do anything but stare.

No, no, no. Stupid. So stupid to die like this.

Shadows whisper across the gravel, filled with grunts and growls and angry mutterings. A sniveling figure looms above me, its grotesque face curled into a snarl. Sharp teeth flash, shiny with saliva. Its breath is thick and putrid. I can't turn away. I am helpless against the goblins surrounding me.

They grab my arms and drag. Arguing voices become clearer, louder. We pass through the brick wall, into Max's dim lair. They toss me to the stone floor. My head lolls to one side, and I see Max and Istral standing in the corner. She is as elegant as her voice implies, dressed in stealthy black befitting a well-paid corporate spy. Her white-blond hair is perfectly coiffed, her makeup flawless. She reeks of royalty.

"You should be more careful, gargoyle," a strange female says. "We weren't the only ones spying on you tonight." Her words are clipped, harsh, like someone trying desperately to hide a flaw. But it can't be. Goblin Queens don't do their own fieldwork.

"What do you want, Kelsa?" Max asks. "Your kind does not have permission to travel uptown and you know it."

My body jerks. Did someone just kick me?

"The Triads are a little busy tonight," Kelsa says. "They aren't looking for me, and they certainly aren't looking here. Though something tells me I've just found a little piece of leverage."

"She is a rogue," Istral says, pointing to me. "The Triads do not bargain. She is of no value."

"I will decide that, vampire. For what purpose do you haunt the lair of a gargoyle?"

"I do not answer to you."

Cloth shifts. A gun is cocked. Istral tenses. From her position, I assume Kelsa is directly behind me.

"You will answer to me tonight," Kelsa sneers.

"Your plan will fail, Kelsa," Istral says. "You will fail and your people will become little more than slaves, forced back underground to eat the droppings of others."

"And what are we now?" There is fury in Kelsa's voice. She has lost the struggle to maintain a human voice. Snarls punctuate each word as they are forced through a goblin throat. This won't end well.

"The same as you always will be." Istral takes a step forward, back straight, unafraid. "Scavengers."

Kelsa growls, throaty and terrifying. A shot is fired. Istral screams. The bullet propels her backward into the stone wall. Blood spurts from a wound in the center of her chest. It isn't a mortal blow for vampires, so why is she sliding to the floor? Kelsa is laughing.

An anticoag round. How did a goblin get her claws on our ammunition?

I watch because I can't look away. Istral clutches her chest, fingers ripping desperately at the cloth and skin. Blood continues to pour in torrents. She pales quickly, like colored chalk washing away in the rain. She is bleeding to death. Her eyes are wide, glazed, a beautiful shade of lavender. Alive with light, fighting. She looks at me until the light fades, and I am lost in a dead woman's eyes.

"Do you know who she was?" Max asks.

"That no longer matters," Kelsa says. "Our peoples must look to the future."

"I only look to the present."

"Then you may die in the here and now."

"Your bullets can't pierce my skin."

"Perhaps not." A flash of orange light glances off the stone by Max's feet. "But morning sunlight will, and we have mirrors."

Oh no.

Max retreats to the shadows. The reflected light dances just out of reach. I only half see him. He is calculating, pondering the risk of a direct attack. I don't know the numbers behind me. At least three. "The gargoyles will not be your allies," he says. "It is not our way, and no amount of coercion will change that fact."

"I actually expected as much. I do not want your help, only your word."

Max's eyes flicker to me, and back up to Kelsa. "As part of what agreement?"

"Complete neutrality in all matters. You will do nothing and say nothing about this to the Triads. You will report nothing you witness to the humans or the Fey Council. They are off limits." Another kick jostles me. "Talk to no one."

Max is silent for a ponderous eternity. I want to scream, beg him not to agree, but can say nothing.

"What of her?" he asks, pointing to me. *Yes. Yes!*

"She is not your concern. She is wanted elsewhere, and will be paid handsomely for."

Her tone sickens me. If I could move, I would vomit. Kelsa and her goblins are not here for Max or Istral. They were tracking me. I led them to Max. It's my fault Istral is dead. But why do the goblins want me? Who will pay for me? I am a rogue. I have—

"She has no value," Max says.

"On the contrary." Kelsa's feet move into my line of sight. Black boots, soft soles. Silent and deadly. "Your word?"

"What do I receive in return?"

No, Max. Please.

"The same," Kelsa says. "Noninterference. Your

people will be allowed to continue as you are now under our rule."

Max laughs—a deep, grating sound that vibrates the floor. "You assume too much, goblin, but I agree to your terms. You have my word that I will not interfere with the humans or your plans."

"Good."

I am lifted up and slung over someone's shoulder in a fireman's carry. All I can see is sideways. The bricks of the tower as we pass out of Max's lair and onto the roof. Then something is tied over my head, and I see only darkness.

* * *

I wake with no memory of passing out. Dark engulfs me, thick and oppressive. I am on my back, with something soft beneath me. Cold metal encircles my wrists and ankles. I pull. Chains rattle on both sides of my head, more at my feet. Fear twists my stomach. I'm not dead, but this is so much worse.

The dark turns to dimness. A thin line of light peeks from beneath what could be a closed door. The room is small. I can see the outline of the mattress I lay upon, flat on a dirty cement floor. The walls are bare. Handcuffs bind my wrists to chains, which are studded to the wall above my head. Shackles hold my bound ankles, similarly anchored.

I tug. The cuffs bite into my wrists. I rock my lower body and push/pull with all of my strength. Nothing. The chains are solid. I collapse, panting. My body tingles—probably a side effect of the numbing drug.

In the dark, bound to a mattress in a dark closet

of a room, I realize something else—I am completely naked. My clothes are gone, nowhere to be seen. I go through a mental checklist, testing various parts of my body, but nothing aches. Nothing feels violated. The torture hasn't begun.

Gooseflesh prickles my arms and stomach. I don't know how long I've been here. Is Wyatt worried yet? Has he started looking for me?

He won't know where to start. I only told him I was going uptown. He doesn't know Max, and Max won't go to Wyatt. He gave his word to not interfere.

Betrayal stabs my heart with its icy knife. Max owes me nothing, but it still hurts. He let the goblins take me. If what Kelsa said is true, they are going to sell me to someone. Or have sold me.

I watch the line of light beneath the door, searching for shadows. Movement. Any indication of life outside of my little prison that smells of mildew and dust. I swallow, but my mouth is dry.

Time passes.

* * *

Bright light startles me. I squeeze my eyes shut against the glare sending bolts of pain into my head. Feet shuffle. The pain lessens, but never quite dissipates. I slit one eyelid open, testing. The light is bearable. Both eyes this time. I want to rub them, wipe away bits of sleep, but my hands are still bound.

A goblin female crouches next to me. Her black hair is loose and wild, framing red eyes and crimson lips that pull back in a snarling smile. I don't recognize her. I've only ever fought and killed males. Goblin society is matriarchal for two reasons—females are born one in every fifty, and species procreation requires the death of the male. Only the strongest, battle-proven warriors are allowed the honor of mating and continuing the goblin lines. Like a bee and its stinger, fertilization is fast and deadly. Females are revered and honored, and rarely venture out in public.

They certainly don't do their own dirty work.

"Evangeline Stone," she says. It is a challenge as much as a greeting.

I don't know her face, but I know her voice. "Kelsa." It comes out somewhat garbled. I'm thirsty and my throat is tight, but I won't ask for water.

"The great Evy Stone," she says, as though I haven't spoken. "Murderer of goblins and vampires and those you think beneath you. I've long wanted to meet you."

"Lucky me."

She arches a slender eyebrow. Long-nailed fingers slip into her stylish leather coat and produce a straight razor. She opens it with careful precision. I curl my hands around the cuff chains. My stomach flutters. She runs one fingertip down the sharp edge of the razor. I tense, but there is nowhere to go. The cuffs dig into my wrists and ankles. I grunt.

Kelsa smiles. "There is no escape from this, child."

"Why?" I ask before I can stop myself.

"Why what?"

Coy bitch. I won't give her the satisfaction.

"I've seen what your kind does to mine," she says. She trails the tip of the razor down the center of my abdomen, too light to pierce the skin but hard enough that I feel every centimeter of her touch. I look at her, not at her hands.

"I've seen the way you kill, slitting them open from groin"—she presses just below my belly button, slicing the skin, and I cry out—"to sternum." Swiftly her hand moves, drawing another fiery line straight down between my breasts. I hold my breath. Don't make a sound. "It's a shame, really. You humans have such spunk."

Agony spears my left thigh, matched immediately on my right. Tears spark in my eyes. I bite down hard on my tongue, concentrating on that self-imposed pain. I try hard to ignore the inflicted wounds. I feel blood, oozing hot and thick from every cut. I won't scream. I can't.

She must be taunting me. If I'm to be sold, why damage me now? It makes no sense. Collectors rarely pay for broken merchandise.

Kelsa leans down, too far away for me to head-butt her, but close enough to smell her breath—moist and sharp, like metal. "We will have fun, you and I." Fire bursts across my stomach and I wince. "Oh yes, Evy Stone. Two days of fun . . . for me."

Two days? Until my buyer shows up? Until she gets bored and lets me go? Until her vampire alliance hits its boiling point? Questions without answers, agony without relief—this is my life now.

She holds up the razor, its edge coated with my blood. As red as her eyes. She presses the blade to my cheek and, in time, I do scream.

*   *   *

Time is lost to an endless cycle of light and dark. She comes and goes without warning—always her and no one else. I doze; she wakes me. I find no rest between our sessions, no respite from the anguish of her torture. She is creative in her methods. Meticulous in drawing blood. Expert in causing pain. In another life, I may have respected her for it. Today I despise her.

The mattress is soaked with blood and sweat and urine, and it sticks to my skin. Their fetid odors mingle with the wrenching stink of vomit. Burnt flesh lingers on the edge of my senses, but those wounds are old. Fire seems like days ago, though I know it is only hours. Lights come on and the pain resumes. Lights go off and the throbbing takes over.

I think of Wyatt in those brief moments alone. The soft caress of his hand on my breasts. The fullness of him as he slides in and out of me, loving me. He will come for me. He must be searching. I don't care if the Triads find me first. As long as the suffering ends.

The door swings open. I squint, waiting for the light assault. Kelsa stands in the doorway, backlit. Behind her, something shifts.

"You intrigue me, Evy Stone," she says. "You endure so much, and yet you don't ask why. You don't demand a reason for your suffering. Many lesser women would have broken long ago. I admire you for that."

"Go fuck yourself," I hiss.

She laughs. "You just don't see it, do you?"

"Don't wanna. Don't care."

"Of course you do, Evy. You care about him."

A chill worms down my spine. Shivers ripple across

my stomach, harden my nipples. She can't say it. If she says she has Wyatt, too—

"Don't worry, child; he'll find you. Just as he's meant to, but it will be too late to save you. Too late for the poor, lovesick fool."

She's going to kill me and leave me for Wyatt to find. God, this will destroy him.

Kelsa enters the room, but her shadow remains in the hallway, just out of my sight. She crosses to the foot of the mattress and squats. Unlocks the shackles around my ankles. My legs are too weak to use against her. I want to kick, but find no strength in the torn and broken flesh. She drags a nail along the sliced sole of my foot, and I shriek.

"You've been such a good sport, I hate for our time together to end," she says. "The next step needs tending right now, but don't fret. I'm leaving you with a friend."

Leaving me? But why? I haven't changed hands since falling into Kelsa's. Is this lurking shadow the buyer who has yet to claim his prize?

She waves her hand. The backlit figure shambles forward. Bile scorches my throat, threatens to spill down my lips. A goblin male leers above me, his oily skin shimmering in the hall light. He is naked, the hooked tip of his penis dangling low between his crooked legs. His eyes dance with lusty fire, and I understand. There is no buyer. He's here to kill me.

Only once in my career did I serve a warrant on a goblin for the rape of a human female. I'll never forget the blood, or the frozen horror on her terrified face. For two weeks after, she haunted my dreams, the misery of her fate burned into my memory. The creature that killed her became one of Kelsa's groin-to-sternum victims. I took great joy in killing it.

I close my eyes. Kelsa's familiar footsteps whisper across the floor.

"Good-bye, Evy Stone," she says.

The door closes with a thump. A lock snicks into place. The mattress shifts as weight is added to it.

I think of Wyatt and cling to his memory as my world descends into agony like I've never known before.

Chapter Seventeen

47:18

My fists closed over warm flesh, twisting and squeezing and trying to push it away. Blood filled my mouth, metallic and hot. I screamed, but no sound came out. My throat was hoarse, raw. I pushed, but he wouldn't let go.

"Evy, stop! It's Alex."

The familiar voice finally invaded my foggy mind and pushed away the last remnants of memory. The small room in the basement of the train station faded, replaced by the luxury of the Sanctuary. Incense replaced urine; warmth replaced cold. The agony fled as well, leaving me empty. Shivering.

"Evy, it's okay, I've got you."

I fell against Alex's chest, letting strong arms fold me into his embrace. I pressed my face into his neck and sobbed. I cried for the woman who had died in that room, tortured and left for dead. Only one, final piece of the puzzle was missing—my rescue and moment of death.

It would come, just as the other memories had.

It was only a matter of time, and I didn't want to re-member any more today.

Alex stroked my hair and whispered. I couldn't hear him, but it didn't matter. The words were not important. I just needed his strength until I found my own again and the memories drifted back into the past. As I brought my emotions back under control, the torrent of tears subsided. My head ached. My nose was stuffy. My entire face felt swollen, but I could think straight.

"I am sorry," Isleen said. "I did not realize how overwhelming your memories would be."

"It's okay," I rasped. "I needed to do that. I had to remember it."

"You said things while you were in the trance, Evangeline. You mentioned the name Istral. What does that mean to you?"

I studied Isleen's face. The intensity in her stare surprised me. I realized why she had seemed so famil-iar at our first meeting. It wasn't because we'd met before, but because I'd seen someone who looked just like her. "Istral was your sister, wasn't she?"

Isleen nodded. "She has been missing this past week. I have feared for her."

"I'm sorry, Isleen, the goblins killed her. I was there; I saw it."

She bowed her head, and I found myself torn be-tween wanting to comfort her and not caring for her pain. She was a vampire, for crying out loud. Maybe my ally today, but she could easily be my enemy to-morrow.

"The goblins were holding me on purpose," I said, putting the clues in a row, trying to make sense of it all. "The female told me as much. They wanted Wyatt to find me, to know what had been done to me, but why? Why incite his hatred?"

"To divert his attention, maybe?" Alex offered.

"Maybe, but they should have picked a better target. I wasn't exactly the poster child for the Triads, at that . . ." A scenario presented itself, one I had briefly considered that morning with Rufus. One that pointed to so many truths I didn't know how to face.

"What is it, Evy?"

"What if it *was* all a diversion?" I said. "I know someone set me up for Ash and Jesse's deaths. I was framed for their murders, which put me on the Triads' Most Wanted list, right? So they're spending time looking for me, instead of watching the Dregs. Other stuff, like a potential alliance, gets missed. Wyatt finds out about the alliance from Isleen, which makes him a threat. I'm already on the shit list, so kidnapping me keeps Wyatt off the alliance scent and looking elsewhere. They probably hoped that finding me torn to pieces would make him crazy enough to give up the rumors."

"It makes sense, save one part," Isleen said.

"Which part?"

"The part about making him crazy. Goblins do not understand mental illness or grief, but they do understand the concept of revenge. Hence your treatment under their care. They wanted Truman to find you, but not to grieve for you or to lose himself in that grief."

"Then, what?" Her explanation made sense, but she hadn't given me an alternative. "They wanted him to seek revenge for me?"

"Perhaps. But this is merely speculation on my part, as it is speculation on yours."

Damn her and her good points. "So let's end the speculation. We need to track down this Kelsa and extract the truth from her. Preferably with a straight razor."

"We're going to see goblins now?" Alex asked. His look was black.

"The offer to stay behind is still good," I replied. "The things she did to me, Alex . . . If we get caught—"

"I'm staying with you, Evy. I said I would."

I smiled, energized by his steadfastness. "Thank you."

"We require another mode of transportation," Isleen said. "My car is damaged and quite noticeable."

"I guess you don't keep spares in any of the empty storefronts?"

"This is a place of Sanctuary, not a used-car lot."

Sarcasm from a Blood. Who knew? I stood up and nearly fell over when the room tilted. Alex looped an arm around my waist to steady me. I waited for the world to stop spinning before I gently pushed him away. I rubbed my hands over my face and through my hair. I still felt the cuts and burns, even though my skin was unmarred. It was like post-traumatic stress in fast-forward.

"We'll just have to play this by ear, then," I said. "Let's go."

* * *

"There is a serious flaw in your plan, Evangeline," Isleen said as we left the mall the same way we'd entered. "We do not know how or where to find Kelsa."

I rolled my eyes and ignored the statement of the obvious. This time though, I studied what I'd previously assumed to be a wall. It was a cleverly disguised entrance that made me think of the old Road Runner cartoons where a fake train tunnel was painted on a rock and the Coyote smashed right into it. Vampires were clever; I had to give them that.

The sun was dipping low on the horizon. The passage of time alarmed me. "Kelsa may have to wait," I said. "I gotta get to that phone booth before dusk."

"You still trust this Rufus guy?" Alex asked.

"I don't know. I really don't. But I have to do something proactive to find Wyatt. I just need to know that he's still alive."

I started down the sidewalk, unsure of my exact direction, but determined to find a car I could steal. Tufts of grass grew in the cracked parking lot, some of them sporting early dandelions. I plucked one as I passed and started tearing the tender yellow petals off one at a time. Something to keep my hands busy.

Half a dozen yards from the exit, I heard a distant hum. The air stirred. I stopped. Alex crashed into me, and I stumbled a step.

"What is it?" he asked.

"I hear it, as well," Isleen said before I could answer him.

I looked up at the darkening sky. Thick clouds covered much of the blue. A bird flew too high to be disturbed by what had caught my attention. My stomach knotted.

"Get back inside," I said.

Alex blanched. "What—?"

"Just go!" I gave him a shove. He started running, and I followed, Isleen somewhere behind me.

The helicopter rose up over the west side of the mall, ten times louder the moment it was in sight. The pavement exploded by my feet. Alex shouted. The trail of automatic gunfire followed us like a shadow, marking our trail until we burst into the safety of the mall's interior.

We came to an ungraceful stop near the fountain, panting and red-faced. Even Isleen seemed ruffled, disturbed by the change in events. Through the entrance, we watched the helicopter land in the middle of the U-shaped parking lot.

"Who the hell are they?" Alex asked.

"No idea," I said.

Isleen raced back to the car, as light as a shadow. She ducked into the car's interior and withdrew almost immediately, gun in hand. She rejoined us at the fountain. Past the bulk of the ruined car, two familiar faces leapt from the helicopter.

Tully and Wormer, decked out in flak jackets and carrying enough ammo for six men, once again opened fire on the mall's fake wall. Bullets pinged off the car bumper. Surprise colored their faces even from a distance.

"Christ," I muttered.

"Aren't those the guys from my apartment?" Alex asked. He'd gone pale, mouth tight. "They look pissed."

"Wouldn't you be?"

"You know them?" Isleen asked. She aimed at her targets, but didn't fire.

"Triads," I said. "Wyatt kidnapped and tortured their Handler for information. How the hell did they track us?"

"It may be chance. We created a sensation down the street. Perhaps they were patrolling at precisely the right time."

"Or the wrong time."

"Indeed."

A few more random shots preceded their flight toward the mall. And us.

"Shall I kill them?" Isleen asked, keeping someone in her sights. "Or merely slow them down?"

"What rounds?"

"Regular bullets."

"Slow them down."

She tilted the gun barrel down a few degrees. She squeezed the trigger. Tully dropped, blood spurting from his left thigh. Wormer faltered, concern for his comrade overwhelming his instincts. Isleen shot the back of his right thigh, and down he went with a cry. Both were a foot shy of the hidden entrance.

"What about the guy in the helicopter?" Alex asked.

Our collective heads turned. Air hissed and squealed, even above the din of the rotating chopper blades. Smoke, a flash of metal, and then the helicopter exploded in a cacophony of flame and heat and thunderous noise.

The concussion flattened Tully and Wormer to the pavement. Their cries were lost to the roaring fire. Heat rippled the air inside the mall, scorching and thick. Debris pinged against the building and car like hailstones. Flaming bits rained down on the injured men outside. The back of Tully's shirt caught fire and spread fast, like a match to flash paper. He began to scream.

I was on my feet and running to the tune of Alex's surprised shouts. Wormer was out cold, unable to help his companion. They may have been my enemies that day, but I couldn't watch a former colleague burn to death. I tackled Tully and slapped at the oil-fueled flames eating his shirt and scorching his skin. My hands blistered and wept, but I didn't stop until the fire was out. Tully was whimpering, facedown, unmoving.

I felt for Wormer's pulse and found it strong. Good. I pulled my hand back. A red-feathered dart pierced Wormer's shoulder where my arm was less than a second before. I toppled sideways. A second struck the pavement by my foot. Shit. I crabbed backward, driven by pain and surprise, followed by more darts, until the shadows of the mall enveloped me.

Alex was there, trying to look at my hands. The top of Wormer's head exploded from a gunshot I didn't hear, see, or expect. Tully tried to sit up and flee. He collapsed a moment later, half his face gone. I gasped, choking on bile.

"Who did that, Evy?" Alex asked. He looped one arm around my waist and hauled me to my feet. I let him drag me back to the cover of the fountain, still stunned by the rapid-fire change of events. In less than five minutes, things had gone from bad to completely fucked.

Another dart sailed over my shoulder and pinged off the front of the fountain. I dove for cover. Rough tile scraped my elbows. Alex landed next to me, on his stomach. He turned his head, looked right at me, and said, "Damn."

"What?"

His head dropped to the floor and lolled. My heart nearly stopped. One of the darts was lodged in his hip. I pulled it out and threw it. The dart shattered against the far wall. The sound brought no satisfaction. Whoever was out there wanted us alive, and they were willing to murder Triads to get us.

"Evangeline," Isleen said. "You must run."

I glared. Her lavender eyes gave nothing away. Footsteps echoed around us. Small, many, and closing in fast.

"You must. They want you, child."

"Alex—"

"You have no friends, only duty."

A familiar line, one that Wyatt had tried on me once upon a time, back when I was new to the Triads and just learning the ropes. It didn't work back then, and it wasn't working in the mall. I did have friends. Friends I could no longer protect.

Isleen handed me the gun. I took a breath, turned, and bolted back down the mall corridor, toward the Sanctuary, firing over my shoulder as I went, hoping to get a target. No time to look, no time to see who was hunting me.

The only thought in my head was escape. Live to fight another day. I was completely alone. The Sanctuary seemed to call to me, beckon me toward its powerful center. Everything blurred and, for an instant, I was sure my feet left the ground. I saw the interior of the Sanctuary, smelled the incense. Felt the warmth. Two places at once.

One . . . two . . . three stings in my lower back. Cold permeated my legs, my arms, my chest. I fell toward blackness, even as the floor rushed up to meet me.

Chapter Eighteen

43:10

Consciousness returned like an anvil. A headache and queasy stomach dropped out of nowhere and knocked me back to the real world. The dim room and stark ceiling sent a bolt of panic through my abdomen. Adrenaline set my heart pounding. I jerked my hands. Instead of finding them bound above my head, they moved easily at my sides. My back was on something hard and cool.

It still smelled of waste and sweat, but I wasn't in that damnable closet again.

"Evy?"

The familiar voice startled me. I rolled onto my side and drew my knees up, prepared to spring. The sudden movement sent my stomach churning. My vision darkened. I swallowed against the overwhelming need to vomit.

I was in a jail cell of some sort, five-by-eight maximum, with no cot and a bucket in place of a toilet. Iron bars made up three of the walls, with cement blocks the fourth. A bare orange bulb glowed from an open fixture just outside of the cell. Others dotted the corridor every ten feet or so. I could see straight through to the other cells. The two on my left were empty. The one immediately to my right was not.

Wyatt knelt on his side of the bars, hands clenched around the slim poles. I blinked, certain the apparition would disappear. It didn't. A purple bruise colored his left cheekbone. His nose was red and slightly swollen, and his knuckles were flecked with dried blood.

"You're alive," I said.

"So are you."

He smiled, and I nearly broke my nose trying to hug him through the bars. My arms were slim enough to make it through, but he could only squeeze my shoulders and touch my face. I pressed my lips to his forehead, inhaling his familiar scent.

"I didn't think I'd find you again," I said.

"It's not quite the rescue I was hoping for, but I'll take it."

Rescue. Shit. "I screwed up, Wyatt. I let myself get caught."

"Doesn't matter, Evy, we'll figure this out. We always do."

I looked past him, at the cell on his other side. It was empty. "Did they bring Alex and Isleen here, too?"

"You met Isleen?"

"We ran into each other at the train station earlier today." Or yesterday, depending on how long I'd been unconscious. "She's been helping us. She was there when we were captured."

"I haven't seen her." His frown hardened. "Another guy was here for a while. They took him about an hour ago, while he was still unconscious."

Fear twisted my stomach. I grabbed my throat and found bare skin. I gazed at the floor of my cell, even down the front of my T-shirt. The cross necklace was gone. God damn me for losing it. "They? Who's doing this, Wyatt? It can't be the Triads."

"It's not them, Evy. After they picked me up at the burger place, they took me to one of our holding stations near the Anjean. It was mostly Kismet and Willemy, and I spent an hour or so not answering their questions. Rufus showed up and said he wanted to talk to me. The door opened again, and suddenly he was shot. . . ."

He looked down. I squeezed his hands, urging him to finish.

"I remember a flash grenade and a lot of shouting, and then I woke up here. Broad daylight and they're running around like it's nothing."

"Vampires?" I asked.

He shook his head. "Halfies. I didn't even see them until they brought you two in a few hours ago. No questioning, no talking."

It was still the same day, probably evening. Not as much time had passed as I'd thought, but that still didn't explain— "What do Halfies want with us?" They'd gone through a lot of trouble to capture us alive—just a little more proof that they had, in fact, been targeting my partners at the train bridge. Not me.

"I'm not sure, Evy. The Halfies aren't organized enough to be the brains of this, whatever this is. They're following someone else's orders."

"Orders like setting me up, getting me hunted down, and keeping us locked down here for God knows how long?"

"Something like that."

"What about your Gift, Wyatt? Why haven't you used it to summon a key or something?"

He pointed toward the far wall of the corridor. At first, I saw only more cement blocks. But dangling from a nail, wrapped in twine, was a slender orange crystal. "It's blocking me," he said. "Every time I try to do something, it zaps me like a cattle prod. I've never been cut off from my power source before. It's so strange, like I'm missing an arm or something."

I realized the distant sense of static I'd felt since my rebirth was, likewise, gone. The crystal cut us off from the sources of magic—what Isleen referred to as Breaks—but how in the blue blazes did a Halfie get hold of one?

"Well, if they haven't questioned you, why take Alex?"

"Dinner?"

I slapped him harder than I intended. He stared, hurt sparking in his black eyes.

"I'm sorry, Evy," he said.

"He's a nice guy, Wyatt. He didn't have to help me, but he did." The idea of Alex surrounded by Halfies, each one taking a bite out of his arm or neck or leg, enraged me. "So what do we do now?"

"I don't know. Have you remembered anything new?"

"Boy, have I." I fed him the details of my *Mo'n Rath* experience, complete with visuals on Kelsa and the reason behind Max's strange reaction to me. I left out some of the torture details, not wishing to relive them or inflict them upon Wyatt, but I saw the anger spark in him—fury at what I didn't say, horror at what I did.

"When you didn't come back to the hotel by noon," he said, "I knew something was wrong. I should have started looking for you sooner."

"You wouldn't have found me. Wyatt, is it possible that the alliance we've heard about isn't with the ruling vampire Families, but with the Halfies? They've always been outsiders, hunted by us, and treated like shit by the Bloods. It makes sense that they'd try for a power shift, if they made out good on the deal."

"I've considered that, too. It certainly puts Ash and Jesse's deaths into perspective. The Triads are too busy chasing you to see what else is happening."

"Something still doesn't make sense."

He tilted his head. "What's that?"

"Me."

"What do you mean?"

"They could have picked any Triad to attack, Wyatt, but they chose yours. They chose me. Kelsa said someone was paying a lot of money for me, but not in the way I assumed. Whoever wanted me paid her to do what she did, and to ensure that you were the one who found me. But why? All they had to do was kill me and hide my body. You would have kept the Triads looking for me for days or weeks until I was found. Why set it up the way they did?"

"I don't know. I really wish I did, but I don't. And it isn't the only thing that doesn't add up."

"Like why keep you down here, alive, and not torture you?"

He quirked an eyebrow. "Are you advocating violence against my person now?"

"No, jackass, just a logical ordering of events. They killed Wormer and Tully this afternoon while they were capturing us. Shot them dead. But they used tranqs on us. Why do they want me alive?"

Aggravation mounting, I stood up on shaky legs and started pacing the narrow length of the cell. Confusion, anger, and remnants of despair all bubbled up through my mouth before I could censor myself. "Why the fuck did you bring me back, Wyatt? Why didn't you just let me rest in peace? Hell has to be better than this."

He wilted in front of me—every bit of light, every scrap of fight in him fled. I didn't regret the words. I only hated that they were true, and how precisely they reflected my feelings. Overwhelmed and frustrated, I took it out on my only available target—a man who'd given up everything for me.

"Why?" I grabbed the bars separating us. He had to say it. I had to hear it.

He retreated to the corner of his cell, as far from me as he could get. Worse still, he turned his back. I had no way to make him face me. He couldn't disappear behind a bathroom door, but he could still escape.

My knuckles ached. I loosened my death grip on the bars—a wall that might as well have been solid rock. I was livid, but not at him. I was furious at myself for not mounting the rescue I'd hoped for. For failing at the happily ever after he so desperately needed to believe in.

"I really am a self-centered prick, aren't I?" he asked. His tone was so mild I thought it was a rhe-

torical question. He turned his head, showing me his
profile and nothing else. "Aren't I?"

"You're not a prick," I said. "A little selfish, but
not a prick. Hell, you did what you thought was right.
You need to know what I know."

His profile disappeared. He grasped the bars in
front of him. Tension thrummed through his shoulders and back. "I convinced myself that was the reason. I convinced everyone, even you."

Nausea struck me so hard and fast my knees buckled. Only my hold on the bars kept me standing.

"Now I'm not so sure anymore."

"I knew something." I repeated words I'd been
told and believed to be true. "I had information we
needed about the alliance."

"I hoped you did."

"Wyatt, stop!"

"I told myself that was why, that I wasn't bringing
you back because it hurt too much to lose you. That a
lifetime without free will wasn't worth three more days
with you. That wasn't good enough. I had to do it for
the right reasons, you know. For them, not for us."

Rage rippled through me. My skin flushed. My
hands continued to shake. "You bastard! Do I know
something, Wyatt? Do I?" My voice grew louder,
angrier, and he flinched away. "Do I fucking know
anything, or was remembering it all for nothing? Did
I just relive the torture and the goddamn rape for
nothing?"

"You never should have lived it the first time."

"That's not a fucking answer!"

"I don't have one for you, okay?" He finally
turned. Color suffused his face. His eyes sparkled, but

no tears fell. "I don't think I remember the truth anymore, Evy. I've been sitting here for hours with nothing but time, and I can't seem to think straight. I don't know the difference between what I told myself and the actual truth. It doesn't seem to matter anymore.

"I know you don't love me, and that's probably the worst of my crimes. I betrayed your trust, Evy. I had no right."

He looked so lost, like an abandoned child. Compassion had never been my strong suit, but even furious as I was at his deceptions, I found myself reaching for understanding. Intention did not outweigh the cost of what he'd given up for me. I had easily accepted the notion of him sacrificing his free will—becoming a slave to Tovin's own will—in order to serve a nobler cause; I had trouble with the idea that he'd done it all for three days with me. I wasn't that special. I wasn't worth the price tag.

"I don't understand," I said. "How can you still be in love with me? With this person? I'm not the same as I was before."

"It's not about hair color or height, Evy; it's about what makes you who you are. The spirit of you. Your memories and the way you talk and your ability to swear like no one I've ever met. They'll never change, no matter what the outside package looks like."

The physical mattered less to him than the emotional and intellectual. The former was a bonus; the latter the only thing he needed. So why was I struggling with the reverse problem? My new body wanted more from him than I was emotionally prepared to accept.

"I think you're wrong," I said. "I think a little bit

of Chalice is still inside of me, and that I'm different than I was." My unusual connection to the magical Breaks was proof enough. Bits of her were leaking into my personality, including her friendship with Alex. "I think you want me to be exactly the same, because it's what you hoped for. Just like me knowing anything pertinent to stopping this alliance is what you hoped for. But hope has no basis in fact."

"Fine." He held out his hands, palms up and open, empty. Defeated. "What do you want me to say, Evy? I made a huge mistake. I did the wrong thing for the right reasons, and now we're both getting burned for it. Is that what you want to hear? That this is all my fault?"

"That's not what I want, you asshole." I slammed my palm against one of the bars. It reverberated up my arm and shoulder. I held tightly to the pain.

"Then what?"

"I want to live, goddammit!"

The words flew out of my mouth unfettered—so unexpected I found myself stunned to silence. Had that been it all along? More than uncertainty over Wyatt's motives, much more than not knowing if I had anything useful to contribute by regaining my memories, was I angry about my lack of time? Angry that I had forty-ish hours left to live? I couldn't bargain for more time. I couldn't prevent my window of opportunity from closing.

Yes, everything in me screamed against going quietly into that supposed good night. Training told me to fight, to find any possible alternative to death. Only, the deck was stacked and the dealer had all the aces. I didn't even have a wild card. I had nothing, except the keen sting of helplessness over my current situation and my impending doom.

"I want to live," I whispered. I pressed my back against the bars and slid to the floor, metal hard on my back and cement cool against my bottom. My anger was gone. All I had left was sorrow. I pushed it away. I could not give in.

Denim rustled. Cool hands brushed my shoulders. I didn't pull away, too electrified by the gentle gesture. He squeezed tense muscles, and I relaxed into the impromptu massage. Bitter tears stung my eyes, but did not gather or spill.

"Dying wasn't so bad the first time," I said. "I clung to you when things got really bad. I never stopped believing you'd come for me. It was easier, because of our happy ending. Easier to believe in a rescue."

"I tried so hard to find you."

"I know." I reached back and threaded my fingers through his, so strong and cool. "But now everything in me is screaming to fight and survive, and I just can't reconcile that with knowing I'll be dead in less than two days. I don't want to die again."

"I wish I could take it all back, Evy." His voice was so quiet, barely above a whisper. "But I can't. This was wrong. All of it's wrong."

He kissed the back of my head. A warm tingle danced down my spine. I thought of the library stairwell and the way I'd reacted to his touch, his kisses. All of this had been complicated by Chalice's overt attraction to Wyatt, which had, in turn, become my attraction. It elevated my existing affection into something else, into something close to actual desire. Something

I couldn't bear to give in to when no chance of happiness existed for either of us.

"We can't undo it," I said. "We can't change it. Maybe we never could. My part was over, and I was never supposed to be here to stop the goblins or the Halfies or whoever the fuck is involved in this shit, but I am. We're both in it now, and I'm not going to spend the rest of my limited lifetime rotting away in this stinking cell. It's not me, and I know it's not you."

"You have any bright ideas on getting out?" He thumped the top of my head with the tip of his finger. "Because that crystal is keeping me from using my Gift, and unless you've learned how to bend metal . . ."

"I'm working on it."

I pulled away, just far enough to turn around. I knelt in front of the bars and took his hands. "No more about the past," I said. "We have to think about right now and nothing else. No more why's or how's or who's, and definitely no more self-pity from either of us. Deal?"

"Deal."

"Are you lying?"

"Are you?"

I glared. How the hell did he do that? "Self-pity is your thing, not mine."

The hard line of his mouth remained. No hint of what he was thinking. Just an enigmatic stare that was getting on my nerves.

"What, Wyatt?"

"It's just something you mumbled while you were unconscious. You were asking someone to forgive you. Was it Alex?"

"No." I should have gone along with it and

pretended. Opening up wasn't my strong suit, but I had to tell someone. Wyatt would understand. "I shot an innocent today. He got in the way, and I shot him."

"Did he die?"

"I don't know. I don't think so."

"But it was an accident?"

"Yeah, but he'll never know why he was shot, or what that thing was that was chasing us through the streets."

"He's better off not knowing."

"Doesn't take away my responsibility."

"In my eyes, it does. You can't dwell on one mistake, Evy."

"Like you?"

He grunted, not pleased by the reversal. "I'm your Handler. Dwelling and self-indulgence are job prerogatives—especially when you're the only surviving member of a team that I led for four years, surviving intact longer than any other Triad. I have put everything into this job, and everything else on the line for you. Forgive me for being self-indulgent with my emotions."

I quirked an eyebrow. For someone usually so reticent with his feelings, he was doing an awful lot of sharing. Getting things off his chest and airing some dirty laundry. It had to feel great. He watched me for a minute, mouth pulled into a taut grimace. I wiggled my eyebrows. His mouth twitched. I crossed my eyes.

Wyatt laughed out loud. He tugged me forward, and I initiated our awkward, bar-infested hug. His hands were warm around my shoulders, protective and loving. I never wanted to let go, but cold metal was digging into my left breast. I grunted; he loosened his grip. I pulled back a few inches.

Our faces were so close, mouths nearly aligned. His breath was hot on my cheeks, gently caressing the skin. I stared at his lips and remembered how they felt, how he tasted. The fire his kisses had lit in my belly. I wanted it again, that consuming ache. Knowledge that every inch of his body wanted me, every muscle thrummed with need. I had never felt that before, in my first life. As a Hunter, I didn't have time for anything personal. Life was about work; pleasure was always secondary. And pleasure with a co-worker was forbidden.

I leaned back on my heels, putting cold distance between us. It wasn't the time or the place to indulge in such things. An inch of solid steel every four inches was an unbeatable obstacle. Not to mention a painful one.

"No more self-pitying. Right?" I asked.

He nodded. "Right."

"Good." I made a show of looking around the cell, pretending to admire my surroundings and take in every (nonexistent) detail of the spartan space. "So, what do you do for fun around here?"

"Shadow puppets."

"I'm amazed you're still sane, Mr. Truman."

"You could count the number of cement blocks that make up your back wall. I've done it twice."

"I'll pass."

"Strangely, my count was off by one the second time."

Once again, his delivery was perfectly deadpan.

"I'd only start worrying if it's off the third time, too."

"Want to count with me?"

"I'd rather go around my cell and test every single bar for a weakness I might be able to exploit."

"I tried that, but good luck."

"Have fun counting."

*   *   *

The jail cells were old, probably hadn't been in regular use for fifty years, but they were still solid. Not a single bar jiggled or shimmied, and the lock on the door was sturdy. No scraps of metal to pick it with; nothing but a bucket waiting to be pissed in. My diligence paid off in exhaustion and an hour of time wasted.

Wyatt lounged on his back in the middle of his cell, staring at his cement wall. Probably counting the blocks, as he'd said. I couldn't tell and didn't much care. I was geared up, and nudging inches closer to claustrophobia. I couldn't stand being caged. Tied up was one thing, but walled in was quite another. Just enough room to move around, but not enough to truly stretch my legs.

Metal clanged nearby. Wyatt scrambled to his feet, and we moved to the front of our respective cells. At the far left of the corridor, the cells ended with a steel door. It had a handle on our side, but no lock or window.

More noise from the same direction.

"Someone's coming," Wyatt said.

A lock clicked back. I winced at the tight squeal of rusty metal. The door swung inward, casting a rectangle of yellow light onto the bare cement floor. Three figures entered the room.

The two standing upright were Halfies, easy enough to recognize. True vampires look like Isleen: tall, willowy, white-blond, with pronounced fangs and lavender eyes. The process of infection cannot change a person's height or build, but it does change hair and eye color. Halfies end up with mottled hair, like a peroxide job gone bad, and opalescent eyes that look purple from one direction and their natural shade from another. Half of two worlds, but welcome in neither.

Between them, they supported Alex by his arms. His head hung low, and his bare feet dragged along the floor. He'd been stripped down to his boxers. Bruises, welts, and dozens of shallow cuts covered his torso and legs. There was little blood. I imagined the Halfies didn't waste a drop.

A guttural snarl tore from my throat. This seemed to startle the Halfies. They paused and exchanged a look. Teenagers, I'd guess, with less than a week's experience in their new lifestyle. They looked better suited for a homecoming football game than doing interrogation dirty work. Fury hit me so hard that my stomach ached. I clenched the bars until my knuckles cracked. If I could have escaped my prison, I would have gleefully ground their faces into the floor.

"What the fuck did you do to him?" My voice bounced around the narrow corridor and reverberated off the metal bars. One of them—the larger of the pair—winced.

They dragged Alex into the cell next to mine and let him go. His head cracked off the hard floor. I bolted to the shared wall of bars, reaching through for one solid swipe at one of those arrogant assholes, but missed. They knew enough to stay out of arm's reach.

Tall Jock, the more skittish of the pair, squared his shoulders and looked me up and down. A noticeable bulge grew in the front of his tight jeans. Definitely a high school student who strayed to the wrong side of the city at night. He whispered to his friend, and Short Jock offered me the same visual appraisal.

I didn't turn around, but could imagine the poisonous glare on Wyatt's face. I couldn't take my gaze off Alex. His ribs moved a fraction of an inch. He was breathing—small comfort. He was still unconscious, at the mercy of the Halfies and their infectious bites.

"Shoulda turned her," Short Jock said, eyeballing me.

My stomach dropped down to my feet. Blood rushed from my face and set my heart racing. The Halfies laughed as they left the cell. I didn't look at them. I eyed every cut, every scrape on Alex's visible skin, looking for a bite. All it took was one. Their combined laughter was cut off abruptly by the door slamming shut.

I slid to my knees and reached through the bars. He was too far, by at least a foot. He was facedown, half his body hidden from my inspection. He couldn't be bitten. They'd said that to goad me, piss me off.

"Alex." I pressed against the cold barrier until my shoulder ached. "Alex!"

"Evy, is he alive?" Wyatt asked.

"I think so. I can't see!"

He didn't have to ask what I couldn't see. I tugged at the bars, as if I could pull them apart like putty. I tried the other arm, stretching and bruising it in vain. I screamed Alex's name over and over, but he didn't stir. Wyatt didn't interrupt my mininervous breakdown, remaining quiet in his corner, watching.

Minutes later—or an hour, it no longer mattered—Alex's left hand twitched. I went completely still. Then he groaned, low and muffled. I held my breath, afraid to break the spell. Another groan, another twitch. His head tilted . . . the wrong way.

"Alex," I said.

After a moment's pause—and probably some superior effort on his part—Alex turned his head in my direction. Both of his eyes were puffy, swollen half-shut. Red tinged both nostrils. A fresh cut decorated his forehead from his tumble to the floor. His old gunshot graze was unbandaged and oozing. He blinked bleary eyes that remained at half-mast, hidden from my desperate need to see their color.

"I'm here, Alex. It's Evy."

His nostrils flared. He squinted. His lips moved, tried to form words. No sound came out, but I recognized the shape. It was a name. I bit the inside of my cheek, crouched down, then reached through the bars.

"It's Chalice," I said. "Take my hand, Alex, I'm here."

A pained smile ghosted across his lips. His left hand inched toward mine, dragged there by fingers missing their nails. I swallowed back a small scream, but he didn't seem to notice. His attention was fixed on my hand. One small task. One centimeter at a time. He closed the gap.

My fingers brushed his. He stopped, satisfied with his progress. Panting hard, his cheeks flushed bright red against a deathly pallor, he gazed at me with shadowed eyes.

"Alex, did they bite you?" I asked.

He squinted, but didn't seem to understand the question. "Asked me," he managed, each word a single, wheezing breath. "Don't know . . . anything."

"I'm so sorry, Alex. So sorry."

"Guess won't . . . bury . . . you after all."

I couldn't stop the tears from falling. They scorched my eyes and throat, burning with the sorrow in my heart. I had taken a gentle soul, thrust him into my violent world, and he was dying. Dying because I didn't stay dead the first time.

"You're fine," I said, choking on the words. They stank of lies. I forced them out anyway. "We're going to get out of here, and we'll get you to a hospital. They'll take care of you. All of the junk food you can eat while you get better."

The corner of his mouth quirked. "Ice cream?"

"Any flavor."

"Strawberry."

"That's the best you can do? Strawberry? What about chocolate chip?"

"Gross."

I laughed and lost it inside of a sob. My fingers stroked his, light enough to let him feel me, but not hard enough to cause him more pain. "Fine, strawberry it is. Lots of it, with strawberry sauce and whipped cream. You just have to hold on, okay? You can't have it if you die on me."

"Better not die."

"Yeah, you better not."

All I could do was sit there and touch Alex's hand. A few drops of blood leaked from his nose and pooled on the cement. He didn't seem to notice. His eyes were barely open, but his hair was still solid brown. Maybe I'd get away with only killing him once.

"You," he said.

I shook my head, not understanding. "Alex?"

"You did this."

A gunshot to the stomach would have hurt less. Agony squeezed my heart so tightly I couldn't breathe. He withdrew his hand and left me grasping for air.

"Alex, don't. I'm sorry."

He closed his eyes.

"Please!"

His chest stopped moving. I stared, my entire body trembling. Silence pressed down, louder than a thunderclap and deadlier than a lightning strike. He didn't stir. I'd let him die. It was my fault. I'd done it, and he knew it.

"Alex."

I dissolved, sobbing harder than I'd done in my life. Curled into the tightest fetal ball I could manage, I wrapped my arms around my knees and wept. Hatred and sorrow and loss and helplessness, all rolled into one broiling emotional cauldron. Rising above the rest was despair, sharp and painful, a thousand splinters in my heart.

"Evy, please, come here."

I heard Wyatt's voice, but couldn't conjure the energy to respond. Crawling five feet to his side of the cell was too hard. Staying on the floor was easier. Pretending it wasn't happening was easier still. Maybe if I stayed there long enough, the floor would open up and swallow me whole. End it all. Stop the suffering and doubt.

The hysteria subsided on its own. Choking grief

was replaced with faint whimpers. My head weighed fifty pounds. My nose and eyes hurt, and my throat felt raw. Every muscle ached from lying on the cement ground. I wiped my face. I didn't sit up.

"Evy." The alarm in Wyatt's voice parted the fog in my brain. I uncurled and lifted my head. He stared past me, lips parted, eyebrows knotted. His eyes widened. "Evy, move!"

I followed his barked order without thought, rolling toward him, over and over until I slammed into the bars of our shared barrier. I pulled into a crouch too quickly, and nearly keeled over. Then the dizziness passed, and a nightmare came into focus.

Alex smiled from his side of the cell, straight-backed with hands clasped in front of him. Cuts and bruises littered his chest, but he seemed not to feel them. He ran one hand through his hair. Brown powder streaked his fingers and dusted his shoulders, revealing the blond peppering beneath. He wiped his hand on his shorts. Eyes finally open wide enough to show a flash of lavender, he grinned like a fool satisfied with a cruel joke.

I waited for more anger to bubble up and spill over. Righteous indignation at his deception. Hatred for the show he'd just put on. Already a Halfie, pretending to die, just to hurt me. Instead, I only had pity. Alex was gone. The half-breed creature in front of me didn't change that fact. Vampiric infection irrevocably alters a person, not just physically, but also their brain chemistry. His little show had only proved how much the vampire had already overtaken the human.

Alex Forrester was dead, in all ways except physically. The creature in front of me was just another rogue that needed putting down.

Slowly, I stood up. Wyatt hovered behind me.

"You should see your faces. This is priceless," Alex said.

"What was the point?" I asked.

"Boredom. The fellows upstairs don't have much to keep them entertained while they're guarding your sorry asses. I was only interesting for a short while."

"I'm sorry."

"For what? Getting me into this? We had that conversation, remember? I'm still Alex, just a little improved."

"You're not Alex."

"Sure I am." He strolled out of his cell and came around to the front of mine. "I still remember everything, Evy. I've just never felt like this before, like I could run a marathon and never get winded. Like I could take down an armored car with my bare hands."

"But you can't, because you aren't a vampire. You'll never be one, you'll never have their strength or their powers. You're infected by a saliva parasite that's altering your DNA. You're a half-breed, nothing more."

"It's better than being dead, isn't it?"

"Sometimes dead is better."

Wyatt grunted.

"Do you really think that?" Alex asked.

"More than ever."

"Cheer up, sweetheart. Your clock runs out in thirty hours, and then everyone gets what they want."

"What the hell does that mean?" Wyatt asked.

Alex gave Wyatt a hard stare. "She talks so highly

of you, and you still haven't figured this thing out? That's pretty pathetic."

"I'll give him one thing, Evy, he's got the cryptic-speak down pat."

"I've got at least forty hours left," I said.

"Wrong," Alex said. "Hate to break it to you, beautiful, but your boyfriend forgot to clarify one point when he made his deal, and that was when precisely the clock started."

Wyatt made a strangled sound.

I gaped at Alex, quickly doing the math in my head. It came out to an answer I should have anticipated, and that instantly infuriated me. Had Tovin somehow fucked up the resurrection spell? "Son of a bitch, he started the clock at the time of death of the host body."

"Bingo. Sucks for you, doesn't it?"

"So we're supposed to do what now? Just sit down here until my time is up? That's the plan?"

"In a nutshell. But just think, Evy, it's your fondest wish. You get to spend the rest of your life with him. Short though it is."

"Step into this cell with me, asshole," Wyatt said, "and we'll see whose life is going to be shorter."

Alex laughed—a hard sound lacking warmth or mirth. "Please, I'm not that stupid. I may be reborn, but that doesn't mean I suddenly know how to defend myself. You'd wipe the floor with me, help your girlfriend escape, and then he'd be pissed."

"Who's he?"

"Nice try, but no. It'll ruin the surprise, and trust me, no one's going to see this coming."

More questions died on my lips. He wouldn't answer them. Asking was a waste of time. The Halfies wanted us down here until my time ran out. They had a crystal in place that interfered with Wyatt's Gift. It had been planned meticulously. Yet as simple as it all seemed, I couldn't see that final piece of the puzzle. The final "who" and "why" that completed the picture.

"And lucky you," Alex said to Wyatt. "You get to watch the love of your life die twice." Wyatt growled; Alex laughed. "But you two won't be alone. An old friend will be back around midnight, and she's bringing her favorite straight razor. That healing thing you do fascinates her."

My stomach trembled. Anger flared bright red in my vision. Kelsa had been here recently, and she was coming back. Passing threats against her health to Alex was a waste of breath, but it didn't stop me from thinking them. If she even pointed her razor at me or Wyatt . . .

"We probably won't meet again," Alex said. "Good-bye, Evangeline Stone."

"Fuck off, Halfie," I said, offering him a one-fingered salute.

He smirked and strolled back to the iron door, as breezy as a man on an afternoon stroll. He hit it twice with his fist. The door opened, and he disappeared through it. The lock squealed back into place.

"Evy?" Wyatt said.

I retreated to the middle of my cell. "If you ask me if I'm okay, I'll belt you, I swear it."

He offered a wan smile. "Sorry."

"He never should have gotten involved in this shit, Wyatt. I kept trying to push him away, but he wouldn't go. This is what friendship got him." I sat down, exhausted and hungry and verging on the need to pee. "So what do we do now? A rousing game of I Spy?"

"Arousing, huh?"

"Cute."

"I know you are, but what am I?"

"A jackass."

"You should get some rest."

The change-up surprised me. I also wasn't about to argue. I needed sleep, as well as the fresh perspective that came with a rested mind. The hard cement floor wasn't conducive to comfortable sleeping, though, as Wyatt could certainly attest. He'd been caged up longer than I.

"Come here," he said.

I did. He stretched out lengthwise on his side of the prison bars, facing me. I did the same, lying on my right side with my back to him. The barrier prevented much contact, but I felt his presence. His warmth and strength and life. He draped half of one arm over my waist. I reached up to clasp that hand, fingers tangling with his. It was the best we could do, but I'd take it over nothing.

We were together again, and we made a hell of a team. Faith in that helped me find some restless sleep, once again devoid of dreams or nightmares.

Chapter Nineteen

25:40

Hours passed in a hazy daze of sleeping and waking. Time spent not talking about anything important, just holding each other without really touching. The more I puzzled it out, the more confused I became, unsure of what was true and what was false. Memory and instinct vied for attention, but neither provided the answers we needed. Or a means of escape from our cells.

No one was left to look for us. Isleen and Rufus were probably dead. Max wouldn't interfere. We had no more allies within the Triads. Hope grew dimmer with each passing hour, marked only by my increasing hunger and thirst.

At some point during our slumber, two bottles of water appeared outside of my cell. I scrambled for them, and nearly wrenched my shoulder out of its socket. No matter how I twisted and tried, they remained outside of my grasp, a full twelve inches from my fingertips.

"Use my belt," Wyatt said, already reaching for the buckle.

"That'll just knock them over." Water had never looked so good, and I didn't want to risk pushing them farther away.

I stood up and shimmied out of my jeans. They caught on my sneakers, so I yanked those off, too. I shook out the jeans, put them through the bars, and knelt. Holding one leg cuff in each hand, I flung the crotch toward the bottles. The makeshift net lassoed them in one try. I gave a cry of triumph and reeled them in, half an inch at a time so they didn't fall over and roll away.

When the bottles were finally close enough to grab, I gave one to Wyatt and nearly dropped mine wrenching off the cap. I forced myself to take only two long gulps. More would make me sick. The tepid, plastic-flavored water sloshed into my stomach, bringing blessed moisture to my mouth and lips. The small gesture of anonymous mercy refilled my energy levels, and I found myself giggling.

"What's the joke?" Wyatt asked, water dribbling down his chin.

"Nothing's funny." I tried in vain to sober myself. "Just never been so thirsty in my life."

"Too bad they didn't send along a couple of cheeseburgers."

"Or some pancakes." It felt like breakfast, but we had no watches. "What time do you think?"

"Morning. The sun's up. I can feel that it's warmer now."

I took another sip and screwed the cap back on. I had half of an eighteen-ounce bottle and didn't know when or if we'd be resupplied. It had to last.

"There's one other thing I still can't reconcile," I said.

"One thing?"

I rolled my eyes. "Me, Wyatt. If they're just waiting for my death, why sit on me until the clock runs out? Why not put a bullet between my eyes?"

"Does the phrase 'don't look a gift horse in the mouth' mean anything to you?"

"I'm serious."

"So am I."

"Why the theatrics if they only want me dead? What happens if I die before the end of the seventy-two hours?"

"Then the freewill contract is voided," he said. "The deal was for seventy-two hours."

"Although it seems the starting point is now in question."

He nodded. "Anything that breaks the contract—"

"Like me being killed ahead of schedule."

"—nullifies the terms, and I owe him nothing."

I allowed a tiny flare of hope. "You keep your free will?"

Another nod. "The only profit and loss is between the two people who made the deal."

"You and Tovin?"

"Right." Then Wyatt's face went slack. His skin paled to a shade whiter than any living human. His lips curled back. Sweat broke out across his forehead. He looked like a man on the verge of a heart attack.

"What?" I asked, my heart beating faster.

"Tovin. It's been Tovin from the start. It's the only explanation."

"For what?"

"This." He swept his arms out. "Us, locked in here instead of on morgue slabs. He planted the idea that we had a happy future. It's the seed that's sown this entire debacle. I believed him, Evy, so when you died I sought him out, and I never thought about how easy he was to find."

A tremor clawed down my spine. "Whose idea was the resurrection, Wyatt?"

He looked ill. "His. Tovin suggested the spell with that line about something still left for you to do. It's what convinced me to accept the deal. I didn't even consider the price. I just wanted him to be right."

I was finally tracking his thought process. Each missing puzzle piece, save one, was clicking into place. Tales of a happy ending when one couldn't possibly exist. Halfies killing Jesse and Ash, and forcing me and Wyatt together. Kelsa admitting someone else had a purpose for me and that Wyatt was intended to find me dying.

The plan for the resurrection was to put me into the body of a dead Hunter—a Hunter who'd already been dead two days. If the clock had started then, as planned, the whole ordeal would have been over yesterday. Except something had drawn me to Chalice—a fortuitous turn of events I still couldn't explain. The final piece of the puzzle.

"That son of a goblin whore," I said. Another more terrifying thought occurred to me about the powerful elven mage. "Christ, Wyatt, does that mean he's part of this alliance? And what about Amalie and the other Fey?"

"I don't know." His fists clenched and released, clenched and released. He seemed to vibrate like a live wire. "We can't trust anyone, can we?"

"What about the Triads? They're still human, run by humans. Surely someone can help us."

"Maybe, if we had any way to get to them."

Good point. "So what the hell does Tovin want so badly with your free will?"

"I have no idea."

Wyatt was Gifted, sure, but his abilities were no match for Tovin's. And there were easier ways of getting access to the Triads. Handlers had no high-level influence. If Tovin had truly gone through the trouble of setting this up from the onset, the payoff didn't seem to match the effort. Not even close.

"Then I guess we'll have to ask the bastard when we see him," I said, relatively calm, considering.

"Thinking positive again?"

"I'm thinking I don't like being manipulated. I'm thinking I don't want the clock to run out in this cell without ever knowing the truth about my death. I'm thinking we'll get out of here, because I don't want to die. I believe we have a future, Wyatt, and I want it."

Wyatt went absolutely still—an amazing feat that seemed to go on endlessly. Intense black eyes stared at me, through me. Sought the truth of that final statement. Giving him no reason to doubt—and suddenly very aware that I was still standing there in my panties—I stepped toward the bars. He mirrored my movements.

"I do love you," I said. "I don't know if it's romantic love, or just because of our history, or if it even matters now if it's mine or Chalice's or gratitude for everything you've done for me—"

He silenced me with a finger across my lips—a simple touch that unleashed a swarm of butterflies in my stomach. His finger traced a line down my cheek and hooked beneath my chin. The subtle hint drew me forward the few inches he needed to kiss me.

It was tender and awkward and painful. The bars bit into my cheekbones and left little maneuvering room. The spicy taste of him, familiar and foreign, invaded my senses. His tongue probed forward. I parted my lips to allow entry, meeting his with mine. My hands tangled in his short hair.

As our mouths danced in what little space we had, a subtle warmth built low in my stomach. It spread lower. I clenched my thighs. The movement elicited a pleased growl from Wyatt.

Cold metal continued to press into my face. Cold, like a goblin's skin.

Irrational fear drove me back, out of the safety of Wyatt's embrace. His hurt surprise quickly turned to understanding.

"Evy?"

"I'm sorry."

"No, I am. I shouldn't have—"

"I'm glad you did." And I was. Glad and terrified and turned on and a conflicting mess of other things. "A little awkward through the bars, though."

"Maybe if we ask nicely, they'll put us in the same cell."

"Sort of a final request?"

Darkness flickered across his face. "I thought we were thinking positive here."

I shivered at the chill in his voice, yet another reminder of my lack of clothes. My jeans were still on the other side of the cell. I padded across the cold cement to fetch them, then put them and my sneakers back on.

Fully clothed once again, I sat back down against the bars. Wyatt hadn't moved and he didn't reach for me. He was still waiting for an answer, and I had none to give. Positive or negative, I was tired of thinking. I wanted to lock myself into a room and let Wyatt hold me until this nightmare was over. I wanted to eat pizza and beer and donuts, and do tequila shots until I threw up. I didn't want to spend the rest of my life staring at him through iron bars, waiting for Kelsa to show up and the clock to run out, wondering if I'd escape or wither away.

"I'm thinking," I said, turning to face him. "I'm thinking I'd like to get out of here."

"Ditto, but unless we can shatter that crystal, or discover a hidden escape route, we seem to be stuck."

"What happened to thinking positive?"

"I—"

The ground trembled, distant and soft, like a train passing too close. It couldn't be an actual train—we'd have heard one passing sooner. The miniquake silenced itself after only a few seconds. Maybe a truck, or an airplane flying too low.

"That was odd," Wyatt said.

Odd repeated itself a moment later. The second tremor was closer, stronger. The floor vibrated like an electric wire. Whatever it was, it seemed to be moving toward us. Sideways, upward, backward, I couldn't tell. Through the cement floor.

The unfinished cement floor.

I whooped, pumping one fist into the air. Wyatt stared. "What, Evy?"

"The cavalry is here."

The cell floor hummed and shimmied. The tightly packed particles began to thrum with kinetic energy. They pulled apart and shifted, like quicksand. I backed to the corner, careful to not get sucked into the maelstrom. A hand formed, the size of my leg. It braced on the unmoving section of the floor and pulled a second hand out of the liquid cement. A familiar face coalesced. Basketball-sized eyes blinked at me, but did not see. Only sensed.

"Smedge," I said.

"Stony."

"How did you find us?"

"Know scent. Spells . . . cannot block."

"But why?" Wyatt asked. "What are you doing here?"

Smedge grumbled, a familiar sound of dislike. **"Save. Sent."**

"By whom?"

The bridge troll grumbled again, but did not reply.

"Who sent you to save us, Smedge?" I asked. I didn't dare hope it was true, that we were on the verge of getting out of there. Hope was a dangerous thing. Like gargoyles, the trolls had always presented themselves as a neutral race. Stories about trolls hiding under bridges and eating children are highly exaggerated.

Smedge curled his stony lips in some attempt at a smile. **"Amalie. Friend."**

"Amalie?" I repeated. The sprite Queen was sending trolls to find us? I recalled yesterday's conversation with Smedge about Amalie. He said she was consolidating her power in preparation for choosing sides. Had she seen this coming, or was she working with Tovin? Sprites and elves were distant cousins after all.

"Friend."

"Smedge, do you trust her?" I asked.

"Yes. Trust. Friend. Save Stony. Save Truman. Save world."

Save world? Gee, no pressure.

"Can you get us out of here?" Wyatt asked.

"Trust me. Must."

"We trust you," I said.

Smedge's head lowered back toward the floor, flattening out until it appeared to be little more than an anthill. His eyes disappeared as his mouth opened and expanded. Wider until it was a three-foot hole in the floor, outlined by cement hands. I peered over the edge. It descended into complete darkness. Into the heart of the earth and the world that trolls inhabited.

I looked at Wyatt. He seemed dubious, but shrugged, leaving the choice up to me.

"I've always wanted to see how the other side lived," I quipped.

"Just don't forget to come over here for me."

"Never. See you down there."

I inhaled and held it, summoning up the courage it took to leap off a cliff with no sign of the bottom. I closed my eyes, stepped off the edge of Smedge's lip, and plummeted into his belly.

Chapter Twenty

25:12

Free-falling into utter darkness turned into a sensation of floating. At some point, I stopped moving. Pitch surrounded me. I tried to move, but couldn't. I opened my mouth to scream, only to realize that I couldn't breathe. Something filled my mouth, thick like gel, but with no taste or actual consistency. It was in my ears and nose.

Great plan, Evy. You're going to suffocate in the gullet of a troll.

I tried to spit out the offending substance. It was like forcing air out of my mouth without actually exhaling. My lungs ached. I tried to move, claw, fight, anything but hover there. Alone.

Wyatt! I screamed in my mind. Was he down here with me, slowly choking to death on some viscous fluid with no real properties? Had it all been another of Tovin's tricks?

My chest spasmed. Lungs burning, I prepared to open up and suck in that fluid and just end it all. Then floating turned to actual movement. Free-falling again, this time headfirst, toward light. I held on, fighting against the need to inhale.

I hit something hard. My left shoulder burned and I cried out, which forced an intake. I coughed on the fluid and something else—air. I inhaled greedily, alternately spitting out the mucus, which was foul-smelling and gluelike now that I was . . . somewhere else.

Rubbing the mess out of my eyes with equally messy hands, I tried to get a look at my surroundings. I felt dirt beneath my knees and caked on my skin. Mixed in with the stink of the goop was the heavy odor of earth. Dark shapes coalesced in the gloom.

Something slammed into my back. I fell over again, this time with Wyatt tangled up in my arms. Dirt scraped my elbows and face. I grunted. He wasn't coughing. I rolled him onto his back. He was slathered in the same clear goo from head to foot, but his eyes were shut. He was perfectly still, and not breathing.

"Shit!"

I wiped off his face as best I could and tilted back his chin. With muddy fingers, I scooped some of the gel out of his mouth. CPR training was years ago, lost along with most of those first few, intense weeks of training at Boot Camp. I did what I remembered, hoping it was accurate. I pinched his nose and blew twice. One hand over the other, five compressions. Two more breaths. Five compressions. Each motion performed with careful precision. No panic, no haste, just absolute faith that he would—

Wyatt coughed. I rolled him onto his left side, so he could vomit onto the floor. His entire body shook as he expelled the offending goo. He coughed for a long time, and I held his head, content just to have him breathing again.

We were in a tunnel of some sort, probably an abandoned construction shaft, part of last year's attempt at creating a city subway system. There were dirt floors and walls, with a hand light strung every ten feet or so. It was cold and quiet. I listened for the sounds of traffic or running water, anything to identify our location.

Wyatt rolled onto his back, still coughing. His grimace melted into a smile when he saw me. I cupped my hands on either side of his cheeks. "Do not scare me like that," I said.

"Sorry." He cleared his throat and spat to the side. "I tried, but I guess I didn't take a deep enough breath."

"Well, Smedge could have warned us."

"Did not ask."

His voice, less than a foot to my right, scared the shit out of me. He had emerged in the wall, features more pronounced in the softer earth. I considered arguing with him, but failed to see the point. Trolls were very literal, and he was right. We didn't ask what to expect before leaping into his mouth.

"Halfway."

"We aren't there yet?" I asked.

"No. Halfway. More air."

"No kidding."

"We have to go back into that?" Wyatt asked.

"He said halfway. So we just need to take deeper breaths." And a shower, once we got where we were going. In the open air, that fluid smelled like rotten eggs.

I helped Wyatt sit up. He threw his arms around

my shoulders. Though slick and smelly, and uncomfortably chilly, I still hugged him tight. Together again and away from the blocking crystal, the sense of power returned. It tingled through me like a static shock, energizing and comfortingly familiar. I started laughing for no good reason. He did, too. Smedge probably thought us a pair of loons.

"Must go."

We both stood. I held Wyatt's gaze as I inhaled, matching my breaths to his, prepping like a deep-sea diver. I nodded when I was ready. He winked. Mucus trickled down his cheeks like tears.

Smedge had shifted, creating another mouth-shaped hole in the dirt floor. I took a deep breath, held it, and jumped.

* * *

Halfway my ass. The second trip felt interminable, and even with the prep, I was screaming for air by the time I was finally ejected. I coughed and spit and gulped in oxygen. This time, I had the good sense to roll a few feet and avoid Wyatt's crash landing. He hit the sand a few seconds after I did, alert and gasping.

No, the stuff on the ground was finer than sand. Like confectioners' sugar, without the white residue and dust. It didn't scrape my skin like regular dirt, but it still stuck to the goo and made a gross, pale brown paste on my arms and hands.

"Evy, are you okay?" Wyatt asked. He tried to wipe his face and succeeded in smearing muck across his forehead.

"Yeah. You?"

"Yeah. Where the hell are we?"

Awareness of my surroundings set in with the nearby thunder of falling water. We were in a cavern. Its roof towered over us at least twelve stories high, the very top lost in dimness. The water flowed from a break in the upper rock, straight down in a stream as thin as my arm, and splashed into a pool the size of a small car. The water in the pool was black as pitch and glossy as a mirror, despite the constant ripples. The sound should have echoed louder, given the enormity of the cavern. Instead, it created a rhythmic white noise.

Dotted here and there on the craggy walls around us, flowers grew. Nothing I'd ever seen before—blue and purple and red, trumpet-shaped like lilies, but with dozens of petals like a daisy. I couldn't imagine how such a stunning flower grew underground without sunlight. The sandy ground around the pool was peppered with small pockmarks, like thousands of tiny feet had once run across it. Glowing orange orbs stood on rock poles, acting like street lamps and casting a glow on the underground world we'd been vomited into.

"Holy . . ."

Awe crept into Wyatt's voice. I twisted around, away from the falls. My mouth fell open.

A city rose up behind us. Carved directly into the rock, hewn stairs connected level after level of doors and windows and walkways. Their sizes varied, but few were larger than five feet tall. Curtains of shimmering material covered them all, cutting off their interiors from prying eyes. It reminded me of photos I'd seen of Mediterranean villas, but built up instead of out. Other varieties of flowers grew among the stones and doors and steps.

More impressively, abstract murals covered every inch of rock on that side of the cave. Scrolls and filigrees surrounded doorways and repeated on the windows—splashes of red, green, orange, blue, purple, and yellow, twisted into a thing of beauty. Dotted among it were silver and gold and bronze, and I had no doubt that it wasn't paint creating those rich, shimmering colors, but the metals themselves. Spheres the size of basketballs dotted the walls between windows, along the stairs, and in the stone face of the cave itself. They glowed with the same burnt orange color. But more than the visual aesthetic, I felt the power of the place. Stronger than I'd ever felt in the city; keener than just those vague wisps of energy.

I stood up on trembling legs. There was no sign of Smedge, or of the cave's inhabitants. No, "village" was more appropriate than "cave." Cave did not do the space's majesty any sort of justice. The air was rife with the scents of flowers—lavender and roses and honeysuckle—none of the stale, humid air I expected.

Wyatt's fingers slipped around mine, and slimy as they were, I held tight. My heart sped up a few beats, but not from fear. Nothing about this place scared me. It was exhilarating, like coming home after a long absence—a feeling I didn't quite understand. Wyatt's wide-eyed, slack-jawed gaze indicated similar feelings.

"I've never seen anything like it," he said. He whispered, as though afraid speaking too loudly would destroy the peace around us and bring a horde of angry locals down on our heads.

"It's amazing. Empty, but amazing."

The burnt orange spheres glowed brighter, becoming first yellow, and then shimmering ivory. The colors of the wall murals sparked and lit, creating rainbow washes that almost hurt my eyes with their beauty. It bounced off the cavern walls all around us, making it seem somehow larger than before. Like a football stadium, minus the fake grass.

A curtain in one of the ground-level doors pulled to the side. A petite figure emerged, walking slowly, but with purpose and intent. Barely four feet tall, her sky blue skin radiated light and life. Her flaming red hair was done up in fancy spirals and held in place with crystals. More crystals dotted her face and cheeks, creating lazy paths down her shoulders and arms and across her stomach to her legs. Her breasts were faint mounds on her chest, with no discernible nipples. The sharp V between her legs was smooth and sexless. She was the perfect re-creation of the female figure, on a slightly smaller scale.

As she closed in on us, her cobalt eyes fixed on me. She smiled with ruby lips, showing off a perfect line of pearly teeth. I melted under the warmth of that smile, and all I felt from her was peace.

"Amalie," Wyatt said.

I gaped. I'd seen Amalie and, save the piercing blue eyes and flame-red hair, the small, sparkling woman-wannabe was not the sprite I knew.

Her smile and laughing eyes turned to him. "Wyatt Truman, my friend," she said, her voice commanding and feminine and disproportionate to her small frame. "We finally meet."

"How's that?" I asked.

"Apologies, Evangeline," she said. "My people prefer to avoid the cities, but our abilities allow us to send our spirit through the body of an avatar. It helps us communicate with the outside world, without exposing ourselves to it."

"Avatar?"

"Usually a human whose mind is already open to possibilities. It allows us to take them over for a short period of time, often without their knowledge. They wake as though from a dream and remember nothing of their possession. It is how Wyatt knows me, and how you have previously seen me. Few have ever seen my true self."

She spun around in a circle, her delicate arms spread wide. "In fact, you are the first humans to be welcomed here in our most private home. Welcome to First Break, where the Fair Ones reside."

Her announcement created a flurry of activity. The shimmering curtains covering the carved doors and windows drew away. Bright light spilled out. Hundreds of creatures exited those doors, and some flew from what were actually not windows, but smaller doorways. Some were proportionate like Amalie, their skin and hair colors as varied as the rainbow, but none possessed as many crystals as she. Others were squat, or had heads too large, arms too short, or bodies too slim. The smallest, no larger than a chipmunk, flew on filament wings, even more delicate than a butterfly's. Lights the size of fireflies gathered high above us, a cloud of pearly light that never stopped moving.

They assembled on the sandy floor, creating a semicircle around us. Inhuman chatter, like the gentle buzzing of bumblebees, rose above the din of their arrival. With them came more sweet smells, like the garden of the gods had just opened up to us. It was intoxicating, invigorating.

"Fair Ones," Wyatt said.

"You have other words for us, of course," Amalie replied. "Names of human myth that do nothing to explain what we are. Pixies and nymphs and sprites and faeries are only titles. Human constructs of literature, to help explain how they saw things they couldn't possibly have seen."

"Sort of like Bram Stoker?" I asked. He'd done a lot to create false myths about vampires.

"Precisely, but there is time later for explanations. I must apologize for your conveyance, but I could see no other way to retrieve you and avoid being followed here. The Dark Ones must never find this place."

I didn't have to ask who the Dark Ones were. "I never realized trolls were friends with sprites," I said. "But thank you, all the same, for the jailbreak."

For a moment, Amalie seemed puzzled. Understanding elicited another heartwarming smile. "The being you call a troll is one of our Earth Guardians. They are our eyes and ears in the world."

Earth Guardian. I liked that.

"May I ask," Wyatt said, "why you brought us here?"

Her cobalt eyes flared. "As I said, the time for stories is later. We have prepared a place for you both to bathe and rest."

An orange sprite with lime green hair sprinted to my side. She beckoned me forward with jewel-encrusted fingers. Wyatt squeezed my hand and let me go. I followed her through the parting crowd, toward the high rise of dwellings. I glanced back and saw Wyatt attended by two of the disproportionate ones—heads twice the size of their puny bodies, features distinctly male. I didn't know what to call them, and it felt inappropriate to ask.

My sprite guided me to the second tier of homes and through one of the tallest doors. I still had to duck to enter. My skin tingled. The room was impossible given the outer façade. A palace would have been less impressive.

I had stepped into paradise.

The floor was gold, the walls brushed silver and polished to a shine. A bed covered with colorful silks stood against one wall. Opposite it, two tapestries curtained off a footed tub. Hot water steamed. I inhaled the delicate aromas of sage and lavender. It was a small room, but decorated with a luxury I had only dreamed about in my waking life. I still wasn't convinced I was fully awake.

"Is this a dream?" I asked.

The sprite giggled. The blissful sound made me smile in spite of myself. "You are in First Break, dear one. Anything is possible here."

"What is First Break, exactly?"

"A place where magic is born. Now please, rest and clean up. There are clothes near the tub. Our Queen will summon you when she believes you are ready."

"Okeydoke."

She didn't seem to understand, but took my words as a dismissal. A curtain was pulled across the door, giving me privacy. I wandered toward the center of the room, expecting to wake up at any moment, find

myself still trapped in that forsaken prison cell, await-
ing my second death.

I avoided the bed and its delicate fabrics. My shoes
left dirt smudges on the pristine floor as I approached
the bathing area. The scent of flowers was stronger
here, and I realized the water was scented, not the
room. It was hot, but not scorching.

"Might as well enjoy the illusion."

I stripped slowly, trying to keep the majority of
the drying ooze in one place. I tossed the ruined clothing into a small pile by the tub. It felt great to get it all
off and free my stifled skin. I appreciated the rescue,
but the conveyance left a lot to be desired.

Two plush towels sat on a stool by the tub. Next
to it were several bottles without labels. I ignored them
and dipped one leg into the water. A soft sigh escaped.
It was the perfect temperature, hot and soothing. I sat
on the smooth bottom and slipped down until only
my head remained above the surface. Heat cocooned
me in its gentle embrace. The scents and oils siphoned
the day's stresses away and replaced them with con-
tentment.

I held my breath and slid down beneath the water,
submerging my entire body. I floated for a moment,
content to be cut off from the rest of the world. Eager
to simply exist. Never had a bath felt so much like
heaven. It was a place I wanted to stay forever.

Or at least until I started to prune.

Chapter Twenty-one

24:01

She ran around naked, so I had to laugh at the sprite's definition of clothing. The dress I found draped on a hook was little more than two silver curtain sheers held together at the shoulders by jewel-encrusted brooches. It would have been more at home on a Greek goddess. It looked downright silly on me and did nothing to protect my modesty. Maybe the Fair Ones—seeing how they didn't possess genitalia of any sort—didn't care if they ran around in the buff, but I sure as hell did.

I washed out my panties and wrung them as dry as possible. I'd rather run around in damp underwear than do without. It helped, but the gown still billowed all over the place. I located a small vanity next to the bed, and when I rummaged through the drawers, I found dozens more bottles of scented oils and perfumes, and then a handful of colorful ribbons, probably meant for my hair, in all lengths and widths.

A thick, purple velvet sash became my belt, tied tight around my hips. After a little trial and error, a second, thinner purple ribbon crisscrossed my chest and back. It created some support for my breasts, even though the fabric of the dress was still uncomfortably sheer. I briefly considered stuffing some ribbons down the front, but as long as I didn't get chilly, my nipples wouldn't be saluting anyone.

I stared at myself in the polished wall, surprised at the vision reflected back at me. The woman in the mirror was no longer a stranger. We smiled at each other, and she wasn't Chalice anymore. We were Evangeline, and we looked fabulous in our Grecian dress. My hair was drying on its own, creating thick brown waves that framed my face and shoulders. Even without makeup, my cheeks blazed with color. My eyes were bright. A trick of the environment, no doubt, but still mesmerizing.

For the first time in two days, I truly felt alive. And hopeful.

A bell chimed, the tiniest tinkle. "Evangeline?" I turned toward the door and the familiar voice. My orange sprite stood in the doorway. "Amalie requests your company."

Finally, some answers. The sprite stepped aside and led the way. The stone pathways were smooth beneath my bare feet as we ascended another flight of carved steps to the third level, then up to the fourth. Fair Ones of all species buzzed and flew and scampered. Many just watched. I felt scrutinized, but not unwelcome.

"What's your name?" I asked.

"Jaron," the sprite said.

I blinked. This was Amalie's bodyguard? The sprite that Wyatt had once described as a man big enough to intimidate a professional wrestler? Avatar ability or not, it was a disparity I couldn't quite wrap my brain around.

Jaron led us all the way to the top level of the complex. I paused and looked down at the circular pathways below. Activity surrounded me. We were closer to the source of the waterfall, and the pool seemed so tiny, like an onyx eye peeking up from a distance.

"It's the Anjean River," Jaron said. "It flows above us."

"Cool."

She stopped in front of a circular doorway, its border decorated with an intricate pattern. It could have been a language, but I definitely couldn't read it. Jaron pulled back the curtain.

I ducked to step through and felt the same encompassing buzz of magic inside. The room's physical simplicity surprised me. The main piece of furniture on the smooth, tan floor was a long, polished stone table, covered with platters of fruit and vegetables and nuts and grains. Pitchers of liquid stood amongst the feast. Another sphere hung from the ceiling, casting the perfect amount of light.

Amalie lounged in a stone chair decorated with living flowers and vines, placed at the head of the table. Her bright smile made me giddy. She waved me forward.

"Please, help yourself," she said.

I gaped at the table's bounty, too timid to touch anything. But the smells were tantalizing, and my stomach grumbled. I inhaled deeply, identifying the heady, sweet scent of wine from one of the pitchers. The bottle of tepid water seemed so long ago.

A throat cleared. I pivoted, hair swirling in a loose

flurry. Wyatt stood just inside of the doorway, hands clasped behind his back. My heart sped up at the sight. His keepers had cobbled together slacks in much the same manner as my dress. The thin, bronze fabric was belted at his waist, cut and tucked to create a make-shift crotch, and cinched with velvet ribbon at both ankles. The sides of the legs were completely open, flashing toned muscles and tanned skin.

His hair was tousled, finger-combed, and allowed to dry, and his face was freshly shaved. His bare chest glistened, showing off a roped torso and tight abs. The new scent of fruit—apples, maybe—hinted that he'd used the oils provided. More than his physical attractiveness, though, I stared at his flawless skin—stared until I realized what bothered me.

The array of parallel bruises I'd seen two days ago were gone. The knife wound from our previous fight with the goblin scouts was likewise gone. Not healed—there would have been some faint residual marks. They were just gone, as though they'd never existed.

"Evy," he said. I looked up, met his smiling eyes. "You look like a goddess."

My cheeks heated. "You, too," was all I managed.

"Do I? Should I be in that dress?"

"You know what I mean, jackass. What happened?" I pointed at his chest.

"I'm not sure. One of the gnomes put something in my bathwater that smelled like peppermint. When I got out, they were gone."

Note to self: gnomes have big heads and small bodies.

"They possess great knowledge of healing," Amalie said. "Consider it a gift."

"I feel like I owe you so much already," I said.

She shook her head side to side, as elegant as it was forceful. "You have done much for us without knowing. I feel I cannot offer you enough recompense."

Not particularly inspiring. Wyatt joined me at the table and eyed the goodies spread out in front of us. I picked up one of the largest strawberries I'd ever seen and inhaled its tantalizing aroma. Perfection in a piece of fruit.

"Why did you rescue us?" Wyatt asked.

"As I said, Wyatt Truman, you have been a service to us without your knowledge. I could not see allowing you to wither in those cells, apart from each other, until her time is up."

"You brought me here to die?" I asked, the strawberry halfway to my lips. A small flare of fury lit deep in my belly.

"I cannot change what has been put into motion, Evangeline. I do not possess that sort of power."

"So that's it? Your compensation for a job well done—so well done I didn't even know I was doing it—is to die down here with the faeries? To sit on my ass, drink wine, and let Tovin win?"

Amalie bristled when I said his name. Her skin darkened to the color of her eyes. Every crystal glittered and winked. "You proved Tovin a traitor. He sees nothing, except potential gain for himself. There will be no peace for the Fair Ones, or anyone else, should the goblins come into power. Even the vampires know the potential cost of this fight."

"Isleen," I said, thinking of her for the first time in hours. "Do you know what happened to her? She was captured along with me."

"Then she is likely dead. Vampires do not suffer threats, nor do they bargain for their people. She will have no value to the half-Bloods who captured you."

My shoulders sagged. I dropped the uneaten strawberry onto the delicate silver platter from which it came. Wyatt slipped his arm around my waist. I melted into the warmth of him and the apple-sweet scent of his body.

"This whole time," I said, "I thought the Bloods didn't give a damn, that they were our enemies, but they were trying to help. Isleen wanted to help, just like her sister, and now they're both dead."

"She did her part," Amalie said. "As we all do ours. Each has a role to play in coming events—some more than others."

"Then what makes you so sure my part is over? I'm not done fighting, dammit. I will not give up and just let Tovin take Wyatt's free will for whatever god-forsaken purpose he has in mind."

"You cannot undo the bargain they have created, Evangeline. A freewill pact, signed in blood, can only be voided by the spilling of more blood."

"What the hell does that mean? Do I have to sacrifice a goat?"

Her color tone lightened. "That is not what I meant. This is not within the scope of my powers, but I am told that there are three ways in which this pact can be voided in blood."

My stomach quivered. Wyatt's other arm came around my waist, and I clasped my hands over his. I needed to hear this, but was terrified to know.

"If Evangeline dies before the end of the seventy-two hours, it is voided," Amalie said.

"We came up with that one on our own," I said. "But the fact that I've healed after every little scratch and bruise means that Tovin put some extra effort into making sure that didn't happen. If the hound attack didn't kill me, few things weaker than a beheading likely will."

"And not an option," Wyatt said.

Yet.

"If Tovin dies before the contract expires, Wyatt is free of his obligations," Amalie continued.

"Makes sense," I said. "And definitely a more plausible scenario, since he's proving to be a number one asshole anyway."

"Tovin's well protected," Wyatt said. "Few ever know where to find him, and he conjures. He could make you see things you can't even imagine."

I patted his hand. "And you can only summon the power of the sun. Weakling."

"Very funny."

"The caveat to killing Tovin," Amalie said, "is that at the moment of his death, Evangeline's time is also up."

"If he dies, I die?"

"Yes."

Terrific.

"What's the third option?" Wyatt asked.

Amalie's cobalt eyes burned. "If Wyatt dies before the end of the time frame, then Evangeline is freed of her constraints and may continue to inhabit her new body."

A tremor ran up my spine. I'm sure my mouth was hanging open. In two days, no one had ever presented me with an option that included me living past the seventy-two hours. Three days was it, so no use in making plans. Knowing the option existed exhilarated me, even though the price was impossible to pay.

"Evy could live," Wyatt said. His soft, contemplative tone alarmed me.

"Fuck you, Truman," I snarled, disentangling myself from his arms. "There is no way that's happening."

"Evy—"

"No!" I stalked to the other side of the room, hit the wall, and rounded to the opposite side of the buffet table. I glared at him over the display of uneaten food and drink. "Absolutely not, so fucking forget about it. If you even think it, I'll have someone bring you back just so I can kill your ass myself."

His eyes narrowed. "That's not funny."

"No, it isn't, and I'm dead serious."

"You could keep on living, Evy."

"I died, Wyatt." My voice rose to just below screaming, but I didn't care. "I'm supposed to be dead right now, so who cares if I'm dead again in a day? I don't want it, but that's the way it's supposed to be. I will not spend the rest of my afterlife worrying if you're going to try and commit some sort of noble suicide. I'd rather take a flying leap off this walkway and land on my head."

"Please," Amalie said. "Now is not the time for such arguments. Now is the time for eating and resting. You need your strength if you are both to find a solution to the puzzle facing you."

Wyatt and I glared at each other for seconds that stretched into minutes. Neither of us wanted to back down. Wyatt wanted me to live. But as much as I wanted it, too, I couldn't knowing everything he'd given up for me. I'd lost Jesse and Ash. I'd lost Max and Danika. I'd lost Alex. I had nothing without Wyatt. Even the gift of life wasn't enough.

He blinked and looked away. My anger deflated. We silently filled silver plates with food and crystal goblets with wine. I stayed on my side of the table and sat down on a long, granite bench. Wyatt sat on his side, still opposite me. He began slicing a pear into halves, then quarters.

I bit into the strawberry first. Its sweet juice splashed over my tongue, the most exquisite thing I'd tasted in days. I ate it in slow bites, savoring the flavor and texture.

"Why is this place called First Break?" Wyatt asked.

"The waterfall outside is not for show," Amalie said. "Its waters mask a gateway, much stronger than the Sanctuaries guarded above, and it is why we settled here belowground. It is the main source of power for the Fair Ones. It is what allows the Gifted, such as yourself, their unique talents."

"Do all Dre—do all nonhumans know it's here?"

"Most can sense it, yes; however, only a select few outside of the Fey know of its precise location in the forest."

"Is that why all the nonhumans move to this city? The power source?"

Amalie shook her head, a patient teacher. "First Break existed here centuries before a city was built in the valley; the gateway since before my peoples' memory begins. Many travel, but they always return, as we have always been here."

"They just haven't been so obvious about it as in recent years."

"Precisely."

"Where does the gateway go?"

"Are you familiar with the writings of John Milton?"

"Mysteries?" I asked.

Wyatt snorted; I glared.

"No," she said. "He wrote of the fall of man and the journey through Hell. Milton disguised his work as fiction, but he was not just a man. He was companion to a gnome prince who lived through that journey and thought to tell others about it. We considered masking the work, but there is no better place to hide than in plain sight."

"So that pool is what?" Wyatt asked. "A gateway to Hell?"

"Precisely."

I stopped chewing a mouthful of almonds and stared. Cold dread trickled through my body. Wyatt puckered his lips and scrunched his eyebrows. Amalie seemed unaffected. She sipped a goblet of wine like she'd rehearsed this conversation a hundred times and found it dull.

"What's on the other side?" Wyatt asked.

"Creatures long ago banished from walking the Earth. The Greeks called them Titans. The Christians call them demons. We call them the Tainted. They are driven only by instinct and pure emotion—desire and rage, lust and need."

"And you keep them from crossing over?"

"The Tainted cannot cross the Break on their own. They have no free will, you see, only instinct."

I was definitely starting to see. I swallowed the almonds and chased them down with a gulp of wine—sweet and pungent—as Amalie continued.

"Someone with knowledge of First Break and its powers can summon the Tainted across it. Our duty here is to protect it from those who would try. Summoning even one across the Break could be devastating to this world."

"These Tainted," Wyatt said. "Can they be controlled by the summoner?"

"They are uncontrollable—pure beings of consumption and need. Once the Tainted enters its host's body, it is unleashed and the host is no more."

"Host?"

"They possess no physical form on the other side. They are energy and emotion. Part of the summoning is the presentation of a host."

I dropped my goblet. It clattered to the table, splashing maroon liquid on the front of my dress, but I didn't care. "That's it," I said.

"What's it, Evy?" Wyatt asked, standing up. Alarmed.

"All of this, Wyatt. Tovin and the Bloods and me dying and you giving up your free will for it and them holding us prisoner. It all makes perfect sense now."

Wyatt frowned, not understanding. I sought help from Amalie, and she nodded sagely. She'd known it all along; she was only waiting for us to figure it out. Damn her and bless her both.

"Tovin wants power, which means ensuring his dominance," I said. "What better way to do that than by summoning a demon to possess a man whose free will he already controls? He'll have a lethal weapon that can't disobey."

I'd heard the expression "all the blood drained from his face," but had never actually seen it in person. The color bled out of Wyatt's face, leaving him deathly pale. His black eyes shimmered, a stark contrast to the pallor of his skin. Even his lips turned white as he pressed them together. Nostrils flaring, he clenched his jaw so hard I thought his teeth might snap.

"We believe that is his plan," Amalie said.

Her words seemed lost on Wyatt. He stared at the table, hands in his lap, his entire body rigid. I was on my feet and by his side before I registered moving. He vibrated with tension, maybe even fear. The demon would have his powers, as well as his body.

I touched his shoulder. He jerked as though stung. I turned his face toward me. He avoided eye contact, looking everywhere but forward.

"Wyatt," I said. "Look at me, damn you."

He did. Some of the tension fled, but he remained pale and trembling. His eyes were obsidian pools, never-ending and full of uncertainty. I had never seen him so vulnerable, not even when I died the first time.

My heart pounded. Because sitting next to him, at the turning point of this entire freaking mystery, I finally remembered my death.

Nothing as dramatic as I'd hoped for—no remembrance of important words or necessary information. Just flinching away from the light, as I'd always done when the closet door opened. Numb, unable to move, and without the energy to do so. I'd hoped to bleed to death before anyone found me like that, broken and ruined.

I remembered Wyatt kneeling over me, releasing my hands from the cuffs that bound them. Unable to feel my arms or legs. Looking into his heartbreaking eyes, seeing the measure of his devastation. Hating myself for causing him so much pain. My tongue had been thick, my mouth dry. I couldn't speak, couldn't say I was sorry or that I loved him. I only managed a high-pitched keening sound. I had gazed at him until his face went dark and the agony was finally over.

He had looked much the same as he looked in Amalie's home—ravaged, betrayed, alone. I wondered if my own expression was that much different.

"I didn't say anything," I said. "When I died, all I saw was you, and I never said a word. You couldn't have known what I did or didn't learn, could you?"

His head turned slowly left, right, back to center. A simple shake. An even simpler affirmation that left me cold. We had both been betrayed and manipulated by people we trusted. I had been rustled out of my afterlife and fed lies disguised as good intentions. He had been fooled into a fate worse than death, tricked into playing a pawn in Hell's chess game.

But we weren't done playing, and Knights knew how to sweep in sideways. "This is not your future," I said. "If Tovin ever said one truthful thing to you, Wyatt Truman, it's that we belong together. Whether it's in life or in death, we'll prove that one thing right. You hear me?"

He blinked. Some amount of recognition sparked. Bright circles of color flared in his cheeks. The lines in his face smoothed out, and determination replaced terror. "I hear you." His voice was thick, not as convincing as his expression. "I feel like such a fool."

"Tovin played on your emotions and manipulated you from the start. It wasn't your fault."

His left eye twitched. "Don't patronize me, Evy."

"Then quit feeling sorry for yourself and help me figure out how to fucking do something about it, okay?"

He pushed my hand away and faced the table.

Okay, fine. To Amalie, I asked, "Once this thing possesses a host, can it be expelled?"

"The death of the host body ejects the Tainted, yes," Amalie said. "It will be momentarily weakened, rendering it vulnerable to expulsion beyond the Break. However, sending something back across, as bringing it forward, requires great knowledge of the inner workings of our oldest magic."

"Can you do it?"

She shook her head, light sparkling off her jewels. "Few possess the knowledge, and I am acquainted with none of them, save Tovin."

"What about the other elves?"

"At this late hour, attempting contact will take too much time, and there is no guarantee they will share their knowledge."

I blew hard between clenched teeth. "Okay, so what about capture? Let's say it infects someone and the host dies. Can we catch the Tainted before it finds another host? Like in a crystal or something?"

"I know of no such method of capture, but that does not mean none exist."

Wyatt snorted. I glared, but he didn't acknowledge me.

"Can you find out?" I asked the sprite leader.

"Of course."

It wasn't much, but it was a start. Only, Wyatt didn't seem willing to acknowledge the hopeful information. I gave up. He could wallow for a while, but I didn't want to see it. I put some food on a plate and poured another goblet of wine.

"Amalie, my apologies," I said. "May I finish my meal in my room?"

The sprite nodded, her demeanor cool and calm, as if our argument had never happened. We'd figured it out. We knew who our enemies were. We just needed time to plan a counterattack and beat Tovin at his own twisted game.

At the door, I spared a look back at Wyatt. He didn't turn around. I sighed and left.

Chapter Twenty-two

23:25

My patience vanished with the last of the wine. The assortment of fruit, nuts, and raw vegetables had filled the ache in my stomach and refueled my energy, but could do nothing for a different ache. That went deeper, the wound more raw.

So many things had happened in the last two days that Tovin had never factored into his plan. I had woken up in a different body than planned—a fortuitous, if unexplainable, turn of events—so Wyatt and I hadn't been imprisoned immediately and for the duration of the pact. Being out in the world, I'd managed to gather more evidence of the coming power shift and shown Tovin for the traitor he was. I had hurt people along the way—my heart still ached for Alex—but had it been worth it? All of the pain, both physical and emotional, in order to prevent the Break from being crossed?

I paced the length of the room, hands clasped behind my back. Melodies of harmony and peace, not quite real music, danced in the air. I hadn't noticed it before, and yet it seemed like the background noise had always been there—part of the lives of the Fair Ones who lived in an underground cave and guarded the gate to Hell.

It sounded absurd, but no more so than the idea of a twenty-two-year-old who served unofficial warrants on vampires, goblins, half-Bloods, and weres for a living. Or a twenty-seven-year-old barista and part-time college student who committed suicide in time for a murdered girl's soul to possess her body. Why this body? Why Chalice and not the Hunter Tovin chose?

The answer was probably in her past, but that had been erased—except for the hard copies Wyatt had requested. Was it worth getting her history? Did it really matter why Chalice? Not really, not when possessing her had been a stroke of sheer luck. The first wrench in Tovin's wheel.

On one pass from the bed to the far wall, I spotted a shadow by the door and stopped. Wyatt stood just inside, half his body still covered by the curtain. His color was back to normal. He'd lost the shell shock and seemed almost sheepish, both in his half smile and the slump of his shoulders.

"Can I come in?" he asked.

"You're already halfway in. Might as well come the rest of the way."

He did, but stayed close to the door. Ten feet of empty air separated us, but it might as well have been ten miles. He shifted from foot to foot as he gazed around the room. My attention kept dropping to his chest—rippling with perfectly toned muscles, glistening with scented oil, the scars of the last few days washed away by gnome magic. Too bad the gnomes didn't have an oil to heal the internal wounds, too.

"You were right," he said. "Tovin manipulated all of this, and by sitting and wallowing in self-pity, I'm letting him manipulate me again. I won't do that anymore, Evy. I may not see a way out of this yet, but if this really is our last day together, I want to spend every second of it with you."

"Preferably not fighting?"

"Doing anything except fighting."

"Did you have something else in mind?"

He didn't reply. Not long ago, he'd said I looked like a goddess. Even with the wine stain and our most recent argument, the sentiment was reflected in his expression. I remembered yesterday's kiss. The heat of his lips, the spicy taste of him. The way my heart had raced, and how strongly this body wanted him. Then I remembered the moment memory overcame desire, and I'd pulled away. God damn Kelsa for what she'd done.

So many words perched on the tip of my tongue. Reasons why and why not. Words of comfort, and words to shut him down. Standing one day from oblivion, I didn't know what I wanted, so I chose silence. Words were useless while my mind remained uncertain, muddled by fear and indecision—two weaknesses I despised, both in myself and others.

I sat on the corner of the grand, silk-covered bed. The sheer dress whispered around my ankles. An answering rustle of fabric accompanied Wyatt across the room. He knelt in front of me, eye-level now, warm hands gently grasping my thighs just above the knee. The touch of his skin, both innocent and urgent, loosed those damned butterflies. Heat speared my abdomen, as welcome as it was uninvited.

"You know what I have in mind, Evy," he said, a husky edge to his voice that made my heart hammer. Onyx eyes seemed to look right through me. I wanted to ask what he saw there, if he could read me better than I could read myself. Could he see the real Evy buried deep inside? The one he loved so much?

I licked my lips, mouth dry. He interpreted it as an invitation. I closed my eyes and allowed the kiss. His lips moved against mine, soft but insistent. No clashing teeth, no inhibiting steel bars. Just us and the tingling heat everywhere we touched. His fingers caressed my throat and wandered back to tangle in my hair. My lips parted, allowing him entrance to my mouth, and for a moment we shared the same breath. His tongue traced along my upper lip, sending delicious tingles through my belly.

I parted my knees, allowing him closer. He shifted forward. The flimsy material of our clothing created a meager barrier. I felt the heat of his arousal straining against my inner thigh. A tremor surged through my chest, down to my legs, but it brought no warmth—only a bracing chill and a weak cry deep in my throat.

His tongue darted into my mouth, stroked across my teeth, misinterpreting that cry. I tried to meet his tongue with mine, but no longer felt his heat. I felt only cold and a new, terrible ache deep in my gut. He trailed cool fingertips along my back. I raked my fingers down his bare chest and earned a soft moan. His hand stopped to caress the sensitive small of my back.

No longer so sensitive. Phantom agony speared my stomach, from belly button to spine. I felt cold skin all over me, and putrid breath in my face. Misery and death moving in and out of me with brutal strokes. Memories of torture awoken so innocently by the love of a man who had risked his life and bargained away his free will, and all for me.

I shuddered. He broke the kiss. Warm hands cupped my cheeks. Thumbs brushed away tears I hadn't felt fall. I grabbed his wrists and squeezed. My chest was tight. My legs trembled. I didn't open my eyes.

"Evy?"

I concentrated on breathing, on keeping those memories at bay, lest I break into unfixable pieces. I couldn't acknowledge them, not while Wyatt held me in his arms. If I did, I would never see him, only the goblin. I wouldn't feel Wyatt's skin or taste his mouth or know his touch without remembering.

"Please, Evy, look at me."

The anguish in his voice, so like what I'd heard as I lay dying, drew me out. I opened my eyes and blinked away a film of tears. His cheeks were flushed, twin roses of color that highlighted the tumultuous emotions warring in his eyes. His entire body seemed to vibrate.

"I'm sorry," I whispered.

He blanched and, for the briefest moment, I thought he would burst into tears. "You're sorry? Evy, no."

"I want to, Wyatt."

"It's not your fault."

Truth, in so many ways, and yet the simple platitude did something entirely unexpected. Instead of tamping down my emotions, I exploded into a rage. It bubbled up from a place I never knew existed, as scorching and destructive as magma. My face heated, and I pushed Wyatt away with shaking hands. He tumbled backward, unprepared, and fell on his ass with a surprised cry. I stood and stalked to the other side of the room, bare feet making unsatisfying slaps on the stone floor. I balled my fists, but could not stop them shaking.

"Evy—"

"Don't tell me it's not my fault, Wyatt," I said, rounding to face him. "It *is* my fault, because I'm fucking stronger than this!"

He didn't move from the floor, frozen there by the fury of my outburst. I couldn't read his expression, nor did I care to try. Fuck what he was feeling; it wasn't about him. It wasn't even about me. It was about the goddamned goblin and getting the goddamned thing out of my head.

"Do you remember the Halfies we took out last summer?" I asked, words streaming from my mouth. "Remember how one of them held me down and systematically broke every finger of my left hand? I healed; I moved on. Or the were-cat who stabbed me two years ago, or all the broken bones when I was pushed off a three-story building three Christmases ago?

"It's what I do, Wyatt, I heal. I bounce back, and I go on with my life. Hell, this time I didn't even have to heal. Fate just gave me a new body and said, 'Have fun again, girlfriend.' She was even cruel enough to give me one that insists on knowing how we fit together naked, and I can't even kiss you without remembering that fucking goblin. Goddamnit!"

He slowly stood up, but smartly kept his distance. My fists ached to slam into something soft, and he was the only available target. I clenched and unclenched my hands, nails digging into my palms. The room tilted. I clung to my fury, the only lifeline keeping me from shattering.

"Why did I have to remember it?" I whispered— a plea to whatever gods existed to give me some answers. To help me understand why I'd traded oblivion for purgatory, and forgetfulness for the memories of a living Hell.

"I wish I could take it back," Wyatt said. "All of it. Erase everything that happened in that closet, but I can't."

I snarled. "Why, so you can kiss me without triggering a flashback?"

"No, Evy. Because I couldn't save you from it the first time, and because now I'm making you relive it. You don't deserve this."

"Maybe I do."

His jaw dropped.

I didn't give him a chance. "I'm a killer, Wyatt. I've done horrible things to living creatures, deserving of it or not. I shot an innocent man yesterday. I got Alex killed. I got the Owlkins wiped out. So many have died because of me, and I keep bouncing back. The unkillable Evy Stone. Why the hell do *I* get nine lives?"

"Don't do this." Wyatt crossed the room with long, purposeful strides. I retreated until my back hit the wall, hands up, ready to strike. He kept coming, stopping with only a foot's distance between us, never touching me. I flinched, nowhere left to go.

"What Kelsa did to you?" he said. "You didn't deserve it then, and you sure as hell don't deserve it now. You're a good person. You've saved lives, a hundred times as many as you've ever taken."

I turned my head, fixing on a spot by the curtained tub. I didn't want his placating words. I wanted to stew in my own rage, to give in to the despair in my heart. To mourn everything I'd lost.

He touched my cheek. I punched him in the mouth. My fist ached, and he was on the ground before I realized what I'd done. He stared up at me, a thin line of blood beading on his split lip. I watched the blood rise until it trickled down his chin. I couldn't look away from what I'd done. Hurting someone I cared about out of anger. Blind rage, if I was honest with myself. I closed my eyes. Twin tears scorched down my cheeks. When I opened them again, he was starting to stand. At a safer distance.

"I think I deserved that," he said.

I snorted. "I think I should have broken your nose."

"Evy, you can break every bone in my body if it helps you forgive me, just please, don't do this to yourself. What happened to you . . . it's not like the other times. You were hurt, and then you died. You never got the chance to heal. It's not something anyone, even you, bounces back from in a day. It takes time. You need time."

My throat closed. "What if we don't have any more time?"

"Then we take what we do have and live it. No more regretting what we can't change."

I finally met his eyes and looked into such depths of sincerity and affection that my knees buckled.

Wyatt caught me around the waist. My rage was gone, stripped away by understanding, leaving exhaustion in its place. Strong arms looped beneath my legs and lifted me up, cradling me against his chest. I closed my eyes and pressed my face into his neck.

We were moving. Silk sheets fluttered around me, against my skin. The mattress sank. In my mind, his warmth turned to cold; dry and human skin to slick and oily skin. *No!* I inhaled, could smell the apples and soap and heady scent of male. I clung to it. And to Wyatt.

He turned me onto my side, my back to him, then stretched out behind me. His left arm snaked beneath my head, a warm pillow. The other lay lightly across my right hip. I threaded my right hand through his left and held tight. His breath tickled my ear. We lay together for a while, not moving, not talking. Everything had been said. All that was left was this—tender moments in an underground paradise.

My tears dried. The soothing scents of the room relaxed my tension, and soon my breaths matched his.

We dozed a while, and I woke still in his arms. An innocent embrace that made me feel perfectly protected. I could have stayed like that for the rest of my afterlife . . . only I had to pee. He muttered in his sleep as I slipped out of the warm bed.

Our clothes were neatly stacked on the vanity stool, freshly laundered and dry. I was a bit unnerved by the idea of a sprite or gnome or whatever wandering in and leaving things. Still, I hadn't expected to see those goo-drenched jeans again, and getting back into civilian clothes would make me feel more like a functioning Hunter, and less like a princess. They reminded me of what remained to be done aboveground.

I couldn't sit down here and wait to die.

A quick search of the room made one thing abundantly clear about our hosts—the Fey don't have toilets. The empty tub, however, had a drain. It wasn't elegant, or even moderately sanitary, but I did my best, and then fetched my clothes.

I started tugging my jeans back on. One leg in, I realized I was being watched.

"You're getting dressed?" Wyatt asked. Sleep made his voice thick, husky.

"As much as my inner goddess appreciates the compliments, I feel more comfortable in my own clothes. You?"

"I'm comfortable."

"Suit yourself. Just get a move on."

He sat up and scrubbed one hand through his tousled hair. "What for?"

"So we can talk to Amalie."

A frown creased his forehead. "Talk to Amalie? For what?"

I stopped with the purple sash mostly unspooled, gauzy dress material hanging loose around my shoulders, and gaped. "What do you mean? I do care for you, Wyatt, but I don't intend to spend the rest of my life, short though it may be, in this room talking about our feelings. There's still something left to be done. We just have to find out what."

His jaw twitched. I finished dressing and finger-combed my tangled hair to the tune of Wyatt's pants zipping up. Moments later, we left the comfort of my room for the activity of the outer cavern.

Activity that continued much as it had before, with the Fair Ones flittering to and fro. They paid us no mind, as though human visitors were a normal occurrence, and parted to allow us to pass. A small pack (school? swarm?) of creatures buzzed by, no larger than dolls, their batlike wings beating the air. They flew up toward the source of the waterfall and disappeared into the shadows. An exit, perhaps.

No one stopped us on our journey to Amalie's chambers, and we arrived quickly. Jaron stood outside and pulled back the curtain. I ducked inside, with Wyatt close behind.

Amalie still sat at the head of the food-laden table. At the other end, an elderly gnome sat on a cushioned chair. His white hair was tufted around the edges of a bald head and nearly connected with his bushy eyebrows, creating a comical mask. Tiny eyes peeked out from below those eyebrows. Gnarled hands gripped the edges of a spiraled wood cane.

"Please, join us," Amalie said.

I stepped farther in, but didn't sit. "I apologize if we're interrupting."

"Not at all. Horzt was discussing an unusual message he received through the emergency communiqué channels."

"Message?" I had no idea what an emergency communiqué channel entailed for her people, or for the gnomes. "From whom?"

Amalie looked past me. "He's one of yours, I believe," she said to Wyatt. "His name is Rufus St. James."

Wyatt stepped forward, lips parted, fists clenched. He had a bead on Horzt, and I could practically see the bull's-eye on the elderly gnome's chest. I put up a hand to keep Wyatt still.

"He was wounded when the Halfies took me," Wyatt said. "How do we know he wasn't taken and turned? It could be a trick."

Horzt grunted. It sounded more like a gurgle, given his stature. He wrinkled his button nose. "We can smell humans no matter their disguise, and vampires are even more disgusting. Trust me, human, he was not turned, or my cousin would have known it."

"Your communiqué channel is your cousin?" I asked. It was definitely less impressive without the mystique.

"The Apothi see and hear things others do not," Amalie said.

"Apothi?"

"Those you call gnomes. I trust their judgment, and you would do well to do the same. This man, Rufus St. James, requests your presence in order to share information. He says that he wishes to help."

"He said that once before."

"When?" Wyatt asked.

"Right before you were arrested. He said he believed us. He helped me escape, and I believe he was going to help like he said, only the Halfies attacked."

Wyatt was not convinced. "Two-thirds of his team is dead, Evy. He was shot less than a day ago. How's he going to help?"

"I don't know, but Nadia is still out there, and you can be damned sure she wants revenge on the people who killed her Triad mates and wounded her Handler. We should go see him."

"Returning to the city," Amalie said, "is both dangerous and foolhardy. You will be captured again."

"Don't count on it." I looked around the room. Something else the Fair Ones lacked was a clock. "Amalie, what time is it?"

"It is quarter until eight in the morning," she said without looking at anything for confirmation.

"I have twenty hours, then."

She nodded. Wyatt winced.

I turned to Horzt. "Can your cousin get a message back to Rufus for us?" At his nod, I continued. "We need him to get Nadia to meet us. She could be helpful."

"The decision is unwise," Amalie said.

"Well, then, call me stupid and get it over with," I said, hands on hips. "I thank you for what you've done for us, Amalie, and for giving us a safe place to rest. I just can't give up on this, not when I know there's a piece to the puzzle I'm not seeing."

Her face darkened to cobalt. Not good. "And if you are captured again, despite your confidence? What if Tovin claims his prizes? Will you take the chance of him summoning a Tainted from the other side of the Break?"

"Yes," Wyatt said. He slipped his hand into mine. "Isn't there a saying? You can't win at chess without risking your pieces first."

I squeezed his hand. "I always thought it was that you can't make an omelet without breaking a few eggs."

"You risk more than eggs," Amalie said. "You risk all of our lives and the safety of this city."

"I thought you said you were here to protect the

Break. Even if, by some miracle, Tovin gets us again, he still has to get by you. Right?"

Amalie's skin lightened to a pale, ice blue. She looked down the length of the table to Horzt, who seemed interested in his wine goblet. They neither refuted nor acknowledged my statement. The small sprite leader seemed almost . . . embarrassed.

"Don't tell me," Wyatt said. "Your kind are pacifists?"

"I said only that we guard First Break," Amalie admitted. "I did not say we could defend it with physical violence. We will do everything in our power to prevent it from escalating to that, and the Earth Guardians keep us well protected, but they are fallible. Their access to the outside world is being slowly cut off, and our contact with the other races is limited."

"Maybe you should get out more," I said. "Look, I understand where you're coming from, I do, but I can't do what you want. I appreciate the soft bed and good food and opportunity to live out my last day in peace, but this is just a layover, and now it's time to get back to work. We need to figure out how to get to and kill Tovin."

"Elves are difficult to kill, even if you get close enough," Horzt said. "They're wily buggers and fast healers."

"I remarked earlier that I may require another favor of you, Evangeline," Amalie said.

I held up my free hand. "Sorry, but I'm not going to hide underground just to keep Tovin off my scent."

"That is not the favor I was going to request." Her nostrils flared, and her skin returned to its normal dusky blue shade. The gems in her skin seemed to have lost their glitter. "You can end this, Evangeline, before it has a chance to begin. There is no need to risk any other lives, save your own."

"We are so not back to this conversation." Anger flared in my cheeks and surged in my belly. "I am not going to slit my wrists in a preemptive strike against Tovin's plan. If we're captured again, sure, maybe then, but not right now. Not when we've got time and a chance to end this a different way."

I glanced at Wyatt, whose silent fury was focused on the floor. Whether his rage was directed at my wrist-slitting comment or at Amalie's continued suggestion of suicide, I didn't know. Probably both.

"You humans do foolish things for love," Amalie said, somewhat sadly. "I once envied your pure emotions and your ability to love, but no more. It makes you lose sight of that which is most important."

"From my perspective," Wyatt growled, "there isn't anything more important."

"Not even duty? Your duty to your people, Wyatt Truman, to ensuring their continued survival? Above other humans, you have been blessed with a Gift. Use it to do what is required."

"And what is that, exactly?"

Cobalt eyes burned, first at him, then at me. The air snapped and crackled. Amalie had power of her own, and it simmered around us like an impending lightning strike. "Protect the Break," she said. "Do not let Tovin succeed, no matter the cost. A life without love will be paradise compared to a world ravaged by a loosed Tainted One."

"We have to kill Tovin," I said.

"Evy—" Wyatt tried.

"Stop it," I said, ripping my hand away from his. I stepped sideways, several feet from him. "Look at this objectively, for Christ's sake, Wyatt. Killing you might stop his plan for now, but what's to stop him from trying again? Once a power mad dictator, always a power mad dictator, right? You don't stop a weed by chopping it off at ground level. It just comes back. You have to attack the root."

"Attacking the root sometimes kills the flowers around it," he said quietly.

"But doing nothing allows it to spread and choke out everything."

He held my stare for several long moments. A train wreck of emotions raced across his face. Neither one of us liked to give up; it wasn't in our nature. We fought until the very last breath. And sometimes you had to give that final breath (again) in order to achieve something worthwhile.

"Wyatt, it doesn't matter if you brought me back for selfish reasons or noble ones. What matters is that I'm here and I'm part of this fight, and I know I was always meant to be here. We are playing the parts chosen for us. In the end, all will be as it should be."

He closed his eyes and pursed his lips. Seconds ticked by, and then he opened them. "One step at a time," he said. "First we contact Rufus, see what he knows, and go from there. No second-guessing, no noble gestures of suicide."

I smiled; he didn't. "Agreed." Another thought struck me. "Amalie, did you have any luck with ways to capture an unhosted Tainted? In case it comes to that?" I doubted the use of such information, because using it hinged not only on Wyatt's possession, but also on his death while hosting the Tainted. Twin scenarios I'd do anything to prevent.

"None still live who witnessed the first defeat of the Tainted, so long ago," she replied, "nor do those who witnessed their reign."

"Not my question."

Her skin momentarily darkened with annoyance. "Human mages of that age had a spell they believed protected them from possession."

"Please tell me. . . ."

She plucked a small, drawstring pouch off the table. It was hidden behind a pitcher of wine, and I hadn't noticed it until now.

I caught it easily—the brown leather soft as silk and smelling vaguely of mustard—suddenly angry. "If you had magic that could protect us—?"

"You misunderstand," she said. "Their magic was flawed. A strong enough Tainted can possess anything it desires, under the correct conditions."

"So what the hell's this do?"

"How do I explain the intricacies of magic to such a young mind? The spell inside will act as a temporary binding agent, holding that which is the Tainted in a solid pattern for roughly six hours."

I eyed the pouch, said, "Cool," and meant it.

"If we even get the chance to use it," Wyatt said.

He was right. It required a sequence of events that would probably never take place, but I'd done this long enough to know the value of a Plan B. I tucked the pouch into my back pocket for safekeeping, doubtful I'd ever need to use it. "Thank you," I said.

Amalie smiled. "Of course."

"We'll need passage back to the surface."

"Very well. However, once you leave our cavern, you are no longer protected by our magic. You are wanted by many, with few friends left to assist you. My blessings to you both."

"Thank you."

Wyatt grunted something. I wasn't entirely convinced he would abide by our agreement and not do anything rash. Conversely, I wasn't convinced that I wouldn't do something rash to save him. He hated the idea of giving me up as much as I hated the idea of losing him, but save a miracle, nothing could change the fact that one of us would be dead in twenty hours.

Chapter Twenty-three

19:40

Leaving First Break would take longer than our arrival, but the mode of transportation proved far less messy. Horzt led us to a doorway at the very top level of the stone settlement. He hobbled along quickly for someone of his apparently advanced age, his cane clicking on the stone.

"Follow the left juncture until you come to a split," he said. "Then bear right and keep going until you see daylight."

"Where will we come out?" I asked.

"The northernmost outskirts of the city, in what you call Mercy's Lot. The Earth Guardians will be watching, though there's little they can do to interfere." His tiny eyes flickered back and forth between us. "You young ones shine like the sun itself. You have old souls, and I hope they'll soon find the peace they seek."

He reached out his small hand and I took it. Expecting a handshake, I instead received a hard object. I palmed it, and examined it. A sliver of crystal, the length and width of my index finger, its sides rounded and perfectly smooth and peaked to a single point.

"A gift," he said, "from the Apothi. It's not enough for the suffering I have caused you."

"You?" I asked.

Thin lips pursed. "Knowledge of healing magic is Gifted only to my people. Tovin took me for a fool once. It was I, Evangeline, who helped him add your regenerative powers to the resurrection spell. He said you needed the advantage in order to fulfill your destined task. I know now he meant only to prevent you from dying before his plan was enabled. I'm so sorry."

I stared at the little man in front of me, so small and yet reeking of power—a different sort than I felt while around Amalie, but still present. He was the only gnome I'd had a real conversation with, and I found myself hoping we'd meet again.

"You've still given me a gift," I said. "Your regenerative powers have helped me survive this long when I should have died multiple times. I do still have a task ahead of me. But thank you for this second gift." I slipped the crystal spike into the back pocket of my jeans. "May I ask—?"

"When the time comes, you'll know how to use it. Go on careful feet, and may the ancestors keep watch over your journey."

I didn't know if he meant his ancestors or mine, so I merely nodded and ducked through the doorway. Unlike the others, this door did not lead into a room, just a tiny space, no larger than a coat closet, with three potential corridors. I started down the farthest to the left, led by more glowing spheres, placed every ten feet and roughly the size of lemons. It was dim, but enough to see by.

Wyatt followed, keeping a distance of several feet. We didn't speak for the first leg of the journey. My thoughts consumed me. Training told me to never walk into a situation I couldn't walk out of again—exactly what we were doing. We had no plan of action beyond contacting Rufus, who may or may not be able to provide Triad assistance. If not, we were up shit creek without a boat, never mind a paddle. None of the other species would help us without proof.

Yet another great difference between humans and the majority of Dregs—a complete lack of, or simple inability to use, imagination. The very fact that Tovin had orchestrated our steps up until that very moment, that he had every piece in place to summon a Tainted into Wyatt's body, would not sway them. They judged on action, not intention. Until Wyatt was actually demon-possessed, our chances of persuading them to assist us were less than zero.

The Bloods were the only wild card in the deck. Istral and Isleen had already acted on their suspicions about the goblins, which meant they were on the list for proactive potential. But I hadn't spoken with Isleen long enough to know her intentions, and her people likely held me responsible for her death. Still, if we could contact the heads of the Blood Families—

"Penny for your thoughts?" Wyatt's voice bounced through the narrow tunnel.

"It'll cost you at least a dollar," I replied.

"Got change for a twenty?"

I smiled. The tunnel bent sharply to the right—

our assigned direction. I almost missed a left-bearing junction, its entrance less than half the height of the tunnel. The floor was rougher, the walls spotted with roots and loose dirt.

"Must be the split that Horzt mentioned," Wyatt said.

"Looks like. Where do you think it goes?"

"Somewhere else in the city."

"Duh." I crouched in front of the rougher entrance, intrigued by its age and the faint breeze trickling out.

"Evy, come on."

I looked at him over my shoulder and winked. "It's the path apparently never taken, Wyatt. Where's your sense of adventure?"

"Hiding behind my free will."

I wasn't serious about exploring the rocky tunnel and only meant to tease, but his comment startled me. I stood up, heat in my cheeks and hands on my hips, and managed to scrape both elbows on the rocky wall. Ignoring the pain, I glared at him. It was rendered somewhat ineffective by the near-dark.

"What the hell, Wyatt?"

"What? I don't think we should go exploring a strange tunnel when Horzt told us to go this way." He jacked his thumb down the right curve.

I didn't particularly want to, either, but that was no longer the point. "You used to trust my instincts."

"I still do, Evy. I just don't trust mine."

"Since when?"

"Since now. Since all of this."

"I still trust you."

"How the hell can you? Everything happening

now is because of me. You're in Hell again when you should be at peace, making choices no one should have to make, because I let someone manipulate my emotions. I did this to you. How can you trust me?"

Shadows darkened his face, making it nearly impossible to read. Only his eyes sparkled brightly. I reached out, but he shied away from my touch. The simple action, more than any of his words, hurt.

"Accepting responsibility and casting blame aren't the same things, Wyatt. I know why this is happening, and I know who's responsible, but that doesn't mean I blame you, because I don't. Blaming you won't change it, won't find a solution, and it won't make me feel better." I poked him hard in the chest. "And I will not let you use my imaginary blame as an excuse for your own self-hatred. You were made a fool of and there's no changing that, so get the hell over it."

"Get over it?" The dug walls vibrated under the force of his angry tenor. "You aren't the one being prepped to host an ancient demon, Evy."

"No, I was the one brought back from the dead to relay important information I don't fucking have." Another circular argument, getting us nowhere. "Can we please stop playing Who Got the Worse Deal? Our primary goal has not changed, and that is stopping Tovin before he can bring something across First Break. The rest of our personal bullshit can wait."

"For when, exactly? The day after tomorrow?"

"If I have anything to say about it, yes."

He frowned, glittering eyes searching my face. "Don't tell me you believe in a happy ending now?"

"I believe that the next twenty hours are still mine to do with as I wish. Am I prepared to die again to stop Tovin? Yes. Would I rather find a loophole that lets both of us live? Most definitely yes. Until I am faced with death or a demon, I'm going to keep looking for that loophole. How about you?"

His hand slipped around my waist, and I pressed close, my arms encircling his neck. I received his answer in that hug. It offered the promise of hope. And, in the face of impending death, a promise was better than nothing.

* * *

The tunnel narrowed after thirty more yards. We were reduced to crawling on our hands and knees over packed dirt and the occasional exposed root or rock. I cut my palms several times, but the pain was refreshing, almost invigorating. It marked our progress.

After what felt like a mile, the glowing orbs disappeared. Caught in pitch black, we slowed even more. I swept my hand in front of my face before each step, imagining all sorts of creepy things ahead— spiderwebs or worse. But beyond dirt and more dirt, the tunnel remained empty.

"Too bad you need both hands for crawling," I said. "We could use some sunshine in here."

"Next time, I'll be sure to ask the sprites for a flashlight."

"And a bottle of water. I think I've swallowed enough dust to shit a brick later."

Wyatt started laughing. The sound echoed, painfully loud, but it was contagious. I found myself giggling as I limped along on hands and knees, waiting for that elusive light at the end of the tunnel. The kind I was prepared to follow.

It appeared, as if out of nowhere, twenty minutes later. I blinked, sure I was hallucinating. But it seemed to get larger the closer I got, and I realized soon that I could see my hands in front of my eyes.

"Finally," I muttered.

"Go quietly, Evy. We don't know where we are."

I swallowed a "Duh," and plodded along. Every breath seemed too loud, every heartbeat like thunder. The tunnel never widened. The light remained steady, its yellow glare marred by a black pattern. Something was in front of the exit. A bush, maybe?

The refreshing coolness of moving air whispered across my cheeks. I inhaled deeply, savoring the sweetness. Anything was better than the damp, basement air we'd been breathing for two hours. Then I became aware of something else new. Music thrummed all around us, a steady rock beat that was all sound and no words. Dance music. Strange for that hour of the morning.

And it wasn't a bush that covered the tunnel exit; it was a wire-mesh grate. I scooted closer and squinted out. We were in a weed-filled ditch, half lit by the cloudy morning sun. The pulsing music came from somewhere behind—probably a nightclub that never closed. I smelled cigarettes and gasoline and exhaust. Definitely near the parking lot.

I pushed at the grate, and it gave without hesitation. I moved it only a few inches at first, then stopped and listened, but heard no voices or footsteps. I pushed it a bit more. Still nothing, so I pushed until I could slide through, into the dry ditch bed. I peeked out, expecting a red-feathered dart at any moment.

The ditch did, indeed, border a nightclub parking lot. T.D.'s was a popular joint, more because guys got a kick out of saying the name than for its class or dollar-per-beer value. The other two sides of the parking lot butted up against the bare brick sides of other buildings. The only street access was from an alley between T.D.'s and its neighbor. I knew the place.

"We're in the Lot," I said.

I scuttled farther down the ditch so Wyatt could climb out. The sky was overcast and threatening rain. Moisture hung in the air like a damp sweater. Once Wyatt was by my side, we made a mad dash for the nearest parked car.

"I think I know where we are," Wyatt whispered. "Rufus's apartment is six blocks from here."

"Won't they be watching it?"

"They who?"

"Any they. The Triads or the Halfies?"

"The Triads won't watch it; they won't see the need with Rufus in the hospital. If he wants to contact us, that's probably our best way."

"What about the Halfies?"

"They left him for dead."

"Doesn't answer my question."

He turned his head, winked. "Where's your sense of adventure?"

"Smart-ass. Let's go, then. If nothing else, we can clean up. You have dirt all over you."

"You were rolling in it, too, you know."

We hit the ground running and made it into the shadows of the alley without notice. Each step raised my anxiety level a fraction. This part of the city came alive after dark, but daytime saw just as much activity. Even the back alleys and side streets received heavy foot traffic—mostly teenagers keen on skipping school and young adults who couldn't afford college. We probably blended right in.

No one paid us any mind, not really. But every time someone's eyes acknowledged me, I cringed and expected attack. When you don't know who your friends are, anyone can be an enemy.

I counted the blocks. After six, Wyatt turned us toward a stinking, rotting alley that ran next to a seven-story brick apartment complex. One of the low-rent styles with one fire escape per floor, no balconies, and bars on all the windows. He found a back door with no outside knob. It was locked tight.

"It's hard to pick a lock without a lock to pick," I said.

"Want a lock?" He held his hand out, palm up, and closed his eyes. Sweat beaded on his forehead. The air above his hand swirled and crackled. He was summoning something. A lump of black metal materialized. He opened his eyes, face pale, and held up the object.

It was the door's locking mechanism.

"Have I said lately you have a pretty cool power?" I asked.

He grinned and pocketed the lock, then nudged the door. It creaked open without protest. He led me into the bowels of the tenement, through a dank hallway to service stairs that reeked of sweat and urine. I was careful to not touch anything on our ascent, horrified by the vile substances that seemed to coat the railings and walls. Rufus St. James wasn't well paid as a Handler, but certainly he could afford nicer digs than this dump.

Wyatt peeked out into the fifth floor, then waved me forward. Stark walls of ivory-painted cement blocks proved no homier than the outside of the building. The hallway was bare concrete, the doors a heavy, gray metal. A television blasted a laugh track as we passed one door. Several more apartments went by until he stopped in front of 512.

"You going to summon a key, too?" I whispered.

Turned out we didn't need one. The apartment door swung open, and we found ourselves staring down the barrel of a shotgun. Across the length of it, past the sight and the arm holding it at shoulder level, I recognized the brown hair and deadly eyes.

"Look what I caught," said Nadia, the last surviving member of Rufus's Triad.

Wyatt groaned. "God—"

"—dammit," I finished.

Chapter Twenty-four

16:05

The standoff lasted the space of a breath, then Nadia lowered the shotgun. Her coffee-colored eyes darted to the hall behind us, searching. She stepped back and cocked her head. "He is waiting for you," she said.

"Who is?" I asked.

"Rufus, idiot." Her disdain was palpable. She pointed the muzzle of her weapon toward the interior of the apartment. "Go on, then."

Not quite the welcome of Kings, but she didn't shoot us on the spot. I walked down a short entry hall that smelled like tomato soup and bleach—two cloying and somewhat nauseating odors. The hall opened into a surprisingly spacious living room/kitchen combo. Plain roman shades covered both windows in the living space, and the sofa had been pushed up against the shared wall. Light flared down from a single overhead fixture.

Rufus lounged in a wheelchair parked next to a small wooden side table. His left shoulder was in a sling. Bloodstained bandages poked out beneath his unbuttoned shirt. He was pale, with dark circles lining both eyes, and he was sweating like a junkie long overdue for his next score.

"Jesus, Rufus," Wyatt said. He scooted past me and approached his old friend. "Why aren't you in the hospital?"

"Not safe," he replied, slurring his words. Nadia had him hopped up on something. "Halfies followed me to finish the job."

Nadia swooped past me and knelt next to Rufus, shotgun across her lap, protecting her Handler. She continued to glare at me with open suspicion, so I glared right back. She had nothing to fear from me unless she got in my way.

"He insisted we come here," Nadia said, her faint accent sharpening her S's and R's. "I told him it was not safe, but he is stubborn. He said you would know to find him here, so here he must stay."

"And I was right," Rufus said. "I'm sorry I didn't believe you, Truman. I should have helped you sooner."

"I didn't give you much reason to trust me, pal," Wyatt said. "But at least I didn't shit on my friends for nothing. We finally got the answers we wanted, and none of them are good."

"About the alliance?"

"More like a conspiracy," I said.

Wyatt and I took turns narrating the events of the last twenty-four hours, right up through Horzt leading us out of First Break, and Wyatt ended with our arrival at their doorstep.

Rufus had gone impossibly paler during our description of Tovin's ultimate plan for Wyatt's free will.

His breathing seemed erratic, almost panicked. Nadia remained a sphinx, her internal thoughts impossible to guess by her body language. I might as well have told her the grocery store had a half-price special on laundry detergent, for all of the interest she displayed.

"That's unbelievable," Rufus said after a brief pause. "I mean, I knew it had to be something big, but from the elf? I never would have guessed."

"He's playing everyone," Wyatt said. "Putting up a concerned front about a possible alliance that was all bullshit. He's been using the Halfies, and the goblins, too. The Bloods are on to him, but the Families won't act without proof. No one will."

"Are we not overthinking this?" Nadia asked. Her chilly voice sparked goose bumps across my skin. "Save lying, Tovin has committed no real crime. All we need do is void your contract. Simple, no?"

Wyatt glared at her with unmasked fury. "No, not so simple, Nadia. And if you even contemplate putting buckshot into either one of us, I'll summon your heart right out of your chest."

Her eyes widened to comical proportions. The threat worked; she backed off. Lucky for us she didn't know Wyatt couldn't summon living tissue.

"We need to find Tovin," I said, "but he could be anywhere in the city, and we don't exactly have time for a door-to-door."

"You can always have a go at the babbler," Rufus said.

I blinked. "The what?"

"The babbler in the next room." He waved his right hand at a door to the left of the kitchen. "The Halfie who tracked me to the hospital. Nadia brought him with us, but he's pretty useless. Must be newly turned, because it didn't take well. He's losing it."

"Lost it," Nadia said.

One in five humans infected by a Blood doesn't take to the change. Most adapt to their new cravings and lifestyle and limitations and powers, but some don't. They can't quite grasp that life will never be the same, and often lose their tenuous grip on reality in a mighty scary fashion. I'd cleaned up after many feral Halfies who turned their insanity against helpless innocents.

Rufus wiped his hand across his chin. "Keeps on muttering about his lost goblet, or some such nonsense. Can't get anything else out of him."

"Lost goblet?" Wyatt asked. "You sure know how to pick useless hostages. But I'm surprised that just one Halfie came after you. They tend to travel in packs."

"Not if one of them's gone feral," I said. "Usually they kill them outright, to prevent them from weakening the group."

"You want a go at him?" Rufus asked. "See if you can get something else out of him besides 'goblet'?"

"Chalice," Nadia said. "He said chalice, not goblet."

My lips parted, and every muscle in my face went slack. Blood rushed down and set my heart pumping hard and fast. "Chalice." The word slipped from my lips without thought.

"What is wrong with her?" Nadia asked.

Wyatt's hand looped around my wrist. I forced my head to turn. Concern lined his face. I stood up and tore my hand away from his. He matched my steps to the bedroom door. I spun around and put a hand out that nearly clipped him in the jaw.

"Stay," I snapped. "I'm not going to freak out. I'm going to talk to him. See if I can help him find his missing chalice, and maybe get a few answers."

I opened the door, slipped inside, and closed it before Wyatt could drum up a good retort. I didn't need him talking me out of it or following me inside. Help appreciated, but not necessary.

The light was off. I palmed the wall until my fingers found a switch. Harsh yellow light filled the room, courtesy of a garish floor lamp, all bulb and no shade. The bed was pushed to the far wall against a mirrored closet door. A wooden dining chair lay on its side, a naked body strapped to it with a queer tangle of shoelaces and ripped sheets.

Covered in bruises and dried blood, his skin red and rashed wherever it touched the chair, Alex Forrester was easy to recognize. I had never expected to see him again, much less tied up, sporting a pair of gleaming fangs, and babbling to himself. Spittle ran down his chin and had pooled on the scuffed wood floor. Everywhere, he was surrounded by unfinished wood—one of the greatest irritants to vampires and their kin.

I crouched in front of him, but he didn't seem to notice. His eyes remained wide, staring straight through me.

"Alex? Can you hear me?" Not even a twitch. "I'm going to get you sitting upright, okay? Don't, you know, bite me or anything."

He didn't react to the change in elevation. I expected something during the fiasco, but amid my groaning and straining, he made no noise. Nothing. His lips continued to move, but no sound came out.

Old wounds on his arms and legs were swollen and infected from contact with the chair, some weeping and others necrotic. All looked extremely painful.

I touched his shoulder, and he blinked. Nothing else. "Alex, it's Chalice," I said.

He stopped muttering. He looked up at me, really saw me. Wonder and awe softened his features and widened his eyes.

"You're dead," he said. "Am I in Hell? Am I finally dead, too?"

"Almost, Alex." I inhaled, held it, let the oxygen strengthen me. It wasn't really Alex. He had died yesterday. This was a shell that had information I needed; I just had to manipulate it out of him. "You're in a place where you can still do some good before you pass on. I can help you."

His face crumpled. "I should have known you were depressed. I should have seen the signs. It's my fault you died."

"I killed myself, Alex. It's no one's fault but mine."

"Friends don't let friends commit suicide."

Heartbreaking though it was, the conversation wasn't helping us. "Do you remember my friend Evy? You gave her a ride once, did her a favor?"

He pursed chapped lips. Shook his head.

"She looks kind of like me. She was looking for someone she loved. You helped her find him, but you got hurt. That's why you're here."

"You do look like her, Chal. It's creepy. Is she dead, too?"

"No, but she could die if we don't help her."

He chewed on his lower lip. His fangs punctured the skin and drew blood. Glittering eyes flitted to the bedroom door, to the ceiling, the covered window. "They're in the walls," he said.

I tensed, listened hard, but heard nothing save the occasional creaking floorboard from the living room. I imagined Wyatt standing there with his ear pressed to the door, straining to hear every word.

"Who's in the walls?" I asked.

"Them. You know."

"I don't know, Alex. Who are they?"

"Millions of them, crawling through me, Chal. Making me want to hurt people. Making me want blood, but I don't want blood. Can I please just go? I want it to stop."

The vampire infection; that's what he saw in the walls. The parasite that turns them into monsters. He was trying to fight those instincts, to reclaim his body again by disassociating. I hadn't the heart to tell him it was a losing battle.

"You can go soon, I promise, but I need you to help me first. Just answer a few questions, okay?"

His chin trembled. Tears filled his eyes and spilled down both cheeks in twin streams. He pursed his lips and shook his head. "They're everywhere, Chal. Make them go away. Make it stop."

My heart went out to him. I wanted to end his suffering. I just couldn't. He knew something, and big or little, I had to know what it was. When I didn't reply, he started to cry in earnest. I'd never seen that sort of utter terror in the face of a grown man. Strike that—I'd seen it once before, as I lay dying the first time.

A sharp knock on the door stole my attention. I opened it a crack, revealing half of Wyatt's face.

"You want to put a pause on that for a minute?" he asked, "The package is here."

"What package?"

"The one I asked the gremlins to assemble before they wiped out all hard traces of Chalice Frost."

I perked up. That was certainly worth a short recess. I slipped through the door, back into the living room, and pulled it shut behind me. In his hands, Wyatt clutched a bulging legal folder, held together by two large rubber bands. "Why did they bring it here?" I asked.

"It's where I told them to bring it," he said, as though it was the most obvious question in the world.

"Duh, genius, but why here?"

Wyatt had the good sense to adopt a hint of chagrin. "I thought I'd still have Rufus in custody when we swung by to collect it."

Across the room Rufus grunted. Nadia had disappeared somewhere—a blessing I wasn't about to ponder. She gave me the willies. I snatched the bundled folder from Wyatt and ripped off the rubber bands. Dozens of newspaper clippings tumbled to the floor and scattered, along with photographs and a few slips of printed paper.

I dropped the remaining contents of the folder on the dining table, freeing my hands to collect the information.

"A little eager?" Wyatt asked.

My mature response was to stick my tongue out at him. I snagged a column dated twenty-seven years ago. The headline stopped me short: "Woman Gives Birth in Mall." I scanned the article and sucked in a breath.

"What is it, Evy?"

" 'Six people trapped in the women's restroom at Capital City Mall soon became seven,' " I read, " 'when one woman unexpectedly went into labor. Part of the ceiling outside the restroom collapsed, authorities say, making it impossible for the women to exit for several hours. During that time, Lori Frost, eight months pregnant, went into preterm labor. Charlene Williams, an off-duty trauma nurse, helped Frost deliver the baby without complications. Upon rescue, both mother and daughter were rushed to St. Eustachius Hospital, where they are listed in good condition.

" 'The Frosts were not available for comment, but Ms. Williams described the experience as "the easiest birth of my life. Though that's not saying much, since I work in the Emergency Room." ' "

I looked up, mouth agape. "That's the same place Isleen took me to for that memory ritual. I was born . . . Chalice, I mean, she was born on a magical hot spot. Holy shit, Wyatt."

He plucked the article and read it for himself. His eyes grew wider with each sentence, letting the full meaning settle into his brain. Hot spots existed all over the city. Many were so faint they couldn't be detected. A few, like the vampire Sanctuary, were unmistakable and made their presence felt. It wasn't the coincidence of the location that scared me—it was the implication that Chalice had been born above a hot spot, just like Wyatt and the handful of other human beings considered Gifted. It meant she (and in turn, I) was Gifted.

"Is that possible?" Rufus asked.

"Not only possible, but it solves the last mystery," I said. "It's why I came back in Chalice's body, instead of where I was supposed to. My resurrection was made possible by Tovin's connection to the Break, so I was attracted to a body that also had that connection."

"Do you have the birthmark?" Wyatt asked.

"How the hell should I know?"

"You've been in that body for two days."

I stood up and tossed the rest of the gathered clippings onto the table, annoyed by his silly argument. "Sorry I haven't penciled in time to stare at my own ass, Wyatt."

"Drop your pants."

"Now's not really the time. . . ."

"Evy."

Okay, wrong time to joke. He was dead serious. Giving little thought to my audience across the room, I tugged the button and unzipped the fly, then pushed the dirty jeans down to my ankles. I bent at the waist and placed my palms flat on the table. The pose was both submissive and suggestive, but I felt no thrill—only slight apprehension of what he might find.

Wyatt hooked a finger into the waistband of my panties and pulled them down. Cool air caressed my exposed skin. I shivered. Halfway down, he stopped. Pulled back. I yanked my pants up, my suspicions confirmed by his silence.

"I can't believe we never guessed it before," he said after a moment's pause.

"We still don't know what I can do," I said, "or if I can even access Chalice's Gift."

"You said you felt the power of the Break when we were down with the Fair Ones, right?"

"Yeah, and I've felt it ever since my rebirth, but I just thought it was a side effect. It never occurred to me it was something more."

"You're already tapped into the Break, Evy. Now we just need to find out what you can do with the tap. Knowing the well is down there doesn't help if you don't have a shovel to dig to it."

"But how are we supposed to do that?"

He held up a handful of Chalice's file. "Keep looking. There has to be something here."

We sifted for several minutes, through school records and doctors' notes and copies of report cards. I found more newspaper clippings. "Toddler Missing; Found in Toy Store" caught my eye.

"Listen to this," I said, skimming the article for salient details. "When she was three years old, Chalice disappeared from a sandbox where three other kids were playing. No one reported seeing her get up on her own, or anyone take her. She was discovered a few hours later by police, in the stuffed animal section of a local toy store ten blocks from the park. The owner didn't see her come in with anyone, and security cameras showed no front door entry." I scanned the rest. "It was a shop that the mother frequented. She said Chalice loved the big stuffed lions and tigers."

"There are more like that," Wyatt said. He held up something with a Child Welfare stamp on it. "She also disappeared from her preschool classroom six times over a four-month time period. Same as before, with no one seeing her get up and leave, and no one taking her. She was always found outside on the playground, away from the other kids."

Our eyes met over our individual sheets of paper.

He was thinking the same as me, but I hesitated to say it. It seemed impossible, given what we knew of the Gifted and their limitations. But not so impossible when you factor in a return from the dead.

"Is it even possible?" I asked.

"Teleportation?"

"Yeah."

"Theoretically, yes. Practically, I have no idea."

"How do we test something like this?"

"Concentration?"

I balled up the article and threw it at his head. It bounced harmlessly to the floor. He didn't react, seeming lost in thought. I stared at the pile of records, hoping to make sense of everything now swirling dangerously through my head. I pulled out a slim folder sporting the seal of a public school district more than a hundred miles away. High school records.

"Alex told me she moved back to the city two years ago," I said. "He said she was fine for the first few months, and then gradually she started getting depressed. It wasn't an overnight thing, so being back here affected her negatively. She obviously grew up elsewhere. Maybe her parents moved away because of the disappearances and, without that localized connection to the Break—"

"She lost her Gift," Wyatt finished. "Which starts coming back when she returns to the source, only if she doesn't remember it from childhood, or have any idea how to tap into the Break—"

"She ends up wallowing in depression without knowing why. It gets so bad she kills herself."

"Then you find her body, because even though she's dead, it's still a tap into the Break."

"Do you think that's how the Halfies tracked us to the mall? Someone gave them information on Chalice and they had the place watched?"

"Possible, but not likely. I had the gremlins start wiping her out a day before that happened."

"Right, okay." I turned, marched back to the bedroom door.

"Where are you going?"

"I'm not done talking to Alex. Keep sifting; see what else you can find that might help us."

"We need to talk about this teleportation thing."

"We will, when I'm done."

I slipped back inside before he could argue, and locked the door. No more interruptions.

Alex hadn't moved. Tears had left stains on his pale cheeks. His cut lip left a red smear on his chin. Clear snot dripped from his nose. He didn't look like a dangerous, half-Blood traitor, just a scared young man without a friend in the world.

I imagined a similar look on Chalice's face near the end. Completely at odds with herself, feeling alienated and uncertain as to why. So depressed that she saw no way out of the well of pain she'd fallen into. I found no common ground with that sort of emotional agony and no sympathy for the choice she'd made— only commiseration in feeling trapped inside a body that didn't seem like her own.

"Alex?" I asked. "It's Chalice."

He blinked, didn't look at me.

"I'm sorry I left, but I still need to talk to you."

"Are you going to set me free now?"

"Soon, but first, do you know a man named Tovin?"

"Tovin's not a man," Alex said, his demeanor

changing instantly. Like I'd flipped a switch with a single word. His face hardened, mouth drawn in a tight line. Every scrap of misery was gone. "Stay away from him, Chal."

"Tovin wants to hurt someone I care about, and I need to stop him. I have to find him first, though. Do you know where he is?"

"I've only heard things. The others, they talked about him. He's like the boogeyman. He's powerful."

"I need to find him, Alex." I cupped his cheeks in my hands, amazed at how cold his skin was. Cold and clammy and rough. "Where is he?"

He held my steady gaze, his tinged with disgust. "Do you promise to let me go?"

Across the room, on top of an antique dresser, I spotted a discarded gun belt. Several boxes of ammunition were laid out on top of it. Nadia had certainly brought along an arsenal. Good news for us, since I had no weapon on me, save Horzt's crystal shard. I eyed the gun and hoped one of those boxes held what I needed.

"I promise, Alex."

"The old mill."

"What old mill?"

"They kept talking about an old mill, said that's where he was. The old mill. That's what they said, Chal. Does that help?"

I searched my memory, thinking about the city's waterfront properties. No mills came to mind.

"I told you where he is," Alex wailed. Tears pooled in his eyes. Bright spots of color flamed in his cheeks, standing out from his pallor. Blood dripped from his cut lip to his chin and dappled his shirt.

"The old mill," I said.

"Let me go."

I stood up and walked to the dresser. Each step echoed like thunder. I found the box of bullets labeled "A.C." and fed two of them into the gun's chamber. Anticoagulant rounds were hard to come by outside of the Triads. I walked to the back of Alex's chair and held up the gun. His shoulders shook. My finger twitched.

"I'm sorry, Alex," I said.

"Does dying hurt?"

My eyes tingled. I bit the insides of my cheeks, tried to ignore the heartache in his voice and keep focused. Alex was already dead; this wasn't Alex. I was stopping a monster, putting down a rabid dog. Nothing more, nothing less. Lie to him, shoot him, and get it over with.

"Dying didn't hurt the first time," I said. "It's all the shit leading up to it that's painful."

He bowed his head. I pressed the muzzle to the back of his neck. Clean shot, perfect kill, even for a Blood. My finger twitched. I couldn't pull it. I couldn't rationalize the kill.

"Do it, Chal."

I closed my eyes.

"Let me go."

I couldn't breathe.

"Save me."

My finger squeezed. The gun roared. I screamed.

Chapter Twenty-five

"This is useless," Nadia said, fingers tapping away at the keyboard of a laptop. "There are no mills in this city. No paper mills, no flour mills, not even a puppy mill. He lied to you."

"Check anyway," I snapped.

I had taken refuge in Rufus's kitchen with cling peaches and a can opener while Nadia and Wyatt made themselves useful by looking into our only clue. The teeth of the opener cut an uneven path around the edge of the can. Thick syrup pooled. My stomach rumbled. Rufus really needed to shop more often.

Nadia shot me a glare over the edge of the laptop, which I promptly matched. With a brief nostril flare, she ducked her head. Wyatt stood behind her at the dining table, arms crossed over his chest, reading over her shoulder.

The file on Chalice had revealed nothing else useful in determining the actual existence of a teleportation Gift. She had a list of child psychology evaluations as long as my arm, as well as a handful during her teen years. And medical records for two E.R. visits in high school—drug overdoses that seemed more teen-related than Gift-related. It only confirmed that she had been a lonely, troubled woman long before Alex met her.

"The old mill," Wyatt said, uttering the words for the tenth time since I'd relayed them. "Could it be a code for something else?"

I rolled my eyes. "Sure, maybe Tovin's location is hidden in the text of the Hardy Boys' *The Secret of the Old Mill*."

"I'm serious."

"Me, too. He said 'old mill,' okay?" I tossed the serrated can lid into the sink and plucked a fork out of the dish drainer. The peaches were warm and too sweet, but I ate them anyway.

"Nothing," Nadia said. "No mills within city limits."

"Did you search the suburbs? The mountains north of the city?"

She grunted and typed something else. I chewed on a peach, somewhat unnerved by the faint metallic taste of the fruit. Oh well. If Tovin didn't kill me first, then botulism would.

"There's nothing relevant there, Evy," Wyatt said, after gazing at another page on the computer screen. "Nadia, try searching the maps for street names or buildings."

"How about company logos?" I said.

"One moment, please," Nadia said.

Fingers flew. The laptop buzzed. She and Wyatt leaned closer. The blue light of the monitor reflected in their eyes. I slurped down another peach. On the other side of the room, Rufus continued to sit quietly in his wheelchair. Patient, watching, not participating. It was downright spooky.

The rest of Rufus's apartment was as spartan as a motel room. I found myself looking around for personal artifacts. Photographs or paperweights, even an old take-out bag that had missed the trash can. Something to prove a human being had lived here for a reasonable amount of time. He chose to live in a crappy part of town, but didn't even make an effort to nest?

Then again, Wyatt lived in efficiency apartments and motel rooms rented by the week. Maybe all Handlers had nomadic tendencies.

My attention strayed to a simple white wall clock next to the ivory refrigerator. It was after two o'clock. Fourteen hours until smack-down, and we were still chasing our tails. Not even in the amusing-to-passersby way, just in the we're-pathetic-and-have-no-leads kind of way.

"Except for a farmers' open-air market that runs every Saturday morning from nine to twelve," Nadia said, "we have nothing. No Old Mill Road, no symbology that makes sense. Tovin cannot logically be hiding in any of these places." She quirked an eyebrow at me. "Perhaps you were too fast to execute the prisoner."

"He didn't lie," I said. The peach can joined its lid, making a mighty clatter as it hit the stained sink.

"He is a half-Blood. They all lie. You were a fool to believe him."

"I knew him before he turned, you Russian bitch. The change wasn't taking; he was losing it. I was talking to Alex at the end, not the Blood, I'm sure of it, so back the hell off."

She started to stand, fists balled by her sides.

"Will you two quit?" Wyatt said. "The bickering might be fun for you, but it's not helping." He put one hand on either shoulder and pushed Nadia back into the chair. She didn't fight him.

I felt a strange twinge of jealousy at the manner in which he was touching her. Cursing myself a fool, I focused on the clue at hand and not on my hatred of Nadia. Our current need to join forces didn't erase the fact that she'd once hunted me and been perfectly willing to kill me.

If folks thought regular bounty hunters had it hard, they should try serving warrants on goblins for a living. We made the most hard-core dog hunters look like pussycats.

"Olsmill," Rufus said. It was his first contribution to our conversation in over thirty minutes. He still stared at the floor, a newfound alertness in his pale features. His eyes moved back and forth as if reading. Searching for an elusive memory.

We waited, a trio of blank stares.

"Is there more to that, or are we supposed to guess?" I asked.

"North of the city," he said, strength in his voice. He looked up, right at me. "The Olsmill Nature Preserve closed down twenty years ago. The owners went bankrupt after their animals kept dying. No disease or apparent cause; they just up and died."

An imaginary lightbulb went off in my brain. I bounced off the counter. "I know where that is," I said. "It's three miles out, along the Anjean. I've never been up to it, but I've been past the gate. If it's the right direction, it can't be very far from the location of First Break."

"Which makes sense," Wyatt said, excitement creeping in his voice. "The energy output of both First Break and all of the Light Ones living down there probably affected the animals and their heart rhythms."

"Are the buildings still there?"

"I have no idea, but if they are, it's a perfect hiding place."

"Not to mention near a magical doorway."

"You do realize," Nadia said, "that all of this could be a trick? To send in someone you trust to lure you to a place above this Break, from which Tovin intends to summon this Tainted creature? Bravo for walking right into his trap. Again."

Wyatt intercepted me before I could punch her. He herded me to the other side of the kitchen, away from her smirk and annoyingly angular face. He grabbed my chin with one hand and held me still. I stared right back.

"Don't let her bait you," he said. "She's in pain, Evy, just like you were."

I yanked my chin out of his grasp. "Was I that much of a bitch?"

"Aren't you always?"

"Very funny, Truman."

"I know you are, but what am I?"

"A pain in the ass."

"Sorry to interrupt the happy time," Nadia said, "but we have not yet decided upon a plan of action."

"You mean, do we play right into Tovin's hands again and head up to the nature preserve, or do we stand around and insult each other some more?" I asked.

She nodded.

"We'll need help," I said. "I'd feel better going up there with some Triad backup, especially if Tovin's got a herd of Halfies guarding the place. The three of us won't be much good against more than a dozen."

Nadia snorted. "Three? You assume a lot."

"You're telling me you don't want to kick a whole lot of Halfie ass on behalf of Tully and Wormer?" Her silence confirmed the opposite, so I switched my attention to Rufus. "How about that backup?"

"Kismet owes me a favor," Rufus replied. "She can probably get Baylor's team on board, if I ask nicely. Maybe Willemy, too, if he's forgiven me for Turner Street."

"Do I even want to know?" Wyatt asked.

"Nope."

"That's good backup," I said. "Weapons?"

"Standard. I've got a stash. Hall closet, black trunk."

To Nadia: "Map?"

She returned to the computer and typed. I passed Wyatt to stand behind her. She was in a great position for me to wring her neck. I quashed the urge. Wyatt was right. I'd been in her shoes, and had no business judging her anger.

The computer displayed a map of the forest north of the city. Nadia dragged the mouse to the location of the defunct nature preserve. Cherrydale Road wound along the banks of the Anjean, passed the turnoff for the preserve, and continued deep into the mountains.

"There should be a gas station here," I said, pointing to a spot where a secondary road branched off from Cherrydale, half a mile from our destination. "You and the others will meet us there at three A.M., fully armed and assault ready."

"Wait, who's you and who's us?" Wyatt asked.

"Us is you and me. We're leaving early to go on recon. No sense in planning a blind assault on an unknown compound."

"You are both wanted targets. Is this wise?" Nadia asked.

"Probably not, but I don't want us separated. As long as we know what's going on with the other person, we can control the game." And I could keep Wyatt from acting on his damned guilt.

"Three o'clock is cutting it close," Wyatt said.

"We need to rest a little. I don't know about you, but I haven't slept much in the last few days."

"And we still need some time to figure out your Gift. Teleportation could be pretty damned useful, you know."

"If we can find the trigger."

"I have an idea on that. Let's go up to the roof."

I tilted my chin. He quirked an eyebrow.

"Fine." Over my shoulder to Rufus, I said, "Make the calls. We'll be back in a bit."

*   *   *

It took several hard shoves to open the roof access door. Rusty hinges squealed angrily. We only managed to move it three feet before it stuck on the tarred surface.

The city hummed all around us. Car engines and

the occasional bass line drifted up from the streets below. A city that never seemed to sleep, no matter day
or night—consequences of a population that preferred
coming out after sundown.

I followed Wyatt across the spongy surface. It was
the strangest roof I'd ever walked on, and I imagined it
leaked like a son of a bitch during storms. "So what's
the trigger?"

"You tell me, Evy."

I rolled my eyes. "You said you knew."

"I have the same pieces as you. Just put them together."

He was going all Sphinx-like Handler on me
again. I hated that. Straight answers were simpler, but
he liked proving his point. Challenging me to do the
work myself.

"She was in the sandbox with other kids," I said,
thinking back over the information I'd read. "Probably
not having fun. She wanted to go to the toy store and
see her favorite animals. It was a place she liked and
felt safe. She didn't like her preschool, so she went out
to the playground. She was shy, an introvert."

"By nature, shy people are more likely to be
what?"

I worked the question over in my mind until the
answer came screaming at me. "She was lonely. You
think loneliness is the trigger?"

"It's a logical trigger."

"Is yours logical?"

"Not really."

"What is it?"

"Also not telling."

"Come on, Wyatt, you need to teach me how to

do this. I can't just drum up loneliness and hope I land ten feet away. What if I reappear in between walls? That could hurt."

He heaved a sigh dramatic enough to make a professional actor proud. "It's arrogance, okay? Haughty, highbrow arrogance at its worst."

My lips twitched. "So what? You forget to put your arrogance away when you're done with it?"

His eyebrows scrunched. He opened his mouth to retort. I stuck my tongue out—a gesture guaranteed to force a smile. It worked.

A shadow passed my peripheral vision—a large bird shape that was gone before I turned my head. Too big for a pigeon, but what else? I thought of Danika and was struck by a sudden pang of sadness.

"Evy?"

"Yeah?" Had he been talking?

"Do you feel the Break right now? You said it felt tingly, like static."

I closed my eyes, took a deep breath, exhaled. It was there, but more distant than in First Break. The faintest hint of static just below the surface. I latched on to the buzz and urged it closer. Asked it to burn just a little brighter.

It ignored me and remained far away, the palest notion of power. "It's there," I said. "Barely, but it's there."

"Use your trigger to bring it forward. Concentrate on feelings of loneliness."

"Uh-huh." Hard to feel lonely when he was crowding me. He wouldn't always be there, though. At the end of this day, one of us (or both) would be dead, forever parted. Alone.

Tears stung my eyes. Nostrils flared. Instinct told me to push those thoughts away and stay positive, but I needed that emotion. Needed to feel the loneliness. I held on, trying to imagine living without Wyatt. Spending the next five or ten or thirty years without him in my life. Without his voice in my head.

The faint buzz crashed on top of me like a waterfall, zinging through from head to toes and back out again. The hair on my arms tingled. My skin flushed, at once hot and cold. Every single cell in my body seemed to vibrate, threatened to fly apart at any moment and scatter me to the four winds.

"I feel it," I said, tears spilling down my cheeks. "I've tapped in, Wyatt."

"Picture the other side of the roof, Evy. Just a few feet. Let the Break take you there."

I thought of a spot ten feet away, next to the edge. The tar seemed thinner there, ready to wear through at any moment and leak into the cheap apartment below. My body vibrated. The oddest sensation of movement was punctuated by a blinding headache. I wobbled, then toppled sideways when my hands found no traction.

Something slammed into me. I fell a short distance and hit the soft tar roof with a body on top of me. My eyes snapped open. Wyatt stared down, his eyes wide and fearful, mouth open and panting. The pain in my head subsided to a dull ache and settled between my eyes.

"What happened?" I asked.

"It worked. You overshot a little, though."

We had landed on the soft tar roof, arms nearly touching the ledge. Ten inches to the left, and I'd have missed completely. My stomach knotted. "Holy shit, I almost killed myself."

"We just need to practice."

"Easy for you to say."

He settled in, making no effort to get off me. I pushed my hips against his. He grunted and pushed right back, teasing. Jerk.

"You going to get off me?" I asked.

"You can get out from beneath me."

Drumming up the loneliness took longer the second time, due in no small part to Wyatt. It was difficult to imagine being without him when he was on top of me, seriously affecting my concentration.

I thought about our time together in Amalie's home. What if that had been our last opportunity to be together? Annoyance melted into sadness. I latched on and turned it until the tap opened. The static poured through me again.

Wyatt's face faded. The ache increased. My vision blurred into a mass of swirling colors and unfocused shapes. I was moving again, but realized too late I hadn't focused on a destination.

The ache flared into a sharp spike of agony that threaded through my skull from top to bottom. I shrieked. Movement stopped. I fell and hit a cool, slick surface and curled up into a little ball. The headache didn't relent. Pain speared through me. Bright spots of color burst in my eyes.

It dulled in time and awareness returned. Familiar smells and voices. A hand on my shoulder, another on the small of my back, rubbing in gentle circles. I focused on those movements, let them calm my nerves and frazzled brain, then cracked one eye open.

The kitchen in Rufus's apartment. Lucky transport. Wyatt was behind me, whispering soft words of support. And apology. I turned my head. Each muscle in my neck protested. Wonder and pride shined in his face.

"That was impressive," he said.

"Hurt like hell," I replied.

"Side effects are a bitch."

I groaned an affirmation. "How'd you know I'd end up here?"

"I didn't. When you didn't reappear, I panicked and started looking. Nadia found me in the stairwell." His hands continued to massage my back and shoulders. "But on the plus side, we know you can move through solid objects."

"Yeah, and it feels like I'm being ripped apart."

"Want to practice some more?"

"Fuck you, Truman. I need aspirin and a nap."

He scooped me up into his arms, and I let him. The blinding headache had turned to a debilitating throb. My stomach swirled and threatened to empty. I imagined it was some sort of magic-induced migraine. Only time would fade the pain enough to let me think properly. Until then, I simply allowed Wyatt to settle me on the sofa, tuck a blanket around my shoulders, and watch over me while I tossed on the edge of agonized slumber.

*   *   *

The nap lasted longer than I'd planned—the bits of sunlight that had peeked through Rufus's dark curtains were gone—but I woke refreshed. The ache still lingered on the very edge of my senses, no longer strong enough to affect me. I focused on the room and the soft hum of nearby voices.

Wyatt, Nadia, and Rufus were gathered around the dining table. I couldn't hear the conversation, but Rufus had his cellular phone out and open. The apartment was otherwise quiet, almost serene.

"What time is it?" I asked.

Wyatt's head snapped in my direction. He grinned. "Almost eleven at night, Sleeping Beauty. We need to go, if we're going to manage any recon before reinforcements arrive."

"They're coming?"

Rufus angled his wheelchair to face me. "I called in a few favors. Three o'clock at the gas station, like you said. They trust me enough to trust you."

"Great." I sat up and swung my legs over the side of the sofa. Dizziness blacked out my vision for a short span, but I covered with a sunny smile. "You said something earlier about weapons?"

As promised, the hall closet hid a large black trunk. Nadia produced a key to the arsenal. Wyatt and I delved inside without waiting for permission. I strapped a pair of serrated knives to my ankles; their weight was familiar and comforting. Always more secure with guns, Wyatt slipped into a pair of shoulder holsters and checked the ammo on two modified Glocks. I tucked a similar gun into the back waistband of my jeans. We found six clips of anticoagulant rounds, took two each, and gave the other two to Nadia.

Wyatt opened a small metal case. "The hell, Rufus?" he said. "Where did you get grenades?"

"Took them from a Halfie nest once. Be careful, they're pretty old," Rufus replied.

"Nice." Wyatt closed the lid and put it back into the trunk.

I plucked two more clips of fragmenting rounds. The back pockets of my jeans bulged with the ammunition, creating a false sense of security. In the past, having those weapons made me feel powerful, invincible. Knowing I wasn't invincible anymore—and in fact, likely to die again very soon—made me feel like a fake. I was putting on a good show for Wyatt, even though we both saw the only real outcome of today's planned assault.

"We're going to need a car," I said.

"So will we," Nadia said. "We have ours. Good luck with yours."

Helpful as always.

Wyatt pulled a light jacket off a coat hanger and slipped it on, effectively hiding his weapons. He walked over to Rufus, offered his hand, and tilted his head. Rufus looked first at the offered hand, then at Wyatt. The two men shared something in that look—silent encouragement, a parting of ways, maybe even an apology—and shook.

"See you on the flip side, man," Rufus said.

"Yeah, you too," Wyatt replied.

We left as cautiously as we'd entered and exited through the rear door of the building, back into the stink of the alley. It had cooled off significantly, enough for me to wish I'd borrowed a jacket, too. We headed for the street end of the alley.

"We'll go a few streets over," Wyatt whispered, "then look for something we can drive."

"You ever hot-wired a car before?"

"I've seen it on television. How hard can it be?"

The explosion shook the ground. I pitched sideways and found myself on the mucky concrete, with Wyatt on top of me. Heat swirled around us. Bits of wood and brick and rubble peppered my exposed shoulder and cheek. He grunted. The roar of fire pushed through the thundering of my heartbeat and drowned out all other sounds. I turned my head, hazarded a look up. Windows and chunks of wall had blown out. Smoke billowed, acrid and thick.

The fifth floor was engulfed in flames.

Chapter Twenty-six

4:04

We watched the grisly scene from the roof of the building across the street. Tenants were evacuated into the street, many in nightclothes. Some clutched small children wrapped in blankets. Fire trucks arrived and poured water on the spreading flames. Police put up barricades, herded reporters, and tried to keep order amid chaos.

Wyatt and I stood side by side as the last of our allies were taken from us. I wanted to cry for Rufus and the brave spirit he had been, only I had no tears left. Wyatt was not so lucky. Unshed, they pooled in his eyes, creating a glassy, faraway look.

"Ten years," he said quietly. "I worked with him for ten years, and now . . ."

I tried to think of something sympathetic to say, but it all felt hollow. Trite. "Could it have been those grenades?" I asked instead.

"Doubt it. I don't buy this as an accident, Evy. The timing was too perfect."

"Do you think Nadia was right? Are we walking

right into another of Tovin's traps by going to the preserve?"

"I don't think we have a choice anymore."

"As if we had one before."

He grunted.

"We still stick to the plan," I said. "We recon the preserve and get our bearings, and then we retreat to formulate our attack plan and hope the other Triads don't blame this on us and really do show."

"If they don't show? Without any help, it's suicide."

He seemed to miss the irony in his words. "Wyatt, we don't have a choice, even if there's no one left to help us."

"I would not say that," said a lilting, female voice. It came as though carried on the wind, and might as well have been a phantom, since we hadn't heard anyone approach.

We pivoted in tandem. Wyatt reached for one of his guns, while I crouched and wrapped one hand around the handle of a knife. Twenty feet away, in the middle of a gravel roof she'd made no noise walking across, stood Isleen. Alive. She held out empty palms. Her calm expression never changed.

"I am no threat to you," she said.

"Holy shit, I thought you were dead," I said, standing. I quashed the very real urge to race across the roof and throw my arms around her neck. Never in my life had I been so happy to see a Blood.

"Even half-breeds know better than to kill one of their royalty, Evangeline."

Royalty? No shit. I'd have to ask her about that. Later. "How did you escape?"

"I was never taken, only drugged and tied up in one of the empty mall storage rooms. It took my Family time to locate me, and it took me almost as long to locate you."

"And how *did* you find us?"

A soft sigh escaped, as though the litany of necessary questions bored her. "I was following your friend. I spotted him earlier today on the street. The change was easy to recognize. I trailed him to the hospital, and then here when the humans took him. I was correct to do so."

Her story made sense, even though the foundation lay on her happening upon Alex in the street. I hated coincidence, but didn't necessarily discount her explanation because of it. She'd always showed a keen interest in discovering the truth. That didn't appear to have changed.

"You've been watching the building the whole time?"

"No, an hour ago, I spotted an osprey on the roof of the building. It flew away, and I attempted to track it. I failed. When I returned, the fire had already begun."

"I wasn't accusing you—"

"You said an osprey?" Wyatt asked.

Isleen nodded. Dummy me finally caught on. "The only osprey in this city are weres," I said. "It was a surviving Owlkin?"

"I believe so," she replied, "so I attempted to follow it. We are not friendly with shape-shifters of any ilk, but we know what your Triads did to them."

I flinched.

"Do you think the survivors blame Rufus's team?" Wyatt asked. "That they're targeting them?"

"The Owlkins were always peaceful," I said. "I can't imagine them burning down an entire apartment building out of spite."

"Watching his people being slaughtered by supposed allies can change a man's perspective on vengeance, Evy."

Good point, and we finally knew Owlkin survivors existed. But it didn't help us in our impending fight, not even a little bit. If Wyatt was right, the Owlkins may have just cut us off from our only backup. Unless . . .

"Can you help us, Isleen?" I asked.

"That depends on the information you share. Why did the half-breeds take you, and how did you escape?"

We fed Isleen the highlights of our captivity and escape and time in First Break. Its existence seemed to surprise her, if the quirk of one slim eyebrow was any indication. I left out details of its location and our exit through the tunnels. The Fair Ones had trusted us enough to let us leave; I wouldn't betray their trust by giving them up. I also left out the discovery of my Gift; some information I just won't give to a Blood.

"You are certain Tovin is at this nature preserve?" she asked after a long pause.

"No," I said, "which is why we're on our way there now. We had hoped for some Triad backup, but I get the feeling that's on the rocks once this gets around."

Her attention flickered to the fire behind us. I turned and felt the heat of it on my face. So much destruction, so much loss.

"Until they get it out and get the fire marshal in," Wyatt said, "there's no way to know how or where it started. I just know that we could have walked out sixty seconds later than we did."

"You two were either very lucky, or you were intentionally spared," Isleen said.

"I'm banking on luck," I said.

"I thought you didn't believe in luck," Wyatt said.

"I also said I don't believe in fate, but look at me now. I feel like a character in a fucking Greek tragedy, where all the gods are sitting back and having a good laugh at my expense."

"Not gods," Isleen said. "Mortal creatures with a thirst for power. The Fey have waged a silent war against my people for centuries. If Tovin succeeds in his plan, this Tainted One will help him destroy us." She stepped closer, a spark of anger in her violet eyes. "My people will not act on suspicion. You know this as well as I, but the half-breeds are abominations, and assistance will come if I say I have seen a nest in this place. Tell me there is a nest, and I will take you at your word."

The improbability of that statement struck me momentarily speechless. Wyatt squeezed my arm, silent encouragement, and I said, "There's a nest of Halfies there."

"Good enough. Where is this location?"

I told her about the preserve and the gas station, all the while observing her for signs of deception, some hint she would pass this along to the wrong person. I found none. "Three o'clock," I said. "We'll meet you there."

"Agreed. I will bring all of the help I can. Good luck to you both."

"We'll see you in a few hours."

Her willowy frame bolted to the side of the roof, and she vaulted to the next building. She moved like a shadow, disappearing the instant she landed. I had always envied the Bloods' ability to move like water—smooth and silent, or fast and furious, but always with intent.

"What do you think?" I asked.

Wyatt pulled me against his chest, arms wrapping around my waist. I leaned back, content in the warmth of his body for as long as I could have it.

"She's lying," he said.

"You think so?"

"Not her intention to help us, but her reasons. She isn't in this to stop Tovin; he's just an excuse. A way to justify it to her kin and get them to help her in her real goal."

That much I could have guessed. Vampire royalty put on airs, much worse than any Fey, and thought humans beneath them. Pure bloodlines, they said, kept them strong—another reason the half-Bloods were so hated by the Families. The Bloods I knew tried to differentiate themselves from humans by suppressing their baser emotions: lust, greed, hate, envy. The human sense of vengeance was seen as most distasteful of all, because it drew on desire rather than logic.

I was tickled to see a daughter of the royal lines so hell-bent on revenge for the death of her sister. As much as I wanted to believe she was trying to help us, we were simply a foil. A means to an end, and that end was finding Kelsa, the goblin responsible for Istral's death. And mine.

"On the bright side," I said, "we know she'll show with her people."

"We just can't be sure she won't stab us when our backs are turned, just to save guessing on whether or not we can beat Tovin."

"Then we don't turn our backs." I spun us so I could see the razed and ruined tenement that held the bodies of our allies. It was a terrible way to die, and I prayed they'd died quickly. An entire Triad—three Hunters and their Handler—wiped out. The Triads would recover their losses; they always did. Bastian was excellent at recruiting Hunters. I just didn't know how they'd replace Rufus.

If a Tainted was loosed, how long before the rest of the city learned of its Dreg neighbors and our mission of secrecy became obsolete?

We stood together, our faces caressed by the heat of the fire. The odor of smoke and wet pavement made me want to sneeze. I held tight to Wyatt's hands—the only calm we would get before the oncoming storm.

Activity on the street increased. Paramedics emerged from their ambulance with a stretcher and medical bag. They pushed it closer to the front entrance of the building and waited. I strained to hear the shouts of frenzied voices. Moments later, two firemen burst from the front doors in a cloud of gray smoke, carrying a grown man between them. The man was badly burned on his hands and chest, and his face was streaked with soot and sweat, but I still recognized that hair.

My mouth fell open. "Holy hell."

Wyatt grunted.

I watched the paramedics strap Rufus St. James to

their stretcher and wheel him toward the ambulance. He was tucked inside, and it sped away with its precious cargo.

"I don't believe it," Wyatt said.

"How did he survive that?"

"I don't know, but Rufus used up the last of his nine lives on this."

We waited a few more minutes, hoping for one more miracle to be carried out of the burning building. After a while, it became obvious she wouldn't. Nadia was gone.

"We should go," I said.

Wyatt nodded. "You know, I just realized something."

"What's that?"

"We still don't have a car."

* * *

Cars ripe for stealing were in easy supply on the streets of Mercy's Lot. Hot-wiring skills, however, were lacking. After I broke into a late-model Chevy POS, Wyatt tried unsuccessfully to start the damned thing. Finding the correct wires was harder in real life than on television, so we moved on to Plan B.

"We are so going to Hell for this," I said as I struggled to hold on to our victim's legs while Wyatt carried him by the torso. A few more steps and we had the unconscious man in the alley, nestled comfortably among a pile of plastic trash bags and empty crates.

"You doubted that anyway?" Wyatt asked.

He palmed the man's car keys and led the way back to the street. I kept expecting someone to shout at us, or police sirens to break the quiet of the night. Music still drifted in from far away, but this block seemed mostly asleep. Good news for us; not so much for our randomly selected victim.

Wyatt unlocked the small, blue car and I slid into the passenger seat. The vinyl was cracked and foam puffed out. The floor was sticky, the carpeting worn completely through. I glanced at the dash. At least it had a full tank of gas.

"I feel like I should leave an IOU or something," I said.

"I feel like we're doing him a favor by stealing this piece of shit." Wyatt turned the engine. It sputtered, strained, sputtered again, and finally roared to life. The "check engine" light flashed. Thunderous rap music blasted from the speakers; I turned the radio off.

Towering tenements and crumbling businesses were replaced by trees and gently sloping hills. Soon we would pass the city limits, enter the scattered homes of the valley's end, and wind our way up into the mountains north of the city—a majestic sight I often admired from a distance and rarely ventured into. Nature was nice, but I was a city girl.

The clips of ammo in my pockets made sitting still uncomfortable. I squirmed, aware of warmth against my backside. A hand on the seat found nothing amiss there, but did locate the source in one of my pockets.

Curious, I fished out the crystal Horzt had given me. It was warmer than it should have been. I turned it over in my fingers, careful of the sharp tip. The size and shape reminded me of high-caliber rifle ammunition, but I had no gun with which to fire it.

"What are you thinking?" Wyatt asked.

I lifted one shoulder in a noncommittal shrug and held the crystal lengthwise between two fingers. Bits of light refracted onto the dash in colorful patterns. "I hope this comes in handy at some point, because as far as weapons go, it's kind of tiny."

"Horzt said you'd know."

"Yeah, well, until then, it makes a pretty prism, don't you think?"

"It could make a nice paperweight."

"Yeah." I pocketed the crystal. Front pocket this time, point angled up so I didn't stab myself in the thigh.

We passed the gas station a few minutes later. Carved into a rocky spot on the side of the road, it had limited parking and two badly lit pumps, anchored by a dingy convenience store. The store was closed, and we hadn't passed another car in ten minutes. It was a good place to meet.

Another mile up, the road widened a bit and provided a gravelly shoulder. Wyatt pulled off and maneuvered the car into a ditch. Not ideal, but the best we could do by way of hiding our transportation. Someone would have to be searching for a parked car to notice.

The chilly mountain air bit into my exposed skin. I slammed the car door shut and stood for a moment in the weeds, breathing the fresh air. Inhale, hold, exhale. It energized me as we began our mile-long hike up the road. A peeling sign advertising the preserve and its entrance a quarter mile ahead was our marker. We veered off the road and into the woods.

I'd never been in the forest at night. Darkness blanketed us, broken only by thin shafts of moonlight between the towering treetops. Fallen branches and logs marred our path, hidden by layers of last year's fallen leaves. The breeze whispered past us. Crickets chirped; insects I didn't know called to one another. Our footsteps were lost to the symphony of the night.

We followed the descent of the mountain. The preserve was in a valley, half a mile from the shore of the Anjean. One of the park's two hiking trails ran past the river itself. They'd be grown over by now, but good guideposts if we found one.

"You smell that?" Wyatt whispered. He stopped next to a towering elm and inhaled deeply.

I did the same. Hidden on the edges of rotting leaves and dirt was the faintest odor of tar. "We're close," I said.

Not as close as I thought, it turned out. We walked another couple dozen yards before the trees thinned out and the night sky opened up. The odor of tar was traced to fresh blacktop—a sea of it, in fact. It extended far beyond the borders of the old parking lot, on which we stood, to cover every inch of what had once been bare soil. It butted up to the tree line on our side, and into the dim distance. Three buildings stood in the middle of the pavement, the largest and closest being the Visitors' Center. Just beyond it was an open-air pavilion for picnickers and planned parties. To the right side of the pavilion stood the two-story, bricked Olsmill Natural History Museum.

More blacktop massed out behind the museum, where the petting zoo had once stood. It appeared to be bulldozed, paved over, gone. Everything on the property, in fact, was paved. Very smart. No better way to keep out the Earth Guardians, especially when your home base was so close to the Break they were commissioned to protect.

Over the stench of tar came another, equally rank odor. The air shifted. I pivoted, dropped to one knee, and plucked a knife from my right ankle sheath. I thrust up, right into the throat of an attacking goblin male. The point came out the back of its neck. Fuchsia blood oozed and gurgled from its mouth. I stood up and yanked the blade back. The dead creature slumped to the ground, having never uttered a single sound.

"Think he raised the alarm?" I asked quietly.

The buildings remained silent, the night air otherwise undisturbed. "Hard to tell," Wyatt said. "But at least we know for sure that they have perimeter guards."

"And that goblins are here."

"Best guess is they're in the Visitors' Center. Let's see if we can get closer."

Wyatt crept down the perimeter line. I hung back and gave myself permission to crush my heel into the dead goblin's crotch. There wasn't much of a target, though. Like dogs, a goblin's penis only protrudes when aroused. Otherwise, only the barbed head remains exposed. My stomp was satisfying, but not quite so much had it still been alive and aroused to feel the excruciating pain.

I caught up with Wyatt a few yards down. He stood behind a thick tree, shaking his head.

"What?" I whispered.

"Some spies we are, Evy. We didn't even bring binoculars."

I would have smacked my own forehead, if I weren't afraid of the loud clack it might make. Any sort of actual surveillance equipment would have been useful, if we'd had access. Being out in the metaphorical cold certainly had its unique set of disadvantages.

Bright lights flashed across the trees. I ducked behind Wyatt and pressed up against his back, out of sight. Damn me for not hearing the engine. A car drove erratically across the ocean of pavement, toward the front of the Center. It was too far away to see in the window. It pulled past the Center and parked beneath the darkness of the pavilion—I couldn't help wondering how many other vehicles were hidden there.

Three shapes emerged. Two were hunched over, short, with moonlight glinting off their black hair. Goblin males. Between them walked a female, her black hair flowing down to her waist and red eyes uncovered by contact lenses. She wasn't trying to pass, but even without the decoration, I recognized her.

Kelsa.

My heart almost stopped. Anger and terror clenched my stomach, at once icy cold and fiery hot. I hadn't seen her since she left me for dead. Rage bubbled above the terror. My nostrils flared.

Wyatt grunted. I let go of my grip on his shoulder, forcing myself to relax. Flying to pieces would get us both into trouble. As long as Kelsa was here, I had a shot at killing her with my own two hands—if I could keep Isleen away from her.

"That's her," I said.

His entire body stiffened. "The goblin who tortured you?"

"Yes."

I caught his elbow before he could reach for and retrieve one of his holstered guns. His head turned;

fury danced in his eyes. His jaw was set, and I could practically hear his teeth grinding.

"One shot will bring them down on us. It will wait," I said. Besides, killing Kelsa like that was way too impersonal. And quick. When I killed her, I wanted her to know who was doing it and for it to last. Return the favor in a big way.

One of the males scampered ahead and pulled open the Center's front door. Kelsa swept inside, her bodyguards right behind. The Center itself stood in the middle of an ocean of pavement, with absolutely no cover. No way of sneaking in closer to have a peek inside.

We moved farther down the perimeter. No more guards jumped at us. No one sounded any alarms. I wondered several times if Tovin had concocted any magical security measures that we couldn't detect. While possible, it seemed likely we would have been apprehended by now if he had. Unless they were busy preparing our cages.

The treetops rustled, singing their familiar tune— only louder and faster than before, as if a strong wind was building. I looked up, waiting for the answer to present itself. Instead of sight, it came through sound— a gentle pattering.

"Do you hear that?" I asked.

Wyatt tilted his head to the sky. "Is it rain?"

"I don't think so. Sounds like a—"

He grabbed my arm and yanked me to my knees in the damp leaves. Overhead, the patter became a whir, and then a constant stutter. Twin helicopters hovered over the parking lot. No police markings; they were private. Had we been discovered? Was this an emergency escape plan?

Doors on both sides of the helicopters slid open as the machines dropped to twenty feet from the ground. The air whipped around us, swirling spring leaves and stinging my face with dirt particles. I waited for rappelling lines. None came. Twenty-one black-clad figures, dressed to the nines with armor and weapons and protective face gear, jumped gracefully out of the sides of the helicopters.

The figures landed on the hard blacktop with the ease of a step off a staircase, split into three groups, and surged toward the Center. One group left, one group right, the third directly up the center. Guns drawn and ready.

"Bloods," I said. "Goddamn Isleen."

"Guess she got tired of waiting," Wyatt said.

Chapter Twenty-seven

2:10

Twenty feet from the Center, the three groups of Blood forces engaged a force field that knocked four of them backward onto their well-armed asses. The field shimmered briefly—a flicker of blue light. Someone called out an order, and they retreated en masse to the porch of the museum.

The Center remained quiet. No lights came on; no alarms blared. The Bloods didn't open fire, but simply formed a protective circle, weapons still trained on the other building.

A slim, black-clad figure stepped from their ranks and into the open. It was impossible to tell if the Blood was male or female. My best guess, based on the walk, was male. He hefted something in his left hand, wound up, and hurled it at the Center. The object shattered against the barrier, which fritzed and snapped like water on an electric fence. Blue light sparkled. The stink of ozone filled the air. In seconds, the blue field dissolved and blinked out of existence. The Bloods surged forward again.

This time, an upstairs window opened and gun-fire rained down on the advancing Bloods. Several faltered and jerked. Blood splattered the pavement, but they pressed onward. Had to be regular bullets if the Bloods weren't staying down. Two stopped in mid-advance, dropped to one knee, and concentrated return fire on the window. Wood and glass shattered. The onslaught stopped.

Isleen's people were well trained, I had to give them that.

They had advanced within twenty feet of the Center's front door when they faltered again. Many bent, hands clutching their ears, screeching in pain. Something tickled the very edge of my hearing. The back of my neck prickled.

"Dog whistle," Wyatt said.

With the Bloods distracted, the opposition enacted a rear attack. The front door of the museum building opened. Halfies poured out, armed with knives and hatchets and their teeth. They moved too fast for recognition, surging toward the Bloods, thirty or more with one goal in mind.

I shouted for them to look out, but my voice was lost in the Halfies' echoing battle cry. The crash of bodies was thunderous. The Bloods reacted immediately, overcoming the squeal of the dog whistle—if it was still being blasted, which I doubted, because it should have affected the Halfies, too—and turned weapons on their attackers.

Every single gun possessed by the Bloods flew into the air, lifted by invisible hands. Shouts of surprise mixed with screams of pain.

"What the fuck?" I asked.

I saw him then, standing on the second-floor balcony above the Center's front door. Instinct told me it was Tovin, even though I'd never met him. He stood almost five feet tall, the tallest Fey I'd ever seen. His lean body seemed too thin, like pulled taffy, something a stiff breeze could knock over. Silver hair stood in short spikes, reaching high to the sky like his sharply pointed ears and eyebrows.

Small like most Fair Ones, he overcame that by radiating power. Even from where we stood in the cover of the forest, Tovin dwarfed everyone in front of him. I felt the power of the Break all around me, but Tovin lived it. He was born part of the Break. He was power. For the first time since I discovered his plan, I was genuinely afraid of him.

He levitated the weapons into the sky. The Bloods compensated by pulling blades, and the surface attack became more vicious, almost feral. The weapon cloud began to coalesce and spin. Each individual gun melted into the one next to it, until all that remained was a ball of metal the size of a washing machine. It fell and crushed two battling Bloods.

Wyatt had his gun out and aimed at Tovin before I could stop him. He squeezed the trigger, and for one brief, shining moment, I thought it would work. Tovin was watching the battle. The bullet roared at its target.

The world seemed to slow down, each second taking thirty. The bullet telescoped forward. Tovin turned his head and seemed to look right at me. I was certain he saw me. I felt deadly cold under that hateful gaze. He smiled, raised his hand, and plucked the bullet from the air.

Sound and action roared back to normal time.

Tovin was gone. The balcony doors slammed shut behind him.

"Oh my God," Wyatt said.

"He knows we're here."

"I've never seen that kind of power."

I squeezed his bicep, trying to offer comfort and calm my own nerves. I could kill mortal creatures, and I never had a problem with the morality or with the actual task. Killing something that plucked bullets from the air? Not exactly within my realm of experience, Gifted or not.

"Should we help them?" I asked, tipping my head toward the battling Bloods.

"They seem to be doing okay."

They were. I spotted Isleen in the fray. She'd removed her protective headgear, and her brilliant white hair flashed in the moonlight. She moved with the speed and grace of a dancer, each motion calculated for maximum damage as she spun through the battle bearing twin blades. Cutting and slicing, drawing blood from her most hated enemies. Dead or dying Halfies littered the pavement, but the battle was far from over.

In chess, you sent in the pawns first. We hadn't yet seen the big guns.

"We need to get inside the Visitors' Center," Wyatt said.

Headlights flashed across our position. Vehicles approached from the access road. They'd turned a curve and would enter the open parking lot in moments.

"What now?" I asked, more to myself than to Wyatt, and took off.

I ran down the tree line, sticking to the shadows

and dodging underbrush, Wyatt close behind. Four Jeeps were on the road. The first one crashed through the closed gate and turned sharply to the right. Three more followed, each tailing the other until they formed a wall of trucks by the gate, a good hundred feet from the actual fight. Men and women, armed for a fight, flooded out the passenger-side doors.

"Triads," Wyatt shouted.

We had backup after all. No sense in waiting for three o'clock if they thought we'd died in the fire with Nadia or if they thought we'd set it and run. No way to know which they thought was true without asking, so I blundered forward and burst through the trees just behind the last Jeep.

Two familiar faces stood out among twenty-odd strangers.

"Tybalt," I shouted, hoping to catch his attention. Tall and lean, Tybalt Monahan always seemed better suited for the pro-basketball court than our down and dirty job. He heard his name, turned, and saw me. Suspicion and confusion flared, and I realized my mistake too late. He didn't know me as Chalice.

None of them did.

Wyatt put himself in front of me, but even his familiar face didn't stop someone's itchy trigger finger from twitching. The gun of a fresh-faced Hunter—probably a week out of Boot Camp—roared. Wyatt stumbled backward into me. Air hitched in my lungs.

"Hold your fire, goddammit," Tybalt commanded.

Wyatt gained his balance. I ducked around to stand in front of him. My heart nearly stopped when I saw the blood on his shirt, with more oozing between his fingers. It was all I saw, hot and crimson—something meant to be inside of his body, not outside.

"It's okay," he said. "It went straight through, it's fine." His voice startled me back into breathing. He'd been shot in the bicep—not a mortal wound. Our eyes met. Pain had glazed his, and I could only imagine what he saw in mine.

Gina Kismet appeared, with Milo and Felix—the rest of her Triad team—in tow. Kismet was the only female Handler I'd ever met. She was built like a gymnast—short, muscular, and not an ounce of extra fat anywhere—but looked like a pixie, with short red hair, angry green eyes, and a voice like a Marine drill sergeant. She seemed more suited to being a Hunter than a Handler, but I'd never bothered to ask her story. It had never mattered.

"We thought you were dead," Kismet said to Wyatt.

"Not for lack of trying," Wyatt said through gritted teeth.

"Rufus?"

"We saw him taken away in an ambulance, but Nadia never got out."

She nodded, then gave me her full attention. A quick sweep with her eyes preceded a terse, "Stone?"

"In someone else's flesh," I said.

"When Rufus called and asked for our help, he said you'd . . . ah, changed."

"He's a master of understatement." I had to get their brains back on the continuing bloodbath on the other side of the Jeeps. "The Bloods are on our side right now. We know Tovin is inside the Visitors' Center.

Goblins are here, too; we just haven't seen their numbers yet. Anyone got a bandanna or something?"

A nameless Hunter whose face I barely remembered handed me a red-checked cloth. I pulled Wyatt's hand away from his still-bleeding arm and tied the bandanna around the wound. I tightened it, until he hissed.

"Big baby," I said.

"We need to form a perimeter around the Visitors' Center," Kismet said. "Just in case Tovin gets any ideas about leaving. Morgan, Willemy, take your teams to the north side of the Center. Nothing gets past you."

Eight people tore away from the group. One of them was the baby-face newbie. I tapped him on the shoulder as he passed. He looked up. I punched him square in the mouth. Teeth cut my knuckles. He yelped and stumbled back, blood seeping from his lip. Someone snickered, but no one reprimanded me.

"That's definitely Evy," Tybalt said.

"That idiot could have killed him," I said. Maybe ended the fight sooner, rather than later, but I was not giving up hope of an alternate solution to one of us dying. Not yet. We had time, dammit.

"Once Morgan and Willemy are in place—" Kismet started, only to be cut off by a raucous war whoop that started as one voice and rose into dozens. Screeching and inhuman, it signaled a fresh attack.

Goblin warriors streamed from the cover of the trees behind us. Too clumsy for guns of their own and too fast for us to shoot them down, they swarmed over and around the Jeeps. The sight of them, barely clothed and aroused by bloodlust, flooded me with fury. Hatred pushed pure adrenaline through my veins, and I found myself looking forward to the carnage.

"Use your blades!" Kismet ordered, barely audible above the din of the war cry.

Claws swiped; teeth gnashed. Serrated knives in hand, I dove in.

Movement blurred around me as I searched for the hunched shapes of goblin males. They were faster than they had any right to be and outnumbered us four to one. I still heard scattered gunfire as I plunged one knife into the back of a goblin. Fuchsia blood spurted in stinking jets. Thoughts of anything but slitting throats and spilling blood fled with my first kill.

One of them jumped on my back, its razor teeth sinking into the flesh of my left shoulder. Muscle and skin ripped. My right hand swung sideways and buried a blade into its skull. It dropped away, taking some of my shoulder with it, and two more goblins quickly took its place. I killed them with fast slashes across their throats.

"Don't kill her!"

My head snapped toward the familiar, tingle-inducing voice. Kelsa stood on top of the last Jeep, hands on hips, like the battle had already been won. She seemed unconcerned with the rate at which her warriors were falling. She bared her teeth and held out her hand. Light glittered off a silver chain and cross. I dropped one knife and reached for the gun still tucked in the back of my jeans. Bitch had my necklace.

I hadn't seen it since the mall. I'd written it off as lost during capture. But Halfie-Alex had said Kelsa was at the jail while I was unconscious. She may have taken it then. One of the Halfies who captured me may have given it to her. The details didn't matter. I wanted it back.

Teeth clamped around my right ankle like a bear trap. I shrieked, pulled the gun, and fired, splattering the goblin's head against the pavement and my jeans. I yanked my leg free. A red-tipped dart struck the ground, barely missing me. Hell, no, I was not going to sleep again. Not this time.

Loneliness, that's what I needed. Wyatt was shot. He could have died. That fear remained fresh and close to the surface, and I latched on to it. Focused on Kelsa atop the Jeep, and felt the familiar tingle of the tap. The power of the Break. Dissolution. Movement.

The pain was duller this time, likely due to the shorter jump distance. I gained my bearings quickly. On the Jeep roof, right behind Kelsa—exactly where I wanted to be. She was still staring at the fray, dart gun in hand, seeming unsure where I'd suddenly gone.

I smashed the butt of my gun against the back of her head. She dropped like a stone. The necklace fell from her hand and clattered to the Jeep's roof. I rolled her over and knelt down hard on her arms, knees against elbows, until I heard one snap. She shrieked. Gleaming red eyes glared up at me, pained and slightly unfocused.

"You're not so tough when I'm not tied down," I said.

"I killed you once. I can do it again," she snarled.

I popped the anticoag clip out of my gun and replaced it with the fragmenting clip. Snapped one into the chamber. "This isn't going to be fast. You aren't going to enjoy this, but you will remember it in whatever hellish afterlife your kind goes to."

She spit in my face. Her saliva smelled like sea-water. I wiped it away, but the stink lingered. I reached back and placed the barrel of the gun against her foot. Her eyes widened. Lips parted in a fang-baring snarl.

Two goblin males slammed into me sideways. I tumbled over the roof of the Jeep and hit the blacktop on my back. The impact exploded oxygen from my lungs and left me dazed. A dark blur leapt from the Jeep. I rolled sideways, barely missing Kelsa's landing —precisely where my head would have been.

I tucked and came up on my knees and fired a wild shot. It glanced off her right arm and took a chunk of flesh with it. She kept coming, too fast to shoot again. She kicked the gun out of my hand and fol-lowed through with a serious swipe with her left hand. Sharp nails furrowed across my ribs and belly. Agony flared hot and immediate. Blood flowed.

My high kick connected squarely with her nose. The crunch rang out, mingling with her scream. Her head snapped back, but she refused to go down. I dropped to one knee and thrust upward with my knife. She blocked it and her good elbow smashed into my ear and set my head spinning. She had my wrist in her hands and was trying to turn my knife against me. I fought, but I had lost leverage.

She hissed, baring her bloody incisors, and snapped at my face. I gave her a well-deserved head-butt that drove her broken nose a little deeper into her snarl-ing face. She faltered; I wrestled the knife away and plunged it into her stomach. Putrid blood pumped over my hand. She slashed again with her claws, catching me across the left cheek. Pain ripped open with the soft flesh. I shoved against the knife handle, and she fell backward.

I was on top of her again, ignoring my own pain, operating on fury and adrenaline and a very selfish need for personal vengeance against this monster who'd held me captive for days. Who had tortured me mercilessly. Ordered me raped. Allowed me to die.

I yanked out the knife and ground down with my knee until her other elbow popped. She squealed—a sound unbecoming a leader. Blood coated her face, but wild, animal eyes still shone brightly through the mess. I pressed the tip of the knife against the underside of her chin.

The air shifted behind me. I slashed sideways with the knife and cut an approaching goblin male straight across the belly. It screamed and ran the opposite way, past where my gun lay, lonely on the pavement. Too far to reach. I wanted it so badly I thought the desire would rip me to pieces. I wanted to press the barrel against her foot, pull the trigger, and shatter it into blood and bone and muscle and goo. I wanted to do it with her other foot and with both hands. I wanted to take her a piece at a time, just as she'd taken me.

Only I didn't have the time. Bloods and Halfies still battled in front of me. Humans and goblins battled behind me. At some point, the twin fights had mingled into a single war zone. And time was running out.

"You don't deserve this," I said. I gripped the knife with both hands and held it high above her throat. "You deserve a hell of a lot worse, you bloodsucking bitch."

I plunged; she gurgled. Blood pooled from her

mouth, down her cheeks and throat. I pulled the knife out and wiped it on her clothes.

I'd heard people say revenge is a dish best served cold. I had no idea what that meant, but I doubted it was meant to describe the chilly emptiness I felt at what I'd done. There was no satisfaction, no joy or sense of closure. It was just another kill. A notch on my belt.

"No!" Isleen ran toward me, easily dodging the few senseless goblins who tried to stop her. Rage painted her pale cheeks with orbs of crimson. Lavender eyes snapped and flashed.

I stood on shaky legs. My wounds ached and smarted. I didn't back down from Isleen as she closed the distance between us.

"She was mine," Isleen snarled. "She killed my sister."

"And she killed me, so I killed her. Get over it."

Bad move on my part. Covered in blood and trembling from head to toe, Isleen was so tightly wound from the battle raging around us that she was one pull from snapping. And it turned out my little retort was that final pull. She tried to punch me, but was sloppy about the windup. The blow glanced off my temple, more annoying than anything. I raised my knee and caught her square in the stomach. She doubled over. I jammed my elbow into the small of her back, and she dropped.

"Sorry about that, but I'm too busy to fight my allies," I said.

I retrieved my gun and stuck it down the back of my pants. The second knife was lost. It didn't matter; I still had one left.

The tide of the battle had shifted in our favor. With their leader dead, some of the fight had gone out of the goblins. They attacked with less fury. Small groups had pulled away toward the trees, wounded and bloody and lost. I spotted Wyatt on the edge of the fray, unharmed beyond the preexisting gunshot wound. His shirtsleeve was stained red, a severe contrast to his pale, sweaty complexion. He shouldn't have been out there fighting, but he was on his feet. Tybalt stood close by, surveying the battlefield and speaking into a walkie-talkie.

The remaining Halfies, maybe a dozen, were in the process of retreating to the entrance of the Center. The Bloods followed at a distance, apparently not keen on chasing them into close quarters. The Halfies, however, stayed on the porch and made no move toward the door.

I had a bad view over the sea of bodies between me and the Center, some standing, most not. The Bloods surged forward. Something silver was lobbed into the air from the porch. The Bloods scattered—too late. It exploded on impact. A ball of fire billowed into the sky, consuming everyone within ten feet of it. Bloods shrieked in agony. Flames beat against a brand-new force shield that sparkled aqua blue.

The heat blasted across the paved lot. I raised my arms to shield my face. The actual fire dissipated quickly. Melted pavement and scorched bodies marked the blast zone. The handful of surviving Bloods retreated, joining the ranks of the Triad teams regrouping by the Jeeps.

I climbed atop the last Jeep, its roof a colorful palette of blood smears and skin bits. In the mess, I found the cross necklace, its delicate chain somehow unbroken—a small reminder of everything Alex had given up for me. I tucked it into my pocket, glad to have it back, and jumped to the ground.

Kismet appeared by my side. She was bleeding from a deep gash in her left leg. The rest of the blood on her clothes was fuchsia. She gave me a once-over and quirked an eyebrow at my impressive array of wounds.

"I've had worse," I said.

Tybalt jogged over. "The rear teams report killing half a dozen goblins that tried to run," he said, "but no other activity on that side of the building."

"We're picking them off as best we can, too," Kismet said. "With their leader dead, they don't know what to do. Goblin males don't traditionally do much thinking for themselves."

"And Tovin's still got himself locked inside," I said. "I don't know if he's just biding his time until my clock runs out, or if he's daring us to come in. What time is it?"

"Quarter till three."

An hour left. I looked around for Wyatt, keen on getting his advice. He wasn't mingling among the battle-worn. My heart skipped a beat. Kismet was speaking, but I walked away. Pushed past people, worry planting its icy seed in the pit of my stomach.

I found him on the other side of the Jeeps, standing amid a grisly scene of dead bodies and noxious blood fumes. Back to me, I saw weariness in the slump of his shoulders and bend of his knees. He trembled—barely noticeable if I wasn't looking for it. Above the hiss of his ragged breathing, a steady plopping sound stood out. I followed it to the red-stained tips of his fingers.

Blood dripped in a steady stream from his wounded arm.

Fear and bald understanding almost knocked me to my knees. The bullet may have gone right through like a normal round, but it hadn't been normal. Not even close. Triad teams heading into an unknown situation involving Halfies or Bloods always entered with anticoag bullets chambered and ready.

Wyatt had been bleeding to death for the last half hour.

Chapter Twenty-eight

00:58

As though my sudden understanding had robbed him of the last of his strength, Wyatt fell. He was too far away for me to catch him before he hit his knees. I caught him around the waist and eased him down onto his back. He looked like a ghost, pale skin stretched taut over his face. His lips were dry and colorless. Glassy eyes blinked up at me. Hard, shallow breaths dragged in and hissed back out.

My stomach twisted, tightened, and my heart nearly hammered right out of my chest. Fear blasted through me like a winter wind. I knelt beside him and cupped his cold cheeks in my trembling hands.

"Wyatt, look at me. Wyatt!"

He blinked twice, hard, and saw me. "Sorry."

"Why didn't you say something?"

"It's better this way."

I wanted to slap him, punch him hard until he took it back. Force him to stand up and dress me down for hitting a superior. Instead, I reached down and clasped his good hand. He squeezed back, so weak. Something thick clogged my throat. I swallowed hard, unable to dislodge it.

"Better for you, maybe, but I can't do this alone." My voice sounded strange—high-pitched and desperate. The din of the fight faded away until nothing existed but us.

His pale lips stretched into a tired smile. "You can, Evy. You have to."

"This is my death, goddamnit, mine. Not yours."

"You'll be whole. Force his hand. You can win."

I leaned over and pressed my forehead to his, as though I could keep him there by touch alone. His cool breath puffed against my lips, each exhale a struggle. I didn't understand. Didn't want to understand. I only wanted him to stay. Stay by my side and help me fight.

"Stay with me," I whispered.

"I can't. Evy, promise me."

"Anything."

The hand holding mine squeezed harder. "Live."

My insides quaked. Everything in me screamed to get help, to fight and save him—even though I knew I couldn't.

"Evy?"

"I promise." I brushed my lips across his. When I pulled back, a single tear had marked a slick track down his cheek. My chest ached. Scorching tears pooled in my own eyes, stung my nose.

I held on until his hand loosened around mine. His eyelids drooped, forever hiding his glimmering black eyes. His chest rose once more and stopped. He lay so still I thought the world had frozen in place.

Then an anguished scream broke the spell, and I realized it was me.

Until that moment, I'd never known the word "heartbroken" as anything other than a metaphor. Yet as I gathered Wyatt in my trembling arms and held him to my chest, I felt it happen. Something inside me shattered, releasing rage and anguish unlike anything I'd ever felt—whole and feral and never-ending. I pitched headlong into the despair of loss, with the last person I cared for in the world dead in my arms.

My descent into grief, however, was cut short rather rudely by a blinding gray light. Even with my eyes closed, it was all I could see. It blasted through me like a lightning bolt, electrifying every nerve ending. I was falling into consuming fire that did not burn. It invigorated me and, within the chaos of pain and ecstasy, a life played out in my mind's eye.

A little girl so lonely she prefers playing with stuffed animals to other children, misunderstood by unknowing parents, misguided by well-meaning counselors. A misfit in high school who acts out and makes bad choices and ends up in trouble more times than her beleaguered parents can bail her out. Coping with the loss of everyone important to her and the desperate need for a fresh start.

They could have been my own memories, save the faces of the players and the point at which they diverged. For while my story ended in a fulfilling job with the Triads, this girl's story ended in a tub of hot, bloody water. It was Chalice's life that I experienced, all of her memories coming to the surface as the pact made between Wyatt and Tovin shattered.

Wyatt was dead. I got to live. Forever trapped in

someone else's body, with her life tucked into the back of my mind. Alive. Whole. And furious.

I see her walking across a college campus, balancing too many books and a coffee cup. A clumsy, harried young man knocks the books to the ground, getting coffee on his khakis. Alex. He gathers her books, smiling his sunny smile at her. I felt her love for him—genuine affection for a gentle soul who accepted her, warts and all. So undeserving of his violent fate.

How was I seeing these things? Chalice Frost was long dead, her soul at rest. Was memory more than just consciousness? Had some of her remained behind, her body as much a part of memory as her soul had been? I had enough trouble with my own memories and emotions; I didn't need someone else's crowding my head.

The gray light faded. Still holding Wyatt, I no longer felt the hard pavement beneath me. The cloying odor of earth and leaves clued me in before I got a good look. I had transported us both, quite by accident, into the woods. I could still hear the distant hum of voices, the occasional spatter of gunfire, the residual stink of the explosion.

Had my release from Tovin's spell made me powerful enough to transport not just myself, but others? The evidence was in our new location, and the very faint ache between my eyes. My entire body thrummed with energy. It cycled up into me, like a lifeline to the earth itself. With full possession of Chalice's body, I had tapped into the Break and was helpless to turn it off.

I eased Wyatt to the carpet of leaves. His head listed to the side and lay still. I touched his cheek, his forehead, memorizing his face. Revenge hadn't felt so good when I enacted it for myself, but I had a feeling revenge was going to taste wonderful when I tore it out of Tovin's ass.

Something poked my thigh as I rocked back on my heels, preparing to stand. I dug into my jeans pocket, the tips of my fingers sliding around something solid and hot. The crystal Horzt gave me. I pulled it out and held it between my forefinger and thumb. The clear crystal had turned cloudy white and was fiery to the touch. It seemed to pulse with life of its own.

When the time comes, you will know how to use it.

A tiny flare of hope burned bright in the back of my mind, but I refused to acknowledge it. It was too much to expect. I had lost everyone I loved. Wyatt was no different. So why did the crystal burn with life of its own?

I untied the blood-soaked bandanna from Wyatt's arm and ripped a hole in the sleeve of the shirt. The wound was small, maybe the size of a dime. I poised the pointed tip of the crystal above the bullet hole. My stomach fluttered. I couldn't dare to hope. I pushed the crystal in, down through torn flesh, until its length disappeared and blood oozed out to cover its presence completely. I kept my hand over it, uncertain what to do next.

"Please," I said.

The skin beneath my hand warmed—from the crystal or my pressure, I didn't know. The hard butt of the crystal softened until I no longer felt it. It seemed to melt into him. Hotter still, for only a moment, and then it cooled. I let go and brushed away the drying blood. The skin on his arm, once torn, was mended. I checked the other side—no exit wound.

My heart dared to hope, pounding hard, threatening to choke me, but Wyatt didn't move. Didn't open his eyes or suck in a ragged breath. Hope shattered into despair.

I put my right hand on his chest, threaded the fingers of my left above it, and depressed. One, two, three, four, five. "Come on, Wyatt." One, two, three, four, five. "Come on, damnit."

Again, nothing. I pounded with a closed fist. Fury and tears blinded me, choked me. No reaction. The crystal had been too little, too late.

"Fuck!"

I collapsed against his chest, too exhausted to sob. No more energy for grief. I couldn't make his heart beat. I couldn't force him to breathe. I couldn't do anything, except finish the task we'd started together. Tovin had lost his vessel for the Tainted, but I had no illusions that he'd just roll over and give up. Creatures that cunning always had a failsafe.

Force his hand. You can win.

"I hope so." I touched Wyatt's lips with the tip of my finger, positive the warmth I felt was a figment of hope. "If I don't, I'll see you soon."

I stood up, tapped into the Break with little effort, and thought about the line of Jeeps. Colors swirled. The world dissolved into a pale ache that lasted only until movement ceased, and I found myself face-to-face with a very stunned Kismet.

"Where the hell did you come from?" she asked. "Where's Wyatt?"

"Dead," I said, surprised at the even tone of my

voice. "What's our situation here?" She frowned, but I didn't care how she interpreted my question. I had to finish this before I let myself fall to pieces.

"No movement inside the Center," she said. "The Halfies aren't attacking, but the Bloods are getting itchy, and we still can't get past that barrier."

"What about the thing they used the first time?"

"They only had the one, and getting another takes both time and money."

"What if I can get us through? Well, me and maybe two others."

"How?"

"A little trick I picked up along the way, but I don't think I can carry more than two. Hell, I might not even get us across the barrier, so I'd pick two volunteers who don't mind the distinct possibility of being smashed into putty when we try and spectacularly fail."

"I'm in," Tybalt said. He fell in next to Kismet, his mouth set in a grim line. "How about you, boss?"

She gave him a sideways look. Nodded. She pulled her walkie-talkie. "Baylor, come in."

It crackled briefly. A male voice said, "Go ahead, Kis."

"You're point on ops outside. We may have a way in. I'm going in with Tybalt and Stone."

"Acknowledged."

She slipped the walkie-talkie back into her belt without a reply, checked the clip on her gun, then turned to me. "Ready when you are."

"Do either of you know the layout of the Center?" I asked.

Tybalt nodded. "I came here a few times as a kid. The first floor is an open lobby, with a lounge and information booth. I think the second floor is offices and a couple of activity rooms. I never went up on the third, but the basement should be all storage."

"And Tovin's likely location. Underground gets him as close to the Break as possible. So I'll aim for the lobby. It's an open area. We're less likely to land inside a desk or a wall."

Kismet blanched.

I held out one hand to each of them and clasped theirs tightly. They reached to each other, completing the circle without being asked. I fed the thrum of energy through me and into them. Tybalt's hand jerked; I held tight. "This might feel weird," I said.

The world melted. The pain was immediate, because of the added weight and distance traveled. It furrowed between my eyes like a red-hot spike. We floated until the world turned blue. Power crackled around us. Agony exploded in my head. I screamed, pushed through it, and came out the other side, intent on the lobby.

As soon as I felt hardwood form beneath my feet, I let them go and fell to my hands and knees. Something warm and wet stained my upper lip. Drops of red hit the floor between my hands. The horrific pain faded, but the migraine-esque symptoms remained. My stomach tried to turn itself inside out. A hand touched the small of my back. I focused on the contact, used it to push the pain away and focus on standing.

"How did you do that?" Kismet asked.

"I'm Gifted now," I said. "The girl whose body this was, she was an unfound tap. This is her—it's my power. It's never been this strong before, but Chalice and I . . . we're truly one person now. Everything that was individually ours is mine."

"So your emptying hourglass?"

"Busted."

"Great. Now that you've solved that quandary for us, I—"

A low growl cut her off. I paid attention to our surroundings for the first time, cursing myself for not doing it sooner. The lobby was the length and width of the building itself. Freestanding walls had long since fallen over. The wood floor was warped in places, and scored in others. The main desk that dominated the very center of the lobby was covered with writing that, upon first glance, appeared to be graffiti. A better look revealed an actual language—albeit, one I couldn't read.

And I didn't have time to try, because the desk wasn't the source of the growl. From the shadows of the rear corner of the lobby came a hulking shape— one that had become very familiar over the last three days. The snarling hound hybrid shambled into the light, saliva dripping from its bared fangs. It stopped, balanced on two legs, then drew up to its impressive height.

My fingers clenched around the hilt of the knife. I'd killed two of them. I could use one more notch on my belt.

"What rounds do you have in?" Kismet asked, her voice a hushed whisper.

"Anticoags," Tybalt replied. "You?"

"Same."

"Mine are frags," I said. "Mix them up. It'll kill that thing faster."

Kismet reached behind me with precise movements, doing nothing to startle the hound into attacking faster. It was still fifteen feet away, approaching like it was on a Sunday stroll. She pulled my gun and tucked her own into its place.

"Get downstairs. We've got him," she said.

"Destroy the desk, too. It could be the barrier spell," I replied.

"Got it. Now go." She stepped to the left. "Hey, ugly!"

I turned and ran as gunfire erupted behind me. Fast, toward the door marked EXIT. I crashed through the fire door and descended the dank, cement steps two at a time. The weapons play faded into the distance. I hit the basement level and was presented with two doors, made of the same heavy metal as the door upstairs, but these felt different—ominous and dark, the keepers of terrible secrets. The thrum of energy was strong. It crackled all around me. Whatever Tovin was doing, he'd already tapped into something.

My hand closed around the bar handle of the door on the left. A thunderous explosion from above shook the walls and trembled the ground beneath my feet. Dust drifted down. I sneezed and looked up, as if I could see up through the floor at what had happened.

"I hope that was the desk blowing up," I said, wishing they could hear me. The barrier was beyond my powers or ability to detect, even through the Break. It didn't matter, though, because Tovin had to know we were inside.

I pushed down on the bar. The door opened without resistance or noise. I slipped through into what, at first, looked like a high school science lab, or something out of a hokey television horror movie. Long metal tables covered with laboratory equipment straight from *Young Frankenstein* filled the center of the room—microscopes, petri dishes, flasks and vials, and intricate setups of tubes and burners and bubbling liquids.

The smell nearly felled me—a fetid mixture of waste and blood and rot, made sour by chemicals and lemon-scented cleaner. Fluorescent bar lights gave the entire room a sickly yellow cast. While my brain caught up to the stink, I scanned the perimeter of the room. The right wall was all open shelves and locked cabinets, fully stocked with supplies I couldn't identify. The left and rear walls looked like dog kennels, each section four feet wide and the height of a man, partitioned by cement blocks. Iron bars more suited to a prison cell-block made up the fronts.

Something growled inside one of those kennels. A chill wormed its way up my spine. The hounds. They were artificially created hybrids, the source of which was right here and had been for quite a while, given the intricacy of the lab and its contents.

I made my way to the nearest cage, curiosity edging out common sense. The kennels weren't lit, leaving the interiors cast in shadow. I remained at arm's length and squinted through the iron bars. Matted, moldy straw covered the floor, which extended less than six feet to the rear.

Huddled in the corner was a creature the size of a five-year-old child. If it had ever been human, it had long ago ceased being so. Oily black skin glinted in the dim light. Short, connected spikes, like the dorsal fin of a pickerel, ran down its spine. I saw no face, no hands, only the backside of it.

The kennel had no label or designation, only the letter A painted above it. Each kennel was similarly lettered, all the way to N. Fourteen kennels, fourteen potential experiments. I forced myself to the next one. In the center, nestled in soiled straw, was a teenaged boy. Half of a teenaged boy. The entire left side of his body was stone, fixed in place and anchoring him to the ground. He blinked at me with one brilliant blue eye, an image of perfect despair.

"Holy shit."

I backed away, unable to bring myself to look into the rest of them. I didn't want to see the abominations created by mad scientists—or more precisely, a mad elf—for reasons I could never hope to understand.

Something squealed. My head snapped up and right, to the very last kennel. The door had swung open. I slipped sideways, putting the rows of lab tables between me and it, fixed on the shadowed interior. The occupant snuffled. Straw shifted—a dry and wheezy sound. My knife hand twitched.

The thing that finally showed itself shouldn't have been able to move. It shouldn't have even been alive. The size of a house cat, sans fur or distinctive markings or muscle mass of any kind, it had twin incisors at least four inches long. Like the living skeleton of a saber-toothed tiger kitten, it trotted out of its cage and leapt onto the nearest lab table.

Claws clicked on the metal surface. I watched it sniff a petri dish. It hissed—a horrible sound like steam escaping. One step at a time, I backed toward the door. It continued its forage along the table, paying me no heed. Only a few feet to go and I would escape the waking nightmare. My heart pounded so loudly I was sure the thing could hear it.

I closed my hand around the door handle and pushed down. The gentle clack was all it took. Skele-kitty raised its head, sunken eyes looking right at me. It yowled, and the screech made my teeth ache. It raced toward me, faster than it had any right to move. I pushed against the door, went through, and shoved it closed again. The critter hit with a thump. Unless it knew how to open doors, it was trapped.

"Okay, let's try door number two."

With perfect silence in the stairwell and lobby above, I pushed through the second door and into another stairwell. The basement had a basement. Interesting. It also had no light of any kind. After a moment fiddling with the door and finding no way to prop it open, I gave up and let darkness envelop me.

The stairs were steeper, wood instead of cement, and still held a hint of pine fragrance. They were new enough that I doubted they were part of the original floor plans. I dragged my fingertips along the rough, packed-dirt walls, each step taking me farther into the gloom.

My foot finally landed on something harder than wood. I scraped the toe of my sneaker around. Cement floor. I'd hit bottom. I fumbled until my eyes adjusted enough to make out a thin line of light on the floor, roughly the width of a door. The metal frame was embedded in the dirt walls and within it was another steel fire door. Another handle. Another room.

I pressed my palm against the smooth metal. It hummed beneath me like a living thing. The short hairs on the back of my neck prickled. I was there, on the precipice of solving my entire three-day ordeal. Facing Tovin, and getting what few answers he might reveal before I cut his black heart out with my knife. But standing there, so close to what I wanted, I hesitated.

Wyatt was supposed to be by my side for this. We should have been facing Tovin together. A pang of loneliness loosed a flood of power through my body. I had to maintain control. The last thing I needed was to teleport out in the middle of killing the bad guy. I inhaled deeply, blew out through my mouth, and pushed down on the door handle.

Showtime.

Chapter Twenty-nine

I felt like I'd stepped out on the other side of the world. The walls were dug roughly from the earth. Roots protruded from both walls and ceiling, and the air was heavy with the odor of fresh dirt and incense. Sage, maybe, or some similar herb. It was about thirty feet in diameter, a perfect half-circle with the door at the top of the arch. In front of me, all along the straight wall, were dozens and dozens of lit candles, perched in the notched earth.

Six metal crates, the type people carry large-breed dogs in, stood along the wall, beneath the candles. The crates were half covered in dark cloths and vibrated with movement—scratching, growling, living beasts wanting to get out. After what I'd seen upstairs, the possibilities of what were in those crates chilled me.

In the center of the dugout space was a brick-lined circle the size of a hula hoop. Still, black water filled it—the same as the pool at the base of First Break's waterfall—dark and mysterious, and seeming infinitely deep. Energy crackled and snapped in the air, and standing a few feet inside, I felt as close to true power as I'd ever come.

I stepped closer to the pool, drawn by its convergence of energy and uncertain why. Was water somehow part of the equation? It made sense, given what I knew and what I'd seen both in the mountains and the city. The majority of the Dregs were concentrated in the downtown area—a peninsula of land with a river on two sides and the mountains directly north. Location was just as important an ingredient in magic as emotion, it seemed.

I gazed into the onyx pool, at my tangled hair and bloodstained face and wide, searching eyes. Searching for someone seemingly not in the room.

The door slammed shut, its report echoing loud enough to set my ears ringing. I pivoted on one ankle, hand immediately on the grip of Kismet's gun, and my heart nearly stopped. Tovin stood inside the room, as unconcerned by events around him as he'd seemed earlier on the balcony. In front of me, three paces away, he seemed unimpressive. But physical stature meant little. I had seen his power at work.

"You don't know what you've done," he said, commanding and firm. I hadn't expected a forceful voice from such a small, unassuming body.

I arched an eyebrow. "What I've done? Those aren't my science projects upstairs, pal. Even I'm not that sick."

"Unfortunate mistakes that I've grown rather fond of. I doubt you've ever had a pet in your short, meaningless life, but I can't bring myself to destroy them." He didn't speak like I suspected an elf would. He had no practiced cadence or high-brow inflections. He spoke like any other person on the street.

"What are they for?"

"You were but one cog in this grandly designed wheel, Evangeline. You and Truman both, necessary parts to play, but not the only ones that mattered. I needed proper vessels."

"Is that what's in those cages? Vessels?" I wasn't going to bother trying to puzzle that one out. Both my deductive reasoning skills and my patience had been left aboveground. Down here, I wanted fast and simple answers, so I could kill him and get it done.

Tovin nodded. "The perfect vessels for hosting the Tainted."

Rather than walking, he seemed to float past me, along the curved line of the room, toward the nearest crate. He yanked off the black sheet. Inside, crouched on its haunches, was a man-sized version of the hound. Its snout was less pronounced, but its razor teeth just as plentiful. It looked able to stand and run on two legs, instead of four.

"We were missing the human element," Tovin said, as if discussing a beloved child. "The vampire and goblin hybrids weren't enough, even with the added canine traits. We had to mix in the right amount of human DNA. The result was startlingly perfect, as you can see."

And startlingly ugly. "Perfect for demon possession?"

"You can't possibly comprehend what will possess them."

The final puzzle pieces came crashing into position. Our theory was correct: the freewill deal was meant to get Wyatt under his control. With a controlled mind, Tovin had the perfect vessel for his Tainted One, and a being of unbelievable power would be at his command. He had his hound-hybrids caged and ready to accept their own demons—probably lesser in power and controllable by the first. The only X-factor in this fucked-up situation was Tovin's next move now that Wyatt was dead. And I had one last question to ask before we danced—a final confirmation.

"So this was all you?" I asked. "Every single moment, from the murders of my teammates to my kidnapping to Wyatt and the resurrection? You did this?"

"Yes. Humans are so malleable when it comes to their emotions. So many of my Fey brethren desire your range of emotional imbalances, but I've never seen the appeal. Love will always be your kind's greatest flaw. It makes you do truly stupid things."

"Like this?" I whipped out the gun and fired at his head. As before, time slowed and, after an eternity of anticipation, stopped completely. Just like on the balcony, he plucked the bullet out of the air.

With nothing to lose and no more tricks to try, I started squeezing the trigger a second time. An invisible hand yanked the gun from my fingers and pitched it across the room. My body was flung backward, and the sudden stop against the rough-hewn walls took my breath away. A thick root dug into the small of my back. I couldn't move, held there by some invisible force, feet dangling two feet from the ground.

So not good.

Tovin stepped closer to the black pool, sparing me a pitying look before gazing down. The mirrored water began to ripple and, as I watched, came to a rolling boil. "These events have been in motion for some time, Evangeline," he said, his voice difficult to hear over the roar of the pool. "I can no more stop it than I can change the color of the sky. This Tainted requires a vessel more controllable than the soldiers I've created. With my puppet Truman gone . . ."

He cast a contemptuous glare at me, and I swore I saw uncertainty hiding just below the surface. "My soldiers do not possess a human's free will to choose. It's something your people stupidly take for granted as you live your meager lives. I can't manufacture it, but I can steal it and bind this Tainted with it."

I finally got it. Amalie had said the Tainted were beings of pure emotion and instinct, unable to make moral choices. They simply acted. Humans, on the other hand, had been making moral choices ever since Eve supposedly bit into that damned apple. Free will was Tovin's apple, and owning Wyatt's was his guarantee of control. So how—?

"You won't be as easy to manipulate as one whose free will I own," Tovin continued, turning back to his bubbling pool, "but the Tainted's crossing cannot be stopped, and your body will have to do."

My stomach knotted. *Oh hell no.* He was not putting a demon into me. I struggled in vain against my barrier, fear bordering on panic.

The boiling water began to swirl, until its entire surface was a maddening whirlpool. Energy snapped and spit in our underground dungeon. The candle flames flickered, but the air remained completely still. Tovin recited words in a language I didn't know. He was doing it—bringing a Tainted across the Break. Turning a demon loose on me and the rest of the unsuspecting world.

Blackness rose up from the center of the whirl-

ing vortex, like a jet of ink through water. It hovered
several feet above, a shapeless web of pitch no larger
than a volleyball. Tovin's mouth kept moving, speaking words unheard above the screaming in my head.
He swept his hand out, indicating me. The black blob
shuddered, and I swear it looked right at me. Then it
floated forward.

No!

I reached for the threads of the Break, so faint behind the wall of magic holding me down. I caught it
and pulled, fixated quickly on loss and loneliness, and
then I was moving. Every fiber of my existence felt
pulled part, vibrated, stretched to the point of shattering. I shrieked, hoping only for a destination far from
here and the demon intent on possessing me.

My face hit dirt first, and I tumbled to the ground
in a shuddering heap. Tovin snarled, an angry sound
more befitting a wild dog than a revered—and slightly
insane—elf mystic. I rolled onto my left side in time
to see the black blob slam into Tovin's midsection and
disappear. He froze in place, his aged face a contortion
of anger and confusion. And pain.

I sat up and blinked hard in the dim light, positive
he had grown a few inches in the last five seconds. It
didn't seem possible, but it was happening.

To the tune of strangely melodic screaming, his
entire body expanded to the bulk of a professional
wrestler—height and weight and expanse of muscle.
The short, white hair that had crowned his head fell
out, revealing bald, oily skin. His complexion darkened to a slick violet, not quite dark enough to be purple. Fingernails grew and sharpened. Incisors dropped

down over his lower lip. Anything once elvin about him was gone, save his eyes.

Something else leered at me from across the half-moon room. Something evil.

"What the hell are you?" I asked, standing with caution, fear choking the words.

"The thing you mistakenly call a demon, girl." Its voice was impossibly deep and completely inhuman. "We are older than the Earth, part of Her long before your wretched kind crawled from Her womb."

"The Tainted."

His laughter was a thunderclap. It vibrated the floor and sent bits of the ceiling trickling down. "We have many names. We are Legion. We are the Horsemen. We are the Titans. We are the Maladies. We are myth and legend and story. We are Hell, girl, and we're coming home."

"Over my dead body."

"Your dead body is what this elf once desired, but his plans to control us are as lifeless as he. This body suits me. I taste freedom for the first time in millennia, and I will not leave my family imprisoned on the other side of the Break—not when life on Earth is so much sweeter."

A crazy noble idea coming from a . . . well, whatever he was. It was time for this demon, Old One, Titan, or just plain Crazy Ugly Thing to go back across the Break to Hell. For me, for Wyatt, for Alex, and for everyone else who'd died along the way.

"I have to admit, demon, that Tovin had a good plan." My fingers flexed around the knife's hilt. I didn't have to reach far to feel the Break's power and grasp it. "But he didn't count on one thing."

His bushy eyebrows arched. "And what is that, girl?"

"Me."

The teleport destination was so close that the blur, ache, and swish seemed to happen instantaneously—from across the room to right in front of him in a blink. I plunged the knife into his chest—given his great height, it was nearly his abdomen—and twisted. He roared and the thunderous sound shook the room.

I was flying through the air and hit the opposite wall before I registered the blow. My head cracked against the rough dirt. I tumbled to the floor, bright stars of color bursting in my vision, and came to rest on my side, too stunned to move. I heard the knife clatter. Shambling footsteps. A shadow fell across me. Shit.

Meaty hands closed around my throat, hauled me up by my neck, and slammed me against the wall. My sore back protested. Oxygen rushed from my lungs. My feet kicked a foot above the floor, unable to find purchase. He squeezed. I raised my knee and hit nothing but rock-hard muscle. Slowly, painfully, he was choking me to death. Blood rushed to my head. Dizziness spread. My eyes seemed to bulge, threatening to pop out of their sockets.

His leering face was close to mine. His hot breath stank of rot and death. Lust gleamed in his eyes and pulled his pale lips into a taunting snarl. "I'll put my wife into you, girl," he growled. "I look forward to getting to know her again."

Rage jolted through me. Drawing on the last of my energy, the last of the Break's spark, I concentrated on the far side of the room, by one of the crates . . .

. . . and found myself lying there, gasping for air, sucking oxygen greedily down a bruised and battered throat to the tune of an elf-demon hybrid's angry snarls. It was a small victory. He'd be on me again in moments. My head spun and ached. My body felt like liquid. I had nothing left with which to fight him.

I watched him come with black blood oozing down his chest, each footstep falling like an anvil. A thudding pattern interrupted by the unexpected—and wonderful—sound of an ammunition clip snapping into place. He stopped, and his oily head snapped toward the dugout room's only entrance.

A gun roared. The Tainted took a frag round in the center of his forehead. Bone cracked and splintered, and meat shredded. A second shot followed the first, and the back of his head exploded, coating the floor with black and pink gore. I gaped. He continued to stand, a thin trickle of blood dancing down the bridge of his angled nose. Eyes wide, lips parted, stunned.

A third shot caught him in the throat, followed immediately by a fourth that destroyed his neck and severed his head. Body and head dropped to the ground and hit with a sound like spaghetti plopping to a plate—wet and soft and disgusting.

Thank God for the Triads; they'd finally found their way down.

As I gaped, all of the blackness in the dead thing's blood and body seemed to melt together in a single puddle by its severed neck. As it left, Tovin's body returned to normal—shrinking and regaining actual color, until all signs of the Tainted were gone.

The black puddle shuddered and swirled like a

beached jellyfish, stunned, but far from finished. Right where I never imagined it would be. I fished out the pouch containing Amalie's spell, loosened the drawstring, and spilled the contents over the squirming Tainted.

White powder dusted down, reeking of mustard and blood and crushed rose petals, and like salt on a slug, the Tainted shriveled into an onyx rock the size of a baseball. And didn't move.

Holy shit, it worked.

Footsteps shuffled in my direction. I rolled onto my left side and stared at the black sneakers in front of me. And at the blue jeans above them—not Triad standard for an assault. My savior crouched in front of me, the left sleeve of his shirt stained red.

I swallowed, unable to believe it. Unwilling to give in to the illusion. I was delusional, seeing what I wanted to see, not what was in front of me.

Strong arms wrapped around my waist and drew me up against his chest. A familiar, wonderful heartbeat thrummed steadily against mine. I pushed back so I could see. Brilliant onyx eyes looked down at me over a mouth stretched into a joyous smile. Color flushed his cheeks. Life vibrated from him like a live current.

"Wyatt." I said the word like a prayer, afraid he would vanish in a puff of smoke.

He nodded. "It's me." He stroked my cheek with the tip of his finger. "I don't know what you did to my chest, but it hurts like hell."

I started laughing and flung my arms around his neck. He was alive—truly alive and well and in my arms. His scent filled my nostrils; his existence invaded every sense. My chest ached, but it was a sweet ache. The gentle pain of something broken that was on the mend.

His laughter mingled with mine and we held each other. We had wallowed in shit and, against the odds, had come out clean on the other side. Clean, alive, and together.

"Amalie's magic pouch worked," I said.

"I see that. What do we do with it now?"

"Nothing. I say we contact Amalie and let her people deal with it. They're the ones who were supposed to keep this from happening in the first place."

"I like that plan."

"So does this mean we get to compare our death experiences?"

He grinned. "Absolutely not. You win, hands down. Although I do know how you feel now, scaring the shit out of people who think you're dead."

"Kismet?"

"Tybalt, actually. I never thought a grown man could shriek like a girl."

I tucked my head beneath his chin, content in a place that, only a week ago, I never thought I'd want to be. "I thought I lost you, and I hated it."

"I know, Evy, but I think it's finally over."

"Not quite." Over his shoulder, past the contained demon, I spied the six crates. "It isn't quite done yet."

* * *

I couldn't bring myself to go back into that laboratory. Seeing those wretched, tortured creatures once was more than enough. Some had been human, most not. But all were living creatures, and they didn't deserve what Tovin had done to them.

Wyatt and I hung around the Visitors' Center lobby while Kismet, Baylor, and two other Handlers conferred with their bosses, via cell phone, over the hybrid problem. I kicked at the charred remains of the front desk. Destroying it had knocked down the protection barrier, as I suspected, and allowed the Bloods and Triads to continue their assault on the last of the Halfie forces.

The battle hadn't lasted long. Tybalt had a few deep lacerations on his thigh from the hound getting too close, but he would live. The Triads had only suffered six deaths—the least of any side. The pavement outside was littered with corpses. The Halfies and Bloods would burn with the morning sun. A bonfire would deal with the rest.

"Evangeline."

I turned toward the Center's entrance. Isleen strode toward me, her body armor somehow blood-free, every white hair tucked firmly into place. I was almost sorry I'd hit her in the gut. Her ghostly white face needed a little color.

"You going to try and deck me again?" I asked.

She shook her head. "I am certain you, of all people, understand actions taken in the heat of battle."

"Kelsa killed your sister."

"Yes, and while not by my hands, she paid for that crime."

"And a few others."

Isleen half turned, as if to go, and paused. Over one shoulder, she said, "I cannot guess where our paths may cross next, Evangeline Stone. I hope it continues to be as allies."

"Ditto." I offered my hand. She eyed the dirt and bloodstains and shook it anyway. Her grip was firm, cold, and truthful.

She spared Wyatt a nod and a terse "Truman," and left. Probably to gather her troops and leave us humans to clean up the carnage.

"Did anyone tell her about the critters downstairs?" Wyatt asked.

"Nope," I said.

"Think she'll be annoyed at being left out?"

"Maybe."

"Do you even care right now?"

"Not even a little bit." Kismet strode past. I took a step toward her and asked, "What will happen to the hybrids?"

"We'll take them out of here," she replied. "We have a secure facility south of the city."

My mouth fell open. "You're taking them to Boot Camp?"

"It's a secure facility, and it's the best we've got on short notice. We need someplace to sort them out."

"You mean kill them?"

"I don't know, Stone; I really don't. We'll do what we can for the ones that can still function. The others . . . It's wait and see. I'm sorry."

"Thanks."

She started to walk away. Stopped. "By the way, Rufus will live. He's got some pretty bad burns, but he's tough. Just thought you'd like to know."

Relief settled warmly in my stomach. Score one more for the good guys.

Kismet disappeared into the mix. No one paid us much attention. Wyatt slipped one arm around my waist. I leaned against him. We were both splattered in complementary shades of red and fuchsia. My shoulder had stopped bleeding, and the gashes on my stomach itched like a bitch. Overall, though, we'd come out ahead.

"So you going to get your old job back?" I asked. "Seeing as you're a hero and no longer a hunted criminal?"

He grimaced. "I doubt it. Having everyone turn against you and try to kill your girlfriend kind of sours a working relationship."

"Girlfriend? Presume much?"

"Probably, yes." He turned his head, breath tickling my cheek. "I told you yesterday, Evy, you have healing to do, and I'll be here for you. Whatever it takes."

My physical body seemed to be healing on its own, but only time would tell if the healing gift was as permanent as my new body. The emotional wounds, though, were more plentiful and harder to reach. I was just glad to know I wasn't alone. "And in the meantime?"

"I'm sure we can find something to keep us occupied and out of trouble."

"Like what?"

"Ever wanted to open a nature preserve?"

I punched him in the shoulder.

"How about a Grecian dress shop?"

"I am never wearing a getup like that again, so kiss that fantasy good-bye."

"Not even if Amalie invites us down for tea?"

I could only imagine how Amalie and her people felt about tonight's victory. Anger at the Tainted's successful crossing into our world. Joy over the continued security of First Break. Annoyance at being tasked with babysitting the Tainted we'd captured. Relief at never getting her own blue hands dirty in its protection. Then again, all of those reactions were emotional. Human. Beneath her kind, and yet something I would never give up.

"If I ever set foot in that place again without her asking for a favor, suicidal or otherwise, I'll eat that damned dress."

·He kissed my temple. "That's the Evy I know. So, what do you want to do next?"

I faltered. I hadn't given any thought past today and the events I had felt certain would end in my death. Tomorrow was a gift, and I was glad to have it. I just didn't know what the hell to do with it.

"I think I want to go get a bag of cheese puffs," I said.

"You . . . what?" His expression—openmouthed and eyebrows arched—was priceless. "Since when do you like cheese puffs?"

"Remember the part where you died and, instead of renting, I got full and permanent residence of Chalice's body?"

"Yeah."

"Well, it seems like the body comes as a packaged deal with residual memories and odd food cravings."

His eyebrows arched higher. "Really? Think you'll be brave enough to try sushi now?"

"Never."

"Where's your sense of adventure?"

"Waiting to take a hot bath and a weeklong nap, along with the rest of me."

"And after that?"

I shrugged and smiled, unwilling to think that far into my after-afterlife. "I think we'll just wait and see where the day takes us."